A Tryst in Paris

Anne Armistead

SOUL MATE PUBLISHING
New York

A TRYST IN PARIS

Published in the United States of America by Soul Mate Publishing
P.O. Box 24
Macedon, New York, 14502 ISBN: 979-8-218-25499-5

Print imprint Sandra Havriluk   www.annearmisteadauthor.com
Digital imprint Soul Mate Publishing   www.SoulMatePublishing.com

The publisher does not have any control over and does not assume any responsibility for author or third-party websites or their content.

To Jan Agnello,

*A kindred soulmate & fellow "Storyologist," whose antique
coin purse jewelry helped inspire my story.*

Acknowledgments

Thank you, dear reader, for choosing to read A Tryst in Paris. Thanks to Deborah Gilbert and Soul Mate Publishing for believing in my story and bringing it to you.

I owe appreciation to so many who helped me in the writing of this story. Thanks to Jan Agnello, to whom this book is dedicated, who shares my love for Paris and stories that end happily-ever-after. Thanks to my amazing critique group, Ginger Garrett, Sharon Pegram, and Johnna Stein, whose support and friendship never wavers and whose insightful comments always push my writing to the next level. Thanks also to Anne Beth Presley, Ph.D., Associate Professor at Auburn University's Department of Consumer and Design Sciences, for her generous assistance in the details of 1900 Parisian fashion. Thanks to Ulrich Fleming, Professor of Architecture (Emeritus), School of Architecture, Carnegie Mellon University, for his beautiful translation of the poem "Das Karussell" ("The Carousel") by Rainer Maria Rilke, which inspired my carousel scenes. Thanks to the Library of Congress for archiving the Actualités of the 1900 Paris Exhibition, filmed by James H. White of the Thomas Edison Manufacturing Company. These silent films transported me back in time and helped me place Mirabelle in that historical setting. Thanks to author Janelle Dietrick for her expertise about Alice Guy and the filming of La Fée aux Choux. Thanks to the elegant and lovely Sylvie Gould for proofing my use of French throughout the story.

Lastly, and most of all, thanks to my family. If not for your encouragement, the blinking cursor on the empty page would win out.

ONE

"There's no telling what tomorrow may bring."

"Aren't you the philosopher, Sylvie." Mirabelle accepted the mug of café au lait. She sank into the soft leather club sofa in her godmother's Paris apartment.

"My PhD in Philosophy did convince the Sorbonne to hire me." Sylvie sat opposite Mirabelle, a demitasse in hand. She'd tucked her legs to the side in the antique French tufted chair. "That's neither here nor there. I'm merely translating the saying on your coffee cup, dear. *Les jours se suivent et ne se ressemblent pas.*"

Mira studied the French script her forehead creased in concentration. "Oh, I confess. I'm hopeless in foreign languages." She rolled her eyes. "I can tell you what tomorrow will bring, though. A long day of antique shopping and lingering doubt over Rob." She slouched against the sofa's back. "I barely slept on the flight. I kept second-guessing myself. Maybe Rob was the one for me, and I blew it."

Sylvie finished her espresso and placed her china cup on the yellow damask top of the carved oak nesting tables next to her chair. "*Coeur qui soupire n'a pas ce qu'il desire.* Translation? The heart that sighs has not what it desires."

"You hear my heart sighing, do you?" Mira placed her mug by her phone on the large glass-topped vintage iron- legged coffee table. She scanned the residence, admiring its understated elegance. Her decade of working in film set design honed her appreciation of its decor. Sylvie filled her home with priceless objects, yet it projected an atmosphere of welcoming warmth.

Mira kicked off her flats and stretched her legs prone on the couch. She rested her head against antique Aubusson tapestry pillows, which she coveted. Dramatically exhaling, she announced, "There it goes again. My sighing heart."

"So be it, Mirabelle Montgomery. Better to recognize boring and pre-dictable Rob was not your heart's desire before marrying him. *N'est-ce pas?*"

"*Je suppose.*" Mira rearranged to a sitting position and grabbed one of the pillows to hug.

"Tell me about your studies." Sylvie clasped her hands in her lap, prepared to listen.

"Film history mesmerizes me. No secret there. The career change is intim-idating, but I'm glad I decided to go ahead. The NYU film preservation program is perfect for me. And, I finally have my own place, minuscule as it is, to call my home, complete with my dog. When I come through the door, she wriggles with joy."

"A gal's best friend is her dog. Though a couple of close human friends are nice, too."

"Message received." Mira knew her mom and godmother worried over her being such a loner. It worked for her.

"Don't get testy." Sylvie sighed. "What's your pup's name?"

"I call her Guy." Mira emphasized the French pronunciation of the name, with the *u* pronounced as a long *e* sound. "I named her after the French pioneer filmmaker, Alice Guy-Blaché, the subject of my thesis." She tossed the pillow aside and showed Sylvie a photo of Guy on her phone.

Her godmother responded with an admiring *ahhh*. "Guy is part pom, pap, and poodle. Fifteen pounds of joy. Everyone loves her. My boarding place spoils her. I miss her." She kissed two fingers and placed them against the dog's photo. "He never liked Rob much. When he taught me Jujitsu, she barked nonstop defending me."

"You must trust your dog," Sylvie said in a solemn tone.

"Don't tease."

"I'm not, dear." Sylvie held out her hand for Mira's phone. "Do you have photos of your place?"

"I thought you'd never ask." Mira scrolled to them and handed Sylvie her phone. "Swipe away."

The photos reminded Mira of how much she loved her efficiency in Brooklyn, even though it meant siphoning money from her savings to stitch her budget together. Commuting to campus could be vexing. Hopefully, she'd find the sacrifices to change careers at age thirty worth it.

I stepped out of my comfort zone by taking a chance, not my strongest personality trait, but the change feels right.

"An adorable home, Mirabelle." Sylvie returned her phone. "You are happy with your life's new direction?"

"Absolutely." Mira closed her photos and placed the phone on the coffee table. "I loved creating sets for films. The older the period setting, the more I adored it. But it was a hard existence, meandering from one film location to another, never having roots anywhere, and worrying about another gig."

Sylvie nodded. "You bond on a set with a team, and then everyone disperses. Why become close to anyone if you'll soon part?"

"You've psychoanalyzed me." Mirabelle snorted a laugh. "You and Mom have talked. She's convinced I focus on finding the 'wrong' in 'Mr. Right' to avoid commitment. She worries I guard my heart. I keep myself to myself, is all."

At the mention of her mom, Mira noticed the spark fading from Sylvie's eyes.

"How is Eleanor?" Sylvie's voice quavered. "Any word yet?"

"Not yet." Mira grabbed the pillow once more and hugged it tightly. "It isn't fair that chemo and radiation required for treating breast cancer can damage your heart. We knew cardiomyopathy to be a risk, but we optimistically assumed Mom would not develop it." She forced her next words through her tightened throat. "Dr. West, her cardiothoracic surgeon, says she needs that heart transplant now."

Sylvie frowned. "She's been on the transplant list for months. Why hasn't she received a heart?"

"For those with type O blood, the donor must be the same blood type. The wait for such patients extends more than a year. We're six months into that timeframe. Mom is strong enough now for the transplant, but each day she grows weaker."

"Oh, Mira. I'm so sorry. Should she keep her store open, considering?"

"Mom says she'll die with her boots on. Preferably Victorian-era ones, with mother-of-pearl buttons." Mira forced a smile. "She's a determined woman, as you very well know."

"Oh, yes. As Eleanor's best friend since age five, I have first-hand experience with that character attribute of hers. She's a tough one. She'll hang on until a donor is found. She must."

"Agreed. We can't lose hope. She's only sixty." Mira blinked away her welling tears. "We both know Mom sent me on this antique shopping trip to get a break from my hovering. I insisted I would come for only a long weekend. I can't be away too long, in case."

"There's nothing wrong with hovering over one you love." Sylvie joined Mira on the sofa and drew her into a hug.

Mira gratefully leaned into it.

Sylvie brushed Mira's bangs to the side as she had when Mira was a little girl. "Think positively, my little one." She stood, placing her hands on her narrow hips. "I think your trip here is a good thing, for Eleanor and for you. You need a breath of Paris, considering what's been happening with your mom, not to mention with Rob."

Sylvie gathered her demitasse cup and Mira's mug and disappeared into the kitchen.

Mira's reality of her once-again single status brought disconsolate thoughts.

What if Mom doesn't survive until I fall madly in love, celebrate my wedding day, give her grandchildren?

With force, she threw the pillow into the corner of the sofa.

Sylvie re-entered, tying a blue-and-white striped apron around her. "You know I am going to London tomorrow for the conference I must attend. I'll return very early Monday." "Yes." Mira jutted out her lower lip in a pout. "I'll miss you, though. I suppose it's selfish of me to ask you to cancel?"

"Not selfish at all. But I am the substitute for a colleague of mine, who most inconveniently broke her leg while skiing the Alps. I owe her a favor and can't leave her in the lurch. I'm so sorry, *mon petit chou*."

Mira grinned at the strange French endearment: Little cabbage.

"No need to be sorry. I should have coordinated my trip better. Mom's friend Carolyn offered to stay with her this weekend, and before you know it, my ticket's booked."

She didn't add that she absolutely had to get away from New York this very weekend. Rob had invited her to spend it at his parents' place in the Berkshires. He'd hinted about a proposal. She broke up with him before the trip to avoid that possibility.

Sylvie's understanding expression told Mira her mom had explained. *No secrets among family.*

"At least we'll have Monday to enjoy, before you fly out in the late afternoon." Sylvie pointed toward the bookcase by the fireplace where a framed photo sat of Eleanor with two handsome men. "Remember our antique dealer friends, Tobias and his husband, René? When Eleanor visits, they always go antique shopping."

"Yes. Mom talks with them frequently." Mira walked to the bookcase and held the photo to study it closely. Energy and happiness shone in her mom's eyes. How she loved Paris. Antiques. Life.

"I've arranged for them to meet you early in the morning and squire you around to the antique markets." Sylvie opened the china hutch's door. "Your mom says they have the best eye for unusual items. They found these gorgeous dishes for me. You will have a wonderfully successful shopping trip with them."

"Oh, Sylvie, thank you. I need help to complete what Mom has planned."

Mira prayed once again what she prayed many times daily: *God, please send Mom a donor heart.* Her insides chilled. Life for her mother meant death for another. A cruel paradox. She hated paradoxes.

Her tears once again welled. She replaced the photo on the bookshelf and traced her fingers against the book spines of Sylvie's tantalizing library. The one entitled *The Triumph of Art Nouveau Paris - Exhibition 1900* drew her attention. She pulled it from the shelf for bedtime reading and crossed the room to place it on the coffee table.

Her godmother stood before the china cabinet, choosing the dishes.

"May I help?" Mira grinned, knowing Sylvie needed no assistance. She always set a gorgeous table.

"No, thank you. Except for your bit of antique shopping, enjoy this short vacation. I will not allow you to lift a finger, sweetie." Sylvie finished choosing dishes, silver, and linens, and she began the table landscaping.

"I love how you spoil me. With Tobias and René's help, I'll power through tomorrow's shopping and relax Sunday." Mira mumbled her words through an enormous yawn.

"Oh, my, dear." Sylvie chuckled. "The jet-lag monster is acting up. Why not nap while I prepare our dinner?"

"A nap sounds divine, but I think I'm too fidgety. A walk should revive me." Mira grabbed her phone. "I'll stroll Rue Galande. I love that quaint street. Maybe that's my solution to my love life. Go back in time like in the movie *Midnight in Paris* to meet my soulmate."

"If you do, please travel back from your adventure by six?" Sylvie removed a bottle from the dining room wine rack. "I'll have a marvelous charcuterie appetizer paired with wine awaiting you, followed by *poulet provençal*."

"Oh, wow. You haven't gone to trouble on my account, have you?"

"*Les balivernes.* Nonsense. It's the least I can do since you'll have to fend for yourself after I depart. We must enjoy the most fantastic lunch together Monday before you leave." "We must. And, next trip, Mom and I will come together, with both of our hearts mended." Mira dug into her carry-on bag to retrieve a black cape.

Sylvie lightly gasped. "How gorgeous."

Mira wrapped it around her and swirled to model. "One of Mom's finds she gifted me for my big 3-0 birthday. She explained the curlicue pattern of embellishment and the high dog collar date it from 1900, when the Victorian was transitioning into the Edwardian style. The double layers keep me cozy."

"Not to mention stylish. You need a gorgeous dress of the era, buttoned-up boots, and a parasol. Of course, you'd need to accessorize with a fabulous hat perched upon your Gibson girl bun." Sylvie tapped on the art book placed on the sofa's side table.

Mira loved the painting displayed on its cover, one of her favorite Mary Cassatt paintings, appropriately titled *Woman's Head in Large Hat*.

Sylvie pointed at Mira. "I stand by my opinion. You favor her. Auburn-reddish hair. Blue eyes. Beautiful."

"Thank you for the compliment, but I wish." Mira patted her head. "I'm not sure about wearing such a phenomenal hat."

Her smile faded. Thinking of Cassatt's collection of mother and child paintings pressed upon her more worry about her mother's health. She absently twirled the moonstone ring she wore on her right ring finger. After a moment, she realized her action. Her mother never failed to point out this nervous habit.

"It's your 'tell,' Mira. The more upset, the more you twirl."

Mira held her hand out to admire once again the gray moonstone set in the Art Deco filigree platinum band. This last gift from her father, a vintage René Lalique from the Belle Epoque era, ranked as her most sentimental and valuable possession.

She recalled the moonstone's many symbolisms—new beginnings, mothering, easy childbirth, safe travel, exposing the emotional self to love and forgiveness. The gray one symbolized healing.

Please invoke your healing power now.

After securing her phone and small wallet in the cleverly hidden pocket in the cape's liner, Mira stopped in front of the heavily framed wall mirror hung in the foyer to study her reflection. The April weather in Paris could be as temperamental as she was when jet-lagged. She fastened the top button of her cape, hoping her black bodysuit, jeans, and boots topped by the outerwear would stave off the chilly late afternoon temperature.

This outfit must do. Mom made sure I packed light to leave room for packing the antique purchases.

With a quick brush of her fingers through her wavy hair, Mira justified her less-than-put-together appearance by the fact she had survived a long flight. It was what it was at this point.

"I'm off, Sylvie. À *bientôt.*" She headed out. Sylvie's à *tout* à *l'heure* floated in the air behind her.

TWO

Mira loved that Sylvie called the Left Bank's 5th and 6th arrondisse-ments near Sorbonne as her home. The location on Boulevard Saint-Germain was walking distance to many of Mira's favorite places, including Le Jardin du Luxembourg. She turned from Saint-Germain north on Rue Saint- Jacques and then made a right onto Rue Galande. The window display of tasty treats at Odette's drew Mirabelle in for a raspberry cream puff. While demolishing the delicate yet chewy pastry, she headed to Shakespeare & Company to pay homage to the spirit of its now-deceased owner.

She continued walking on Rue Galande for less than two minutes before turning left onto Rue Saint-Julien le Pauvre. The crunch sounded as her feet traveled the pea gravel in front of the store. She'd arrived.

Mira took in the sight of adjacent Notre Dame as she joined the always-long line at the bookshop's door. She knew by heart the motto posted above the entrance to the reading library. "Be not inhospitable to strangers lest they be angels in disguise."

An angel in disguise.

Whenever in a crowd back home, Mira wondered if one of those strangers would become Mom's heart donor. Mom's angel. As usual, the thought provoked the paradoxical emotions of gladness and sadness. She hated paradoxes. She preferred straightforward and simple communication.

"*Excusez moi.*"

The deep voice behind her claimed Mira's attention. *Great. I hope I won't be trapped into inane chitchat.* She turned and faced an elderly man wearing a huge Stetson. "Hello."

"You're American?" His friendly grin cut deep grooves into the sides of his wrinkled face. "Thank goodness. I'm from Dallas. You?"

"New York City," Mira answered. The man appeared to be around her mom's age. "I thought I heard Texan in your French."

"Guess the cowboy hat confirmed, huh?" He touched the brim of his Stetson and tipped it toward her. "Stetsons say Texas."

"Your hat is impressive," Mira said. "I've never met a cowboy before, and here I am meeting one in Paris."

"I'm happy I can be of service."

"Me, too." Mira raised her eyebrows. "You have a question, I think? Ask away, and maybe I can answer."

"Yes, thanks. Is this the line to enter the store? Or, am I in line for an amusement ride?" He let out a hearty laugh.

Mira surprised her normally aloof self by joining in. His friendliness was contagious. "You're in the right place to enter the bookstore. It's a very well-visited landmark. No rides at the end of the line, though."

"Thank you, ma'am." He tipped the hat's brim again.

On a whim, Mira retrieved her phone from inside her cape pocket, surprising herself yet again. "I'd love a photograph with you."

"Well, little lady, I'd be honored."

Mira snapped one of them together.

"I have an idea." The Texan placed his Stetson on Mira's head.

"Perfect." Mira laughed, and she snapped another photo. She handed the hat to the owner. "What a big load to carry around."

"Well, they say everything's bigger in Texas. Are you enjoying your stay?"

"To be honest, I'm jet-lagged from having arrived today after my all-night flight. You?"

"I'm flying back tomorrow night, first to New York City for business, then back to Dallas. My late wife loved coming to this bookstore, so I wanted to visit. I plan a stroll through Luxembourg Gardens, too, another of her favorite locations."

When he mentioned his "late wife," the break in his voice reminded Mira of how when her mom said her dad's name, her voice did the same thing even after twenty years. *Do you ever stop grieving for the love of your soulmate?*

The man adjusted his hat and sighed. "Take it from me. Enjoy time with loved ones while you can. I wish I had taken time to accompany my wife on her jaunts while we were in Paris, but I allowed my business duties to intrude."

His sentimental words panged Mira's heart. She offered her right hand for a greeting, one more surprising behavior for her, especially with complete strangers. "I have your picture, but not your name. Mine's Mirabelle Montgomery." The Texan grinned. Laugh lines crinkled around his light amber-brown eyes. He took her hand, and they shared a firm handshake. "William Cody, ma'am."

"William Cody? I must ask. Are you any relation to—" "Nope." He smirked good-naturedly. "Don't mean to interrupt, but everyone asks. Although I am ancient, I'm not Buffalo Bill. Not related to him, either. I don't even eat bison burgers." He pointed toward the shop. "Our turn to enter." "Why, so it seems." Mira wished the line had moved slower.

They parted ways.

Mira browsed through the store, thinking about the tradition established by the owner years ago to allow people to live at the shop. These so-called "tumbleweeds" slept in bunks and earned their keep by helping run the store. After her nomadic life working set-to-set, being a tumbleweed did not appeal.

Her eye landed on H. G. Wells' *The Time Machine*. Flipping through it, she heard her father's voice reading it to her. Her ring caught her attention and set her emotions reeling.

When Mom found this vintage René Lalique moonstone ring, why did you ask her to give it to me on my eighteenth birthday? Did you have a premonition you would not be with me to celebrate?

She re-shelved the H. G. Wells book next to a first edition of *As I Lay Dying*.

You are right in what you said about the past, Mr. Faulkner. It truly won't stay past.

She'd been vacillating for twenty years among the first four stages of grief over Dad's death: denial, anger, bargaining, depression, and acceptance. The last stage of acceptance eluded her. She'd never accept how his choice that day robbed her mom and her of him in their lives.

What about when Mom dies?

Mira broke from that treacherous line of thinking before it rushed like high tide into the crevices of her heart and mind. A quick look at her watch advised her she'd spent far too long at the bookstore, as usual. She headed toward the exit and noticed the Texan making his way out.

He sent an oversized wave of his hat in her direction. "We meet once more."

"We do." Mira smiled. Bill Cody had a sweet spirit. She'd love her mom to meet him.

Maybe my turn to play matchmaker?

She plucked her mom's business card from her wallet. "My mother owns the Montgomery Antiques at 4th and Lexington. Her name is Eleanor." She handed Bill the card. "When you are in the Big Apple, stop in to visit."

"I'll be sure to do so. Thank you for the invite." He pocketed the card and gave her one of his own. "If you're ever in Texas, look me up." He tipped his Stetson and walked off.

Mira studied the man's business card. Mr. William Cody, Cody Jet Charters. She presumed he flew on his own private jet.

Pretty convenient.

Fingers crossed he'd visit her mom's store. He'd be an interesting suitor.

On her way back to Sylvie's, Mira mused over being drawn to the Texan. It was such an unlikely reaction from her typically aloof self. Since her dad's death, she'd struggled to be open to others, but it never came easily.

You are an emotional mess, Mirabelle. Why can't you escape your introverted shell and live a little?

Poor Rob chipped a bit through her shell. Although she loved him, she was never in love with him. Never felt he was the one to risk the "til death do us part" thing. Never felt passion in his kisses she longed to feel. But maybe that kind of passion existed in romance novels and movies.

Her grumbling stomach claimed her attention. Mira purposefully shifted her focus to three things: Sylvie's delicious food awaiting her, the antique buying errands to be accomplished tomorrow, and of course, as always, her mother's heart. She'd need to tell her about sending Bill Cody to her shop for them to meet. Who knows? Maybe grieving lost spouses wouldn't be the only thing the two held in common.

THREE

Sunlight filtered through the closed draperies, encouraging Mira to open her eyes. She resisted until the incessant chiming of her phone demanded attention. Her hand found it, and she silenced the annoying alarm. She dreaded parting ways with the cozy down comforter under which she contentedly snuggled. The canopy held aloft by the bed's tall posts created a royal atmosphere. To complete her life as princess, she needed a maid to appear, breakfast tray in hand.

Her wish must have been Sylvie's command.

Her godmother's cheerful greeting followed her rap at the door. *"Bonjour, bonjour. Are you awake, ma chérie?"* *"Bonjour,"* Mira called out.

Sylvie entered, balancing a breakfast tray complete with flowers in a vase.

"Oh, Sylvie," Mira murmured, stretching out and propping her head against the voluminous pillows. "You do spoil your goddaughter." She smoothed her covers and set the book from Sylvie's library she'd fallen asleep reading on the nightstand. She'd gotten to the chapter on the 1900 Exhibit's entertainment. Montmartre's Moulin Rouge, the Rat Mort, the Chat Noir—*oh là là.*

Sylvie placed the tray across Mira's lap. "I must leave for London in a few minutes, so we can't eat together. Delivering to you breakfast in bed is the next best thing, right?"

"*Merci, merci.*" Mira took a sip of the orange juice. "Hmm. Freshly squeezed."

"There's more in the refrigerator, and I've filled the bread bin with croissants for tomorrow's breakfast." "You're amazing."

Sylvie beamed at the compliment. "I hope my conference attendees will agree."

After a sip of coffee, Mira mock-punched the air. "You'll knock 'em dead, I'm sure."

"I'll float like a butterfly and sting like a bee?"

Mira laughed.

Sylvie perched on the bed. "Tobias and René will meet you at the Marché aux Puces de Saint-Ouen. I have arranged a driver for you, who will arrive in an hour."

Mira swallowed a bite of the brioche bread with jam before managing, "Merci."

"They will steer you through the Paris Flea Market, then on to Puces de Montreuil, and finally to Puces de Vanves. From there, on to the nearby Intemporel Antiquités located on Avenue Denfert-Rochereau. The shop is near the Catacombs entrance. Tobias and René can accompany you on a tour of it. We know how you adore scary places."

Mira rolled her eyes at her godmother's sarcasm. She could justify breaking up with Rob solely based on his insistence on binging horror films, which he knew she avoided.

"I'm teasing, my dear." Sylvie laughed her throaty laugh. "At end of day, you may relax in a long soak in my fabulous clawfoot tub while enjoying glass upon glass of wine."

"A delightful idea," Mira acknowledged before taking another sip of coffee.

"I have arranged for my good chef friend, Victor, to stock the refrigerator while you shop today. Awaiting you this evening will be bread, cheese, his specialty of roasted chicken with potatoes and carrots, and a delectable pear for dessert. *Miam, miam.*"

"Yum, yum, yes. Sylvie, you are absolutely the best. Thank heaven for my escorts for this buying trip. Otherwise, I'd be lost, and not only geographically."

"I must scoot." Sylvie rose. "Take care while I am away, *mon petit chou.*" She patted Mira's head. "My little cabbage. Fall in love while I'm gone, eh?"

"Not an issue. I am sure my soulmate awaits me on the sidewalks of Paris."

"Let us hope. After all, *c'est Paris*." They blew kisses to one another.

Mira's insides warmed with gratitude.

I'm so lucky to have Sylvie in my life, especially while my heart aches with worry.

~ ~ ~

Mira found Tobias and René to be the perfect guides to the antique markets. When they arrived by taxi at Intemporel near the Catacombs entrance, her day with them ended. Mira pushed away the thought of six million people's bones stored beneath them in the Catacombs. She'd never understand the appeal of touring it.

After exchanging French air kisses goodbye with Tobias and René, along with promises she'd deliver their good wishes to her mom, she exited the cab with her shopping bag and waved the couple off.

The bag, filled with her smaller purchases of jewelry, proved heavier to lug than she'd imagined. Good thing the larger antiques—rolled art canvasses, vintage clothing, hats, shoes, and several antique silver pieces—were being couriered to Sylvie's by early Monday morning.

Between packing the fabulous finds in her suitcase and carry-on, she'd arrive home with everything from the trip. Flying on airline points, staying with Sylvie, and transporting the purchases in this manner meant turning more sales profit, lessons learned from her mom.

The display window of the Intemporel Antiquités caught Mira's attention. She viewed the mannequin with a slow, disbelieving shake of her head. It wore the same outfit she'd seen in a sketch dated 1900 by the famous Parisian haute couture dress designer, Jeanne Paquin. Turquoise, lavender, and rose embroidery accented the crème-colored bodice and skirt. The wide-brimmed hat sported effusive turquoise plumage. Mira mentally clicked through the IMDb listings of multiple films she'd worked on for which Paquin designs were copied for actresses' wardrobes. If this original existed in such sublime condition, she'd know.

The fabric appeared to be *mousseline de soie*, an extremely fine, soft muslin made of silk. A wide turquoise satin band encircled its waist. The skirt's hem, decorated with diamond-shaped dentelle applique inlay outlined with braided crème cord work, brushed against the ground. The same appliques decorated the high-necked bodice, which had a scalloped turquoise overlay with embroidered floral rose and lavender designs. A broad swath of netting protruded from the hat's top and encircled the mannequin's head.

Mira entered the shop, eager to inquire about the mannequin's clothing. The door chimes provided the singular charm to the dank and dark environs. An involuntary shiver raced through her, as if somebody walked across her grave, per the old saying.

Don't be so morbid, Mira.

She drew her cape closer around her. The store's musty smell reminded Mira of the antique shops she'd grown up visiting with her mother during their summer road trips. Other children might have gone to summer camps or family beach vacations. She and her mother traipsed through antique shops searching for unusual or rare finds. They starred in their own version of *Antiques Roadshow* with one major difference. When her mom identified the true worth of something, she negotiated a fair purchase price, one that didn't cheat the owner but left room to resell at a handy profit. Those finds kept them afloat financially.

Mira approached the older shopkeeper, who stood behind the counter. He continued to examine a ring he held under the jeweler's loupe, ignoring her. She thought he seemed familiar. He dressed the part of an antique shopkeeper. His collar was high, stiff, and upright from which hung a tie. He wore a black four-buttoned *sacque,* or sack coat. The jacket buttoned at the top, with the rest open to show a matching waistcoat underneath. A gold chain, probably connected to a pocket watch, dangled in a loop, attached to the matching suit trousers. A suspension chain worn around his neck connected his pince-nez spectacles to his lapel. A pronounced 1900-styled mustache fringed his upper lip, with the rest of his face clean-shaven. His attire reminded her of her father's dapper style.

"*Bonjour,*" Mira called out the cheery greeting.

The shopkeeper put away the ring and loupe into a cabinet drawer behind him and adjusted his spectacles. "*Bonjour. Comment puis-je vous aider?*" His voice had the scratchy hollowness of an elderly person.

Mira answered with an arms-out shrug. "I do not speak French."

He bowed, unsuccessfully masking his annoyance. "I am M. Le Veille. How may I help you?"

"I'm Mirabelle Montgomery." She projected her most high-wattage smile.

His expression remained solemn.

Mira elevated her charm. "The dress on the mannequin in your window. Is it an original Jeanne Paquin?"

"You know of her?" He stroked his mustache.

Without hesitation, Mira launched into her knowledge of Paquin. "Maison Paquin stood at 3 Rue de la Paix, next to House of Worth. She used red as her signature for clothing and marketing techniques. At the Exposition Universelle of 1900, she served as President of the Fashion Section and had her own exhibit with a mannequin of herself on display. A Paquin design inspired the clothing on the statue La Parisienne mounted on top of the Porte Monumentale entry to the Exhibit."

"*Oui.*"

"*Oui?*" Mira's voice rose, confused at his answer. "The dress is an original Paquin?"

The man brushed his mustache again. "May I help you?"

Mira shifted her heavy shopping bag into her other hand and tried not to scowl. For whatever reason, Le Veille refused to discuss the dress. She'd collect her mother's purchase and leave. The idea of a long soak in Sylvie's clawfoot tub called to her.

"I'm here for my mother's coin purses she purchased from you. Her name is Eleanor Montgomery. I'm her daughter." Thank heaven she needed only to verify the purchases and approve her mother's digital money transfer, sparing her from haggling price with the dour Le Veille.

"*Oui. Un moment.*" Le Veille disappeared into the back of his shop. He reappeared with a bag. The shop's name was imprinted on it in a flourish of cursive along with the shop's logo of a heart with the infinity symbol.

Clever.

"You will find everything in order, Mlle Montgomery."

Mira pulled each coin purse from the bag and checked it against the illustrated purchase receipt she'd brought with her. The selection included small souvenir purses from the 1900 Paris Exhibition and art nouveau sterling silver mesh purse chatelaine ones, always popular with her mom's customers. "All accounted for. They are lovely. My mother will be pleased."

Le Veille reached into his waistcoat pocket and held out another coin purse. "*Mon coeur me dit que tu es elle.* I translate. My heart tells me you are she: the one for whom this coin purse has awaited."

"Me?" Mirabelle bit back a knowing smile. She recognized a clever sales technique. She accepted the purse from his outstretched hand and examined it.

Its box frame closed with a kissing lock closure. The mother-of-pearl exterior boasted mint condition, with minimal fading of the painted designs on both sides. The words *L. Gaumont & Cie. 57 rue Saint-Roch* were painted in two lines in dull gold cursive script. The dots above each letter 'i' were smudged.

Mira's heart stuttered at the other side's design of a fanciful cabbage painted in a subtle green tone with the words *La Fée aux Choux,* painted in the same dull gold cursive script. She knew the title to be Alice Guy's film, *The Cabbage Fairy,* arguably credited as the first narrative film ever made and the topic of her thesis research.

The film's dramatization of the birth of babies in a cabbage patch struck her as strange until she read the popular French fairy tale in which baby boys were born in cabbages and baby girls were born in roses. Sylvie used the French endearment of *mon petit choue.* My little cabbage.

When Le Veille said the coin purse had been awaiting her, what did he mean? He referred to the purse as if it were an animate object with wishes and dreams, a sort of talisman. She smiled at such superstitious nonsense.

When Mira opened the small purse, her insides vibrated at the sight of a yellowed slip of paper tucked into it. Many antique coin purses contained mementoes. Locks of hair, which she thought sentimental. Baby teeth, which she thought disgusting. But no antique coin purse her mother purchased contained an aged, handwritten message.

With a light touch, she extracted the paper and unfolded it carefully, fearing it might disintegrate. A tingling, spidey sense worked its way up her spine. The bold, masculine handwriting, though faded, proved legible. *Rendez-vous avec moi au Carrousel du Luxembourg à midi.*

She placed the note onto the glass counter. Even though she believed she understood the message, she wanted to be sure. "Please, translate?"

"*Certainement.* Meet me at the Luxembourg Carousel at noon." He inserted the paper into the purse and again handed it to Mira. "Do not ask me more. Take."

"Take?" Mira's voice breathed out the word, surprised. She'd assumed he expected a considerable sum for such a one-of-a-kind object.

"*Oui.* Take. I have done my part." He pushed the bag of coin purses across the counter. With a theatrical whisper, he announced, "The carousel awaits. Go to it tomorrow, at the appointed hour. *Au revoir*, Mlle Montgomery."

He disappeared once more into the back of his shop.

Mira realized the old man had dismissed her. She tucked the *La Fée aux Choux* purse into her interior cape pocket, added this store's bag into the larger shopping bag, and left. Lifting her face toward the sun, she inhaled deeply to cleanse the stale odor of the shop from her nostrils and to settle her nerves.

She replayed Le Veille's words when he gave her the *La Fée aux Choux* purse: *My heart tells me you are she: the one for whom this coin purse has awaited . . . the Carousel awaits . . . go to it à midi . . .*

Had Le Veille cursed her? Blessed her?

"Don't be ridiculous, Mirabelle."

At a passerby's curious look, Mira realized she'd spoken her admonishment aloud.

Get it together, girl.

Le Veille and her mother both sought audiences with whom to share stories about the antiques they loved. Yet, why had he given her free such a priceless object? With a shake of her head, Mira decided it pointless to figure out motives of such an obviously strange man. She faced the shop for one last admiring glance at the Paquin outfit, but the mannequin no longer stood in the window. The display space contained nothing, and on the door hung a closed sign. She'd been outside the shop for less than a couple of minutes, not long enough for Le Veille to have moved the mannequin and closed the shop. Had she imagined the dress? Had she imagined the *La Fée aux Choux* coin purse?

Mira checked her pocket, relieved to find the purse still there. She studied the message again. *Curiouser and curiouser. Mom, you'll love this.*

She slid it back into the coin purse and retrieved her phone to glance at the time. Her exhausted body groaned at the idea of walking the short distance to Sylvie's. The taxi line at the nearby Metro Port Royal rank beckoned. She made her way to it. Settled into the cab's backseat, Mira reclined her head and closed her eyes. She'd suffered from jetlag before tackling her arduous day. Now, total exhaustion claimed her.

Once rested, she'd laugh about Le Veille's mysterious ways, the disappearing dress, and the message in the coin purse.

Just wait until I tell you about this guy, Mom.

Mira bolted upright. Had Mom and Sylvie played a practical joke on her? Was Le Veille a hired actor?

I'll play along, to let you both think I fell for it.

The driver delivered her to the front of the building.

The old-fashioned elevator clanked and churned its way to Sylvie's floor.

Mira entered the apartment, placed the heavy shopping bag on the floor, and massaged her aching shoulders. She drew water for a long soak and poured a glass of wine, dismissing the strangeness of her visit to Intemporel Antiquités.

Clawfoot tub, here I come.

FOUR

Mira slipped under the cover of bubbles generated by Pre de Provence bubble bath. The smell from lavender aromatherapy candles perched on the window ledge by the tub, the sensuousness of the bath, and sips of red wine drew the stress from her body.

After a long soak, she pried herself from the tub and bundled into a soft terry-cloth robe. Ravenous, she devoured the delicious meal Victor-the-chef prepared for her.

I could get used to this life.

Satiated with food and wine, Mira removed the day's purchases from the shopping bags and arranged them on the dining table, except for the *La Fée aux Choux* coin purse and the message. She placed those on the coffee table.

I can't wait to catch you on this joke, Mom.

Mira realized with the time change between Paris and New York, it would be four in the afternoon there, a good time to call. Carolyn answered instead.

"Eleanor's napping, sweetheart. Can we call you later?" "Absolutely."

After Carolyn reassured her that her mom's condition remained status quo, Mira ended the quick conversation. The day's whirlwind and the glasses of wine sent her to an early bedtime. She snuggled under the comforter beneath the canopy and lifted prayers for her mother's healing, anxious to speak with her. When she fell into an exhausted sleep, she dreamed about riding on a carousel, round and round, unable to get off.

Mira awakened before dawn, dizzy and disoriented from fitful, strange dreams. She checked her phone, but no call had come from her mom. Wide awake with worry, she stretched long under the bed's lovely canopy and realized she was starved. Sylvie had spoiled her yesterday with a lovely breakfast in bed. No Sylvie this morning, though.

You're on your own today, kiddo.

After downing the delicious orange juice, Mira munched on a croissant and sipped hot tea while she scrolled through the weather app. The forecast called for another chilly spring day. She donned once again her lone packed outfit of the black turtle neck and jeans.

With time to fill because of her early rising, she perused through her social media, emails, and texts and worried about why her mom hadn't called her. The time would be close to midnight there, too late now. When her phone erupted in her mom's ringtone of "Flight of the Bumblebee," Mira almost dropped it. She clicked on Facetime, trying to hide concern over how exhausted her pajama-clad mother appeared. "I was just thinking of you, Mom. It's so late there. Why are you up?"

"Hey, sweetie. Carolyn said you phoned while I was napping. I slept quite a long time, so I'm wide awake now. It's great to see you. I didn't even think, though, about it being so early there. It's what, six in the morning and you're already dressed for the day?"

"Yup. I must be messed up from jet lag. Or maybe I was too excited to sleep much because of my successful shopping yesterday. Look." Mira turned her phone onto the purchases on the dining table before zooming in on the list of the deliveries coming the next morning.

She allowed her mom's ooh's and ahh's before turning the phone back to herself and shifting the conversation to Le Veille, leaving out he reminded her of her father. She described the Paquin outfit on the mannequin before explaining how Le Veille insisted she must take the *La Fée aux Choux* coin purse.

"The entire visit to the shop was surreal. He said his heart told him the coin purse awaited me." Mira widened her eyes. "If I didn't know any better,

I'd describe his demeanor as ominous." She bit her lower lip, controlling her laughter.

"I agree, Mira. It's odd."

Her mother's sincere tone and the questioning expression in her eyes destroyed Mira's theory of a practical joke. "Wait. You and Sylvie didn't set this whole thing up?"

"Not at all. I've never met this man nor visited his shop. He emailed me the offer of the coin purses, saying he knew of my interest from my website. I thought at the time how the French word *veille* can translate as *the day before*. We antique dealers do focus on the days before, don't we?"

Her mom paused to catch her breath before adding, "It can translate as *watch*, such as *keeping watch*. He said the coin purse awaited you? When he found my website, he might have found your blog online as well. You have been posting on Alice Guy, so maybe your interest in her inspired him to give you the coin purse."

"Maybe." Her mom's weakened voice and difficulty breathing dismissed Le Veille from Mira's attention. "Never mind Le Veille or anything else. Let's talk about you, Mom. How are you? Really?"

"I'm fine. Don't worry."

Mira bit her lip. How could she not worry? Dr. West and the transplant team had explained hospitalization would be required as her mother's heart continued to weaken. Had that time come?

"Show me the coin purse and the message, sweetie." Her mother sounded even more breathless.

Mira padded into the living room and switched her phone's view to the coffee table. She zoomed in on the writing on the purse and on the message. "I'm sure it's nonsense. *Les balivernes,* as Sylvie said. "The coin purse is in remarkable condition. Its connection to Alice Guy-Blaché must be a fantastic coincidence." Mira flipped the phone's view to herself. "I can't wait to show my professor. He'll not believe it."

"I bet. It's hard to believe, especially the note. You've always loved the Luxembourg Carousel. You should visit it at noon today. For the fun of it. Promise me you'll have fun?" Her mom's voice faded.

Seeing her mom every day must have camouflaged her mother's sharp decline, but now Mira clearly noticed. "Mom, I'm changing my flight to come home tonight."

"Mirabelle Montgomery, you will do no such thing. Carolyn is staying with me."

Carolyn popped into view behind her mom. "Hey, Mirabelle. Your mom is doing fine. Stay for your trip as planned."

"I told you." Her mom straightened in her seat. Her vigorous reaction brought color to her face and strength in her voice. "The cost of changing flights is exorbitant. And, if you do leave early, you'll miss spending Monday with Sylvie. Plus, you would leave before the purchases arrive tomorrow for you to pack. Sylvie would have to ship them." "Oh, Mom, that is not a problem. Sylvie has people who can help."

"Your flight will get you here late tomorrow evening. Nothing will happen between now and then." She paused, once again breathless, before adding, "So, it's settled. No more discussion."

A debate of logic versus emotion raged within Mira. If she changed the flight, her trip would exceed its careful budget. And, though Sylvie had people—she even had people who had people, as the saying went—she'd hate to burden her.

Mira swallowed her misgivings. "You win. I'll keep my original plans."

"And promise to have a bit of Paris fun?" "Yes. I promise."

"Exactly what I need to hear. My best medicine is for you to enjoy yourself. I think I'll go to bed now. We'll talk later, honey. Love you."

"Yes, you need to go to bed. It's after one in the morning now. I love you too, Mom."

The call left Mira gutted. She texted Carolyn for reassurance.

Hey. Mom looks tired and fragile. Should I come home tomorrow?

Not unless you want your mom to never forgive you. OK, thanks for being there for her. And me.

Keep your promise and go have fun. Maybe go to the Carousel. We're hitting the sack now. Talk later.

Mira prepared another cup of tea and lounged on the sofa reading more chapters in *The Triumph of Art Nouveau Paris - Exhibition 1900* she'd begun last night. Keeping her eyes open became a challenge. The book slipping from her hand onto the floor jolted her awake. A glance at a small, antique clock on the end table showed ten o'clock. She'd napped for about almost two hours.

She swung to a seated position and picked up the *La Fée aux Choux* coin purse to study it and the enclosed message once more.

"Why not?" Mira announced to the room. "I'll visit the Carousel at noon. Who knows? Maybe I'll run into Bill Cody."

She pulled on her boots and swirled into her cape. In its interior pocket she placed the purse with its message tucked inside, her wallet, and her phone. She'd spend her time before the imaginary Carousel rendezvous at the Cluny Museum.

The early Paris morning air possessed a cool bite, but Mira embraced it during her short walk to the medieval mansion housing the Cluny Museum. She never tired of visiting it, especially to view The Lady and The Unicorn, 15th century tapestries. The five tapestries that depicted touch, taste, smell, hearing, and sight took her breath away as usual, but she lingered longest at the sixth tapestry. Its embroidered saying à *mon seul désir* meant *by my own free will*—not something many ladies during the Middle Ages were allowed to act upon.

"Did you embrace your own will, my lady, as I have?" Mira whispered. "Did you find it to be a dangerous thing? For here I am alone, again."

Mira headed to Luxembourg Gardens, taking the Rue Racine route to enter the gardens near the Fontaine Medicis. She came upon a large group led by a tour guide crowding around the fountain. The guide would lead them around to the Fontaine de Leda behind the Medicis, an all-too-hidden gem that unless pointed out went unnoticed. She'd view it before the tour approached it.

Sylvie had shown it to her as a child, explaining its story. "The bas relief tells the story of Jupiter transforming into a swan to seduce Leda, who carries the swan in her arms. The result was an egg, from which Helen of Troy was born."

The myth severely messed with the young Mira's impressionable mind. No wonder she suffered from commitment issues.

Just kidding, Sylvie.

When the guide and tourists joined her, Mira walked around to the Medici Fountain. Flanked by plane trees and giant swags of ivy, its aura projected romance and peacefulness. That combination did not exist in her relationship with Rob. Romance? Yes. But never peacefulness, for her heart never felt at rest with him. She had been right to listen to its argument.

Mira selected two coins from her wallet for wish making and dangled her hand over the wrought-iron fencing to drop the first coin.

Bring my mother a heart. She dropped the second coin. *Bring my heart its soulmate.*

Mira smiled. How many others have wished the same? She replaced her wallet into her cape pocket, and her hand grazed the coin purse. A quick glance at the time on her phone warned she must hurry to the Carousel if she were to fulfill the message's invitation to meet at noon.

Accepting an over century-old invitation smacked of a fool's errand, but she traversed the gravelly pathways, breathing the fragrance of blooming tulips and budding green trees. She paused to enjoy the sight of children setting their sailboats adrift in the Grand Basin before walking by the Théâtre des Marionnettes, where families queued for the next show.

The shrieks of energetic children greeted Mira upon her arrival at the small, green-roofed Carousel next to the park's playground. Of the many carousels in Paris, she loved best this oldest, dirt-floor, weather-beaten one. It played no music. Its smaller-scaled animals dangled from poles anchored into the Carousel's ceiling. Their wooden bodies showed scars from more than a hundred years of children's enjoyment riding upon them.

She pondered a sweet memory of her childhood from when she and her parents visited Sylvie. Her father brought her to this Carousel and recited "Das Karussell," a poem by the German language poet Rainer Maria Rilke. The magic of hearing her dad speak German entranced her.

He recited it again but in English, and the line about the white elephant captivated her. She insisted on riding it and no other Carousel animal. Her father placed her upon the white elephant that day so long ago. After his death, whenever she and her mom visited Sylvie, they made a point of enjoying a picnic at the gardens and of her riding the elephant. She didn't mind how long the wait. Elephants were patient sorts, so she could be patient as well. That elephant brought her dad close again.

With her heart warmed from the memory, Mira searched for "her" elephant. She spotted a young boy astride it, wielding a wooden stick. His face was set with the determination of a jousting chevalier. The children played *jeu de bagues*, the ring game, as she and the generations before her played. Adults cheered the attempts by the boys and girls to spear a dangling tin ring spit from a wooden box held high by the old attendant. His quick agility kept the box loaded without fail. Whoever speared the most rings won bragging rights, nothing more. Mira distinctly recalled the thrill of her own bragging rights.

Her dad called *jeu de bagues* a dizzy and breathless game, a play on a line from the Rilke poem. An ache to be a child again overwhelmed Mira, when her dad was alive, her mom was healthy—and her own belief in true love hopeful. Mira dismissed her maudlin self-pity and removed the message from *La Fée aux Choux* coin purse to study it once more.

Rendez-vous avec moi au Carrousel du Luxembourg à midi.

At that moment, the sun faded, casting a shadow on the slip of paper. Mira inspected the sky, surprised at the suddenness of the overcast. The glorious weather hinted no storm, yet unexpectedly now the wind picked up. Her skin prickled at the distant rumble of thunder.

The ride spun slowly to a stop.

"Descendez, descendez maintenant." The attendant waved frantically at the adults to claim the dismounting children.

The crowd quickly dispersed to avoid the brewing storm, which grew more threatening. The Luxemburg Palace clock chimed, beginning its striking of the noon hour.

Mira snuggled into her cape for warmth against the descending fog's chill. Why had she let this stupid message entice her to the Carousel? With no umbrella, she'd be drenched. She tucked the message into the coin purse and shoved the purse into her cloak's pocket. At the same moment, a text vibrated her phone. She assumed it to be Sylvie. It would be six in the morning back home, too early for anyone to be contacting her . . . unless for an emergency? She pulled the phone from her pocket. When she read Carolyn's text, her heart raced.

Mira, catch the next plane. Your mother has—

The dots flickered on the screen, indicating more words.

Come on, come on. Mom has what?

"Mlle Montgomery."

The powerful voice of the man drew her attention. Confusion clouded her thoughts. Through the foggy air, she recognized him. "M. Le Veille?"

His piercing gaze locked her eyes into his. He wore an old-fashioned top hat and a long cape, reminding Mira of a magician. His outstretched hands beckoned her toward the white elephant. "It awaits you."

How did he know about the white elephant? Her face flushed. She didn't have patience for his foolishness. Besides, the Carousel animals were meant for children. She gripped her phone tighter.

Why didn't the rest of Carolyn's text come through? What is happening?

"Come. Now."

She walked toward Le Veille, relinquishing her will to his control.

The rumbling thunder and the Palace clock, completing its chiming of the noon hour, vibrated within her. Once she stood under the Carousel's ceiling, a cold wind started blowing and the Carousel began turning. With her free hand, she grabbed the pole attached to the elephant, *her* elephant, and swung her body onto it, bending her knees high so as not to drag the ground.

The white elephant line in Rilke's poem raced stupidly through her thoughts. She shoved her phone into her cape's pocket, and her hand again grazed against the coin purse. It now radiated warmth.

Mira squeezed the elephant's pole so tightly her knuckles whitened. The pole glowed with fire but did not scorch her palms. Her scattered thoughts darted this way and that.

Am I dreaming? Has someone slipped me a psychedelic? Am I dying? Is Mom dying? The text . . . why didn't I receive the rest of the text?

The Carousel spun faster. A whooshing, icy wind slammed against her body. Its roar filled her ears with aching fullness. Flames shot from the pole, yet no fire touched her. Instead, it surrounded her body without burning her. She yearned for its warmth against the chill penetrating through her. She spun by where Le Veille stood.

His urgent command reached her, his tone low and forceful. "Vanish into the past which holds your future. Return only if you right the wrong destiny that has befallen him."

The Carousel's unbridled acceleration catapulted Mira from the white elephant into a spiraling black tunnel. Its centrifugal force flattened her into an almost one-dimensional body, sucking her screaming into its dizzy, breathless game.

FIVE

The spiraling ceased.

Screaming, Mira descended from the tunnel, limbs flailing. The rush of air extinguished the flames outlining her almost-flattened frame. Her flesh rapidly expanded over her bones. Waves of pain cascaded through her. She plummeted feet first onto a moving wooden platform.

Losing her balance, Mira lurched sideways into a young woman, sending the girl's open parasol precariously spinning.

She turned her attention to Mira, her mouth moving in rapid-fire motion.

The dull ringing in Mira's ears prevented her from hearing the girl's animated words. Panic reverberated through her sore body. Stupefied, she studied the surroundings and people. She attracted no one else's attention except for this person she'd crashed into and a man, clean-shaven except for a modest mustache. He wore a sack suit of corduroy cloth and a working man's cap. A long, jagged scar marred his left cheek.

He surveyed her mockingly, his eyes narrowing and his tongue traveling his lips before shifting his impudent gaze from her.

Mira shuddered in relief. She'd not be strong enough to fend off an encounter. In her deafened state, the scene before her played like a silent movie. Had she landed in a fabulously constructed set, with hundreds of extras outfitted in fashions true to the turn of the last century?

Or, have I vanished into the past? Impossible. I must be dreaming.

The cape she wore Mira recognized as her own. She groped in its pocket, hoping to find her phone but finding nothing.

A text. I had been reading a text. Why can't I remember? Under her cape she no longer wore her black turtleneck and jeans but a long skirt and bodice. The discomfort of her snug undergarment indicated she wore a corset. She brushed her gloved fingertips against the wide brim of the hat weighing heavily upon her head and then against her bare neck. Her hair must be pinned under the hat.

The snugly fitted cream-colored kid gloves pinched against the finger on which she wore her moonstone ring. Mira removed the glove and flexed her hand for relief. The shine of her ring provided her with an iota of comfort. She struggled on her glove, noticing the intricate turquoise, rose, and lavender embroidery on the gloves' cuffs matched the embroidery on her outfit. The cuff reached to the bottom of her wrist.

A memory surfaced, of being at Luxembourg Gardens and hearing the Luxembourg Palace clock chime the noonday. The noonday sun still shone directly overhead, but in another time era. Her unwelcome transition into the past had occurred in seconds.

The girl she bumped into snapped shut her parasol and tapped it in Mira's direction. Her mouth once again moved. Mira pressed her tongue against the roof of her mouth and swallowed hard, to clear the fullness from her ears. Finally, sounds burst forth. Mira winced at the explosion of noise: loud laughter, animated conversations in French, the clank of a whirring noise from under the wooden platform on which they stood—and the girl's loud reaction to their collision.

"Do you not hear me? I talk to you, but you ignore me." She tossed her head, jostling her wide-brimmed Breton-style straw hat and sending her long plaits flying.

Mira understood the French the girl spoke. *Impossible.*

"You did not apologize for running into me." The girl again tapped her parasol's tip against the walkway.

She reminded Mira of Leslie Caron at the beginning of *Gigi,* when Gigi was an innocent schoolgirl of sixteen or so. The girl even wore a plaid bolero jacket, matching skirt, and white blouse spilling from the jacket sleeves, like Gigi.

"*C'est bon.*" The girl's mood abruptly transformed from anger to friendliness. She moved closer to Mira. "Do you see that man? His attention upon me has been unsettling."

Mira swiveled her head and noticed the same man whose attention she'd garnered.

"I might be overly suspicious. But he is most terrifying, do you not think?" She affixed her attention on Mira. "My name is Bernadette Roget. And yours?"

"Mirabelle Montgomery." Mira's tongue moved heavily in her dry mouth and her voice sounded hoarse. Feverish chills raced through her. Her words tumbled out in American- accented French. "Pardon. I did not mean to knock against you."

I don't know French. How am I speaking and understanding it?

"Ahh, your accent." Bernadette's thin lips stretched into a welcoming smile. "You are American." She spoke now in delightfully accented English.

The adage came to Mira: *Pinch me, I must be dreaming.* If she were dreaming, folklore said she'd feel no pain. She held her arm toward Bernadette. "Pinch me."

Bernadette's face brightened with anticipation. "We play the American parlor game? I love games." She pinched Mira's nose.

"Ouch." Mira rubbed her nose. "Why did you pinch me there?"

"Pardon." Bernadette clasped her hand against her forehead. "Were we not playing Pinch Without Laughing?"

"What? No." Feverish chills again raced through her. If she were not dreaming, then what? Her knees buckled, and she sagged against Bernadette.

"Oh, my." Bernadette wrapped an arm around Mira's waist and led her to one of the waist-high poles evenly spaced apart at the edge of the wooden sidewalk. "Hold on for balance."

Mira gripped the pole and fought against her knees buckling.

Bernadette gazed at her with interest. "We shall speak English, for your French is lacking. Oh, sorry. I do not mean to insult. My English is lacking, as well."

"Oh, no." Mira shook her head. "Your English is excellent."

"Your compliment is kind. Practice will make perfect, no?" Bernadette beamed. "You are in Paris for Exposition Universelle?"

"Paris? Exposition Universelle?" Mira repeated numbly. "What is today's date?"

"Date?" Bernadette raised her eyebrows. "Why, the twenty-eighth of April." "1900?"

"Yes."

"1900?" Dazed, Mira repeated once more. "That can't be."

"But it is." Bernadette giggled. "How you say, *petite sotte?* Silly bird?"

"Goose. Silly goose," Mira said softly.

"Mirabelle, you do not seem well." Bernadette leaned in closely, peering at her intently. "Let me accompany you to your accommodations. Where do you stay?"

The onslaught of questions begins. If I answer with Sylvie's address, what if it didn't exist? Best to plead ignorance. Feign amnesia.

"I don't know."

Bernadette frowned. "Were you traveling with others?"

"I don't know."

Bernadette's eyes widened. "You do not know where you are staying or the names of any companions?"

"I can't remember."

"You poor thing. It is Lethe's fault." Bernadette nodded knowingly. "Lethe is the Greek spirit of forgetfulness and oblivion. You must have fallen under her spell."

Mira nodded, grateful for this young girl's vivid imagination.

Bernadette tapped her parasol emphatically on the walkway. "Do not worry. You will come with me." She jutted her chin forward in a determined way. "My guardian is Jacques Thibaut. He used to be a police detective. I am to meet him at the Eiffel Tower. He can help you."

"Help me?" The girl's words prompted Mira's recall. The intrigue of the coin purse and message enticed her to the Carousel. She checked the inside pocket of her cape once more. *No coin purse, wallet, or phone.*

Snatches came to her: Intemporel Antiques. Le Veille. The Paquin dress on the mannequin. The coin purse and the message. The Luxembourg Carousel. The tunnel sucking her from it. Le Veille's command, "Vanish into the past which holds your future. Return only if you right the wrong destiny that has befallen him."

Le Veille's paradox provided no name, no exact specifics, only she must right a man's wrong destiny.

Have I been deposited next to Bernadette to meet Jacques Thibaut?

"Mirabelle, come with me to meet him." Bernadette looped her arm through Mira's. "Do you think you are well enough to walk with me there?"

"I think so."

"We'll exit at this station, Champs de Mars." Bernadette flashed a comforting smile.

The girl lifted her skirt hem to show laced boots. Mira lifted her own hem and found she wore similar footwear. She looked more carefully at the outfit she wore beneath her cape. Le Veille had deposited her in 1900 in the Paquin ensemble worn by the mannequin in his shop window.

With linked arms, Mira walked abreast of Bernadette while they transitioned from the widest part of the moving walkway to the middle, less-wide part, and then onto its stationary part. They maneuvered from there onto the station's platform and descended the multi-level staircases built from lumber.

Bernadette glanced back. "*Dieu merci!* The strange man remained on the wooden serpent. I hope it bites him, do you not?"

"Serpent?" Mira echoed questioningly.

"Oh, I speak with tongue-in-mouth, as you Americans say?"

"Tongue-in-cheek," Mira corrected in a weak voice. She hoped to reach the Eiffel Tower without collapsing.

"*Oui*, tongue-in-cheek." Bernadette giggled. "Oh, the serpent. The way wooden sections of *le trottoir roulant* move on the circular path reminded a reporter of a wooden serpent with its tail in its mouth."

"Oh, my." Mira gasped, not in response to the vivid description of the moving sidewalk Bernadette shared but in exclamation over the imposing massive structure built of iron, steel, and glass situated behind the station. Standing before it, Mira barely comprehended its immensity.

"La Galerie des Machines." Bernadette announced its name in a huff of disgust. "I nominate this building for the ugly award." She pressed her gloved hand into Mira's hand and propelled her along. "Follow me closely. The exhibition crowds will, how you say, eat you."

"Swallow you," Mira corrected, managing a smile. "The crowds will swallow you."

Bernadette giggled. "English. So confusing."

Not as confusing as finding oneself transported to another place and time.

With her hand firmly clasped with Bernadette's, Mira let the teen lead them through the milling masses on the pedestrian mall of Champs de Mars. People were lolling on park benches, chairs, or the ground. Some were enjoying picnics. The odors of sausage, garlic, dirt, and human stench permeated the air.

Huge iron, concrete, and plaster exhibit halls, each boasting elaborate decorative fronts, lined each side of the Champs de Mars. Mira's heart pounded like a sledgehammer against her chest. The sights before her banished any doubt. She had indeed traveled to the past, swirled back in time by a sucking, tornadic wind.

At one end of Champs de Mars stood the Palace of Electricity, the Water Chateau, and the gigantic Ferris wheel called Grande Roue de Paris, rotating with passengers. Mira's stomach tightened at the sight of it. After a vortex having swallowed her, Mira felt sickened by the circular motion of the wheel.

At the other end stood the Eiffel Tower. It shone not bronze as she knew it, but bright yellow-gold—repainted for the 1900 Exhibit. Mira's pace slowed, overwhelmed by her observation around her and her own exhaustion.

"You walk slowly." Bernadette flung her free hand into the air. "The Exhibition impresses you in the day. But wait until night. The lights. *Oh là là.*"

"*Oh là là,*" Mira repeated. She swayed, dizziness overtaking her feverish body. "Pardon me, but I must sit." Her sandpaper tongue in her still-parched mouth continued to impede her ability to speak clearly.

"Oh dear." Bernadette helped her toward a park bench by the base of the Eiffel Tower. She checked her watch dangling from a gold chain pinned to her blouse next to a gold bar of a design Mira did not recognize. "Sit here and rest. Jacques will arrive soon."

Mira sank onto the bench, breathing deeply. Her heavy clothing and hat, even her gloves, hung hot and heavy, suffocating her. She jerked the gloves off and fanned herself with them.

Bernadette watched her with a quizzical look.

Mira stopped fanning. "What?"

"Do American ladies not know the language of gloves? Fanning them means you wish to meet someone, which you will." Bernadette stood on tiptoes to peer above the heads of the passing crowds. "Once Jacques arrives, I will introduce you."

Mira rested the gloves in her lap.

What other messages are sent by gloves? I'll need tutoring by Bernadette or who knows what messages I might send.

A tall man wearing a homburg called out to them as he approached, walking cane in hand. "*Bonjour,* Bébé."

Even in her ill state, Mira reacted to his handsome appearance.

He belongs on the cover of GQ.

The narrowed suit jacket with its small, high lapels and well-fitting trousers defined his muscular body. On one lapel, he sported the same gold bar as the one on Bernadette's blouse.

He wore his collar turned down with a knotted tie threaded around his neck and his dark hair short. A closely trimmed mustache accented his clean-shaven face. The cane he tapped with every step accentuated his swaggering gait.

"Jaco." Bernadette stood to wave. "We need your assistance." She lowered her voice to whisper conspiratorially to Mira. "I beg you say nothing about the man on *le trottoir roulant.* Jaco will never allow me out of his sight again."

She waved at him once more. "Please, do not mention we met on the walkway. He will know I did not attend my *Lycée's* tour of *Le Vieux Paris,* the exhibit of Old Paris. Instead, I was with *le petit ami,* Siméon. We were—"

Mira shook her hand at the girl to silence her. She had little strength to become involved in the issues between a rule-breaking teen and her guardian.

Bernadette clapped her hand to her mouth. "*Pardon.* Jacques tells me I talk too much. But I advise you to be gloved before I introduce you."

Mira managed to glove only her left hand before Jacques reached them. She watched Bernadette and the man greet each other in the French way, leaning forward, touching cheeks, and kissing the air while making kissing sounds with their lips.

Will I be expected to exchange the same with this man? Or extend my hand for greeting?

Bernadette waved her arm back and forth in introduction. "Jaco, may I introduce Mirabelle Montgomery. Mirabelle, meet my guardian, Jacques Thibaut."

"*Bonjour*, Mlle Montgomery." He bowed, hooking the cane onto his arm. "To clarify, my charge and I enjoy tormenting each other with nicknames, Bébé and Jaco."

He spoke in accented English, the same as Bernadette. His lips parted in a smile that did not reach his eyes. They were bluest-of-blue eyes marked with unusual dark rings circling the irises.

Mira discerned in them little empathy or interest. If eyes were the windows to one's soul, she detected his to be nailed shut.

It will be challenging to gain your trust.

Mira did not trust herself to stand for the cheek kissing exchange nor did she feel comfortable to do so. She held out her ungloved right hand to invite the formal hand greeting.

When Jacques accepted her hand, Mira expected him to place the back of her hand to his lips without making contact. Instead, his lips brushed against it.

The touch vibrated through Mira, shocking her like an electric current. She'd never felt that way when Rob and she touched.

"Jaco!" Bernadette gasped and then giggled.

Mira noticed him staring at her moonstone ring. She rescinded her hand. The presence of this man unsettled her as much as the time travel itself.

"Mirabelle and I stumbled into each other." Bernadette giggled again at the description of their meeting.

Mira frowned with disappointment at the girl's levity. "Oh, I should not joke." A sober expression crossed Bernadette's face. "Mirabelle stumbled against me, ill and lost. She knows her name, nothing else. We must help her, Jaco."

Jacques' eyes lingered on Mira's moonstone ring before he spoke. "You remember nothing except your name, Mlle Montgomery?"

Their eyes locked.

Even if Bernadette had not shared that her guardian used to be a police detective, Mira would have suspected by his suspicious reaction toward her.

Your confident swagger doesn't indicate you need anyone's help, much less a confused and weak time traveler's. "Perhaps you are one of the wealthy young American women who come to Paris while visiting the continent. Or one who professes to reside here to study art." Mira discerned the disapproval in his tone.

"The behavior of those in the second category is well- known as free and easy. Might you be suffering from *gueule de bois*?"

Mira understood his insult. "A hangover? I assure you not, M. Thibaut."

This arrogant, rude man could not be the one Le Veille sent her to help. She needed to find her mission's correct target. Mira struggled to her feet, but dizziness overtook her. She collapsed against the back of the bench.

"Jaco, how dare you." Bernadette sat and placed a comforting hand on Mira's shoulder. "Mirabelle is ill and not suffering from the aftermath of drink. You are a cad."

Mira sensed the girl's criticism landed a blow.

"She may have a fever." Bernadette placed the back of a hand against Mira's forehead. "We should have Susette examine her."

"Not Susette." Scowling, Jacques waved his cane into the air as emphasis.

Mira wished she had the energy to ask about Susette. The woman's name spiked his anger.

A former wife? Girlfriend? Lover?

Susette meant enough to Jacques for him to erupt over the mention of her.

He gave a curt nod toward Mira. "Apologies, Mlle Montgomery. Perhaps we should take you to hospital."

"No!" Panic pulsed through Mira. What if doctors examined her and detected medical anomalies not fitting with medicine of their day? However, she needed a place to rest and recuperate.

"May I rest at your place? Please?" Mira rose quickly, too quickly. She toppled against Jacques.

Jacques caught her. "Ça *me soule.*"

Mira understood his exasperated mutter of annoyance. "Let me go." Her words came faintly.

He scooped her into his arms. She did not fight against him.

"Take my cane, Bébé, and hail a cab. *Dépêche-toi.* Hurry." His words rang out loudly.

"*Oui, je vais me dépêcher.* I hurry!" Bébé rushed off, the cane held high and her shouts fading into the distance.

Crushed against Jacques' chest, Mira's strength ebbed. The mingled scents of his cologne—talcum, sandalwood, and earthy incense—overwhelmed her senses. She relinquished herself to this man she knew next to nothing about. Yet, in his arms, she felt safe.

SIX

Animated voices speaking French awakened Mira. She flipped onto her back and stretched long, wondering if Sylvie's neighbors were having a row. When she opened her eyes, a spackled plaster ceiling greeted her instead of the canopy above her godmother's guest bed.

Mira bolted upright, digging her fingers into the red woolen blanket covering her. Her sudden movement triggered a burst of pain behind her eyes. She swallowed against a surge of nausea. Her body ached as if she'd run a marathon.

The flimsy cotton nightgown she wore did little to dispel her chilled-to-the-bone shivering. The room's small old-timey wall radiator provided little heat. The numbness of her hands caused her moonstone ring to turn loosely on her finger. Shivering, Mira tucked the woolen blanket tightly around herself. She saw only a brick wall from the window. The view provided no hint of her geographic location, but she assumed she was in Paris.

The set designer in her catalogued her surroundings. The room's furnishings reminded her somewhat of the Van Gogh painting, "The Bedroom." Lilac-painted walls. Dull- yellow-painted headboard and matching bureau. Orange wooden table holding a pitcher, basin, and vintage men's toiletries.

A wooden slatted-back chair, with a lady's wide- brimmed hat adorned with plumage and gloves resting on its the seat and her cape folded over its back. In the other corner, an articulated dressing screen with butterflies flitting among vines painted on its panels. A skirt and bodice and undergarments hung from it. Boots belonging to a lady sat on the floor beside it.

The raised voices of a man and woman drew Mira's attention once more. She recognized their names tossed back and forth: Jaco, Bébé. Jaco was insisting Bébé not mention taking "that woman" to Susette again.

I assume he is referring to me as "that woman" but who is Susette?

Mira pressed her fingertips to her pounding forehead. Memory fragments began sorting into place, like pieces of a jigsaw puzzle, until she accepted the unacceptable fact: Le Veille transported her to 1900 Paris to do his bidding.

Vanish into the past which holds your future. Return only if you right the wrong destiny that has befallen him.

A paradox. I hate paradoxes.

Her body trembled, not from the cold but from remembering Carolyn's unfinished text: *Mira, catch the next plane. Your mother has . . .*

That's why she had been searching for her phone. What did the rest of the text say? She closed her eyes tightly, and tears slid from them.

The voices outside the room grew louder. Her breathing became short and shallow. What did she know of these two? What if they held her prisoner for evil purposes? If Le Veille had not given her the antique coin purse with the odd message in it . . . if she had not followed the message's instructions . . . she'd be at Sylvie's, where she belonged.

She must find her way to her own time. What was the law of science she learned from suffering through high school physics?

"For every action, there's an equal and opposite reaction." Mira spoke the words aloud, a plan forming. "If the Carousel's elephant thrust me back in time, it should operate in reverse to thrust me forward, to my present day."

A sharp rap at the door silenced her. Terror shimmied through her. The small room offered no hiding place. Her eyes landed on the large silver hairbrush with a handle amongst the men's toiletries. She leapt to grab it. The chair toppled from her hasty movement. Satisfied with the brush's heft, she stood against the wall where the opened door would hide her.

"Mirabelle?" The door creaked open against where she hid. "It's Bernadette. Are you awake, *mon amie*?"

"May we come in?" The slimly built girl pushed the door open and entered the room.

Mira jumped out from behind the door, wielding the hairbrush against her. Bernadette's scream pierced the air.

Jacques charged through the door and gripped Mira's wrist tightly.

Instinctively, she flew into a Jujitsu move her ex taught her. She rotated her wrist clockwise in his grip, so her palm pointed toward her face. She forcefully thrust her hand onto Jacques', and his hand flew from her. Her move worked like a charm, except Jacques' muscular frame blocked the door.

"She beat you, Jaco." Bernadette burst into nervous laughter. "Mirabelle, do all American women know how to fight? Or only you, a mysterious woman, who suddenly appeared in my path?"

She snapped her fingers in the air. "You were not there, and then you were. A magic trick. *Poof.* In a disoriented state, may I add. You appeared to have been pushed into the wringer."

"Gone through the wringer." Mira whispered the correction, thinking how accurate of a description.

"Mlle, you have nothing to fear from us." Jacques stepped toward her.

Mira surrendered the brush to him. Her face heated at the memory of collapsing into his arms.

He tossed the brush onto the bed, leaned against the doorframe, and crossed his arms. "Bernadette describes you correctly. You are *mysterious*." He slowly flicked his eyes over her.

His lascivious attention reminded her of the nightgown's transparency and of his insulting innuendos when they first met.

Gueule de bois.

How dare you assume the worst of me. Why does Le Veille expect me to help such an utterly disgusting man.

"*You* are rude, M. Thibaut." She wrapped herself into the woolen blanket from the bed and sat stiffly on the edge of it.

Jacques dipped his head, his grin still in place.

"Jaco." Bernadette gave his arm a slap. "So sorry. He's a man, and you are a beautiful woman." She sat next to Mira on the bed. "Everything must be so confusing for you."

An understatement.

"How awful to remember only your name. Jacques used to be a detective. He can help you." Bernadette cast a beleaguered look at him. "Can't you, Jaco?"

Jacques brushed his fingers against his mustache. "If she wishes."

Mira kept silent, struggling with her judgment of the guardian Bernadette adored. When she needed help, he showed kindness and brought her to his home. But his overt stare sent an uneasy and seductive signal, relaying his low opinion of her as a wild American woman, a bohemian.

He must think I have loose morals. Is that why he brashly kissed my extended hand when we met. Does he suspect me of being a prostitute? Or, a coquette?

Jacques righted the toppled chair and replaced the scattered items onto it before turning to address Mira directly, eyebrows lifted. "You claim to have no memories except for your name. I've read about retrograde amnesia. Ripot's Law? Do you know of it?"

"No." Mira bristled at his interrogation.

"During my time on the police force, we studied the latest psychological findings to help us in interviewing suspects and witnesses. Ripot's Law states someone can suffer from amnesia temporarily after a traumatic event, but distant memories are not lost."

So, Jacques doubts my claim of amnesia. Yet I must depend on my cover story. If I try to explain what is happening to me, he'd believe me insane. It's better if he thinks I am a lowlife liar.

After a moment, Jacques frowned. "I cannot help you, Mlle Montgomery, if you keep details from me. Surely, you can recall at least one memory from the distant past?"

"Try, Mirabelle." Bernadette squeezed her hand. "Maybe if you closed your eyes?"

Mira shut her eyes. *What truth can I say that will keep my unbelievable situation a secret?*

"I know my mother is ill. I remember being at the Luxembourg Carousel where a strange man shouted for me to vanish. I remember a dark tunnel swirling around me. I remember nothing else. I do not know how I made my way to *le trottoir roulant*."

She opened her eyes. Her voice grew husky with emotion. "I very much need to find my way home." Those persistent tears once again gathered in her eyes.

"Do not lose hope." Bernadette threw her arm around Mira's shoulder. "We shall help you." Jacques offered his handkerchief.

"Thank you." Mira accepted it, once again noticing the black ringed irises of Jacques' blue eyes and their closed expression.

I'll not easily win over your untrusting, suspicious nature.

"I am sorry your mother is ill."

Mira sensed sincerity. She blotted her tears. "Thank you."

"Your other memories are strange." Jacques ticked his points on each finger. "First, who is this man? Second, why would he want you to vanish? Third, what caused this dark tunnel? We have experienced no storms recently, and your condition does not indicate you have been wandering for days."

"I have no answers." Mira responded with sincerity, for she truly had none.

"We live near Luxembourg Gardens. If you are well enough for an outing, I shall escort you there." Jacques' lips twitched. "Visiting where you last remember being may help you recover your, um, memory."

Mira ignored his biting inference. Her body tensed with worried excitement.

Do I need Le Veille to activate the Carousel portal? Were the coin purse and the message needed? Or, will sitting upon the white elephant instigate time travel? What if I travel to another time, instead of to my present life?

The glint of her ring's moonstone spoke of her father's love and his heroism.

As my father did that night, I must act with bravery. Le Veille, be damned. If I can make my way back to my own time, where I need to be, I will do so. I will not suffer one jot of conscience over leaving this man to right his own destiny. He does not appear to need anyone's help, and surely not mine.

"Yes." Mira nodded. "Please escort me."

"I love the Carousel." Bernadette leapt from the bed. "Let me help you dress, Mirabelle, and we shall be off."

"No, Bébé." Jacques clapped his hands at her. "You may help her dress, but then you go to *Le Lycée*. You will not miss another day."

"Oh." Bernadette sank back onto the bed, color fading from her face.

Mira noticed the teen wore the same blouse and plaid skirt as yesterday. She assumed it to be the school outfit.

"I know about yesterday, Bébé." Jacques' voice projected aggravation. "You did not attend the school trip. You were with that boy."

Mira read Jacques' mind. *Teenagers.* He must have his hands full raising one as spirited and as pretty as Bernadette. She was a knock-out: sparkling brown eyes, rosy complexion, blonde hair. Her tiny waist accented her proportioned figure. But more importantly, her actions showed her to be kind, empathetic, and trustworthy. She hoped the boyfriend Bernadette mentioned—Siméon— appreciated her good heart and not just her beauty.

"Jaco, it is true. Siméon and I did not attend our classes yesterday, but we did nothing wrong while we were together. I promise. Unless you think experiencing the marvels of film with sound is wrong?" Bernadette's face regained its color, slowly reddening with passion. "A stroll with classmates through *Vieux Paris* does not compare to a visit to *le Phono-Cinema-Theatre* with Siméon. Why observe medieval jugglers and knights instead of *célébrités* such as the amazing Sarah Bernhardt on film? Synchronized sound films. The future, Jaco."

Bernadette's answer provoked an irritated sigh from Jacques, yet Mira perfectly understood the girl's excitement about the burgeoning film industry. That very excitement drew her into film preservation. She found herself at the point in time where the early film industry unfolded.

If only I traveled through time under my initiative, for my purpose and not for Le Veille's.

Mira rose from the bed and addressed the pouty Bernadette, who remained seated. "We can agree you belong in class. In your absence, M. Thibaut will ensure my safety." She cast a pointed glance at Jacques, expecting his appreciation for her encouraging Bernadette to obey him.

"Call me Jacques." He jauntily tipped a finger to his brow.

Cocky.

She did not reciprocate with permission for him to use her first name.

Bernadette shifted her gaze back and forth between Mira and Jacques before expelling a defeated sigh. "If that is how it must be. Mirabelle, you are certain you are strong enough for this outing?"

"Yes. I believe so." Mira projected a strength she lacked. The time traveling had slammed her physically. She needed sustenance to survive another time travel trip. "You have done so much for me, but may I ask another favor?"

"Ask." Bernadette bounced on the bed.

Mira patted her growling stomach. "I'm starving."

Bernadette flapped her hands toward Jacques. "*Dépêchez-vous.* Hurry, Jaco, fetch us fresh-baked baguettes while I assist Mirabelle in bathing and dressing."

"*Oui, m'dame.*" A teasing grin softened his sarcastic reply. He tapped his heels together and bowed toward Mira. "I shall leave you . . ." His eyes drifted over her once more. ". . . to dress."

Mira's cheeks burned, but she bit back her stinging retort. Additional negative adjectives effortlessly piled up: chauvinistic, rude, ungentlemanly, egotistical . . . sexy.

Very sexy.

She wondered if Susette found him to be, too.

SEVEN

Bernadette chatted away while she arranged the screen partition to hide the table with the water basin and other bath essentials atop it. "The pitcher is filled for you, and there's soap and towels. I hung your clothing on the screen to air."

"Thank you." The preparations made Mira long for a hot soak in Sylvie's clawfoot tub instead of the "bird bath." She would have to steel herself against the smell of musky body odors and use of shared *la toilettes*.

Hopefully not for long.

Once she arrived at the Carousel, she'd sit upon the white elephant—*her* white elephant—to enact the time portal. She'd find herself returned to Sylvie's Paris, as if this fantastical nonsense had not occurred.

How did the time continuance work while I am trapped in 1900? Does my "present time" march onward in my absence? If so, Sylvie must be so worried about my disappearance. Mom's condition might have deteriorated, or worse, depending on what the rest of Carolyn's text said. Stepping behind the screen to undress, doubt attacked her. Why did she think she could reverse the time travel? She shivered, remembering how the icy wind and fog enveloped her at the Carousel. Merely sitting upon the wooden animal did not thrust her into 1900 Paris.

Le Veille did, luring her with the message in the antique coin purse that she'd placed in her cape pocket. She'd arrived without them. What if she needed them in her hand for the portal to work?

What if she needed Le Veille? He hypnotized her, for lack of better description, to sit upon the white elephant. He shouted the confusing paradox before the dark tunnel took her.

Vanish into the past which holds your future.

How could the past hold her future?

Return only if you right the wrong destiny that has befallen him.

She assumed the man to be Jacques, but Le Veille had not said his name nor how to change his destiny.

The partition's painted butterflies reminded her of the so-called butterfly effect.

"If you alter an event back in time, you potentially alter the future in unforeseeable ways," her dad had explained when they read H. G. Wells together.

Le Veille's paradox implied her actions in 1900 Paris would alter her own future. Her nerves jangled.

What if I unknowingly bring tragedy upon myself, or those I love . . . her mother, Sylvie, Rob?

Mira included her ex among those she loved, even though his touch never sparked within her the physical longing she'd felt from Jacques' touch. Her face warmed, remembering the way his eyes roamed her body, stripping her naked.

She slipped from the nightgown and held it out to the side of the partition. "Bernadette, please fold this for me. I assume you changed me into it?"

Bernadette giggled. "To rest comfortably, your dress, undergarments, and boots needed removing. I struggled with your unconscious body, limp as a dead one. Jaco offered to help."

Waves of embarrassment cascaded through Mira. She poked her head out from the screen. "You didn't let him."

Bernadette pointed at Mira. "Oh, you are horrified." She giggled. "I tease you. I did not allow him to help nor allow him to sleep with you in his bed as he offered." She twitched her index finger in the air. "*C'est un vilain homme.*"

"Yes. A very naughty man." With a relieved sigh, Mira disappeared behind the partition. "I am sorry I turned him out of his own bed. I hope he found another?"

Perhaps Susette's?

Bernadette snickered. "He never lacks a place to lay his head."

"Really."

"Oh, do not pay me attention. He is a gentleman, not a rogue. Last night he slept upstairs in the *chambre de bonne*." "Your maid's room?"

"Our maid?" A belly laugh burst from Bernadette. "No, no. The wealthy family, the Bissetts, who live below us on *etage noble* have maids. They are away to the countryside, to escape the madness of the Exhibition. M. Bissett provided Jacques with a key to supervise his residence and garret. Jacques used it to access the *chambre* for the night. The garret's ceiling slope requires Jaco stoop, and the bed cot is truly short."

Etage noble. Mansard garret.

The words reminded Mira of her set design assignment for the Baron Georges-Eugène Haussmann documentary. His regulations led to the Haussmann-style building regulations of no higher than five floors and strict, symmetrical placements of balconies on the second and fifth floors.

Wealthy families resided on the second floor called *etage noble.* Their maids lived in the claustrophobic garrets called *chambre de bonne,* which were created by the windowed *mansard* roof.

Poor Jacques. A garret must be uncomfortable.

Bernadette made a sympathetic tch-tch sound. "He awoke with, how do you describe, a crooked in the neck." Mira smiled. "I think you mean a crick in his neck." "Yes. Crick. He did not complain, but he may seek a bed elsewhere tonight."

The image of Jacques romping in a luxuriously large bed with a sexy woman, possibly this Susette she'd heard about, flitted into Mira's imagination.

Why should I care what bed he occupies? Yes, I felt a zing at his touch, but that's it. A surge of passion, in the moment. Mira dismissed thoughts about the sexy Jacques Thibaut. "I apologize for imposing upon you both, Bernadette. I hope not to require your help for long."

Please, please, Carousel, whirl me to where I belong.

"We are happy to share our accommodations with you, Mirabelle. I am especially glad you are here." Bernadette's voice turned wistful. "It's nice to have another woman here, to talk with. I love Jacques, but men are so stupid."

Mira laughed. "I can't disagree."

She set about to wash up. Her set decoration knowledge came in handy, for she knew to stand in the tin container supplied by Bernadette to catch the water she poured over her body. She half-filled the small basin, slipped off her ring, and lathered the cloth with a bar of soap smelling of citrus and lavender. Scrubbing away the grime would be heavenly. Mira decided to satiate her curiosity about Jacques by questioning his guardian. "You said your guardian served on the police force. Why did he leave? What does he do now?"

"Ahhh. The answers are complicated." "Do tell me."

"Jacques graduated at the top of his class from École Polytechnique and was chosen for *le policier*. They needed the best candidates to combat the violence in our city. Jacques served as *détective* on the protective force for our then-president, Président Faure."

Mira could see Jacques' physical fitness and swagger fitting that Secret Service type of job. The mention of violence surprised her, though. It was 1900, during Belle Epoque, the Beautiful Epoch of peace before the onset of World War One.

"How has violence disrupted your peacefulness?" Mira asked, squeezing water from the cloth to rinse her legs.

What would Bernadette think if she glimpsed her cleanly shaven legs and underarms? Women were not held captive to those grooming habits in 1900.

Liberating or gross?

Mira directed her wandering attention to Bernadette's answer.

"The violence is within our country, not war with others. We've suffered bombings and attempted assassinations by anarchists. Thefts and crimes by the illegalists. The horrible Dreyfus Affair."

Bernadette's voice heated with passion. "Simply because Captain Dreyfus is a Jew, they convicted him as a traitor, although he is obviously innocent."

"Yes, he is innocent." Mira knew about the Dreyfus Affair from the 1899 films by French film maker and illusionist Georges Méliès. She'd studied the filmmakers from the era, including the Lumière Brothers, the Pathé Brothers, Léon Gaumont, and, of course, Alice Guy, the subject of her thesis.

Her heart skipped a beat.

Have I been sent to 1900 Paris to help Alice Guy? But, Le Veille clearly referred to a man, not a woman. I assume the man to be Jacques. Why else would our paths cross upon my arrival in 1900 Paris? If I cannot activate the portal myself, I must focus on Jacques and complete my mission so Le Veille will re-open it. I hope my return will not be too late.

Mira retrieved the washcloth and focused on finishing her "bird bath." She removed the pins, ribbons, and combs from her disheveled bun. Her hair fell in a tousled mess upon her damp shoulders. She ran her wet fingers through the loosened long strands to freshen it.

Cleaned best as possible, Mira wrapped her shivering body in a bath towel. She redirected the conversation to her original question posed to Bernadette.

"You still haven't explained why Jacques left the police force."

"Must I?" Bernadette heaved a sigh. "Before our late President Faure died from a seizure, someone tried to assassinate him. He survived the attempt because of Jacques, who was badly injured."

Bernadette's voice caught with emotion. "He spent several months in Hôpital Hôtel-Dieu recuperating. If not for Susette's care, he could have died."

"Susette was his nurse?" Mira rubbed her skin dry with the towel.

"*Oui.* The most caring nurse. She treated Jacques with devotion and tenderness." Bernadette's voice faded to a whisper. "They grew close. Until Jacques left the force."

Mira peeked from behind the partition to see sadness cast on Bernadette's face. Her curiosity needled her to ask more, but her questions were clearly upsetting Bernadette.

She let the subject fade while trying to decide which of the clothing draped over the partition to put on first. She thought back to her college costume design courses and remembered dressing began with the chemise, stockings, and the wide-legged, lacy drawers.

With those garments on, she laced on her boots before putting on the corset that restricted bending. She sent silent thanks it fastened on either side instead of lacing in the back. The S-shaped so called "health" corset contraption forced her body into an awkward, embarrassing position of bosom forward and backend out.

How on earth did anyone think this undergarment promoted healthy posture or beauty?

The longer silk petticoat followed by the shorter lace petticoat and the corset brassiere cover weighed on her, and she hadn't gotten her outfit on yet. Before pulling it on, she checked the label of the skirt to satisfy her curiosity.

Paquin.

With trembling hands, Mira stepped into the skirt and secured it with the waist tie. The matching bodice proved to be Paquin, of course. She put her arms through the long sleeves. The tiny buttons in the back required patient securing, as did tying the long tails of the wide turquoise waist sash.

No wonder Bernadette offered to help me with this intricate dressing process.

Mira walked out from the dressing screen to discover the teen at the window staring out at the brick wall. "Oh, dear." She rushed to Bernadette, the ties of the waist sash trailing. "I didn't mean to upset you by asking about Jacques."

"It is not your fault, but your questions resurface terrible memories." Bernadette faced Mira, her expression reflecting sadness. "When Jacques left the force, everything changed about his life. I had thought he loved Susette. She thought so, as well. His actions have proved otherwise."

"I am so sorry, Bernadette."

Jacques' voice rang out from the apartment's entryway. "*Bonjour.*"

Bernadette jumped. "Bonjour, Jaco!" She leaned to whisper into Mirabelle's ear. "Please do not let him know I speak of Susette with you. He will be most upset."

"Again, you ask me to keep information from your guardian." Mira sighed. "Do not worry. I will say nothing." "Oh, Mirabelle. *Merci.*" Bernadette made a swirling gesture with her finger. "Turn around for me to button your bodice and tie your sash. I am jealous you own a Paquin. I saw the labels. Instead of Paquin, I wear the clothes of a schoolgirl. You know Mme Paquin is President of the Fashion Section of the Exhibit? Surely, you must remember shopping at her place, Maison Paquin at 3 Rue de la Paix? I would never forget."

"I don't remember how I came to be dressed in this." Mira turned to face the bureau mirror and studied the outfit, remembering it on the mannequin at Le Veille's store. The color drained from her face.

I don't know how I came to be in 1900 Paris. I do know I don't belong here.

"Oh, please do not look sad, Mirabelle. I do rattle on." Bernadette sighed. "I should not say such things to upset you. Jaco always warns me to think before I say."

"Think before you speak," Mira corrected.

The girl grinned. "Yes, I mean that. Thank you for your help with my English." Bernadette moved Mira's hair to the side to reach the bodice's buttons.

"You look adorable in your school clothes. As pretty as—" Mira caught herself before she said Gigi. What comparison made sense? "As pretty as a young woman in a Mary Cassatt painting."

"Oh, I love Mary Cassatt. I always imagine *ma mère* cradling me close, like the mothers in her paintings. Mama died during my infancy." Bernadette's voice wavered.

Mira fought the lump in her throat.

I'll be at your side soon, Mom.

Bernadette continued chattering while buttoning the bodice. "Before he died, *ma père* took me to the Mary Cassatt exhibit at Galerie Durand-Ruel."

"Now I am the one who is jealous." Mira's heart overflowed with compassion for this orphan.

"You are jealous? So, now we are, um, what is the American saying when one is equal with Steven?"

"Hmmm." Mira's eyebrows drew together. "I think you mean we are even-steven."

"Yes." Bernadette patted Mira's shoulder. "You are buttoned." She positioned the sash to tie it around Mira's waist.

Mira marveled at her reflection in the mirror. With her waist encircled by the sash, it appeared wasp-like tiny. The corset worked a miracle for her figure, if not for her breathing ability.

"There. Done." Bernadette caught Mira's eyes in the mirror. "I owe Jaco so much. *Ma père* died and left me an orphan at age ten. Jaco provided me with a home."

Mira's chest tightened.

How strange you and I share the tragedy of losing our fathers at the same age.

"Jaco did not have to become my guardian. We are so distantly related. He rescued me from an orphanage. He is a good man. No matter—" She pressed her palm to her mouth.

"No matter what?" Mira pressed.

Bernadette removed her hand and forced a smile. "Do you need help with your hair?"

Mira caught sight in the mirror of her bedraggled locks. She'd learned to create a Gibson Girl pompadour from a co-worker who did hair and makeup. "Thank you, but I can manage." She grabbed the pins, ribbons, and combs she'd removed from her hair.

"One moment." Bernadette exited the room and returned with her brush, comb, and hand mirror set. She set the items on the bureau. "Use these rather than Jaco's."

"Thank you." Mira noticed the monogram on the brush's flat back: DB. *Did the initials stand for the first and maiden name of Bernadette's mother?*

"Breakfast will be ready soon." Bernadette hurried to the door but paused to look back. "Mirabelle, thank you for not telling Jaco about the man on *le trottoir roulant*. The one with the hideous scar. *Comme c'est idiot de ma part.*"

"No, Bernadette, you are not silly to be suspicious of strange men." Mira pointed Bernadette's brush at her. "You cannot be too careful."

"*Oui.* My imagination does race from me, Jaco tells me." She blew a kiss and departed from the room.

Working Bernadette's brush through her tangled hair, Mira reflected on Bernadette's protective attitude toward Jacques. The teen owed him much for becoming her guardian, blinding her to his darker side.

Why did you resign from the force, Jacques, especially after your heroic act of saving President Faure's life? If you and Susette were in love, why did you let her go?

She thought again about Jacques' inexpressive eyes. Were they the eyes of a violent man? What was it Bernadette said? "He is a good man, no matter." She obviously meant no matter what people said about her guardian.

What do people say, Jacques Thibaut? But I needn't care. The Carousel portal will re-open, and I will leave 1900 Paris and you behind.

Mira divided her hair into a parted front and back section to create the Gibson Girl bun. Once she secured the updo with the pins, ribbons, and combs, she inspected her reflection. She had no foundation, blush, lipstick, and mascara to camouflage her death-warmed-over appearance. *Oh, well. I'll have to make the best of my natural look.*

Besides, in 1900 Paris, only courtesans painted their faces and lips. I don't need to give Jacques any more ammunition to think poorly of me.

She pinched her cheeks and bit her lips to add color to her pale complexion.

"You are dressed."

Mira jumped at the unexpected presence of the man occupying her thoughts.

"Breakfast is ready. Apologies for startling you." He smiled.

"Not at all." Once more Mira noticed his smile did not reach his eyes.

Should I worry about being alone with you?

She dismissed the worry. After he escorted her to the Luxembourg Carousel, she'd never be around him again.

Nothing dangerous could happen to me in that short interval, could it? In full public view? I think not.

"I am starving. Thank you for my breakfast." She hoped her warm smile masked her uncertainty. She retrieved her hat, cape, and gloves.

He waved his hand to invite her passage through the door. Hoisting her skirt, she swept by him, unable to ignore how his well-muscled build towered above her and how his manly scent—an intriguing mix of talcum, sandalwood, and earthy incense—intoxicated her.

Keep your guard up, Mira. Accept whatever help this man can provide, but do not trust him.

EIGHT

Fortified by the coffee and bread for breakfast, Mira hoped she'd be strong enough to survive another time-travel trip. If the Carousel worked in reverse.

She corrected that thought.

Not if, but when the Carousel worked in reverse.

She descended behind Jacques and Bernadette the multiple flights of the narrow staircase erected in the middle of the building and onto the crowded sidewalk. She noticed Specialities en Pharmacie occupied the ground floor. The painted advertisements on the display windows promoted elixirs, potions, and *flacons*, which Mira knew to be perfumes in stoppered glass bottles. She ran her tongue against her teeth she'd cleaned with her finger and baking powder. If she had money, she'd shop for a toothbrush and toothpaste.

"One moment." Jacques entered the pharmacy, pointing his walking cane toward a man and woman, both wearing merchant aprons.

Bernadette stamped her foot. "He conspires with his spies."

Mira watched as Jacques engaged in conversation with them. "Who are they? And what do you mean, spies?"

"They are M. Verany, *Docteur en Pharmacie,* and his wife. They own the pharmacy and live above it. Jaco has them monitor my comings and goings. They are *les mouchards.* How you say? Stood pigeon?"

"You mean, stool pigeon." Mira bit back her amused grin.

"I am sure they inform on me. They must have seen me meet Siméon here for us to go . . ." When Jacques reappeared, Bernadette's words trailed off.

The girl's words piqued Mira's curiosity.

What were you doing before I descended upon you on the moving sidewalk?

"Bébé, you must not be tardy." Jacques walked ahead of them, calling back, "*Marche vite.* Walk quickly."

The crowds heading the other direction pressed closely against Mira. The reverberating noise of a passing horse and carriage on the narrow cobblestone street deafened her.

How ungentlemanly of Jacques to walk ahead instead of by my side to protect me.

Her thought shocked her feminism, for she'd never expected such behavior from any man before. Her lack of bearings had increased her vulnerability.

Bernadette slung her school pouch over her shoulder and hoisted her parasol. "I will shade us both."

Mira drew closer to Bernadette, battling against the long skirt encumbering her stride and the wide-brimmed hat that required effort to balance. Her gloves and boots fit too tight. She longed for her own century's casual dress. She longed for knowledge of her mother's condition.

Her churning thoughts increased her anxiety and disorientation. "What street is this? Where is your school?" Her questions tumbled out quickly, her voice edged with tension. She blinked with determination to hold back tears that threatened.

"Oh, you poor thing." Bernadette slowed her step. "Have you a handkerchief?"

"It seems I do not." Mira sniffled, disgusted at how easily she teared up. The 21st Century Mira prided her emotional restraint.

Give yourself a break. You aren't in Kansas anymore, Toto. You're allowed a tear or two.

"Here, take mine." Bernadette pulled a white, lace- edged handkerchief from her sleeve. "I have another in my book bag."

"Thank you." When she used it, Mira noticed the whiff of lavender. She tucked it into her sleeve, copying Bernadette. "Having no memory must be disorienting." Bernadette tipped her parasol toward the intersection ahead where the street signs hung mounted on the sides of the buildings. "Our home is at Rue de Bievre and the Boulevard Saint-Germain. In *le quartier latin*."

"Boulevard Saint-Germain." Mira's heart quickened. "The Latin Quarter."

"Does the boulevard bring memory to you?" Bernadette asked in excited anticipation.

How to explain? I cannot share Sylvie lives on Saint- Germain. I wish I could find my godmother's building and walk through its door, reversing this time travel. "No. It brings no memory."

"Do not despair. You will remember once again." Bernadette's disappointed smile fought against her false cheer.

The girl's worry prickled Mira's guilt. She tried to reassure her. "I am sure. Right now, we need to get you to class. We should walk faster, for Jacques is far ahead of us." "I don't care if I am tardy." Bernadette stuck her lower lip out in her typical exaggerated pout. "No worry, though. We are less than ten minutes before arriving."

Mira trained her eyes on Jacques, admiring his broad shoulders and self-confident movement. She observed how the passing women with their lacy parasols aloft sought his attention, throwing flirty smiles in his direction. He tipped his hat to each.

Bernadette laughed. "You notice. It is always such. My Jaco gathers attention of the ladies wherever he goes because he is so handsome and dangerous."

Mira's stomach tightened. Did Susette break up with him because he treated her violently? "Do people fear him?"

"If anyone does, it is because of unproven rumors."

"Rumors? What are the rumors, Bernadette?"

"You will not hear them from me. I will not speak badly of Jaco." Bernadette clamped her lips together.

Mira knew attempting to push farther would meet with further resistance. She smiled, hoping to lift Bernadette's spirits. "You are a loyal ward. Jacques is very lucky to have you believe in him with such devotion."

They walked a few steps in silence before Bernadette spoke again. "I misspeak. My Jaco is not a dangerous man, but he does dangerous things. Since leaving the force, he drives automobiles very fast, making him *célébrité*. I discover people, particularly women, are attracted to men such as Jacques, who dare fate behind the automobile wheel. He will compete in the Olympics motoring events in three days at Bois de Vincennes, and many admiring women will attend to cheer on the drivers."

Mira's breath caught. "The Olympics?" She'd forgotten that Paris had hosted the Second Olympiad of modern times as part of the 1900 Exhibit. "Jacques will be a competitor?" "Yes. He loves speed, but it frightens me. I have not ridden in an automobile. Have you?"

Mira hesitated to answer.

Would it be unusual for me to have done so?

She decided to answer honestly. "Yes, I have."

"You are braver than I." Bernadette adjusted her pouch and shifted the parasol to better cover them both. "I worried enough when Jaco served on the police force. It's more worry since he began working for M. Peugeot. Now I bear the worry alone, since he is no longer with Susette."

"You and Susette are no longer close?"

"I say too much." Bernadette chewed her lower lip.

Mira dropped that subject and focused on Jacques as a race car driver. She had to admit that tidbit accentuated his sexiness.

She knew little about the history of automobiles, but obviously she'd heard of Peugeot. "What does he do for M. Peugeot?"

"Whatever M. Peugeot needs. Race his cars. Be his bodyguard."

"Bodyguard? Is M. Peugeot's life in danger?"

"Famous people prefer protection in case, do they not?" Bernadette shrugged. "Much competition exists among the automobile inventors."

Mira's attention shifted to another woman passing them, who overtly embraced Jacques with her flirtation.

"One more admirer." Bernadette laughed. "I wish I gathered as much attention from men." She pulled Mira to the side for a man to hurry past.

He slowed for a moment, signaling interest in Mira's direction. *"Excusez-moi belle dame."*

Averting her eyes, Mira accelerated her pace. "Jacques walks so quickly."

"Don't be embarrassed, Mirabelle." Bernadette matched Mira's stride. "French men admire beauty, and so they admire you."

"*Merci.*" Bernadette's compliment unsettled Mira. She'd never put herself into the beautiful category. She cleaned up well, so the saying went, but mainly as a result of makeup and a hair straightener. "You garner attention yourself, Bernadette. Siméon finds you most pretty, doesn't he?"

"Ah, my Siméon." Bernadette's eyes took on a dreamy cast. "We are in love, though if I dare tell Jaco, he will banish Siméon from my life."

"Does Jacques not approve of your beau?"

"He does not know him well enough to approve or disapprove. To Jaco, I am the ten-year-old little girl who came to live with him, not the seventeen-year-old woman who in less than a month will complete my ever-boring studies and embark on my own life."

"With Siméon?"

"*Oui.* Again, please I beg. Not a word to Jacques about what I am about to share." Bernadette drew closer to Mira. "Siméon has proposed, and I have accepted. We shall marry once we complete *Le Lycée* this year."

"Does his family know?"

Tears sprang into Bernadette's eyes. "Siméon is an orphan, too. He lost his parents ten years ago, to the deadly Russian flu. Siméon's *grand-père paternel* took him in. He tries to control Siméon, even more than Jaco tries to control me."

"I am so sorry for Siméon." Mira understood both Bernadette and Siméon's pain at having lost a father.

At least I haven't lost my mother. Or, have I? What did Carolyn's text say? I pray you are still alive, Mom.

Mira's thoughts raced forward, to arriving at the Carousel. She knew the negative physical impact of time travel. Traveling through time again in such a short span of time might actually endanger her life. She swallowed at the knot forming in her throat. Her pulse pounded erratically. She forced herself to listen to Bernadette's chatter to distract her fears.

"Siméon's *grand-père* expects him to attend École Polytechnique after he finishes at his *Lycée.* But Siméon has no interest. He is creative, as we are both. We desire to work in the arts. So much is happening now."

"But how will you two get by, Bernadette? Afford a home, a life together?"

"I've been wanting to tell you. Yesterday, I go with Siméon to his work. His *patron* required him to—" Jacques' abrupt stop interrupted Bernadette, leaving Mira's curiosity unsated over the teen and her boyfriend's adventure yesterday.

"We arrive on time." Jacques leaned both hands onto his walking stick and rocked on his heels.

Bernadette directed a scowl Jacques' way. "My prison." Mira studied the building with the words LYCEE FENELON inscribed into the stone ledge above the double entry doors with half windows made of leaden glass. A single elaborate palladium window hung above the width of the two doors. French flags hung from the ledge. The imposing entry smacked of prison. No wonder the spirited Bernadette counted her days to graduation.

"Bébé, you are to apologize to the headmistress. And, behave today."

Jacques' stern demeanor brought a blush to Bernadette's face.

Mira's empathy toward her surged.

"I will be on my best behavior, Jaco. I will say I am as sorry as Icarus, who did not obey his father and flew too near the sun." The girl heaved a dramatic sigh. "I accept whatever punishment I must. I shall not embarrass you again."

Mira turned her head to hide her grin. The reference to Icarus reminded her of Bernadette's comment about Lethe, the spirit of forgetfulness. At least her schooling was not a complete failure, for the girl did know her Greek mythology.

Bernadette handed her the parasol. "You must protect your complexion."

"How kind of you." Mira accepted it.

Jacques reached into his vest pocket and took out his open-faced pocket watch dangling from its gold fob.

Despite how irritating, condescending, and rude she found him to be, Mira admired the taut fit of his vest covering his muscular build. She studied his walking cane made of bamboo wood with a handle carved from the root of a tree.

How you'd salivate over it, Mom. It would fetch a pretty penny in your shop.
Thinking of her, Mira's spirits flagged.
The Carousel must transport me back where I belong.

"Bébé, I have a meeting at the Automobile Club at the time your school day ends." He stored his watch into his vest pocket. "Please meet Mlle at the Eiffel Tower at five today. Perhaps take her to Le Palais du Costume to view the Paquin exhibit. I will meet you for *le diner* at Bouillon Duval at eight this evening."

"Yes, Jaco." Bernadette winked at Mira. "I shall take excellent care of you."

Oh, Bernadette. When I don't show up, you will worry.

"Thank you, Bernadette." Mira's grasp on the parasol tightened. "But I won't need you to meet me."

"*Balivernes,*" Bernadette exclaimed.

Mira's heart twinged. Sylvie often tossed the expression her way.

"Do not pay attention to Mirabelle. I will meet her." Bernadette pecked Jacques on the cheek. "I have a suggestion for you, Jaco. If no memory comes to Mirabelle at the Carousel, schedule an appointment for her to visit Maison Paquin. Her clothing came from there."

"*Merci*, Bébé." Jacques waved her off. "Now, go."

A cluster of Bernadette's classmates called out, "Bébé, *allons-y, allons-y.*"

"*Juste un moment.*" Bernadette exchanged air kisses of farewell with Mira and whispered in her ear. "I can't wait for later. You shall meet Siméon."

Remorse stabbed Mira. "*Adieu,*" she whispered.

"Not *adieu*, Mirabelle." Bernadette admonished. "You say *adieu* if you're leaving someone for a long, long time, or forever."

Yes, I know. And, I do mean a long, long time, sweet Bernadette. Forever.

NINE

“I shall take excellent care of you.” Jacques imitated Bernadette, complete with the wink. “Are you two conspiring?” The hint of a smile ameliorated his aggravated tone.

“Not at all.” Mira swirled the parasol. “Bernadette told me you took her in after her father died. She must miss her mother and father terribly, but she is fortunate to have you.” “It is I who is fortunate to have her in my life.” Jacques’ inexpressive eyes turned more oblique. “We must continue to the Carousel. We are not far.” He walked by her side, offering his arm. “Please, in case a faintness overcomes you.” His offer ignited Mira’s temper. Her adept self-defense moves earlier proved she did not require a man to save her. She wanted to explain fainting to be unusual for her.

Except under the conditions of time traveling. Maybe he should try it and experience what it does to one’s body.

Her mother always said a gal caught more flies with honey than vinegar, didn’t she? Mira took his offered arm and tilted her head toward him, adapting the Steel Magnolia routine. “I appreciated your strong arms carrying me yesterday.”

Jacques regarded her with an amused expression. "You do not appear as the type who usually needs such assistance, Mlle."

Amen.

Jacques' lips curved in a half-smile. "You should be thanking Bernadette, not me. She is attracted to strays who need help."

Strays. A flush crept across Mira's cheeks.

Bernadette must be wrong about Susette or any woman caring for this arrogant man.

A nasty retort begged to fly from her, but she denied its escape. Instead, she would draw his attention to how proud he should be of Bernadette. The vulnerable orphan deserved more praise than she noticed Jacques giving.

"How fortunate someone as generous and kind as your ward took pity on my distressed state. You must be proud of her good heart."

"It's precisely her heart I worry about." Jacques' brow wrinkled with concern. "Bébé has seen little of the world. In her naivety, she attributes good motives to everyone she meets."

"Are you implying she has misread my motives?" Mira's voice took on an edge. "You believe me to be undeserving of her kind generosity?"

"Your words. Not mine."

She recognized the entrance to the Luxembourg Gardens. "M. Thibaut, you insult me for the last time." Mira removed her arm from his, repelled by his negative view of people.

If having been a police detective affected his nature in this way, no wonder his reputation lay in tatters.

I do not regret leaving without helping restore it. Except, I do regret leaving poor Bernadette under your watch.

The young woman did not allow the loss of her parents to turn her inward, doubting the goodness of others. To honor her, Mira vowed to better embrace life, and others.

Has it taken traveling back in time to Paris of 1900 for me to accept my grief? To open up and connect with others emotionally?

"Please give Bernadette her parasol, with my thanks." She shut it, and curbing her impulse to hit him with it, jabbed it forcefully into his hand. *"Adieu."* Mira harshly emphasized her word choice, for she meant a forever goodbye.

She walked from him at the most rapid pace her dress allowed.

I may look wasp thin, but I hate how this fashion binds my movement and my breathing.

"One moment." Jacques stepped in front of her, wielding his walking cane to block her.

Mira slanted her shoulder against him, wishing to move through his blockade.

I can't wait to put more than a century of time between me and this infuriating man.

"You will find it interesting what I did after I undressed you and placed you in my bed yesterday." Raising one eyebrow impudently, he offered her the parasol.

Mira narrowed her eyes. "Bernadette helped me, not you."

"*Comme ci, comme* ça." Jacques tucked the parasol under one arm and with the other swung his cane around in a circle before stabbing it onto the ground. He rested his hands on the handle. "After you were ensconced safely into my bed, I went to the police. I inquired if any American women have been reported missing. None have."

Of course not, you fool.

"The Prefect of Police, Louis Lépine, approved my request to contact the hotels and homes in which Americans are residing during their visit to the *Exposition Universelle*. This morning, I stopped in the precinct on my way to the bakery. They told me they have yet to find anyone who has heard of you." His eyes tunneled into her. "Do you find it unusual no one is missing an American woman as beautiful as yourself, clearly one of moneyed stature?"

His words struck Mira like a fist in her stomach.

If time passed equally in the 21ˢᵗ Century, Mom and Sylvie will be missing me. They'll be searching for me, desperate over my disappearance.

"Now you understand why I have suspicions about your memory loss." His muscular body loomed above her. "Who are you, Mirabelle, and from where do you come?" He dug an object from his vest pocket and studied it.

Mira gasped.

My moonstone ring? I must have left it on the washbasin.

She lunged for it.

Jacques closed his fist around it. "I recognize the jewelry's marking. René Lalique. Not a cheap bauble. If we visit his shop at 20 Rue Thérèse, we can inquire as to what man purchased it for you."

He tossed the ring into the air and caught it. "Then, the mystery of your identity is solved." He tossed it again.

She pounced cat-like and snatched it mid-air. "One thing I definitely know." She removed her right glove, slipped the ring onto her ring finger, and wriggled her hand back into its tight covering. "I have no need to rely upon men to get what I want in life."

Mira stalked from him toward the Carousel, ignoring him when he caught up to her. She pressed a hand against her stomach, overwhelmed by the crowd of families. Relatives cheered the children mounted on the animals, playing *jeu de bagues*.

She sought her special Carousel animal. A young girl sat astride it. "The white elephant," Mira whispered.

"A white elephant?" Jacques repeated, questioningly. The Carousel slowed, then stopped.

Mira ran under the Carousel, pushing aside anyone in her way, until she stood at the white elephant. She touched the pole, expecting it to light with flames, but it did not. Tugging her cape and dress out of the way, she managed to sit sideways upon the carved animal and circled the pole with one arm.

Ignoring the confused exhortations of the crowd, she waved toward the conductor. "Please, please, start the ride."

The surrounding air turned chilled, but the pole grew hot to her touch. The noises faded. Jacques and the other people stood statuesque. A wind blew, bringing a fog that enveloped everyone. Mira tensed her frigid body, anticipating the appearance of the spiraling tunnel.

Instead, a figure wrapped in black appeared. With a dramatic swish, the cloth parted, and Le Veille stood before her, speaking. "You return only if you right the wrong destiny that has befallen him. Save him."

"Do you mean Jacques?" Mira screamed into the thick mist into which he was fading. "How do I help him?" "When the time comes, you will know. I can say no more. After you complete your task, this portal will re-open." With another swish of cloth, Le Veille disappeared.

The fog lifted, and the chilly wind abated. The crowd came to life, and the people were shouting at her.

A young boy pointed at her, crying loudly, *"L'éléphant est à moi."*

Jacques stood before her, coaxing her from the elephant.

Mira slid into Jacques' arms and allowed him to steer her through the throng. In her dazed state, she translated the crowd's cries.

Avez-vous perdu la raison? Has she lost her mind? *Qu'est-ce qui ne va pas avec toi?* What is wrong with you? *Convoquer la police.* Summon the police.

With an arm around her waist, Jacques guided her to sit upon a park bench hidden from the sight of the Carousel. Joining her, he removed his hat and placed it at his side on the bench, propping his cane and her parasol against it.

Mira struggled to breathe against the constraints of her corset. Fury flushed through her. She hoped to end this implausible time-travel experience. Yet, she remained imprisoned in it until she accomplished the mission for which Le Veille selected her—without her consent and with scant information.

Yet, Jacques must be my mission? Surely, Le Veille would have corrected me otherwise?

At least Mira hoped so. She hoped also, as Le Veille commented, she would know what to do when the time came. *How am I going to know? I don't live my life on instinct. I keep myself to myself. I research. I plan. I analyze everything.*

Mom accuses me of analysis paralysis. My intellect guides me, not my heart.

Jacques reached for her shaky hands. She allowed him to hold them.

"The Carousel has affected you terribly, Mirabelle. Did it bring a memory to you? What significance is the white elephant?"

Mira remained silent.

How can I answer your questions without you believing me of unsound mind?

"If you remember, please tell me." Jacques spoke with a quiet, caring tone.

She withdrew her hands from his and averted her eyes, making it easier to speak half-truths. "The Carousel and the white elephant did jar a memory, about someone in danger."

When she looked at him once more, she was surprised to find worry stamped on his face.

"Danger?" Jacques bowed his head. "Mlle, please forgive me for doubting your amnesia. For me, believing in people's goodness does not come easily, as it does for Bernadette."

He placed a finger under her chin and turned her face toward his. "I truly pledge my assistance."

The sincerity of his apology offset Mira's distrust of him. She saw in this version of Jacques what Bernadette must, what the nurse Bernadette said loved him must see. A man with a generous spirit, one capable of gentleness and affection. Her ruse of amnesia brought a pang of conscience.

"*Merci.* Your apology and your assistance mean everything to me." She smiled. "Call me Mirabelle."

"Mirabelle."

The way Jacques spoke her name felt like a caress upon her skin.

"I will help in any way possible. Time is of the essence." He paused, the lines of worry on his face deepening. "Is it possible you are the one in danger?"

"I am not sure." Mira's voice quaked. "You are correct, though. Time is of the essence."

You have no idea. Stay strong, Mom, please.

The reverberation of the Luxembourg Palace clock striking the noon hour startled Mira. She remembered when she last heard the chime. Her pulse quickened, and her palms grew clammy.

"Mirabelle?" Jacques wrapped an arm around her. "You are somewhere, deep in thought. What are you thinking?"

Mira leaned into the comfort of his embrace. She welcomed the warmth of his body, unable to deny her attraction to him.

He tipped her face upward, and his lips met hers.

The heat of their kiss left her breathless and determined to avoid kissing him again.

The last thing I need is to become entangled with a man who lived century-plus years ago. Besides I can tell from his reaction when he hears Susette's name that he still loves her. "Who are you and from where do you come?" Jacques whispered, his gaze holding hers. "What is your life's story?"

Mira discerned the irony of what he asked. She needed the same answers from him. She let his questions and their physical attraction to each other linger between them in the air, feeling the truth scratching within her for release.

She placed a hand upon his cheek and whispered, "What if I told you something about me that you would find impossible to believe?"

TEN

Mira caught her words before they flew from her. She dropped her gaze and removed her hand from his cheek.

I must keep my secret about time traveling. I cannot trust Jacques or anyone to believe me. It's too unfathomable.

"Mirabelle, please." Jacques moved closer to her. "What were you going to tell me?"

"I thought I remembered something, but I do not." She shrugged.

"I am sorry." Jacques stared at her with a disbelieving expression before standing and offering Mira his hand.

She accepted it, her heart hammering from their kiss. She tried to deny how his touch stirred desire within her. Her eyes remained affixed on his lips, unable to stop thinking how kissing a man with such a bold mustache both tickled and excited her.

Jacques opened the parasol. "I may have thought of something. Does the American Girls' Club mean anything to you? Or, the name Elisabeth Mills Reid? She is an American philanthropist whose husband once served as United States Ambassador to France."

Mira recalled a friend from Columbia University who studied set design while abroad in Paris at Reid Hall. "I am not sure." She accepted the parasol from Jacques and held it aloft.

"I hoped hearing her name might jostle your memory."

The disappointment pinching his face invoked Mira's guilt for pretending.

I have no choice but to continue my amnesia charade. We kissed, but I must keep my guard up. Focus on my mission and earn my return home.

"Mme Reid purchased a building once used to house a Protestant school for boys, at 4 Rue de Chevreuse." Jacques studied her with a hopeful expression as he explained. "She calls it the American Girls' Club for American girls who come to Paris to study art. Mme Reid established the Club to protect the reputations of American girls in Paris, given many have fallen into bohemian ways."

Mira bristled, twirling the parasol vigorously. Jacques' first impression of her had been of a free-and-easy American girl, suffering from *gueule de bois.*

"American girls who live freely are called bohemians. However, men demonstrate the most vile and gauche behavior without impact to their reputations." Her words held a brittle edge. "Can you explain the lack of fairness?"

Jacques' stunned silence reminded Mira that her 21st Century attitude showed.

I won't apologize for my outburst. This man needs enlightenment.

After a moment, he regained his composure. "I meant no accusation in my words. I mention the Club wondering if you may be one of the boarders. You might have suffered an incident in which you suffered a blow to the head, perhaps with a speeding carriage in the street. If so, someone at the Club may recognize you."

He paused to allow her to reply.

She remained quiet.

He continued. "If we find a dead end at the Club, we will explore two other avenues: your clothing from Mme Paquin and ring from Lalique's. Records of these purchases should have an affiliated address and, hopefully, your name listed. Do you agree?"

She bobbed her head in agreement.

Resolving my so-called amnesia provides us time together for me to find out the truth behind your dismissal from the police force. Set your life on the right course, whatever the course should be. I must believe I will intuitively know what to do, as Le Veille claimed.

Jacques crooked his elbow toward her. "Shall we walk to the American Girls' Club now? The distance is not far."

Mira placed her arm through his, attempting to ignore her racing heart.

No more kisses. I cannot fall for someone belonging to a different century. Besides, what about Susette, the woman Bernadette says he loves? Or, at least did love.

They walked slowly toward the Garden's exit onto Rue Guynemere.

Mira's cape protected her from the chill of the April day. The sidewalk bustled noisily with pedestrians and the street with some automobiles but mostly horse-drawn carriages. The stench of the horse droppings prompted her to press the scented handkerchief against her nose.

They approached the intersection of Rue Notre Dame des Champs and Rue de Chevreuse.

"The Club is around the corner." Jacques fell silent.

Mira followed his gaze to a couple standing at the intersection who were engaged in an emotional conversation. The woman, obviously distraught, held in one gloved hand a handkerchief with which she dabbed her eyes. Her long brown cape, heavier than the chill in the spring air warranted, hid her figure. She wore no hat, showing a mass of thick, wavy, carrot-red hair. The gauntness of the woman's face and pale coloring disturbed Mira. Did she suffer from consumption?

The man gripped her other gloved hand with both of his own. Mira tried to determine if anger, fear, or confusion marked his expression—or a combination of the three. He wore a sack suit of corduroy cloth and a working man's cap, as did many men of the lower class in Paris.

"Let's allow them privacy." Jacques started to guide her to the opposite side of the street, but a horse-drawn cab blocked their crossing.

The man shifted his attention to the street, and his eyes slanted with anger at recognition of Jacques.

"Do the two of you know—" Mira left the rest of her question hanging. The glaring animosity in Jacques' normally inexpressible eyes unsettled her.

The woman pulled her hands from the man's and walked along Rue de Chevreuse. Jacques' focus remained on the man, who approached them.

When he neared, Mira's hand flew to her mouth at the sight of the curved scar on his cheek. She knew him from the moving sidewalk.

What had Bernadette said? *That man seems to have been following me. I am glad to have you accompany me.*

Suspicion ricocheted through Mira. If this man knew Jacques, then Bernadette's instincts about him must have been correct. He must have been following her.

"M. Thibaut. Our paths cross once more." The man extended his hand, his demeanor brash and gloating. "This neighborhood is more sedate than Montmartre, do you not agree, especially Moulin Rouge, where we meet."

Mira detected Jacques wanted no part of this man. She found it hard to believe he not only knew a foul man such as this one, but he met him regularly at the famous cabaret marked by the red windmill on its roof, where the seductive Can-Can dance was birthed. The posters and paintings of Toulouse-Lautrec immortalized the nightclub.

Scenes from her favorite musical *Moulin Rouge* floated through Mira's mind, especially of the fantastical elephant boudoir. She had seen pictures of the giant stucco elephant positioned in the cabaret's garden for a brief time in its early history. The owners of the cabaret purchased it at the Paris Universal Exhibition of 1889. The alfresco café came to be called the Jardin de Paris Elephant.

A giant staircase inside the hollow elephant's front leg led into the stomach, where men frequented the opium den and belly dancers entertained them. For this abrasive stranger to be one of such men did not surprise Mira, but for Jacques to be among them did.

At Jacques' rejection of the handshake, the man lowered his arm. "Who is your lovely companion?" He leered from under his hooded lids. "Haven't we met?"

Before Mira answered, Jacques jabbed the tip of his cane against the man's chest. "Walk away."

"I think not." The man brushed away Jacques' cane and moved closer into his space.

Jacques gripped Mira's upper arm. "Let us by, Jourdain. We have a rendezvous."

The man blocked their path. "You and I must talk, Thibaut."

Mira felt the anger radiating from Jacques. She attempted to ease the tension. She freed herself from Jacques' hold and boldly offered the man her hand. "May I introduce myself? I am Mirabelle Montgomery."

"Marius Jourdain." He took her hand, bowed, and released it. "I remember now. I saw you yesterday on *le trottoir roulant.* You were with the young girl, the lovely Bernadette."

Marius landed a pointed gaze upon Jacques. "Your ward, Thibaut. I remember her mother well. The Queen of Bohemia."

Jacques grabbed the man at the collar. "*Ferme ta gueule.*" He shoved Marius onto the sidewalk.

Marius struggled to his feet, breathing hard. He straightened his coat before sneering at Jacques. "Still wearing your emotions on your sleeve."

Jacques' body stiffened. "Mirabelle, please continue to our destination. I will join you in a moment."

Mira walked away, her pulse ricocheting through her. She turned onto Rue de Chevreuse and paused to look back. The two men were not pummeling each other, but they remained in a face-to-face, angry confrontation. She needed to learn more about their feud. Did it cause Jacques' dismissal from the police force?

A passing horse and carriage blocked them from her view. She headed toward the address per Jacques' directions and noticed the woman walking ahead of her to be the one with Marius Jourdain. She entered a building with dark wood doors.

Jacques appeared at Mira's side. She had so many questions for him.

How do you know Marius? What caused the bad blood between you two? Why did Marius sarcastically refer to Bernadette's mother as Queen of Bohemia?

Jacques spoke, his voice tight. "Why am I discovering from Marius Jourdain that you and Bernadette saw him on *le trottoir roulant* yesterday?"

Remorse filled Mira.

How stupid of me to not mention it.

"I apologize. I should have. Bernadette begged me not to mention the specifics of how we met. She pointed out Marius to me and wondered if he was following her. He did not disembark from the walkway when we did, so Bernadette blamed her fear on her imagination. Until this moment, seeing him again, I thought so as well."

"But you do not think that now?"

Mira shook her head. "It seems too great a coincidence, especially how the two of you are feuding. He perhaps did follow Bernadette. If so, you must have an idea why, based on the comment he made about Bernadette's mother?"

"The issue is between Jourdain and me. You must promise not to keep anything from me about Bernadette, most especially if she is where she should not be. Such as yesterday."

"Of course." The charged air between them kept her from questioning why Marius upset him.

Jacques halted. "We have arrived at our destination."

They stood in front of a four-storied brick structure with large imposing dark-stained wooden doors, the same building Mira had seen the woman enter. She decided to not mention that. She wanted to observe Jacques' reaction when they crossed paths with her once more.

Mira read the engraved bronze plaque on the brick beside the entrance, which provided the establishment's name, AMERICAN GIRLS' CLUB, and its address and established date of September 1893.

She closed her parasol and waited for someone to answer Jacques' knock. An older woman with an imposing authoritative air opened one of the double doors. She spoke in French with an obvious American accent. Mira's newfound ability to understand the language still confounded her.

"M. Thibaut. Has M. Peugeot sent you to chauffeur our guest to her hotel? If so, you are early. Her seminar has yet to begin."

"*Bonjour,* Mme Newton." Jacques removed his hat. "I am here on a different business today."

"Enter, please. No need to linger on the sidewalk." Jacques stood to the side for Mira to enter first. "*Bonjour.*" Mme Newton smiled at her. "I do not believe I have made your acquaintance, my dear?"

"Allow me to introduce Mlle Mirabelle Montgomery." Disappointment clouded Jacques' face. "You do not recognize her?"

"I am so sorry. I do not." Flustered, Mme Newton studied Mira closely. "Please forgive me if we have met before, but my memory fails."

"Do not worry." Mira spoke in halting French. "It is my memory we are attempting to restore, Mme Newton."

"You are American."

"Yes." Mira lowered her chin. "I apologize for my poor French."

"No apologies, my dear. After all, you are at the American Girls' Club." Mme Newton shifted to English. "You say you have no memory?"

"I suffer amnesia. M. Thibaut is escorting me to various places, in hopes of helping me restore my memory."

"I wondered if she were staying here," Jacques interjected. "As one of your boarders, studying art."

"Mme Newton?" A woman's voice drifted from the hallway.

"*Oui?* I am in the lobby," Mme Newton called out. "Please, Mme," Jacques stepped toward the woman, speaking in a low tone. "Keep what Mlle Montgomery has told you in confidence. For her protection, as you can understand."

"Oh, my, of course." Mme Newton's voice dropped to a hush-hush. "Your story is safe with me."

A tall, elegant woman dressed in black whose graying hair was piled into a pompadour swept into the lobby. She carried a sketchbook.

Mira recognized her. "Mary Cassatt." The name abruptly escaped from her.

"Yes, and you are?"

"Mirabelle Montgomery. A visitor, not an artist. I adore your paintings. I'm thrilled to meet you, Mme Cassatt." Mira pressed her lips together to stop her fangirl tumble of disconnected words.

"Thank you. No formality, please. I am Mary. May I address you as Mirabelle?"

"Yes," Mira said and added in an awed voice, "Mary." The artist turned her attention to Jacques.

"Mme Cassatt, may I introduce M. Thibaut." Mme Newton waved a hand Jacques' way. "He chauffeurs our guests in the most fabulous automobiles, courtesy of M. Peugeot."

"Monsier." Mary extended her hand.

"*Enchanté.*" Jacques politely bowed while holding her hand and approached the back of it with his lips.

Mira noticed his lips did not touch her hand as they had when Bernadette introduced the two of them. She blushed at the memory of Jacques' insolent behavior.

Mary addressed Mirabelle. "Do you model?" Mira's heart drummed. "I have never."

"Come, stand more in the light." Mary grasped Mira's arm and gently pulled her toward the French doors leading from the lobby to an enclosed courtyard.

Mira obeyed.

"May I?" Mary grasped Mira's chin with her free hand and tilted her head upward and sideways.

Mira swallowed against the tightness in her throat, attempting to maintain a still composure under the artist's touch.

"Yes. I planned to use one of the artists in residence here as my lesson's model, but you will do excellently. Your reddish-auburn hair and blue eyes are completely right. Do you have an hour or so to pose as our model?"

Mira nodded, not trusting herself to speak.

I need to focus on my time-travel mission, but how can I reject this offer? When I am with Mom and Sylvie once again and tell them my experiences, they will be amazed.

Her emotions surged at the thought of these two women in her life, and she pursed her trembling lips together.

I will come back to you. I promise.

Mary again turned her attention to Jacques. "M. Thibaut, could you join us for *le goûter* at 4:30 o'clock and afterward deposit me at my hotel? I am staying at the new one, The Ritz, for I have allowed my family who are visiting the Exhibit to use my Paris abode."

"My pleasure." Jacques replaced his hat and announced, "Until 4:30 o'clock."

Mira's rush of anxiety at his leaving surprised her. She second-guessed her decision to sit for Mary Cassatt. It robbed her of time with Jacques and movement toward completing her mission. She followed him to the door. "M. Thibaut, may we speak before you go?"

"Of course." He removed his hat.

"I-I . . ." Mira stuttered, searching for a reason to delay his departure. "Does this unexpected invitation interfere with your schedule? You have an appointment at the Automobile Club at five o'clock."

Jacques leaned lightly onto his cane. His expression conveyed no concern. "M. Peugeot will understand. Providing service to one as well-respected as Mme Cassatt takes priority."

"But I am to meet Bernadette." "I will send a message to her."

Several women swished by them, waving and calling, "*Bonjour*, Jacques."

Mira's cheeks flamed. "You have a gaggle of admirers, M. Thibaut. Are they the reason you have brought me here?" "Perhaps." Jacques' teasing grin faded. "Are you nervous, Mirabelle, to be here alone? Should I remain?"

Annoyance at his offer poked at her.

Needing a man's protection has never been part of my identity. Why should I change because I'm in 1900?

"M. Thibaut." Mira nodded in a dismissive way. Jacques placed his hat upon his head and tipped it toward Mira. "À *bientôt.*"

Mira swirled from him and approached the circular desk in the lobby. Labeled cubbies hung on the wall behind it, providing each boarder a spot for mail and keys. A ledger sat on the desk for signing in and out. The arrangement reminded Mira of the strict monitoring of college girls' movements in and out of dormitories generations ago.

I couldn't stand my independence being so curtailed.

Mme Newton and the artist stood together by the doors leading to the open courtyard.

Mira overheard Mary's question. "Mme Newton, you will serve those delicious macarons you served at afternoon tea the last time I visited?"

"*Oui*, Mme Cassatt."

Mary smiled brightly. "Thank you." She placed her attention once more on Mira, and Mme Newton escaped through the back hall.

Chills raced over Mira's skin. She stood in the presence of the artist she, her mother, and Sylvie adored.

When I return—not if but when I return—I will have an unbelievable story to tell.

ELEVEN

"Come, Mirabelle." Mary opened the French doors. "We shall be working in the garden."

Mira trailed her into a brick-walled courtyard surrounded by a columned wrought-iron fence. Finding such an enticing area secreted in the rear of the building surprised her.

Insets of low brick-walled flowering gardens decorated the large space. Young women were painting on canvases or drawing in sketchbooks. In the center someone had set up an artist easel with a blank canvas and a table. A jar of sketch pencils in varying widths sat on the table along with an overly large woman's hat adorned with blue bow and tulle netting.

Mira recognized it at once, from the cover on Sylvie's art book. She remembered her godmother's words, "I still stand by my opinion you favor her. Reddish hair. Blue eyes. Beautiful."

Mary placed her sketchbook onto the table and clapped smartly. *"Bonjour, bonjour."*

Excited conversation buzzed through the air before the women quieted.

"Today, we will concentrate on sketching the head. My new acquaintance, Mirabelle Montgomery, has graciously agreed to model. Everyone, rearrange yourself for your best view. Let's begin."

She turned to Mirabelle. "You admire the gorgeous hat. Its blue decoration will emphasize your blue eyes, won't it? We must have you wear it. Place your belongings on the table, and we will pose you."

Mira removed her cape, hat, and gloves and placed them with her parasol on the table. The artist positioned her to face straight ahead with her back erect.

The red-haired woman who had been with Marius Jourdain sat close enough for Mira to detect her eyes were green and her complexion freckled. Mira wondered if she may be from an Irish American family. If so, she faced discrimination prominent at the time against Irish Catholic immigrants.

Who are you, and why did Marius upset you? Are you the cause of the animosity between the two men? Are they both in love with you? Is a love triangle at the heart of Jacques' dismissal from the force?

"Now, for your hands, Mirabelle." The artist's touch pulled Mira from her thoughts. "I think folded." Mary lifted Mira's right hand to study her ring.

Mira noted the green-eyed woman affixing a gaze of raw envy on the ring.

"Lovely." The artist released Mira's hand. "Moonstone?" "Yes."

"Lalique?" "Yes."

"Do you know René? Delightful man. So creative."

Not awaiting an answer, Mary placed the hat on Mira's head and tilted the large chapeau before stepping back. "There, I think."

Her expression grew thoughtful. "Mirabelle, I always give my models the same advice. Do not think of yourself as an object we are painting, my dear. As I say, women should be someone, not something. While you pose, free your mind to wander to someone you desire to be."

The artist's words reverberated through Mira's mind.

You'd never believe the wandering I am doing, Mary Cassatt.

~ ~ ~

"Our time has drawn to a close." Mary placed her pencil into the jar on the table. "Everyone to the parlor for *le goûter*."

Mira remained seated with the large hat weighing on her head. Her entire body screamed for release from remaining motionless, but she awaited the artist's dismissal.

She watched Marius Jourdain's acquaintance— girlfriend? lover?—exit the courtyard. How would Jacques react when seeing the woman again? Would she detect a romance between them?

So, what if I did? I am not involved with Jacques. I will not allow myself to be.

"Mirabelle, my dear." Mary swept a hand toward her. "Our session is over. You may relax."

"I wasn't sure . . . in case you needed to complete something . . . thank you." Mira clamped her lips together to cease her nonsensical stuttering in the grand artist's presence. "You may leave your belongings here while we join them for tea in the salon." Mary gazed at her sketch. "You are a beautiful subject. Thank you for posing for the class. I have wanted to paint a portrait of a woman in a large hat. This sketch provides me with a starting point."

"Thank you." Mira stood and stretched her cramped body. "How wonderful my visit to the Club coincided with your lesson."

She removed the hat and circled her neck around to release the strain wearing it caused. A warm glow of wonder spread through her. Here she sat, posing for a sketch of the very same Cassatt painting, *Woman's Head in a Large Hat*, that she and Sylvie had discussed. Her brain ached.

How am I the model in 1900 for this painting I admire in my present life?

Everything about time travel confused her, including the very fact it happened to her.

Mary swept toward the courtyard doors, calling back to Mira. "Shall we join the others, dear?"

"Oui. Merci."

Mira placed the chapeau on the table and hurried after the artist. When she entered the salon, the rumble in her empty stomach reminded her that she'd eaten only part of a baguette earlier. Her mouth watered at the sight of crepes with chocolate, cream cakes, pastries, and fruits. A multi- tiered tray offered the macarons Mary requested.

The artist headed for the tray, trilling, *"Oh là là."*

Several students clustered around Mary Cassatt, vying for her attention. Mira did not locate the green-eyed woman amongst the crowd.

"Did you enjoy posing for Mme Cassatt?"

Jacques' voice behind her startled Mira. "The posing tired me but left me exhilarated. Also, famished."

After selecting a sampling of each item to place on her small china plate, Mira chose a small table near the entrance to keep a watch for the woman.

Jacques joined her and pulled out her seat.

She settled herself at the table and began enjoying the treats.

Mme Newton arrived at their table with a tray offering cups of steaming café au lait. "Bonjour, M. Thibaut." She served the coffee and chatted. "Mme Cassatt is most pleased with Mlle Montgomery as her beautiful model."

Jacques nodded. "Not surprising to learn."

His forward statement took Mira aback.

He thinks I am beautiful?

The china cup trembled in her hand.

"Mlle Montgomery," Mme Newton whispered conspiratorially. "Have you regained any memory?"

Mira sensed the woman enjoyed sharing her secret. "Unfortunately, no."

"Oh, my dear. I am so sorry." Mme Newton clucked sympathetically before bustling away to serve the other tables.

Jacques nodded toward the woman. "We can trust Mme Newton to keep quiet. She is married to Reverend Newton of St. Bartholomew. His Protestant church offers the only English service to the Protestant community of the Left Bank. The church's rear entrance adjoins the courtyard. Mme Reid engaged the church to be the spiritual home of the Club and to keep a diligent moral eye on the boarders."

He paused for a sip of his coffee before adding in a mocking tone, "I assure you Mme Newton takes her responsibility seriously."

"Yes. She seems the diligent and conscientious type." Mira's answer dripped with sarcasm, assuming Mme Newton would not mince her words or discipline on wayward boarders.

Are you such a boarder, Miss Green-Eyes?

On cue, the woman in question entered the salon.

One of the gaggle of girls who earlier flirted with Jacques sat at a circular table with Mary Cassatt. She called out, "Winnie, join us."

Mira raised her coffee cup and pointed it toward Winnie. "Jacques, do you know her?"

After a quick glance, Jacques answered noncommittally. "Only as the woman we saw arguing with Marius Jourdain." "You have not seen her before?" Mira sat her cup onto its saucer. "You know others here well."

"I have made an acquaintance of one or two of these ladies." A smile danced across his face. "When I have been asked to chauffeur them, of course conversation is required."

"Only conversation?" Mira raised her eyebrows.

"Yes." Jacques raised his brows. "Why are you interested in the women I know, Mirabelle? Do I detect jealousy?" His tone teased.

"Do not flatter yourself." Mira folded her hands in her lap and squeezed them tightly. "I am merely curious about what prompted you and Marius Jourdain to come to blows." She spoke with a clipped enunciation. "Of course, I assumed your row to be about her, Winnie-whomever."

"I do not know Winnie-whomever." Jacques' enunciation matched hers. "And, my business with Marius is none of your concern."

"If you confront him in my presence, it becomes my concern." Mira lowered her voice, her tone heated. "Besides, I don't care for Winnie."

"Why?" Jacques' posture stiffened. "Do you know her? Did you regain a memory?"

"No." Mira spat out the word. "I have not regained any memory. The way Winnie focused on me during the lesson was odd. She is trouble."

Jacques shifted in his chair to allow himself a better view of Winnie. "Do you think seeing her is prompting a memory? Does she fit into your life?"

"No, I don't believe so." Mira reached out to touch Jacques' hand. "I think she fits into yours, through Marius Jourdain."

Jacques drew his hand from hers, making a pretense of checking his pocket watch. "We must be on our way."

Mira sighed. She hardly knew Jacques, but she recognized his withdrawal from topics he preferred to avoid. *I cannot wait to question you about Marius. Uncertainty about Mom haunts me. I need to finish my business in 1900 Paris as soon as possible.*

Mira rose from the table. "I'll gather my belongings."

Jacques stood as she did. "Meet me in the lobby." He deposited the pocket watch in his vest pocket and departed the salon.

Mira hurried to the courtyard. The sketch remained propped on the easel. She admired it while putting on her cape and hat. If she had her phone, she'd snap a photo to show Sylvie and her mother. Her shoulders slumped. The thrill of being in the presence of the artist they all three adored diverted her attention. She must find her way back before her mother's heart gave out.

And, before my passion heats up further for this irritating yet sexy Jacques Thibaut.

Mira sensed the presence of someone else in the courtyard.

Was it Jacques, sensing her desire? Was he searching for her, to kiss her once more?

Blushing at the thought, Mira swiveled her head toward the French doors. She caught sight of Winnie, whose brazen glare once again unnerved her. With her parasol and gloves in hand, Mira made her way through the doors without acknowledging her.

Mme Newton greeted Mira in the lobby. She held Mira's parasol to allow her to pull on her gloves while chattering away. "It has been a pleasure to meet you, Mlle Montgomery. Mme Cassatt has taken a seat in the automobile, and they await you."

She held the door for Mira's departure and whispered, "I hope your memory heals quickly, dear. You are welcome back here any time."

"Thank you." Mira felt the eyes of a curious Winnie once more upon her. She leaned into Mme Newton with an air of confidentiality. "May I ask you about Winnie? I do not know her last name."

"Flanagan." A look of disdain scurried across Mme Newton's face.

Irish, as I suspected.

"Mirabelle, has Winifred Flanagan jarred a memory for you?"

"Not at all. Why are you displeased with her?"

"I am not one to tell tales out of school. But that one." Mme Newton made a tch-tch sound. "She has flouted our rules. She sneaks out until the wee morning."

After being with Marius Jourdain, I surmise.

"We have smelt cigarette and liquor on her. She has taken to wearing her dressing gown during the day. Quite Bohemian. We have reprimanded her multiple times." Mme Newton added in a whisper, "You know these Irish Catholics. If you confess, you are free to break the Lord's word."

Mira pursed her lips to keep from reacting to the woman's prejudice.

You speak with such bias, not as a preacher's wife should. "If she receives one more disciplinary action"—Mme Newton held her hands up, in a helpless manner—"Pastor Newton will ask her to leave."

"Oh my. I hope it will not come to that." Mira exited onto the sidewalk and waved farewell to the gossipy woman. Jacques stood next to the shiny red roofless Peugeot. "You hope what does not come to that?"

Mira directed her attention to his automobile, ignoring his question. The elegant styling of the Peugeot swept her breath away. "What a beauty."

She always loved working on a period film requiring these vintage automobiles. She cast her trained eye over this 1900 Peugeot Type 15 Double Phaeton. The name phaeton referred to the horse-drawn phaetons of the era, which the design of these early automobiles closely resembled. The rear-mounted engine replaced the horses. The T-shaped tiller and a tall lever mounted at the driver's side for braking replaced the reins. Large brass lanterns were affixed to the front sides and a brass bulb horn to the driver's side, mimicking the style of horse-drawn carriages.

Mira squeezed the horn and laughed at its loud honk. She glanced at Mme Cassatt, seated on the back bench of red, tufted leather, and then at Jacques. Her antic cajoled a grin from the artist, but not from Jacques.

"Sorry," Mira squeezed the horn for one more honk. "I can't resist."

She traced her fingers along the black chrome fenders which curved over the thin black tires whose burnished gold spokes gleamed in the waning sunshine. The fender flattened between the two tires, providing a step for access into the automobile.

"Mirabelle." Mary Cassatt tapped the edge of the front bench. "You must ride next to Jacques."

Mira's face reddened at Mary's mischievous matchmaking ploy. She offered her hand to Jacques. "May I? I would love to observe how to drive."

"Your preference." Jacques guided her ascent onto the front bench. He leapt into the driver's seat and rested his right hand on the tiller. "After observing, I assume you will request to drive."

"But of course." Mira placed her hand on top of his. The jolt of attraction permeated through their gloves.

"You never answered my question."

She met his smoldering expression with her own. *Quit flirting, Mira. It can go nowhere between you.* "Oh?" She purposefully acted forgetfully.

"You said to Mme Newton you hope 'it does not come to that.' What did you mean?"

"Hmm. You never answered my questions about Marius Jourdain." She directed her attention forward.

Jacques accelerated and swerved them into the street with abandon.

Without the security of a seatbelt as found in modern cars, Mira buffeted about unsafely. She held the brim of her hat and braced her feet against the automobile's floorboard. Bernadette had not exaggerated in her description of Jacques: "My Jaco is not a dangerous man, he does dangerous."

Mira did not fear the speed. She knew the vehicle's maximum acceleration to be twenty miles per hour. She feared how Jacques darted in and out amongst other automobiles, horse-drawn cabs and carriages, bicycle riders, and pedestrians.

She recalled the reason why open air and sporty horse- drawn carriages and these early automobiles shared the name phaeton. The light body atop four large wheels allowed the driver to travel fast and recklessly. She did not need Bernadette's knowledge of mythology to know the name came from the Greek myth of Phaëton, son of Helios, whose attempt to drive the chariot of the Sun nearly set Earth on fire.

Mira cut her eyes toward Jacques and observed his total concentration. He believed in his power to tame the surrounding chaos. She relaxed her body into the moment and believed, too.

Letting go of her hat, she laughed aloud. Unlike Phaëton, Jacques was not setting Earth on fire but her, igniting within her a flame of desire. Why not allow it to burn while here, momentarily, with this man?

Because it is momentary.

I must not play with fire. I will be setting myself up for the heartbreak of goodbye when I travel through the portal to my real life. It would be unfair to encourage Jacques when nothing can come of it.

Besides, his true love is Susette, according to Bernadette and the way Jacques reacts when he hears her name.

My mission could include reconciling these two. If Jacques and I act upon our physical desire it could ruin everything . . . and I may never return to my real life, where I belong.

Mira met Jacques' glance, and all her reasonable arguments left her. When she placed a hand on his thigh, she could not ignore his arousal.

TWELVE

Mira reminded herself again that a love affair with Jacques must never happen. She removed her hand and avoided Jacques' pointed stare while she focused on the sights they passed.

The drive from 4 Rue de Chevreuse to The Ritz rendered Mira stupefied over viewing as new the old Paris landmarks, whose aged existence she held so dear in her 21ˢᵗ Century life. Awe and sadness battled within her.

I know the wars and violence ahead for you, City of Lights.

A terrible thought seized her heart.

What fate befalls Jacques and Bernadette during the bombings of World War One a short fourteen years away?

Tears burned her eyes.

I hate knowing the danger and tragedy each of you will face. But the upcoming years could bring happiness as well, couldn't they?

She dabbed at her eyes with her handkerchief.

"Are you unnerved by my driving?" Jacques projected his question loudly over the engine noise.

"Not at all."

It's being with you in 1900 Paris that unnerves me.

"If not"—Jacques gestured toward her—"then why grasp your hands together so tightly?"

Her ring finger did ache from the pressure of her hands gripped together. She loosened them apart and beamed a bright smile, hoping to appear nonchalant. "I am enjoying the ride immensely."

Jacques grinned. "I have my doubts."

Mira waved her gloved hand in front of her nose. "It is the commingling of the atrocious smells that brings me to tears."

She did not exaggerate. The musky odor of the Seine, the emissions of the automobiles, the excrement of the horses, and the nasty wafts of urine deposited in, on, or around the *vespasiennes* resulted in the city's nickname, The Great Stink. She found it hard to believe what she'd read about Parisians considering this odor "brought under control" for the 1900 Exhibition.

Jacques guided the automobile onto the Pont Royal.

Mira craned her neck backward to view the newly opened train station, Gare d'Orsay. She knew the structure as Musee D'Orsay. She always admired the building's spectacular and opulent Beaux Arts style but seeing it in its virgin state engendered more admiration.

Thank you for rescuing it from tear-down and breathing new life into it as the fabulous art museum.

She often stood before the huge clock on its fifth-floor North-East corner to revel in the view. The lifeblood of Paris pounded in her veins as the clock ticked life's moments. Through the clock's glass windows, she'd look across the River Seine at the Jardin des Tuileries. The row of Haussmann buildings stood behind it on the Rue de Rivoli. On a clear day, she gazed upon the silhouette of the La Basilique du Sacré Coeur atop Montmartre.

Thinking of Montmartre reminded her Marius Jourdain met Jacques there. She glanced at Jacques' handsome profile, wondering what nefarious dealings he had with such a lowlife as Marius, a man he obviously detested.

Mira reset her gaze ahead. The drive across Pont Royal allowed a view of the Louvre facing the Seine. The glass pyramid now standing in the Louvre's courtyard would shock the 1900 Parisians. But the design of the Eiffel Tower built for the 1889 World's Fair created a negative stir at the time. What would Paris be without her now-famous landmark?

Jacques' sharp turn left at the Jardin des Tuileries jolted Mira from her musings. She gripped the edge of the leather seat and dug her heels into the floorboard for balance. The Peugeot's noisy engine added to the cacophony of the traffic through which Jacques threaded. She wished wholeheartedly for their arrival at their destination.

"We are not far now." He careened the automobile to the right.

Mira righted herself in the seat. When the Place Vendôme with its famous landmark column materialized in her view, her annoyance at the uncomfortable ride faded. The square boasted even more magnificence than in her own time. The fashionable pedestrians strolled the sidewalks with polish and panache, drawn by the lure of fabulous shopping on the Rue de la Paix.

"We arrive." Jacques pulled to a stop at the canopied entrances monogrammed with the establishment's name, Hôtel Ritz.

Stories of its intoxicating history set Mira's body a-tingle.

I wish I could share the fame the unfolding years bring to this hotel.

Songwriter Irving Berlin writing the song "Putting on the Ritz" and coining the buzzword "ritzy" based on the hotel's snobbish and ostentatious style.

Author F. Scott Fitzgerald and Zelda partying there with fellow author Ernest Hemingway, who liberated its bar when the Nazis retreated from Paris.

Coco Chanel hanging her little black dresses in the closet of her permanent suite.

And more. Much, much more. But I must not share, for my time travel has made me a stranger in a strange land.

A sharply dressed bellhop met Jacques and assisted Mary Cassatt from the back seat.

"A nice jaunt, M. Thibaut." The artist tossed a wave to Mira. "It was a pleasure to sketch you, my dear. Goodbye, for now."

She walked away, and a bittersweet sadness invaded Mira. She anticipated with delight describing posing for her. The typically unflappable Sylvie would be speechless, as would her mother.

Stay strong, Mom, for I have so much to tell you.

The bellhop assisted Jacques in cranking the Peugeot's rear engine.

Mira watched the process with interest, giving thanks for the invention of the keyless ignition.

Jacques hoisted himself into the driver's seat and turned his attention upon her. "You appear deep in thought, Mirabelle. Is a memory surfacing?"

His sincere concern prodded her guilty conscience.

I hate lying to you about suffering amnesia, but I must distract you before you ply me with questions I cannot answer.

"No memories yet." Flirtingly, Mira placed her hand over his on the tiller. "I am deep in thought about you allowing me to drive."

Jacques' quick acceleration of the automobile bounced Mira against the bench. She glared at him. "I assume you are telling me no."

"How drôle your humor." He laughed. "I don't mean to jostle you. I am speeding to Bernadette. If we are too late, she will find a way to engineer trouble for herself."

Mira assumed Bernadette had found trouble, by the name of Siméon Aubert. The girl planned to introduce her in secret to Siméon. She'd disappoint her by arriving with Jacques.

Oh well. As Shakespeare wrote, "The course of true love never did run smooth."

Neither did the course of riding in a 1900 Peugeot. The swerve of the automobile sent Mira's stomach into a spin. She pressed the scented handkerchief to her nose to mask the smells to allow her to breathe deeply and settle her rattled body while recounting the events of the day to this point.

Worrying about her mother gnawed at Mira. If Jacques was her mission, she achieved little progress toward resetting his life's wrong direction. What part, if any, did Marius and Winnie—and Bernadette's mother, the so-called Queen of Bohemia—play in derailing Jacques' life? Why didn't Le Veille tell her how to get it back on track? Why trap her in 1900 Paris until she figured everything out, alone?

"Damn him."

"Strong language, even for an American woman." Jacques turned the tiller hard to maneuver through the Place de la Concorde's large square. "Damn whom?"

"Oh, um, I . . ." Mira sputtered, flummoxed at having spoken the curse. She pointed to the la Porte Monumentale flanked by two vividly colored minarets.

"Oh, you damn René Binet. Many support that opinion." Jacques' laugh held a hint of derision. "He designed that thing. The gateway to the 1900 Exhibition."

"It is overwrought." She projected interest of an Exhibition sightseer. "The Exhibition does deserve a grandiose entrance, though, and that building is definitely grandiose."

"Most refer to it as a monstrosity. The features of the statue *la Parisienne* were modeled after the famous actress Sarah Bernhardt and the gown is a Paquin design." Jacques made a sharp right turn. "It has been nicknamed *le triomphe de la prostituée.*"

"The triumph of the prostitute?" Mira winced. "I imagine neither Mme Bernhard nor Mme Paquin are pleased with that label."

Jacques swept his arm toward the crowds at the entryway, passing through the ticket-taking turnstiles. "My association with M. Peugeot has provided exhibitor badges for myself and Bernadette to come and go without charge or limitation." He brushed his fingers across the gold lapel pin he wore.

Mira recognized Bernadette wore one like it. "I am impressed to be in the presence of a VIP."

Jacques' eyebrows knitted. "What is this, vee-i-pee?"

"A very important person." "I do not understand."

"It's a . . . never mind."

I need to watch out for anachronisms. His suspicions will grow about where the heck I come from.

They passed the intersection with the eastern end of the Avenue des Champs-Élysées, and Mira took in the beauty of the gorgeous chestnut tree-lined boulevard extending to the Arc de Triumph. At this end, The Jardins des Champs- Élysées bordered one side. She saw the tops of the Grand Palais and Petit Palais, which sat on the side opposite the gardens. Horses and carriages, bicycles, automobiles, and pedestrians crowded the stone-paved thoroughfare, bustling along to whatever activity called to them.

During the rest of the drive, her interest in the passing sights waned. She focused on Le Veille's paradox.

Vanish into the past which holds your future. Return only if you right the wrong destiny that has befallen him.

If she believed in the butterfly effect, her actions she undertook while in 1900 could change future events in lives other than her own. The thought both spooked and intrigued her.

"You have been quiet." Jacques expertly piloted them across the Pont d'Iéna. "I can take you to my place." He slid a provocative glance her way. "To rest."

I doubt rest is in your thoughts, Jacques Thibaut.

His seductive proposal enticed Mira, but she knew she must not accept it. She tossed her head in feigned indignation. "How bold, Monsieur Thibaut, to suggest such intimacy on the basis of our one shared kiss."

"Are you saying no to my invitation?" "I am saying no."

"You won't deny me another kiss, Mademoiselle? Perhaps at the end of this evening?" Jacques cocked an eyebrow. "Perhaps more than a kiss?"

Mira cocked an eyebrow back.

Jacques shrugged. "A bed alone is a lonely bed."

"A bed alone allows much-needed rest, Monsieur," Mira parried back.

I long to fall into bed with you, for you to satiate my body as I suspect you can. But, I cannot. Intimacy with you could derail my mission to help you and trap me in the past. No, I must return where I belong. You must be with your true love, not a time traveler like me. Someone such as Nurse Susette? Does my mission include playing matchmaker?

The Eiffel Tower loomed in the short distance from them, and Mira focused on their activity ahead. "We have arrived. Bernadette is waiting."

Jacques parked the Peugeot curbside on la rue Suffren. He gathered his walking cane and Mira's parasol, adjusted his hat, and disembarked from the automobile. Approaching the passenger side, he held out a hand.

Mira remained still, worried about Jacques' reaction to meeting Siméon.

Should I prepare you, try to convince you not to embarrass Bernadette by treating the boy rudely?

"Did you change your mind?" Jacques leaned toward her, protectively, his eyes focused on her lips. "Shall I drive you to my place?"

Mira leaned away from his closeness. "No, I am fine."

How dare you presume I am fragile. Assume I will fall into your bed, be another conquest for you. If Susette still loves you as Bernadette believes, your womanizing must be chipping her heart to bits.

"Then, shall we find Bernadette?" Jacques opened her car door.

"Yes, but I need to ask something of you first." Mira shifted her body to face him. "Please be understanding of Bernadette. She is a young woman in love."

Jacques frowned. "With Siméon." He tapped his cane vigorously onto the ground. "They are children. They do not know love."

"They know their hearts. They plan to marry. Soon."

His face radiated shock. "I will not allow it. His grandfather will not allow it, either. I have spoken to him. He tells me Siméon is to attend École Polytechnique and become an engineer, or else he will disinherit the boy. What kind of life could Siméon then offer Bernadette? Not the one I hope for her."

"What do you hope for her?"

"More than living in poverty, tied to a failure of a man. Opportunities are broadening for women. They may enroll at their choice of The Sorbonne or Ecole des Beaux-Arts."

His comment surprised Mira.

I'd not suspected you to be supportive of women's equality. What other surprises lie under your chauvinist persona?

"Do you think Bernadette desires to attend either?" Mira doubted it, having observed the girl's boredom with academics.

"Bernadette has a quick mind and artistic talent she should hone instead of living the burdened existence of the poor. If she marries Siméon at so young of age, she will doom herself to a lesser life." Jacques paused to gather his breath before adding, "I have seen too many women eking out lives of desperation."

Mira instinctively surmised he spoke about one woman in particular—one for whom he deeply cared. "Who is this woman you care for whose life has been so desperately horrible?"

"I do not refer to a specific woman. As a police officer, I saw how the unfortunate turn of life's circumstances ruined women's lives. Girls who married young and became old before their time. Grisettes who have been taken advantage of and abused by their Bohemian lovers. Courtesans whose lovers discard them, leaving them to sink into lives of obscure poverty."

Jacques took a breath before adding, "I speak generally of women I tried but failed to help."

Mira could almost feel his heart breaking for one specific woman he felt he'd failed. Her thoughts whirled as to her identity.

From Bernadette's description of Susette, the nurse was an accomplished and successful person. If she'd been married before, Bernadette would have mentioned that, surely. She also doubted Susette could have been a grisette or courtesan before becoming a nurse.

"We must go." Jacques offered his hand to assist her from the automobile.

Mira filed her curious thoughts away to deliberate upon later. She accepted his help to exit the car. After smoothing her dress, she tipped her head up. "If you forbid Bernadette's relationship with Siméon, then you will push her into marrying him. Do not act rashly. Get to know him. Give them a chance to determine the course of their lives."

Jacques opened her parasol and handed it to Mira.

His tensed jaw told her not to pursue further conversation. She took his arm, hoping for the best when they met Bernadette. Winding through the thick crowd, she wondered about what Jacques so passionately shared with her moments ago.

Which woman other than Susette touched your heart so deeply: a young, married one? a grisette? a courtesan? Did you have your way with her? Did you love her?

The image of Winifred Flanagan crept into Mira's mind. Could she be the one Jacques believed he failed?

She glanced at his handsome profile, remembering his lips upon hers. She wished he didn't stir passion within her, tempting her to act upon her desire.

Most of all she wished to know what happened to make him quit the force, walk away from Susette, and associate with someone like Marius Jourdain.

We both hold our secrets, Jacques. I dare not share mine about time traveling, for who would believe me? But I must discover what you are hiding about your past if I am to reset your life's path. And, if I am ever to return home where I belong.

THIRTEEN

"There she is." Mira waved to Bernadette, glad of the distraction the girl presented.

Bernadette waved, but when she saw Jacques, her hand fell.

The young man seated on the bench by her leapt to his feet.

The two engaged in animated conversation. "Let's hurry." Mira accelerated her pace.

Jacques fell in hurried step with her.

Mira waved at Bernadette once more. "I think she is sending Siméon away before we meet him."

"Good riddance," Jacques responded in a rough manner. "Control your animosity, Jacques. The boy looks perfectly suitable. Tall and handsome. I expect he is intelligent, ambitious, and kind."

"Why do you think so? Do you judge him favorably based on his acceptable appearance?"

Mira's spirit bristled. "I judge him favorably because Bernadette does. And so should you."

Jacques nodded curt agreement.

Siméon extended his hand in greeting. "M. Thibaut. *Je m'appelle* Siméon Aubert."

At Mira's nudge, Jacques accepted the boy's offer for a handshake. "*Bonsoir.*"

Bernadette exchanged air kisses with Mira. "Please, meet Siméon."

"*Bonsoir.*" Siméon bowed. "Please excuse my poor English. Bébé speaks much better."

"You mean Bernadette," Jacques admonished the boy. Mira pressed her lips together, amused at Jacques' possessiveness of Bernadette's affectionate nickname.

Siméon addressed her. "Mlle Montgomery, you have my sincere condolences for your suffering."

Bernadette's cheeks reddened with embarrassment. "Oh, Mirabelle. Please do not be upset. I took Siméon into our confidence, for we can trust him."

"I am not upset. Let's not be so formal, Siméon. Call me Mirabelle."

"You may call me M. Thibaut," Jacques interjected.

"I was going to introduce you." Bernadette glowered at him.

Jacques rocked back on his heels. "I have met your grandfather, Siméon. A respected man. He tells me you are to study to become an engineer at École Polytechnique."

Bernadette stamped her foot. "How do you know M. Aubert? When did he tell you of his plans for Siméon? Or, did your *spies* tell you."

"I hope you and Siméon haven't been waiting long?" Mira spoke lightly, attempting to soothe Bernadette's frustration. "Our day became confused, and Jacques did not go to the Automobile Club. Did you get his message?"

"Yes. Did any memory return, Mirabelle?" Bernadette's voice rose in excitement.

"I haven't recovered memories. Let's not discuss me, though." Mira smiled encouragingly at Siméon. "What do you have planned—"

Jacques interrupted. "Mirabelle means you must come with us. Say farewell to the boy and—"

Mira's icy glare silenced him. "Jacques means we are excited to get to know Siméon better."

"You are, Jaco?" Bernadette asked in a quiet, hopeful voice.

Jacques swung his walking cane upon his shoulder in an aggressive manner, his demeanor disapproving.

Mira positioned her parasol to hide the two of them from view. "Do not force her to choose between you and the man she loves," she whispered before raising the parasol aloft.

Settling his face in a neutral expression, Jacques pointed his walking cane toward Siméon. "I will become better acquainted with this boyfriend of yours, Bébé. If that idea meets with his inclination."

"Yes. Very much, sir." Siméon straightened his shoulders. "Thank you."

"Oh, Jaco." Bernadette threw her arms around him. "I love you very much." She stepped from him to hug Mira. "Thank you for convincing him, Mirabelle. You are my fairy godmother."

Mira smiled, a wistfulness overtaking her. How many times had she called Sylvie her fairy godmother? She needed her to sprinkle her fairy dust magic on her mother to keep her well.

Damn you, Le Veille, for giving me only a paradoxical riddle to solve to win my passage back through the portal.

Bernadette took Siméon's hand and swung their clasped hands toward the large blue and gold sphere near the Eiffel Tower. Constellations and signs of the zodiac were painted on it.

"We planned to eat a bite before walking to the top of the Globe Céleste. On its terrace, you recline in armchairs and watch the panoramic view of the solar system rolling past, like traveling through space."

Jacques used his cane again as a pointer, tipping it toward the Globe. "Lead the way."

Mira's stomach twisted in a knot. *I guess if I can survive time travel, I can survive pretending to travel through space.* When they stopped to dine at a vendor's café near the Eiffel Tower, Mira's growling stomach responded to the divine food smells. Her food intake for the day had been part of a baguette and bites of sweets at the American Girls' Club. She set upon her soup and leg of mutton with an appetite while managing to keep the conversation among them light and casual.

Upon finishing the delicious dinner, Mira tucked her arm into Jacques, and they followed Siméon and Bernadette toward the Globe Céleste. Once again, the attraction brought an uneasiness to Mira, for it reminded her of time travel.

A swirl of fog encircled her, further unnerving her. The pressing crowd faded from her sight. She lost her balance and stumbled against the man in front of her.

He turned, with a swish of his black cloak. "Be careful, Mlle."
Le Veille.

The fog lifted before Mira called his name. People materialized again around her, and the chill subsided. Swiveling to search for Le Veille, she lost her footing.

"Watch your step, Mirabelle." Jacques steadied her.

"Did you see him?" Mira gripped Jacques' arm. "The man in front of me?"

"No." Jacques glanced around, puzzled. "I saw no man."

I saw him, though. Le Veille appeared and told me to be careful. Of what? Mira's stomach once more twisted into a knot.

Why won't Le Veille provide more than a stupid riddle? Jacques pointed to a small carved wooden doll. "You must have tripped over that. It's one of the nesting Russian dolls they call Matryoshka dolls. They have been popular at the Exhibition, winning a Bronze medal I have heard." "Yes, I suppose I did trip over the doll." Mira loosened her grip on his arm. "Have we lost our couple in love?" "Please." Jacques grimaced. He gestured ahead. "They have reached the pedestrian bridge to the Globe."

Mira searched the crowd and saw Bernadette and Siméon had climbed midway on the bridge. "Let's join them."

A rumble vibrated through the air. She scrutinized the sky, which held the hue of blue hour, the soft light before twilight. "Oh, my. Is it thundering?"

Jacques jerked her before she could step onto the bridge. "Mirabelle, stop."

The rumble morphed into a roar which drummed through her.

Jacques threw her to the ground underneath him while bits of concrete, sand, gravel, dust, and nails rained on them.

Mira held her breath. Each moment of destruction felt like a lifetime before an eerie silence descended.

Jacques braced himself over her. "Are you hurt?"

She swallowed against the dust in her mouth. "I don't think so."

He helped Mira to her feet.

She unpinned her damaged hat obscuring her vision and dropped it to the ground. Jacques' hatless and disheveled appearance frightened her. "Are you hurt?"

"No."

She gaped around her, dazed. "What happened?"

"The bridge to the Globe. It collapsed."

"Wh-What?" She realized nothing but rubble lay where she last saw Bernadette and Siméon amidst smiling and excited faces. The food and drink she had downed earlier threatened revolt. Forcing away the bile creeping into her throat, she bolted toward the rubble.

Jacques grabbed her arm. "Where are you going?" She struggled against him. "We have to find them." "Yes. I will." He pushed her behind him. "Not you." "Try to stop me." Mira wrested free from him.

Jacques scowled at her. "Stay near me, then. Be careful."

Be careful.

Le Veille cautioned her with those same words.

If you knew the bridge were to collapse, why did you let it happen? Let people get hurt? Killed? Did you stumble against me to slow me so I would not have been on it? Does being a time traveler require me to observe tragedy unfold and do nothing?

The scene surrounding Mira throbbed with the intensity of search and rescue. She followed Jacques into the throng of police, firefighters, and emergency medical people. The danger of the mounds of debris shifting under her feet threatened her courage to join in the rescue.

She breathed in deeply to steel her nerves. The thick dust in the air invaded her lungs. Coughing to clear it wracked her body and brought tears that blurred her vision.

Jacques stopped from where he trod ahead of her. "It is too dangerous. Before you get hurt, stay back. I must help them, but you must stay safe."

Mira's mouth went dry. When she stood with her father before the burning house so long ago on their walk home from the park, he'd said similar words.

"I must help them. Stay back, Mira. Stay safe."

Her legs had rooted into the sidewalk as she watched him rush into the flames. Her fear-tightened throat choked back her cries. It was the last time she saw her father alive.

I never understood why you left Mom and me to save strangers, until now. I will dig to save not only Bernadette and Siméon but anyone who moans and calls out for help, no matter the danger I face. Like you ran into the fire, no matter the danger you faced.

"I am helping." She climbed ahead of Jacques, ignoring his angry mutterings.

When they reached the teams of police officers, the one in charge recognized Jacques.

While the two conferred, Mira snatched a shovel and began digging.

After a moment, Jacques joined her.

The chaos of the rescue effort faded from Mira's attention. She focused on each shovelful of rubble and her prayer.

Please, please God. Help me find survivors. Help me find Bernadette and Siméon. Alive.

FOURTEEN

The blue hour turned to evening's darkness. Mira gave thanks for the Exhibition's electric lights illuminating the rescue and recovery, but a sob hitched in her chest at the mounds of debris.

It's as if we're shoveling with teaspoons. We need 21st Century bulldozers and other machinery.

She removed her dirt-caked gloves, which were providing little prevention from the blisters forming on her hands. Laying the shovel in the rubble, she stretched her weary back and leaned side to side to release its cramping.

Jacques threw his shovel down. "I think it's time to stop."

"No." Mira grabbed his tool and shoved it into his hands. "We will not give up."

Jacques began digging again, his mouth set in a grim line.

Mira lifted her shovel and continued, her strained muscles screaming in protest.

"Aidez moi."

Mira made out the faint call for help.

She tossed away her shovel and grabbed Jacques' arm. "Someone is alive."

"Yes." Jacques' next strike of his shovel hit against a large boulder. "We have to remove this to get to him."

"I'll get help." Mira climbed through the uneven wreckage to reach the remaining group of police. Her call came in a mangle of English and French. "Come, quickly, *venir vite.*"

The closest policeman turned.

She motioned wildly. "Over here, *par ici.* Someone is alive, *quelqu'un est vivant.*"

The policeman barked the information to the others.

With their hands locked to keep each from tumbling, Mira led them through the craggy piles toward where she'd heard the call. When they reached Jacques, the French discussion flew among them faster than Mira translated.

She stood, panting, waiting for the strategy to be decided upon. Hearing the faint call for help once more, Mira crouched and cupped her mouth to answer. "Don't give up, *n'abandonne pas. Je m'appelle* Mirabelle. *Comment t'appelles-tu?*"

"Mirabelle? *Est-ce vous. C'est Siméon.*" "It's me also, Mirabelle. Bernadette."

"Bernadette. Siméon." Mira leapt to her feet and fell against Jacques, who caught her in his arms. "It's them, Jacques! It's them!"

He whispered with trembling breath into her ear. "Thank God. Thank God."

Mira's world collapsed to the two of them. Relief coursed through her. She pulled from his embrace and noted his trickling tears left watery tracks in his dirt-grimed cheeks.

How you love Bernadette. How we both do.

Jacques knelt at the narrow crevice created by their digging. "It won't be long now. We will rescue you."

The thought that one or both could be injured shredded Mira's heart. Her rapid breathing threatened to hyperventilate her. She slowed her breaths, but her racing mind knew what she must do. "Jacques, I am going to get medical help."

Without waiting for his response, Mira picked her through the destruction and ran toward where the doctors and nurses were tending the injured. The wails of friends and families kneeling on the ground at their dead loved ones' sides unnerved Mira.

She'd once knelt on the ground at a loved one's dying side. She pressed her tongue to the roof of her mouth and swallowed hard to repulse the bile returning once again.

One, two, three, four, five, six, seven, eight, nine.

Mira counted the dead bodies she passed, each covered with an improvised cloth of respect: a man's coat, a lady's cape, a blanket materializing from someone's possessions. She prayed for the count of those dead to stop at nine, a miraculous number considering the crowds upon the bridge and the magnitude of the disaster.

Please, God. Don't take either Siméon or Bernadette as the tenth. Don't take anyone as the tenth.

Surveying the scene for a doctor to solicit, she saw none to be spared. A nurse's assistance must suffice. She approached one in charge. "Excuse me."

The woman turned from giving instructions to a group of nurses encircling her. A layer of dust besmirched the whiteness of their nurse caps and aprons.

Mira grabbed the nurse's arm. "I need your help."

"You are American? I shall speak English. My name is Susette Godard."

Hearing the name, the chaos of the scene around Mira faded from her vision. Her breathing suspended.

Susette Godard. Jacques' Susette.

"Are you injured?"

The compassion in the woman's voice felt like a soothing salve over Mira's aching muscles. "You are Nurse Godard? From Hôpital Hôtel-Dieu?"

"*Oui?*" The questioning way in which she answered signaled the nurse's confusion at being recognized. Susette reached to take Mira's hand. "Where are you hurt?"

Mira glanced at her exquisite Paquin outfit, now in tatters and covered with gray dust, and realized she did resemble a victim.

"No, I am not hurt." Her words tumbled out amidst ragged breath. "I am Mlle Mirabelle Montgomery. Jacques and I found his ward and her beau buried in the rubble. Both were on the bridge when it collapsed."

"Bébé." Susette sagged against the young nurse standing by her. "Philomene. It's Bébé."

"Oh, Nurse Godard. I am so sorry." Philomene helped Susette remain standing. "Mlle, Nurse Godard cared for Bernadette's guardian M. Thibaut and grew quite close to them both. This news is quite upsetting."

"*Merci*, Philomene." Susette regained her footing and sent a glance toward Philomene that silenced the young woman. "Mlle Montgomery, is Bébé alive?"

Susette's quavering voice and drawn eyebrows over tear-filled eyes signaled to Mira how deeply the nurse cared for Bébé.

They are lovely black brows arched over lovely hazel eyes. No wonder Jacques fell for her. She's compassionate, gentle, and gorgeous.

"Yes." Mira fought the ache in the back of her throat. "At least, when I left to find medical help, she was calling out."

Susette's professional demeanor snapped into place. "They might be badly hurt. Lead me to her. Philomene, get our medical bags and come with us." She stepped past Mira. In her haste, she stumbled over scattered debris and cried out.

Mira caught her arm to steady her. Susette gave a nod. "*Merci*, Mlle."

"Please. Call me Mirabelle." Mira let go of Susette's arm. "The pathway is treacherous. Be careful where you step. Follow me."

"*Oui*," Susette stepped behind Mirabelle and added, "Mirabelle."

Choosing the least debris-filled ground for them to tread, Mira led them to the rescue scene.

The rescuers had managed to dislodge the boulder over the crevice into which Bernadette and Siméon had fallen. Police officers held ropes dangling into it, but everyone stood motionless, appearing perplexed.

Mira rushed to Jacques, impatience pulsing through her. "What is the delay?"

Jacques peered into the ravine. "We've lowered canteens of water to them and thrown to them the ends of the ropes we will use as pulleys to extract them. We need them to secure the ropes around their waists. Siméon appears in too much pain, and Bernadette is too distracted to follow my instructions on how to knot the ropes."

An unfurled rope lay at Jacques' feet. Mira grabbed it.

Jacques wrenched the rope from her grip. His jaw tightened. "We don't need you requiring rescue as well."

"You should send me." Susette stepped between Jacques and Mira.

"Susette."

The fervor with which Jacques said the nurse's name told Mira everything, even though no emotion broke through his impenetrable expression.

You two were in love. Are still in love. What happened between you?

Mira grappled the rope from Jacques.

No time now to figure that out.

Under the dumbfounded stare of Jacques, Mira created a harness looped under her arms and tied securely around her waist.

Those knot-tying skills I learned at summer camps are finally coming in handy. The yet-to-be-invented carabiner would secure this harness, but I'll have to do without one.

"You." Mira pointed to Susette and Philomena. "Prepare for treating their injuries."

She threw the rest of her rope to Jacques. "Lower me. Now."

Jacques reined her in close.

Mira used her weight to fight against him.

He proved too strong. "Hold still, Mirabelle. I am checking your harness is secure."

His pull on the rope brought Mirabelle even closer against his body. Their eyes connected, and Mira detected raw fear in his.

"Don't worry." She smiled with confidence, hoping she appeared brave. "Bernadette will be safe again, soon."

"She has to be." Jacques gave the rope another tug before releasing his hold. "We descend you slowly. Once you reach them, harness them both and we will pull you up, one at a time."

"Understood." The certainty of her tone belied her fear.

I will not panic. I can do this.

Mira sat on the edge of the crevice and braced her feet against its interior walls. She held her breath and squeezed herself into the narrow opening. Jacques signaled for the men to begin lowering her.

Mira pursed her lips against the pain of the harness cutting against her more tightly as her body dropped, swaying back and forth. The deeper Mira descended the less light filtered in from above. Breathing in the gritty, dust-choked air left a metallic taste of dirt in her mouth. She wished she'd tied a bandana around her face as a filter.

A sudden drop sent her plummeting, and instinctively, she screamed from fear. Her body brushed against the cavern's walls, raining bits of rock and pebble.

Bernadette's screaming mingled with her own.

Mira gripped the harness as tightly as her strength allowed.

Please, please. I cannot die, not lost in time where my mother will never know what has happened to me.

Her moonstone ring bit into her finger, and she welcomed the pain.

Dad, send me strength. Help me succeed in rescuing these two.

"Pull harder. She's falling," Jacques yelled.

The rope snapped taut, wrenching Mira. Her father must have heard her prayers.

Thanks, Dad.

She welcomed the pain of the tightened harness although knowing it would leave her bruised.

"Mirabelle, are you injured?" Jacques cried out. Without awaiting her answer, he roared, "Pull her back up. Now." "No. I am fine. Keep going," Mira shouted. "Mirabelle, no," Bernadette cried out.

Mira called to Jacques. "Let's finish. Slow, though. Please."

Jacques did not argue.

Once her feet touched the dimly lit cavern floor, she yelled, "We have touchdown."

"*Excuse moi?*"

"Oh." Jacques' confused comment reminded Mira to watch her anachronisms. "I've reached the bottom. Slack the rope."

"*Dieu merci.*" Bernadette handed Mira a canteen.

She washed water around in her mouth and spat to rid herself of the grit before taking several gulps to quench her thirst.

"Thanks." She handed the canteen back to Bernadette.

The girl took it in her trembling hand. "Mirabelle, what do we do next?"

"We create harnesses for each of you, using these ropes they have thrown to you. Then they will lift you to safety." Mira knelt by Siméon to check his injuries.

He propped himself on his elbows, and a moan escaped from him.

"Where are you hurt?"

"Do not worry. I am fine." He struggled to his feet, wincing.

Mira expertly created harnesses around each of them. Siméon gave each knot a pull to ensure tautness.

Mira tugged on the rope attached to Siméon and called out to Jacques, "The boy comes first. He needs medical attention."

Siméon struggled against the rope. "I should be last."

"Heave ho," Jacques yelled.

Lifted in the air, the boy's protest faded. When he appeared from the hole, loud hurrahs rang through the air.

Mira tugged on Bernadette's rope and called out, "Bernadette next."

Once freed, Bernadette peered into the chasm. "You next, Mirabelle."

"I'm ready." Mira cleared the crevice opening and leaned into Jacques' waiting arms. Fatigue and stress overcame her, and she sank to the ground.

"Let me untie the harness." He fumbled at it.

Mira closed her hands over his. "I'm fine. Everyone is fine."

Mira read the gratitude in his eyes. She looked past him toward Susette, who knelt by Siméon with Bernadette at her side.

"You and Nurse Godard . . ." Mira trailed her words off, assuming he understood her unspoken question.

Jacques did not answer. He freed her from the harness and steadied her on her feet. "I must thank the officers for their help, if you do not need me?"

"Go. I am fine." Mira watched him amidst the police officers, noticing his ease in a position of authority. He must have been an excellent police detective. Her curiosity deepened.

Why did you leave the force, Jacques? Why are you and Susette no longer together?

She made her way to where the patients lay on the blankets. Susette crouched between them while Philomena stood over them holding bandages.

Jacques joined them. "How is Bébé?"

Susette's smile spoke relief. "Lucky girl. Cuts and bruises, but they will heal. Siméon suffered cracked ribs and a deep gash in his leg requiring stitches. I will have them both admitted to the hospital for overnight observation."

Bernadette, her cheeks wet with tears, lay her hand lightly on Siméon's chest. "It's my fault, poor darling. You cushioned my fall, but I must have broken your ribs."

Susette stroked the girl's hair. "He will heal."

Bernadette raised her head and smiled at the nurse.

Mira saw how much Bernadette adored Susette. She had nursed her beloved Jaco to health. Susette and Jacques shared their hearts and created a family for Bernadette.

I have been right not to act on my passion for Jacques. This near tragedy will reunite him with his true love. Bernadette will have her family once more.

A realization came to Mira. She clasped her hand to her chest, fingers splayed across her heart.

Bernadette and Jacques led her to Siméon. Death would have befallen him if she not overcome her fear of the disaster and been instrumental in saving him. She had been the one who heard the call for help, and she had been the one lowered to help in his rescue.

Le Veille must have sent me here to save Siméon, not Jacques. It was Siméon's destiny I was to ensure would unfold as fate decreed, not Jacques' destiny.

Relief coursed through Mira.

With her mission accomplished, the portal would re- open for her return. Looking at Jacques, her relief turned bittersweet as she remembered his lips upon hers.

Will I meet a man in my real life whose touch—whose kisses—arouses such passion within me?

Bernadette hovered by Siméon, brushing his hair from his forehead. Mira's heart ached with tenderness for their young love. The girl lowered her face, her lips hovering close to his.

Siméon turned his reddening face from the intended kiss. "Not in front of everyone."

Bernadette looked at Jaco. "You understand, don't you, Jaco? You know what it means to fall in love." She shifted her gaze to Susette.

The nurse's thin shoulders sagged.

Jacques stepped to her side. "What are your thoughts, Susette? Should I approve?"

Susette looked into his eyes and gave a slight nod.

"In that case." Jacques loudly called the boy's name. "Siméon. Kiss her."

Bernadette lowered her face into Siméon's again. This time he did not turn his head.

Their enthusiastic kiss invited more hurrahs from the policemen.

Jacques approached Mira's side. "Thank you, Mirabelle," he whispered. "Today you became our angel." He took her blistered hands into his own and gently kissed her palms.

The line from *Romeo and Juliet* flew into Mira's thoughts. "'Palm to palm is holy palmers' kiss . . . let lips do what hands do.'"

Oh Jacques. Even though you love Susette, our bodies crave each other's. How could spending one night together before I step through the time portal be so wrong?

But the look of love exchanged between Jacques and Susette told Mira how wrong—how selfish—it would be. She withdrew her hands from his, her heart pounding under Susette's intent stare.

FIFTEEN

Mira fought exhaustion as they crossed Pont Notre Dame onto Île de la Cité heading to Hôpital Hôtel-Dieu.

She worried about the energy needed to re-enter the portal for her return home. She worried about what the rest of Carolyn's text said. Would she find her mother alive?

Would she remember her time travel and those she met? Sweet Bernadette. Compassionate Susette. Boyish Siméon. Sexy Jacques. She would miss them.

As badly as her heart hurt, body ached, and hands throbbed from blisters, she marveled at her actions. She had reacted as had her father when lives became endangered. Neither of them hesitated to save others.

The idea she might have perished had not entered her decision until she committed herself to the rescue, as it must not have entered her father's that night.

What if my spontaneous actions had killed me? I assume death to be death, whether in my real life or in my 1900 existence. Mom would have never known what happened.

A quiet sob worked its way through her tightened throat.

How could I have been so reckless?

Mira pretended to push back her straggling bangs to hide brushing the wetness from her cheeks. She did not want Jacques to notice her emotional state.

I cannot have a breakdown at this point. I am so close to the portal re-opening, to seeing Mom again.

They neared Hôpital Hôtel-Dieu, which cast a burnished glow created from the Haussmannization of the Île de la Cité. When she'd designed sets for movies based in various times of the city's history, Mira learned about Hausmann's imprint on Paris. Viewing the Hausmann-style architecture in 1900, sparkling from its relative two-decade newness, provided Mira with a different appreciation.

The masterful re-maker of Paris removed residences, including slum areas, and turned this island in the middle of the Seine into administration offices for Paris, including the Police Prefecture.

His renovation created the Parvis de Notre Dame, the open square in front of the Cathedral where to the left stood the entrance to the Hôpital Hôtel-Dieu.

Sadness tinged her admiration of the beauty of the Cathedral and its soaring steeple, remembering its recent ghastly destruction from fire.

So much will happen to you, City of Lights, in the coming years. How I long to protect you from it all.

Jacques parked at the entrance of Hôpital Hôtel-Dieu and aided Mira's descent from the automobile. In turn, she assisted him with Bernadette and Siméon.

When Jacques helped Susette exit, Mira saw an intense glance passing between them, which spoke of their interrupted happily-ever-after.

You can never be mine, Jacques. As a gift of my love, I shall not act upon our mutual desire, so you will feel free to reconcile with Susette. With all that has happened tonight, you must seize the opportunity to correct your fate and live the life you're meant to live with her.

The five of them entered the lobby of the ornately designed building through an arched doorway placed centrally in a line of similarly arched windows. The French motto of *Liberté Fraternité Égalité* carved into the stone touched Mira's vulnerable heart.

Once inside the hospital, Mira shivered in the coolness created by the lofty ceilings and the long, vaulted, window- lined corridors with their smooth, chilly tiled floors and concrete walls. She glimpsed an ornate central courtyard between the two symmetrical facing wings of the hospital. After the chaos, its beauty and calmness beckoned, like a chapel.

The bustle of nuns descending upon them confused Mira. They were in full habit of white tunics with broad triangular shaped wimples, stiff crown bands, and long, voluminous black veils floating from their upper body like wings.

"Why nuns?" she whispered to Jacques.

"The St. Augustine nuns have provided care here since the Middle Ages," he whispered back. "Nurses such as Susette supplement the staff."

Susette took charge of the nuns, sending three for wheelchairs and another to prepare beds on the wards. After dispatching them, she began writing into a book on the lobby desk. "I am admitting each of you overnight for observation and medical care as needed."

"Thank you, but I need no care." As usual, Jacques' determined tone left no room for discussion. "I must check in with the police at the Prefecture, to submit my report on the rescue of Siméon. They are tracking the number of injured and—" He abruptly stopped in mid-sentence.

Mira remembered the bodies underneath the makeshift coverings.

You need not finish your sentence, Jacques. We know.

Bernadette reached for her. "Mirabelle, please stay?"

Mira took her hand, hiding the pain on her blistered palm from the girl's touch. "I shall wait until you fall asleep." She addressed Susette. "If I am permitted?"

Susette's pen hovered above the lobby book. "You do not think an overnight stay for observation is best for you?" "I am not injured. Please, do not waste a bed or care needed for others on me."

Susette inspected Mira's hands. "You must get your hands cleansed and bandaged and let a doctor examine you. Afterward, you may remain with Bernadette for as long as you wish."

She bobbed her head in Jacques' direction. "I cannot force you to accept a medical examination. You may use our showers. I will find you a change of clothing."

Mira cringed at the iciness of Susette's tone.

Jacques sidled close to Mira. His lips brushed against her ear. "Come to the lobby after Bernadette settles into sleep. I shall wait for you there."

Mira's nerve endings tingled at his nearness and the warmth of his breath. *Why does this man elicit such desire in me?*

At Susette's direction, a nun escorted Jacques toward the baths.

When he walked away, Mira felt the void of his presence. *Will you wonder about me, once I am a void in your life?* Another nun with a wheelchair helped Siméon into it. "Take him to Ward D for examination and treatment," Susette instructed.

"I am fine." Siméon's words came through gritted teeth. "Please, take care of Bébé and Mirabelle."

"Oh, my love." Bernadette patted his shoulder. "You mind what Susette says."

"Very well." Siméon pointed down the corridor. "Onward, Sister."

Bernadette cast a worried look toward Susette. "We must get word to his *grand-père.*"

"We shall send a message, Bébé," Susette said. "You and Mirabelle need a warm shower before the doctor's examination." She glanced at herself. "As do I."

Mira's spirit soared at the possibility of a warm shower, but she did not want to take the time. She needed to hurry to the Carousel.

She assessed the disgraced state of her Paquin gown. She no longer had gloves, hat, parasol, or her Edwardian cloak her mother had given her. She'd thrown it on the ground when she began shoveling for survivors.

'My cloak." She half-sobbed the words.

How could I have lost such a sentimental possession?

"There, there." Susette placed an arm around her shoulders. "You are in shock."

Bernadette joined the hug.

Mira leaned into their embrace. "I'm selfish, crying about my lost cloak. Others have lost loved ones." Her words came out in hiccups.

"You are not one bit silly." Susette motioned to the two nuns who remained at standby. "Let's get them to the showers, Sisters. I'll join them after I check on Siméon."

She fixed a concerned look upon Mira. "You need rest. Once you're settled, I will check in on you both."

You will check on Bernadette. With my mission completed, I must go to the Carousel. Le Veille should be waiting there. With a brush of her lips against Bernadette's cheek, Susette hurried away.

Bernadette dropped her arm from around Mirabelle. "I cannot wait to be clean once more." She followed the nun, calling to Mirabelle, "Are you coming?"

"I thought of something to ask Susette. I will join you soon." Watching Bernadette go, Mira's heart contracted.

Adieu, sweet child. Have a happy life. Be safe.

She made her way to the lobby. The wall clock read a few minutes before midnight.

My time in 1900 Paris has been crammed with adventure. Attempting to re-activate the Carousel portal. Visiting the American Girls' Club. Encountering Marius Jourdain and Winifred Flanagan. Posing for Mary Cassatt. Saving Siméon. How he will affect my future, as Le Veille's paradox said, I can't imagine. But my mission is done, and Le Veille must send me home. Has time stood still while I've been trapped in this wrinkle?

The sight of Jacques asleep on a bench by the hospital door froze Mira in her steps. He was minus his hat. His walking cane she'd admired must be lost along with it in the rubble of the bridge collapse.

As was her precious cloak.

His change of clothing, a long-sleeved tunic shirt of rough cloth and black trousers cinched with a belt, lacked his usual high-quality flare. A lock of his damp, mussed hair dangled onto his forehead. A scratch of beard covered his cheeks, contrasting with his fuller mustache.

Your rougher appearance makes you even more handsome and sexier.

She stood before him, watching him sleep.

You have awakened passion within me, and for that I will forever love you. But leave you, I must. I must leave all of you. Hopefully, you will reconcile with Susette and be a family, together with Bernadette and Siméon.

Sadness weighted Mira's heart. The sharp clink of metal against the marble floor startled her. Her moonstone ring lay at her feet. She must have been twirling it on her finger until it dropped from her hand.

Her mother had been right. "It's your 'tell,' Mira. The more upset, the more you twirl."

When Mira stooped to recover it, Jacques groaned.

She knew she must depart before he awakened. In a stealthy manner, she opened Jacques' left hand, placed the ring into it, and curled it closed.

Remember me always. If only I could kiss you farewell.

She clutched her ragged blouse around her and walked from the hospital into the darkened street.

A police officer stood by a horse-drawn police carriage parked at the curb. The horse's soft neigh echoed in the quiet.

Mira approached him, formulating her lie. "*Bonsoir.* You are to take me to the entry of the Le Jardin du Luxembourg, near the Carousel, per orders of M. Thibaut."

The police officer touched the brim of his kepi and aided Mira into the cab.

The rattle of its tires on the cobblestone matched the sorrowful rattle of her heart.

Adieu, Jacques.

SIXTEEN

Mira made her way from the garden's entrance toward the Carousel, thanking the moon and stars for illumination. The domed top of the merry-go-round appeared, and the various animals suspended on poles leered at her. Shivering in the night's coolness, she stood alone at the side of the elephant.

Where are you Le Veille? Why do you play games with me?

The air turned even cooler, and the telltale swirl of fog encircled Mira. She recognized the signs of Le Veille's appearance. When he materialized before her, she climbed upon the elephant. Her grasp on the pole stung her blistered palms, and a muffled cry of pain escaped her lips.

Steadying herself upon the carousel animal, she announced to Le Veille her expectation. "I did your bidding, and now you do what you promised. Send me home."

Le Veille held his arms toward her. "You have shown bravery and accomplished something I did not expect. You once judged your father for his heroic actions, blaming him for leaving you and your mother. Yet, now through your own actions, you understand his, and you forgive."

"Yes." Tears glazed Mira's eyes.

Dad, here I am, once more, on our white elephant. Can you forgive me, for not understanding your bravery, your sacrifice? For sealing my heart from others for so long? For hurting Mom by holding on to my anger against you?

She blinked to clear her vision. "Re-activate the Carousel portal as you promised, Le Veille. My mother needs me, before . . ."

She choked back the rest of her words, remembering Carolyn's text.

Mira, catch the next plane. Your mother has . . .

Her imagination had been filling in the rest since she'd found herself in 1900 Paris. She prayed for its completion to be *your mother has found a heart.*

Le Veille began to fade from view.

"Stop!" Mira screamed. "You cannot disappear. Send me home, now."

"I cannot." Le Veille's presence grew more translucent. "Siméon is not the one. Continue with your mission, Mirabelle." His body dissipated into nothingness.

The air turned warmer. The wind ceased. The fog dissipated.

"No!" Mira howled like a wild animal. "How dare you leave without telling me what I am to do? Am I here to save Jacques?"

"Mirabelle?" Jacques stepped toward her from the shadows. "To whom are you calling? What do you mean you're here to save me?"

At the sight of him, Mira lost her grip on the elephant's pole. Her body collapsed from the wooden carousel animal. "Mirabelle!" Jacques caught her before she toppled into the dirt. "Lean on me. You are chilled to the bone."

He removed his jacket and draped it around her shivering body. "Why did you leave the hospital to come here? You need a nurse's care."

Mirabelle did not fight Jacques pulling her close. "H-H- How did you know to find me here?" Her words came through chattering teeth.

"I fell asleep on a bench in the hospital's lobby, and strange dreams seized me. You were lost and in danger. I jolted awake and found this in my hand."

Her moonstone ring glinted in the moonlight. Heat rose behind Mira's eyelids.

I gave it to you, to remember me. Yet, here I remain. What will happen now?

She took the ring and placed it on her finger. Its touch turned her thoughts to her father, and a tiny flame of resilience flickered within her.

I am my father's daughter. I am not defeated, yet.

Jacques guided her to the bench near the Carousel where they'd sat before.

We sat here only this morning? Have I been back in time only two days? It seems forever. Mom, are you and Sylvie searching for me? Are you still alive?

Jacques' brows tightened with concern. "The guard outside the hospital told me you asked to come here. Why, Mirabelle? What memories does this Carousel and its elephant ride bring to you?"

Mira couldn't quell her trembling.

If I explain, what then? I cannot trust how you will react if I tell you my identity.

"I shall take you back to the hospital." Jacques enfolded her into his arms.

Again, you carry me, and again, in your arms, I feel safe.

They reached his Peugeot. With delicate care, he placed her in the passenger seat.

Before he released her from his arms, Mira drew him close. "No hospital. Take me to your place."

He kissed her forehead. "If you wish."

The way he growled the words signaled his raw desire. Mira's body responded with the pull of wanting him, too. She pushed from him. "I need rest. We both do." His eyes projected hope for more.

She knew she must dash his expectation for their Paris tryst.

I will bring you heartbreak, for my presence here is ephemeral. Our love cannot transcend over a century of time placed between us once I return through the Carousel portal. You are my mission. You cannot be my lover.

You belong to Susette, a woman of your time. A woman who believes in you even though you don't believe in yourself.

Jacques cranked the Peugeot and settled into the car. "I shall drive with care."

"*Merci.*" She braced her feet against the floorboard, not trusting him to put aside his race car driving ways.

The streetlights along with the car's headlights brightened the road. The stars in the sky burned brightly. The moon hung low and romantic, unaware of the night's catastrophe and of Mira's determined resistance against making love with Jacques.

Jacques pulled in front of his building, vaulted from the driver's side, and rushed around the automobile to Mira's side.

Mira placed her hand in his offered one, and again, his touch triggered a pulsing current between them. Her resolve to resist his bed faltered.

If only I had ignored the message in the coin purse, I would not be a time-swept Carousel Traveler, held captive in 1900 Paris, ordered to help a man who could be an assassin, a man who ignites my passion, a man guiding me into his residence for the night.

SEVENTEEN

"I need a moment, please." Mira withdrew her hand from Jacques'. "I feel weak."

She withheld her true reason for refusing his offer to help her from his Peugeot. She knew he wanted to escort her into his home and bed her. She knew she must resist, although her body yearned for the closeness of his.

A shiver overtook her, and she clasped her ungloved hands tightly. She winced at the painfulness of her blistered palms and the pressure of her moonstone ring against her finger. Her downcast eyes assessed the now-tattered Jeanne Paquin gown in which she had arrived at the Paris 1900 Exhibition, topped by the now-lost Edwardian cloak, a thirtieth birthday gift from her mother.

Her conscience spasmed over her ruse of amnesia that resulted in both Bernadette and Jacques caring for her. How much longer could she keep secret the truth about being a time traveler? Dare she tell how Le Veille had turned the Luxembourg Carousel into a time travel machine that whirled her from the twenty-first century into 1900?

The events of my time travel, especially this night, have set my nerves more ajar than I want to admit to anyone, including myself. Le Veille speaks only a confusing paradox. "Vanish into the past which holds your future. Return only if you right the wrong destiny that has befallen him."

He claims he cannot say more. But why? Why did he choose me? How will my actions in 1900 Paris hold my own future?

"Mirabelle." Jacques once more offered his hand. "You are exhausted and chilled. You need warmth and rest. We both do."

Wearily, she accepted Jacques' hand and stepped from the Peugeot. She fought to ignore the spark of their touch.

You must be my mission, for why else have our lives intersected? I must have been sent to save you from the destructive path on which your life now travels, but not to fall in love with you. I cannot allow us to act upon our desire. Mira's exhausted and sore body cried out with each step.

By the time she opened the door to his bedroom, she wanted to forget everything and fall asleep.

Jacques left her at his bedroom door. "I will get you water to bathe."

Mira nodded without speaking and entered the room. She looked forward to discarding the tattered and filthy Paquin outfit. This morning, Bernadette had helped her with the complications of dressing.

When Jacques arrived with pitchers of water, she landed a wary glance upon him, contemplating whether to ask his assistance in undressing. He offered before she needed to ask.

"Allow me." Jacques encircled her waist with his large hands to turn her back to him.

When he unbuttoned her dirt-smudged bodice exposing her bared back, goosebumps raced across Mira.

He untied her sash, and let it slide onto the floor. He unhooked her tattered skirt, and it fell around her ankles. His hands jerked at the corset knot to loosen it before encircling his hands upon her waist to turn her toward him once again, his breath quickening. He unfastened the corset's front hooks, and it dropped from her.

She recognized the hungry look in his eye. Although clothed in remaining layers of chemise, stockings, lacy drawers, and silk petticoats, Mira felt naked. She crossed her arms over her body and whispered, "Please, leave me now."

Jacques took a hesitant step from her. His eyes registered disappointment. "Is that your wish?"

"That is my wish." Mira projected her voice more strongly, to convince him. *I am a visitor to your time. You are my mission.*

Jacques bowed in a haughty manner. "I do not go against a lady's wish. *Bonne nuit.*"

Mira washed the best she could, wrapped washcloths around her blistered palms, and changed into her nightgown. She curled her lonely body under the covers, suppressing the urge to call for Jacques' return.

What would a night with him be like? Sensual and amazing, she imagined. But, would he see only Susette when he touched her, kissed her, satiated her? Would she be a stand-in for the woman he truly loved?

After tossing and turning, Mira fell into a testy sleep peppered with nightmares about the housefire claiming her father's life when she was a girl of ten and the collapse of the pedestrian bridge to the 1900 Exhibition's *Globe Céleste.* The red woolen comforter provided little warmth against a cold wind that swirled through the room.

When the sun slanted in through the window, Mira rolled onto her stomach and hid her face under the pillow in denial of the new day. Her sore body wished to remain in bed.

A sharp knock on her day startled her into flipping over. Her gaze fell upon the butterfly partition on which hung the Paquin outfit in pristine condition. Her Edwardian cloak from her mother lay folded over the chair, against which a parasol was propped. On the seat of the chair lay her gloves and hat.

The cold wind I felt . . . It must have been Le Veille, magically restoring my clothing and accessories and returning my cape.

Another sharp knock was followed by her name being called.

"Mirabelle. May I enter?"

The sound of Jacques' voice spiked her heart rate. The door creaked opened, and he strode into the room.

Mira noticed his clean-shaven face, except for his adorable mustache, and his immaculate dress. Although he was impeccably handsome, Mira missed his disheveled look from the night before.

She shifted her body to sit against the wrought-iron headboard and drew the bedsheet high to under her chin, tucking it under her arms to secure it. Her flimsy nightgown kept nothing about her naked body underneath it a secret, even if part of her wished to share that secret with this dangerously sexy man.

"Good morning." Her gaze lingered on the steaming café au lait and baguette on the tray he carried.

"*Bonjour*. I hope you are rested. I assumed you would be hungry."

"*Merci*."

Surprise registered on Jacques' face at the sight of her restored clothing.

Mira's brain scrambled to produce an explanation. "A knock came after you left my bedroom last night. Did you not hear? A messenger arrived, sent by an anonymous philanthropist who wished to reward my effort by repairing my destroyed clothes. The messenger returned them early this morning."

She tried to decipher the blank expression on Jacques' face. Did he believe this outlandish lie of hers?

With a shrug, he placed the tray over her lap. "This anonymous person employed someone who did remarkable work, almost unbelievably so."

Yes, unbelievably so.

Mira took a sip of coffee. She knew she was half-way to falling in love with this man, but she could not let herself. If Le Veille sent her to correct his fate, then Jacques' destiny must be important.

A romantic entanglement with him could risk everything: him fulfilling his life's purpose and her being stuck in 1900 Paris, never to return home.

Jacques sat by her on the bed. "Where are your thoughts wandering?"

How I wish I could tell you.

She took a bite of the baguette before speaking. "I am thinking of what we shall do today, once we bring Bernadette home from the hospital."

Jacques plucked a piece of baguette from her tray. "We must resume the search for your identity." He placed the piece of bread at her lips.

The reverse. I am in search of your identity, Jacques.

She opened her mouth to accept the bite of baguette, and her lips caressed his fingers. The intimacy of the gesture shook her resolve.

When he lowered his face toward her, she willingly returned his kiss before pushing him away. "We mustn't."

"Why?" He breathed his question into her ear.

Why not say it out loud?

"Susette is why."

Jacques dropped his gaze from hers and stood. "Susette was my nurse when I was injured. Nothing more."

"Bernadette says differently. The way the two of you look at each other says differently."

"You imagine what is not there." Jacques' eyes went expressionless.

"Your denial tells me otherwise." Mira placed the tray to the side and swung her body to sit, grasping the bed covers to her body. Her hair hung loosely around her shoulders. The makeshift bandages hung unraveled from her hands.

"How are your palms?" Jacques knelt before her. "Let me see."

At his touch, Mira's pulse accelerated from the sexual tension between them. Clearly, they lusted for each other. Her body could not deny it, but she mustn't let that physical desire overtake her. He belonged to Susette. She knew that, as did he, deep-down.

"They need attention." Jacques stood once more. "When we arrive at the hospital, I shall wait with the automobile. You see Susette for her to re-bandage you and collect Bernadette."

"You do not fool me." Mira lifted an eyebrow. "You plan to wait outside the hospital to avoid seeing Susette."

Jacques' cheeks reddened. "We both have moved on."

Mira felt his lie.

You pretend to have hardened your heart against Susette. Why? You project the swagger of a womanizer and the cynicism of an outsider. Yet I see through your bravado in the way you adore Bernadette and yearn for Susette.

"Then if you have moved on, why avoid seeing Susette again?" Mira did not push for his answer but walked behind the butterfly-decorated room partition. "If you don't mind, I will need your help to button my outfit. I hope you are as talented in dressing a woman as in undressing one."

"I am a man of many talents." His voice held amusement.

"As I am learning." Mira turned her attention to dressing. She noticed her moonstone ring on the wash table and slipped it on, remembering Jacques finding it and taunting her with it yesterday.

Her ownership of a René Lalique ring raised his suspicions. He'd insinuated she must be a courtesan who accepted jewelry in return for sex. She could not explain how her dad arranged for her mom to give it to her on her eighteenth birthday.

You sensed you wouldn't live to see me grow up, Dad. For so long I resented your heroism, how your actions to save that family from the fire took you from Mom and me. I understand now, after my actions last night at the bridge collapse. If I'd died saving Bernadette and Simeon, I would've disappeared from Mom's life without her knowing how or why. Yet, I put myself at risk, as you did.

Once garbed in her chemise, stockings, lacy drawers, boots, and corset, Mira pulled on her bodice and skirt. Holding the sash, she stepped from the partition and turned her back against Jacques. "Button me?"

Jacques chortled. "I will not say with pleasure, for my pleasure would be for you to remain unfettered from clothing."

"Be a gentleman." Mira's tone held reprimand.

"But, of course." Jacques encroached nearer than needed to fasten the garment.

His warm breath on her neck set her nerves tingling.

He encircled her waist with the sash and tied it. He twirled her around to face him and smiled his approval. "I prefer your hair down."

Mira glimpsed herself in the mirror. "I would frighten others with this mess. Can you try taming it?" She handed him Bernadette's brush, noticing the DB initials on it.

He took the brush and waved it in an *en-garde* motion. "Amusing." Mira blushed, remembering how she hefted the brush as a weapon against him before using a Jujitsu move her ex-boyfriend had taught her.

Had that been yesterday morning? It seemed a million days ago.

Jacques held the brush over her head. "Is it possible to tame a lioness such as you?"

"I believe not, but her mane, perhaps?"

"Let me attempt. It is quite a tawny one." Jacques swiped the brush through her loose, curly, auburn hair.

She watched him from the mirror they faced. His guarded expression vanished. He appeared more approachable. Vulnerable, even.

But she detected a shadow of darkness remaining. A darkness about which she needed enlightenment if she were to complete her mission.

Marius Jourdain knew a different Jacques than either Bernadette or Susette. She needed to find out more about how the paths of these two men crossed. Was Marius responsible for derailing Jacques' life?

"Bernadette tells me you are to race for M. Peugeot at the Olympics, the day after tomorrow."

"Yes." His face came alive with excitement. "I can arrange for you to attend."

"*Merci.*" Mira returned his smile.

If I am not gone by then.

A startling rush of regret attacked her.

If only time travel worked as I wished. I would go back and forth, one foot in present and one foot in past, until . . . until what? I cannot have a complete life straddled between two times.

Jacques handed her the hairbrush. "I will leave you to create the pompadour women wear. Meet me in front of the building by the pharmacy. I shall have the Peugeot ready for you."

The monogram on the hairbrush caught her attention once more, and impulse took over. "Who is DB? Bernadette's mother? The one Marius Jourdain referred to as Queen of Bohemia?"

"Do not speak of Marius Jourdain." Anger laced Jacques' voice. He strode from the room, shutting the door firmly behind him.

Mira traced the DB on the brush with her finger.

If you will not speak of Marius Jourdain, then I'll have to speak to him myself.

EIGHTEEN

Jacques drove them in silence to the hospital.

Mira left him parked in front, convinced he remained in the automobile to avoid Susette. She didn't urge him to reconsider. His absence would allow her an opportunity to question Susette about him.

She hurried to Bernadette, hoping to find the girl recovered from her ordeal.

"*Bonjour*, Mirabelle." Bernadette stretched out and groaned before sitting. "Oh, goodness. Are you as sore as I?" "Yes." Mira perched upon Bernadette's bed. "Jacques and I are here to bring you home. He's waiting in the automobile at the front entrance. Unless you think you need remain for another day?"

"No. Siméon and I have plans for this afternoon. You should join us." Bernadette threw her bedcovers off. "I must go check on him."

Before Mira could question Bernadette about her plans, the drapery partitions opened, and Susette joined them. Behind her stood a nun by a wheeled cart with plates of food atop it. Folded clothing lay on the cart's bottom shelf.

"Good morning, Bébé." Susette took Bernadette's wrist to check her pulse. "Excellent. Did you sleep well?"

"Oh, yes, Susette." Bernadette's aura radiated energy.

Mira noticed how tired Susette appeared. "How are you, Susette? Did you get rest?"

"I am fine." Susette continued scribbling on the charts. "I work the night shift during the week and rest during the day, after I complete early morning rounds."

She snapped her head up, her demeanor professional. "Siméon is quite better this morning. We sent a message to his *grand-père*, but he is in London. May Siméon stay with Jacques and you tonight, Bébé, to be under someone's watch for at least another day?"

Mira bit back her smile. Nothing would please Bernadette or aggravate Jacques more than Siméon staying with them.

"Of course." Bernadette beamed at the proposition. "Mirabelle says Jacques awaits us in the Peugeot out front." "Is that so?" Susette glanced at Mira with raised eyebrows. She added one more note to the chart before placing a hand on Bébé's shoulder. "I wish our reunion had been under less intense circumstances." Her voice thickened with emotion.

"Yes, I agree." Bernadette's face turned into a pout. "Jacques loves you. He's too stubborn for his own good to admit it."

Mira's breath caught in surprise over Bernadette's pointed comment.

The nurse's face went scarlet. She cleared her throat nervously. "The hospital laundry has mended and cleaned your clothing. I will see you again before you leave."

Susette looked at Mira with a quizzical expression. "I see your outfit is clean and mended. I am happy you found your cape. You are looking quite recovered."

"I am better, thank you." "How are your palms?" "Healing, thank you."

Susette motioned to the nun, who reached to the lower level of the cart, retrieved Bernadette's outfit, and placed it on the girl's bed.

"*Merci*, Sister Abilene." Susette nodded at the nun. "Please accompany our patient to the dressing area to change once she finishes her breakfast and then to the courtyard, to meet Siméon."

After Susette excused herself, Sister Abilene served both Mira and Bernadette *petit déjeuner* of fresh orange juice, buttered croissant with jam, and steaming café au lait. Mira found herself eating as if she had not already.

After they finished the breakfast, Mira accompanied the nun and Bernadette to the dressing area. Afterward, she followed Bernadette to the courtyard where Siméon awaited her.

Susette sat by him with her stethoscope to her ears, its bell pressed against his chest.

Bernadette sat on his other side and kissed his cheek. "How is he, Susette?"

The nurse wrapped the stethoscope around her neck. "His heartbeat and pulse are strong. He is making a remarkable recovery."

"I feel fine." Siméon placed an arm around Bernadette's shoulder. He moaned. "Except when I move." He gave a slight laugh and moaned again, more noticeably. "Or laugh."

"My poor darling." Bernadette kissed his cheek.

"Do not rile him, Bernadette." Mira sent a concerned look the boy's way. "He must take it easy."

"Mirabelle is correct, Siméon. You must give yourself time to recuperate. Do nothing challenging physically for a week or so." She stood and leaned to exchange goodbye air kisses with Bernadette. "I've missed you."

"We should meet for *le goûter* one day before your night shift." Bernadette snuggled against Siméon, whose arm remained around her. "Siméon will come also."

"Yes. Contact me with a date." Susette smiled, but her eyes reflected sadness, as if she suspected the invitation would never materialize. "You are both discharged from hospital care. Let Jacques know you are both to rest and recuperate for at least a few days."

She beckoned to Mirabelle. "Walk with me?"

"Of course." Mira didn't hesitate to agree, hoping to query Susette about Jacques.

Once out of earshot of the young couple, Susette spoke in a confidential tone. "I assume you and Jacques are . . . close."

Susette's inference brought an indignant flame to Mira's cheeks. "We are recent acquaintances."

"I see." Susette did not sound convinced. "I ask because I worry about him. Has he mentioned a man by the name of Marius?"

Mira's heartbeat quickened. "Is Marius a friend of his?" "I believe Marius Jourdain to be anyone other than a friend." Susette's voice took on a sharpness. "I believe he is a threat to Jacques."

"How do you mean?" Mira already assumed as much, but she needed to learn more.

"My explanation is long. Can you spare the time to hear it?"

"*Oui.*" Mira contained her relief over the nurse's willingness to confide.

Susette hesitated, as if deciding where to begin. When she spoke once more, she kept her voice low. "During Jacques' extended hospitalization here, the two of us grew close."

"Yes." Mira shrugged. "That is no secret."

"But there are secrets." Susette's eyebrows furrowed. "Jacques' nights proved restless. He'd thrash with nightmares, screaming this man's name. I would ask if he needed me to arrange a visit from him, but Jacques would claim he knew no one by such a name."

"Obviously Jacques was being untruthful. Did you try to find out about this man?"

"Yes. At the time I treated Jacques, I also treated a prisoner. I bartered with him. In exchange for me allowing his wife more visitation time, he would make inquiries about Jourdain. The prisoner found out Marius Jourdain was part of the anarchist movement. More an illegalist, really."

"Illegalist?"

"Yes. They are out-and-out thieves, not true political revolutionaries. They will kill anyone to accomplish their goals."

Mira shuddered. Marius Jourdain did seem capable of murder.

"There's more to what the prisoner told me. He said Jourdain spoke to the surgeon who treated Jacques." "Did you tell Jacques any of this?"

"Whenever I brought up Marius, Jacques would not allow me to continue. He insisted he did not know him." Susette frowned, as if angry with herself. "When Jacques left the hospital, he began courting me. I believed that he planned to ask for my hand in marriage."

Her voice trembled. "But then our new President, Émile Loubet, forced Jacques to resign over rumors he conspired with the anarchists who ambushed

President Faure. The surgeon who treated Jacques insinuated that Jacques' wound had been self-inflicted."

"Did you think that possible?"

"I know that to be impossible. The surgeon's statement gave support to the accusations Jacques let the attacker go and stabbed himself to appear as if he were a hero. Jacques was not arrested or tried for the crime because it could not be proven."

Mira's thoughts went into a spin.

I sense a darker side to Jacques. Dark enough, though, for him to have plotted a heinous assassination attempt? For what reason? Power? Revenge? I cannot believe him capable of such evil motives. Neither do Susette or Bernadette.

"Susette, did you tell Jacques about your suspicions of Jourdain and the surgeon conspiring against him?"

"I tried. Once accused, Jacques stopped courting me. I wrote him letter after letter, telling him I did not believe the accusations and begging for us to meet. In one, I wrote about my suspicions about Marius Jourdain. Jacques never answered any of my letters. Finally, my pride told me to stop contacting him. I convinced myself I must accept we were through. I have not seen him since his dismissal from the police force, until last night."

Mira swallowed hard before she spoke. "How difficult for you to come face-to-face with the man you love under such dire circumstances."

"Our love is no more." The color drained from Susette's complexion, leaving her a sickly pale. "The accusations changed Jacques. I fell in love with a police detective, a man of high morals and ethics. One who fought against criminals. I do not know this Jacques, the one reputed to be a dangerous man. A bodyguard, unafraid of using violence. A ladies' man, using the term *ladies* loosely. A reckless man, shown by his race car driving."

Mira shook her head. "You do not believe Jacques is a rogue. Even though he does not fight against the charges that ruined his career, I can see your faith in him remains strong. I can also see you two remain in love."

"I am not sure. The Jacques from last night was the one with whom I fell in love." The expression in Susette's eyes softened. "You saw how the police officers reacted to his leadership. None of them believe the rumors about him. Most who have known Jacques, including M. Peugeot and even Prefect Lépine himself, believe him to be a scapegoat for those in command whose attempts to find the attacker failed. They needed someone upon whom to focus blame."

Susette's tears welled. "I sensed the connection between the two of you. I hope you can influence him to be the man he is meant to be. I worry his connection with Marius Jourdain places both Jacques and Bernadette in harm's way."

Apprehension flushed through Mira. When she and Bernadette met on the Exhibition's moving walkway, the girl had shared her fear about Marius. She was not wrong. He had been stalking her. He'd bragged about it to Jacques and about knowing Bernadette's mother.

The initials DB flashed into Mira's mind.

It made sense Bernadette would own the monogrammed brush of her mother. The Queen of Bohemia, as Marius called her.

She needed to uncover DB's identity to learn whatever hold Marius Jourdain held over Jacques connected with Bernadette's mother. Jourdain must hold the secret she needed to correct Jacques' destiny.

Is he blackmailing you, Jacques, with information so awful you allowed the criminal to escape from the assassination attempt?

Mira's walk with Susette ended in the hospital lobby.

The hubbub of the hospital provoked Susette's professional demeanor. "Take care of him, Mirabelle. If he will allow you."

She hurried through the hospital corridor, amidst the black-veiled nuns. Their capes reminded Mira of Le Veille and his infuriatingly obtuse words.

Vanish into the past which holds your future. Return only if you right the wrong destiny that has befallen him.

A shiver raced through her.

Proving Jacques to be innocent of the assassination accusation will restore his career and reconcile him with Susette. And allow my return where I belong.

A huge red-winged butterfly floated from the courtyard into the lobby and landed on top of Mira's gloved hand. A red butterfly symbolized intense passion as well as danger, so someone had told her.

She stared into the eyespots on its wingtips, each circular spot layered black, yellow, and blue with a red blotch at the center. It seemed to stare back, like someone spying upon her.

Her father's words came once more to her. "If you alter anything back in time, you are potentially altering the future in unforeseeable ways."

Correcting Jacques' fate would affect not only his life but also Bernadette's. Susette's. Others she did not know of at this point. Her own? Le Veille said the past held her future. Dread crept through Mira.

What if I succeed in what Le Veille has sent me to accomplish? What butterflies will I be setting into motion upon my return through the Carousel portal?

The approach of Bernadette and Siméon startled the butterfly, and it took flight. Mira drew a quick breath at the sight of its underside: black. According to legend, black butterflies were the souls of deceased people who were unable to move on to the afterlife. Had her anger at her father kept him from moving into his afterlife?

You are free to go now, Dad. So sorry it took this long for me to understand and accept.

NINETEEN

Deep in thought, Mira followed Bernadette and Siméon to where Jacques sat parked in the Peugeot.

Flashing a crooked grin, Jacques offered Mira his arm to boost her into the passenger seat. Again, his touch felt electric to her. She could only hope when she returned to her real life, she'd meet a man whose touch would feel like this.

Bernadette and Siméon sat nestled against each other in the back bench, their hands interlocked.

Mira anticipated Jacques' disapproval about Siméon staying with them, and he could not hide it when Bernadette explained. Yet, he reluctantly agreed.

After what the two went through last night, Mira assumed Jacques did not expect them to attend their classes today. Bernadette did not plan to attend anyway, based on the adventure she invited her to join. Mira must convince them to rest, instead, while she and Jacques visited House of Paquin and René Lalique.

Those visits would result in more questions from Jacques about my past. I'm veering into an Oscar-worthy performance with my amnesia storyline.

What she'd learned from Susette was only the tip of the Jacques iceberg. She needed to learn everything about his past if she were to restore his reputation—and his romance with the nurse.

If I cannot convince you to tell me about Marius Jourdain and how he figures in your downfall, I will confront Jourdain myself. And Winifred Flanagan can lead me to him.

Upon arrival at the residence, Jacques assisted Siméon to the attic bedroom. Mira settled Bernadette on her small cot in her tiny bedroom.

"Jacques and I must hurry for our appointment with Madame Paquin." She covered the girl with a blanket. "He has expressly forbidden either you or Siméon to leave here. You will be under the watchful eye of Mme Verany."

Bernadette twisted the blanket in her fists. "Jaco's spies." "Mme Verany is not a spy. She is most kind to take time away from the pharmacy and help Jacques keep an eye on you." Mira stood before Bernadette's bureau mirror and turned side-to-side to admire her tiny waist, as sculpted by the corset.

I am uncomfortable, but my figure looks fabulous.

She swept her Edwardian cape over her, thankful for its return, and squinted her eyes at Bernadette. "Siméon will rest in the attic room, where he is to remain with no visitors. We shall all go somewhere to eat once Jacques and I return." Bernadette kicked off the blanket and crossed her arms, a defiant pout on her face. "You do not understand. Siméon and I have someplace to be at one o'clock this afternoon." "Must I repeat myself?" Mira faced the bureau mirror once more to pin her hat. "You and Siméon are to remain here and rest."

"Must I repeat myself?" Bernadette glowered at her. "Siméon and I—"

Mira raised her hand. "Whatever you and Siméon are to do, it must wait. Besides, if not for the bridge collapse, you both would be in class today. Unless you planned to skip again, as you did the day we met on the Exhibition's moving sidewalk? I am sure you do not want me to discuss this with Jacques?"

Bernadette threw herself back in the bed and covered her face with the blanket. Her accusation came muffled from under it. "You and Jaco are so unfair."

Mira wavered about leaving Bernadette in such an upset state of mind. She thought once again about the initials DB on the girl's hairbrush. After the trauma of last night, Mira knew the comfort of a mother's loving arms would be what Bernadette would have sought. This poor girl had only her guardian. *And me. For as long as I am here.*

"Bernadette, I will return by noon. If you and Siméon are rested, I shall speak with Jacques about allowing you to go out. Chaperoned by me."

"Chaperoned?" Bernadette popped up, letting the blanket fall from her. "By you, Mirabelle?"

"Let's see what happens when I return. Now, I must go." She tugged her gloves on and cast a stern look at the girl. "If I find out from Mme Verany you have misbehaved, such as sneaking to see Siméon, you will be grounded."

A puzzled look crossed Bernadette's face. "Grounded?" *Oh, dear. I must watch my twenty-first century wording.* "I mean to say Jacques will not allow you freedom again, for quite some time."

"Oh." She beamed a smile. "*Je suis sage comme une image.*"

Mira burst out laughing. "Yes, be as good as gold." She picked up her parasol and blew a kiss. "*À bientôt.*"

Upon exiting the apartment, she found Mme Verany entering. "*Merci* for your assistance. Keep a strict eye on them both."

"*Oui*, Mlle Montgomery." The woman's sigh indicated her dread over babysitting.

You must charge Jacques a fortune.

When Mira approached Jacques at the Peugeot, she placed her hand into his outstretched one, as customary with them. His touch electrified her, as expected.

Jacques climbed into the driver's seat and shot an eyebrow-cocked grin Mira's way.

He wanted her.

She couldn't lie. She enjoyed being lusted after by this sexy man, even if his heart belonged to Susette.

If circumstances were different—if I could somehow remain in 1900 Paris yet still belong to my own time (crazy, right?)—if I were able to throw caution to the wind and not care about who I hurt— would I tumble into his bed and let him ravish me?

Mira let her body sway with the swerving Peugeot as Jacques accelerated it through the narrow street. She held onto her hat and let herself pretend the two of them were speeding to a rendezvous of physical pleasure.

I can pretend. Maybe my entire experience here is only a fantasy, anyway. I'll awaken in Sylvie's guest bed and all this will be a dream.

When Jacques turned from Place Vendôme onto the busy Rue de la Paix, her attention refocused from daydreaming about making love with Jacques to being in awe of the fashion houses before her, those of Charles Frederick Worth, Jacques Doucet, and Jeanne Paquin. She admired the symmetrically designed block bearing the Hausmann design.

In my present-day life, five of these adjoining buildings, including House of Paquin, are now the fabulous Park Hyatt Paris-Vendôme. How different it all looks in 1900.

The five-storied adjoining stores, built in cream-colored stone with mansard roofs, boasted the running wrought iron balconies. Large awnings hung over the storefronts, providing shade for the wide sidewalks lined with electric streetlamps that helped establish Paris's nickname City of Lights. The fashionable shopping street was awash in pedestrians, automobiles, and horse-and-carriage traffic.

Mira detected the thrum of anticipation among the throng of shoppers. She knew from her study of the time that bevies of young, wealthy American girls visited Paris twice per year on shopping pilgrimages. Armed with lists of purchases drawn from poring over the latest editions of the Bible of fashion magazines, *Les Modes Parisiennes,* they would meet with their personal *la vendeuse,* a saleswoman who would know their bodies better than their boyfriends, lovers, husbands, or God himself.

Mira hoped to glimpse the mannequin room in House of Paquin. The wealthiest shoppers had bespoke mannequins created with their precise measurements stored at the fashion houses. She smiled, thinking of the shroud of secrecy around those measurements.

Jacques pulled to the curb at the store.

The name PAQUIN was affixed in small letters above the entry and in pronounced larger letters onto the third-floor balcony. Cascades of purple and white flowers entangled into trails of green vines drooped from the symmetrically placed window boxes on the second and fourth floors and poked through the extended wrought iron railing of the third and fifth floor.

Half curtains hung in the display windows, a surprise to Mira, used to the elaborate department store displays of her time. On either side of the double door entry stood columns. Mira noticed the caryatids affixed to the top of each column, draped female figures with their arms uplifted and naked breasts prominently displayed. Obviously, Mme Paquin did not shy away from promoting the allure of womanhood.

"She expects us." Jacques alighted from the automobile and walked to Mira's side to help her exit.

When her hand met his, her desire once again sparked. She gained her footing on the sidewalk and let out a quick breath.

He let her hand go, but his gaze lingered on her.

She did not pull hers away, but let herself pretend once again they were wordlessly plotting their night of passion together.

If only.

Jacques crooked his elbow toward her, and she placed her arm through. He pulled her close and murmured, "Hopefully, we shall learn something to help your memory return."

Mira hated this amnesiac role she crafted. She pushed her cover story from her mind and focused on meeting the famous Mme Paquin. Unlike at the other fashion houses run by men, she served as the couturière, not her husband, Isidore. He managed the business but left the fashion design to his wife. They were the fashion scene's super couple, but he remained in the background while her designs competed against the male-dominated fashion houses of M. Worth and M. Poiret.

All the newspapers and fashion magazines reported about Mme Paquin sending models attired in her designs to the opera, horse races, and any other public event to bring attention to her clothing. If the fashion designer were alive in present day, Mira would follow her on all social media, for Mme Paquin trended in the social media of her own era. When she entered Maison Paquin, Mira's set design vibes went into overdrive, taking in all the detail. The picturesque but subtle exterior of the building did not prepare her for the ornate interior. Ornamental crown dentil molding accented the walls, overlapping onto the ceiling. Columns with elaborate fluted shafts topped with filigree brass set off the hallway toward a curved carpeted stairway with mahogany banisters.

A group of women gathered around the base of the steps in animated conversation, the feathers on their huge hats waving as their heads nodded. The scents of freshly cut fabrics wafted through the air, each unique smell mingling together to create a shopper's desire. The atmosphere felt cordial and elegant to Mira.

Jacques presented a card to the liveried servant, who ushered them into an elaborately partitioned waiting area, divided into equal sections framed by heavily braided wood. Floral striped wallpaper covered three-fourths of each section's wall, with each section's top decorated with a series of oval paintings framed by the same braided wood. Each painting showed lovers in each other's arms in repose in a nature setting.

The partitioned room contained a bench upholstered in ornate dark green silk fabric. A pashmina rug covered the dark wood floor. In front of the bench sat a rosewood marble-top table with scattered newspapers and fashion magazines including *La Nouvelle Mode*, *La Mode Illustrée* and *The Delineator* atop it, along with a tray of two glasses of champagne. On the wall hung a heavily ornate gold arched mirror with electric candle sconces on either side.

With her sensory perception on overdrive, Mira settled next to Jacques on the bench and leaned her parasol against it.

I am not on a movie set. I am truly experiencing this.

Jacques removed his hat and placed it onto the table against which he propped his walking cane and Mira's parasol. He handed Mira a glass of champagne and then lifted the other. "Shall we toast?"

She tipped hers against his and took a tiny sip. After one more sip, her nerves calmed enough to ask, "Toast what?"

"Being at Maison Paquin, of course, surrounded by lovely ladies. May I say, though, none as lovely as you."

Mira took more swallows of the champagne, wondering how many women Jacques complimented with those words. A slight hiccup escaped her, a testimonial to her low tolerance of the bubbly beverage. She lifted her gloved hand to her mouth, and her blush heated her face.

"More?" Jacques filled her glass, not hiding his amusement.
Why not?

She took another swallow. Another hiccup reined in her impetuousness. She set her glass upon the table and swore off having any more. "Do you know Mme Paquin?"

"Slightly, because of M. Peugeot. She has been in attendance at Exhibition meetings where I accompany M. Peugeot. A formidable young woman. Beautiful. Articulate. Charismatic. Determined." His gaze flicked over her. "As are you."

Mira's blush deepened. "You are kind, but I doubt I can compare to her."

"I doubt she would have dug all night for survivors, as did you last night." Jacques returned his glass to the table and picked up *Le Petit Parisien.* "Did you know we are featured on the front page?" He handed her the newspaper.

"What?" Mira looked intently at the front-page picture of Jacques, Susette, Bernadette, and her at Siméon's side. Her features were slightly blurred in the photograph, but unless the champagne played tricks on her, she could clearly identify herself.

When I return to my present time, will I be able to find this edition in archives and see myself in this photograph from 1900?

Mira tossed the newspaper onto the table and reached for her champagne. She quickly sipped the remainder in her glass and held it out to Jacques to refill, ignoring her unsteady hold upon it. "Please, more."

Jacques plucked the glass from her swaying hand and laughed. "I think not."

Before Mira formed a retort, the swish of material announced the arrival of an impeccably turned-out *la vendeuse,* a saleswoman who appeared close in age to her.

"*Bonjour,* M. Thibaut."

He stood and gave a slight bow. "*Bonjour,* Mlle Brodeur."

A light-hearted conversation in French ensued between Jacques and the woman. Their easy banter and unconcealed attraction made Mira wonder what changed him from almost proposing to Susette to seeing every woman as a possible conquest.

I can only imagine how sweet, endearing Susette feels about Jacques' overt womanizing ways. I am sure he's hiding his love for her behind this crafted bon vivant behavior to hide his own broken heart. Does Susette see it that way, also? While listening to the repartee, Mira admired the perfectly coiffed hair of *la vendeuse.* She styled it parted in the middle and gathered low on her crown in a protruding knot fashionable during this era called the Newport. Mira assumed the sheer volume of the bun to be created by a switch, an additional hairpiece created from human hair popular in the era, and that the multi-row of braids sitting on her mid-crown was another added hair piece.

The elaborate hairstyle complimented the gorgeous Paquin design Mlle Brodeur wore. The outfit's center- open long bodice with a trained skirt of pale green silk taffeta sported accents of sequined embroidered appliques in geometric designs, featuring Chinese motifs for which Paquin gained renown. The sleeves hung to the elbow, trimmed with multi-layered silk chiffon ruffles edged in silk ribbon.

A V-shape, wide black velvet ribbon trimmed the bodice's neckline. Black velvet ribbon trim hemmed the silk taffeta underskirt, peeking through from under the lower part of the long open bodice. A thin silk ribbon sash set off the model's tiny waist.

The more Mira admired the dress's detail, the more she fell in love with it.

Jacques diverted the conversation to introduce her, speaking in English. "Allow me to present Mlle Mirabelle Montgomery from America. She has an appointment with Mme Paquin."

When she addressed Mira, Mlle Brodeur adjusted to a professional demeanor. "*Bonjour.* I trust your time spent at Maison Paquin will be extraordinary." She spoke English with a sexy French accent. "Shall we go through? Mme Paquin expects you."

Mira took Jacques' arm. He carried his hat, cane, and her parasol as they followed the accentuated sway of Mlle Brodeur's hips. Her side glance at Jacques confirmed he enjoyed watching the woman's sensual walk.

When they passed the group of women as they ascended the curved staircase, Mira noted their obvious appreciation of Jacques, this man of celebrity and dangerous reputation over whom other women salivated. Their heads congregated together, and their whispers buzzed.

"Isn't that Jacques Thibaut?"

"I heard he consorts with anarchists." "And courtesans."

Jacques placed his hand around Mira's waist. "Ignore their salacious rumors."

Mira moved closer toward him. "Salacious? You must tell me all."

"Must I?" The unusual dark rings circling his bluest of blue irises appeared to darken.

What was it I thought the first time I met you? If eyes were the windows to one's soul, yours are nailed shut.

TWENTY

Jacques guided her up the remaining stairs into a large open foyer. Two hallways extended to the right and left. Each wing opened to two rooms. Opposite the stairs were openings to two additional rooms. Glimpsing into them, Mira noted identical décor in these rooms, with elaborate wallpaper and extensively carved ceiling molding.

In the center sat a circular sofa upholstered in luxurious black velvet. An oversized arched palladium-styled window on the back wall allowed light to stream in, giving the space an airy feel.

Shoes, veils, feather boas, corsets, lingerie, and millinery lay displayed on the open shelf cabinets affixed to the walls adjacent to the back one. An armoire stood in the far corner with its extraordinary heavily carved doors ajar, allowing glimpses of elaborate furs hanging inside it.

In the left room, Mira noticed a beautiful woman with an imposing presence lounging with her back pressed against the circular sofa. Her pale complexion set off her deep-set dark eyes framed by black eyelashes and pronounced thick black eyebrows. Her oval face, with its full lips, straight nose, and high cheekbones, boasted the almost perfect symmetry defining the most beautiful. She wore her jet-black hair in a similar style as Mlle Brodeur, parted in the middle with each side rising in a bouffant of wavy curls.

Mira admired the woman's pastel pink dress, an elaborate velvet and silk concoction embellished with red satin appliques and oversized fabric rose flower garlands at the shoulders. The square neckline allowed enough bared skin for the display of a large ruby solitaire suspended from a golden chain. Matching ruby earrings dangled dramatically and conspicuously since her upswept hair allowed full view of them. An oversized arrangement of fabric flowers, tulle, and tall multi-colored ostrich feathers decorated her hat, cast off onto the sofa by her.

Although the woman reposed in a relaxed manner, Mira sensed she knew the power of her beauty. She appeared capable of striking a fatal blow to anyone who brought her displeasure. Mira feared for the two models floating about in the room.

When the woman shifted in her seat, she caught the presence of them in the hallway. She glanced at Mira before her gaze alighted upon Jacques, interest flickering in her eyes.

"Jacques." She said his name like a tigress growling for her mate.

He propped his cane and Mira's parasol against the staircase banister railing and removed Mira's hand resting on his arm. "I must greet her."

He hurried into the room.

Mlle Brodeur grinned cattily at Mira. "When La Belle Otero beckons, one comes."

Mira recognized at once the name of the famous courtesan and sex symbol of Belle Epoque. The celebrated Spanish actress, singer, and dancer starred at the *Folies Bergère*.

"*Tant pis!*" Mlle Brodeur spit the exclamation before lowering her voice. "So much for the two of us. If La Belle Otero has her eye on Jacques, we both lose."

"Oh, no, Jacques and I . . ." Mira stopped. She decided to let Mlle Brodeur believe what she wanted.

This woman knew Jacques and obviously loved to gossip. She would use her to learn more about him.

Mira leaned toward her. "I assume the two have much in common, a courtesan and a disgraced former policeman. I have heard Jacques can be dangerous."

"I find dangerous to be sexy. Do you not?" Mlle Brodeur placed an arm on Mira to draw her nearer. "So many rumors fly about Jacques Thibaut. He's a violent anarchist. He attempted to assassinate Président Faure. I have even heard he was well-acquainted with the Queen of Bohemia, the model who sparked the riots."

Mira widened her eyes. "Do tell me more. How did this Queen of Bohemia cause riots?"

"It occurred resulting from Bal des Quat'z'Arts seven years ago, during quite the night of debauchery in Montmartre. The absinthe flowed."

Mlle Brodeur's voice dropped to a whisper. "She appeared on stage naked at Moulin Rouge, portraying Cleopatra with four men in loincloths carrying her in a palanquin. They were all arrested for public indecency, but the judge dismissed them with a fine. Yet, the arrests enraged students of the Ecole des Beaux-Arts, who started rioting on the left bank. It is said a police officer killed an innocent bystander."

Mira's mouth went dry.

Was Jacques that policeman?

"You say Jacques knows this Queen?"

"He knew her." Mlle Brodeur's mouth curved upward on one side, as if pleased at the news she was about to share. "I heard her looks faded because of her addictions. She died, about three years ago."

She made a *tch-tch* sound with her tongue. "So young for death. Yet, what does one expect if one lives such a life? Unless, of course, one becomes the wealthy La Belle Otero." Mira remembered the initials of "DB" on Bernadette's hairbrush. "Do you know the Queen of Bohemia's actual name?"

"Désirée Blanchet. She posed for painters of Montmartre." Mlle Brodeur gave a wink. "As Lady Godiva for one artist."

Mira pressed her gloved hand to her mouth and looked away.

DB. Poor Bernadette believes she was an infant at the time of her mother's death. Does she know these stories about her? Both Marius Jourdain and Jacques do. Obviously, Jacques lies to her. To spare her embarrassment? Or, does he have a more calculating reason?

Mira's thoughts raced in too many directions at once.

Slow down, think straight, Mira. Is Jourdain extorting Jacques with this knowledge, threatening to tell Bernadette unless Jacques does—what? Let Jourdain escape for breaking the law?

La Belle Otero dismissed Jacques with a wave. "*A bientôt*, Jacques."

Mlle Brodeur moved away from Mira, ending their side conversation.

Mira noticed Jacques' lips did not touch Otero's offered hand.

The courtesan's mouth curved into a coy smile. "I shall cheer for Peugeot at the motor racing Olympic event. Bring me the medal you shall win for him."

"*Merci* for your confidence in my winning it." Jacques clicked his heels, bowed, and walked from the room into the hallway where Mira and Mlle Brodeur remained, waiting.

La Belle Otero returned her attention to the models, who had melted into the background while she engaged with Jacques.

"I need a mirror. Now. The courtesan snapped at one, who scurried away at the command. "How many times must I say to you? Women have one mission in life: to be beautiful. When one gets old, one breaks mirrors. For me now? Bring the mirror."

Mira's skin crawled over Jacques' deference toward this vulgar and egotistical woman.

How much does Susette know about your actions since the two of you parted ways? She may not forgive you such behavior. I'm finding it difficult myself.

Mira pointedly ignored Jacques' offered arm. Parasol in hand, she spun on her heel and followed Mlle Brodeur into the room adjacent to La Belle Otero.

Mlle Brodeur escorted them to the sofa. "Mme Paquin will be with you soon."

She caught Jacques' gaze and raised an eyebrow. "Of course, if you prefer, M. Thibaut, you may wait in the next room?"

Jacques leaned onto his walking cane, letting the smirk on his face be his reply. After Mlle Brodeur exited, he sat next to Mira.

She shifted to create space between them.

He tapped his cane sharply on the hardwood floor. "Come now, Mirabelle. You cannot believe I have fallen under La Belle Otero's charms?"

"You may fall under any woman's charms of your choice, M. Thibaut. Mlle Brodeur's. Even the Queen of Bohemia."

Jacques' body stiffened, and his expression darkened.

Mira regretted mentioning the Queen in such a flippant manner.

After a moment, Jacques' laughter boomed against the room's quiet. "Carolina Otero's only interest is M. Peugeot. She sees me as a conduit to her successful seduction of him and his fortune."

He murmured in her ear. "I hope it will be you and not La Belle Otero who will cheer for me at the race. I plan to set a speed record."

A vision of Jacques thrown from his automobile onto the track turned Mira's blood cold. "Must you race? Doesn't M. Peugeot have someone other than you?"

"Even if he did, I would not give my place to anyone. I have been training for this event. When I race, I feel most alive, with all cares forgotten." Jacques caressed her cheek with his free hand.

Mira's world shrunk only to his lips near hers. Her heart danced wildly in her chest. Susette's face materialized in her thoughts, and she shifted hers from him.

Remember your mission, Mira. Do not cave into desire. The dramatic entrance of a tall, beautiful woman with notebook and pen in hand drew Mira's attention. Her pulse raced. She recognized the woman at once.

Mme Paquin.

TWENTY-ONE

Jacques stood and bowed toward the elegant woman. Mira admired the woman's gorgeous attire. The high- collared silk bodice fitted to the waist was the color of rose- blush and boasted beautiful textural elements of beige point d'esprit and patterned net lace with light pink silk-wound bead trim. The box-sleeve ruching with silk-wound beaded trim reached below the elbow, accented with a fringe of matching beige point d'esprit.

The A-shape woolen skirt of a lighter rose-blush color flowed from the satin rose-blush sash encircling her waist. Dark beige silk-wound beads placed in asymmetrical rows embellished the flare of the hemline. The outfit was as chic, charismatic, and breath-taking as the woman who designed it.

Mira marveled that at only thirty-one Mme Paquin ran her own house of fashion, with her husband working for her. *I hate knowing you will unexpectedly lose your beloved husband, Isidore, in only seven short years. I wish I could prevent his death, or at least prepare you for it. Knowing the events of what lay ahead for this woman—for Paris—leaves me hollow inside.*

She reminded herself of her mission, to change Jacques' destiny. Or, so she had come to believe.

Should I dare try to change another person's fate?

Butterflies pounded her stomach, warning her once more that what she changed in the past would ripple through the future.

I can't take the chance to change anything except what Le Veille has sent me to change.

Mira stood to greet her. "Thank you, Mme Paquin, for meeting with me. The circumstances are quite strange, as explained in M. Thibaut's request for our visit."

Mme Paquin ignored her greeting. Her gaze was riveted on Mira's clothing. "How can it be possible?" She abruptly rushed from the room.

Mira sank onto the sofa, crestfallen. "Did I offend her in some way?"

In a stalking manner, Mme Paquin returned with a paper in her hand. "Here is the design I drew for the outfit you are wearing, Mlle Montgomery, yet to be sewed. Here you are, wearing it. How?"

Her voice pitched high with accusation. "You stole this illustration and had the dress made by someone. Worth? Poiret? Doucet? I know they were not pleased when I was elected president of the Fashion Section for the Exposition Universelle. But this?"

She rattled the paper at Mira. "Poiret says he is flattering me with his designs closely resembling mine. He calls me an inspiration. Bah. But not even he would stoop so low as to steal a design on paper I have yet to produce."

Through her tightened throat, Mira managed an apology. "I am so sorry, Mme Paquin. I do not know anything about a theft of your design."

How recklessly stupid of Le Veille to put me in a dress not yet made by its designer.

She rose to her feet and held the skirt out with both hands. "I would take this off immediately, but I have no other clothing."

Jacques moved to stand behind the sofa where Mira sat and placed his hands on her shoulders. When he spoke, his tone vibrated with protective anger. "Mme Paquin, I requested the invitation to your House hoping you would have on file the bill of sale for this dress. If so, it could provide Mira insight into her identity. Except for her name, she recalls nothing of her past."

He continued, his speech resonating with conviction. "After spending time with her, I can fully attest to her character. She is not a thief. The circumstances of how she came to wear this dress must be too painful, too vile, for her to remember."

Mira's guilt rose within her over her deception. Jacques' vehement and eloquent support reinforced her determination to prove him innocent of accused wrongdoings. She had to restore his rightful destiny, as well as reconcile him with Susette.

I will not let us act upon our attraction, for I know your heart belongs to her.

After a moment, Mme Paquin's pinched eyebrows relaxed. Although her expression held skepticism, she spoke in a kinder tone. "How terribly frightening for you, to remember nothing about yourself. You must understand, though, how upset I am over my stolen design."

"*Oui*, Mme Paquin." Garnering the designer's sympathy under the false pretense of amnesia riddled Mira with even more guilt. Keeping the secret of being a time traveler clawed at her. "You must believe me, though. I have no knowledge of the theft."

"That remains to be seen, does it not, Mlle Montgomery, once you regain your memory?" Mme Paquin tossed off her comment while she strode with purpose toward the door and tugged three times on a narrow strip of tasseled tapestry which served as a bell pull.

When Mlle Brodeur appeared, Mira hoped Mme Paquin would not command *la vendeuse* to summon the police. She shrank into Jacques' protective hold, fearing an arrest.

Mlle Brodeur curtsied. "Mme Paquin."

The designer continued writing in her notebook. "We shall be putting together a small wardrobe for Mlle Montgomery."

Mira let out a breath of relief. "*Merci*, Mme. How kind." "I have made a list of the selections." Mme Paquin tipped the point of her writing pen toward Jacques. "I shall be seeing Mme Peugeot here, soon?"

So, Jacques inveigled their meeting with Mme Paquin by accepting her demand for Mme Peugeot to visit. The fashion designer knows how to work a situation to her advantage. Good for her.

"I have made arrangements already," Jacques replied. "Mme Peugeot is anxious to choose wardrobe pieces for an upcoming trip to America."

"Excellent." Mme Paquin leveled her gaze upon Mira. "Also, I ask for the return of my design you are wearing and, once your memory returns, an explanation for how you came into its possession."

"*Oui*, Madame." Mira would herself like the explanation from Le Veille.

"Mlle Brodeur will see to your fittings." Mme Paquin re-opened her notebook, pen poised in air. "To what address shall we deliver the packages?"

"My address, Mme Paquin," Jacques said. "Yours, M. Thibaut?" Mme Paquin half-smiled.

Mira felt the embarrassing flame of her cheeks. They assumed her to be Jacques' kept woman.

Mlle Brodeur cut her eyes toward Mira and then toward Jacques. "We have M. Thibaut's address on file. He has purchased from us before, for other ladies."

Mira ignored the innuendo, but she did wonder about their identities.

"*Merci*, Mlle Brodeur." Mme Paquin's cutting tone showed displeasure at the saleslady's impertinence. "I have decided. We shall include what you are wearing as part of Mlle Montgomery's wardrobe."

"But, but," Mlle Brodeur sputtered. "You planned for me to wear this outfit to the Vélodrome de Vincennes when M. Thibaut will be racing for M. Peugeot."

Mme Paquin shrugged. "Mlle Montgomery shall wear it instead." She motioned toward the displays of hats, jewelry, and gloves. "Please choose the accessories while I finish writing this order."

"*Oui*, Mme." Mlle Brodeur swept by Mira, muttering, "*Putain*."

Mira's cheeks burned even hotter over being called a whore.

Jacques gathered Mira's parasol, his umbrella, and his hat. "Mirabelle, I shall wait in the lobby while your wardrobe fittings take place. *Au revoir*, Mlle Brodeur."

She sniffed her goodbye.

Ignoring her rebuke, Jacques addressed Mme Paquin. "*Merci*. Your kindness shall be rewarded. *Au revoir*."

Mme nodded to dismiss him. She finished her entries in her notebook and snapped it shut. "*Au revoir*, Mlle Montgomery. I have an appointment with my husband."

Mira's emotions overtook her rational thought. "One moment, Mme Paquin?"

Her stomach churned, warning her against tempting the butterfly effect. *Don't do it, Mira.*

"You wish to discuss something else with me?" Mme Paquin impatiently tapped her pen against her notebook.

I didn't ask to be plopped into 1900 Paris with knowledge of others' futures. Why not share what I know if it will bring more years of happiness to someone? Let the butterfly wings flap.

"May I have a word with you?" Mira looked at Mlle Brodeur before adding, "In private?"

Mme Paquin waved her notebook toward the door, a silent command for the saleswoman to leave.

Mlle Brodeur directed a look of displeasure at Mira before departing.

"Come, shall we sit?" Mme Paquin settled on the round couch and patted next to her.

Joining her, Mira's words tumbled out. "It is about your husband. He must take better care of himself. I fear for his health."

"My husband's health?" Mme Paquin appeared amused. "You have not met my dear Isidore, yet you are concerned about his health?"

Her expression became reflective. "We both work diligently without concern for the clock. We may not always take the best care of ourselves. But we are enthusiastic and energetic. We love what we do, and we enjoy our success. We do not desire to slow our pace."

"I cannot explain why, but I am worried about him. It's . . ." Mira pursed her lips, wanting to confide about her time travel. "It's a feeling I have."

"I appreciate your concern, but you should direct it toward your own health so that you may recover your memory. I will have Mlle Brodeur escort you to alterations." Mme Paquin rose and walked toward the door with a sense of urgency to be on with her day. She paused at the doorway to look back at Mira, studying her outfit once again. "I look forward to you regaining your memory, for both our sakes. *Bonne chance.*" Walking from the room, she called back over her shoulder, "*Au revoir.*" "*Adieu,*" Mira whispered, deflated.

I did not set off a butterfly effect, after all.

The churning in Mira's stomach ceased.

TWENTY-TWO

The wardrobe fitting session exhausted Mira's patience. She held her tongue against the tart insults flying from Mlle Brodeur and stood as a statue for the alteration woman, who relayed relief that only minor alterations to each piece were needed.

The various layers of the complex fashions of 1900 left Mira pining for the simplicity of twenty-first century clothing. Mme Paquin's generosity equipped her with more than her time in 1900 Paris would allow her to wear, she hoped: chemises and corsets, a dressing gown, exquisite cotton and lace nightgowns, two tea gowns, three day dresses, two evening dresses, evening silk cape, and required accessories. With the fitting session ended and delivery promised as early as that afternoon, Mira descended the staircase to meet Jacques in the lobby. She dreaded their visit to René Lalique. Being in the presence of the fabulous Lalique would be one more astounding experience to add to her list of meeting icons Mary Cassatt and Jeanne Paquin. However, just as no bill of sale existed for the Paquin dress, none would exist for her Lalique ring, which dated to 1905.

How will I explain coming into possession of a Paquin design not yet made and a Lalique ring not yet created? If my amnesia ruse unravels, I need another backstory about myself.

At least these outings with Jacques provided her with opportunity to learn more about him. What she'd learned from both Susette and Mlle Brodeur left her with so many questions.

Did Jacques conspire with anarchists to kill President Faure? Could it be Jacques did kill an innocent bystander the night of the Bal des Quat'z'Arts riots? If Marius Jourdain is blackmailing Jacques about the identity of Bernadette's mother, what does he demand from Jacques in return for his silence?

Another question flew into Mira's thoughts, startling her. Stumbling on a step, she grasped the banister to remain righted.

What if Jacques is not Bernadette's guardian, but her father? Are Jacques and Désirée Blanchet the girl's parents? A woman ascending the staircase swept by Mira, breaking into her shocking conjecture. She descended the steps into the lobby, contemplating how to uncover the truth from Jacques.

He was not in the lobby as planned. The livery attendant opened the door for her exit onto the sidewalk. In front of the fashion house was a *fiacre,* its horse standing placid except for its swishing tail. Mira assumed the taxi to be waiting for a Paquin customer.

The driver tipped his hat to her.

Mira waved at Jacques, who was leaning against his cranked-up Peugeot, staring into space with drawn brow and pursed lips.

She glanced at the clock on the shopfront across the street. It read half past eleven, providing her time to keep her promise to Bernadette about checking on her and Siméon in hopes Jacques would allow an afternoon outing. She assumed he would resoundingly reject the idea, but she had vowed to approach him with it.

After checking on Bernadette and Siméon, she needed to deter Jacques from their visit to Lalique's. She would claim a glimmer of memory about being in a boat traveling along the Seine and beg he take her there. Once they were gliding along the river, she would have the opportunity to explore further what she'd learned about him thus far.

With her plan made, Mira called out to Jacques in a lighthearted voice. "M. Thibaut. You abandoned me."

Jacques' stare adjusted to her. "I visited Lalique's while you were being fitted."

"Oh." Mira felt stripped naked under his disdainful stare. "I hoped—"

Jacques waved his hand to silence her. "The shop has no record of selling anything to anyone named Montgomery. More to the point, they have no record of a ring matching the description of yours having been in their inventory."

His voice sank to a low and accusatory tone. "You wear a stolen Paquin design. You wear a ring forged with Lalique's markings. I assume the cape you wear to be stolen as well. But worst, you have preyed upon Bernadette's good will." His expression hardened. "And mine."

"Jacques, you must believe me. I don't know how I came to be in this dress—"

"Stop." He waved his hand defiantly. "You are using me to survey both Paquin's and Lalique's for the purpose of more theft. You must be working with illegalists, maybe Marius Jourdain. He follows Bernadette, and you appear out of nowhere, bumping into her and claiming amnesia. Coincidence? I think not. The two of us run into him near the American Girls' Club. Another coincidence? Again, I think not. You could be planning a heist from those who board there. With the wealthy crowds in Paris for the Exhibition, the opportunities for theft abound."

Jacques slapped his hand on the Peugeot's bonnet. "Your charade is over, Mlle Montgomery, or whatever your true name. You have played Bernadette and me for fools, plying us with your tale of woe."

"Jacques, please listen." Mira stepped toward him.

He vaulted into the Peugeot. "I have engaged a taxi for you. He will take you wherever you direct him. Do not worry. His bill will come to me, as will the one for Paquin's. I will not cancel your wardrobe pieces. Doing so will bring me embarrassment. Message me with your address, and I will have the clothing delivered there. It is worth the expense to get you out of my life."

Mira's heart lodged into her throat.

If I am to save you from your wrong turn in fate, we cannot be estranged. I can't let you believe such lies about me.

She rushed to the automobile and reached in to place her hand over his on the steering lever. "We must talk, Jacques. Please, let me explain."

He shook her hand from his. "Step aside. I will not hesitate to drag you alongside as I leave."

The lurch of the automobile convinced Mira he meant what he threatened. She stepped from it, its gassy fumes accosting her senses.

He accelerated into the busy street and sped away.

Mira's heart exploded into broken chards. She fought against her tight corset for a deep breath to steady herself.

I must see Bernadette and explain. If Jacques tells her his suspicions, the girl will be devastated.

"Mlle?" The *fiacre* driver called to her, speaking French. "Where shall I take you?"

"To the residential building at the intersection of Rue de Bievre and Boulevard Saint-Germain. Hurry, please."

The driver tipped his hat. Mira settled into the taxi, and his swift acceleration lurched her forward. Their journey moved with a good pace through the traffic. The jostling of the ride heightened Mira's nerves over seeing Jacques once again. Should she reveal the truth?

I'm a time traveler. I am here to help right your destiny so I can return to my own time.

Why would either he or Bernadette believe her? She barely believed it herself.

TWENTY-THREE

As they neared Jacques' residence, Mira assumed he would have already arrived. What choice remained at this point to regain his trust other than confessing the truth about being a time traveler? She must gamble he would believe her. Disembarking from the *fiacre*, Mira did not see the Peugeot. Had he sped to the police precinct to report his suspicions of her being a thief? Were the police looking for her, to arrest her?

She pressed a hand to her throat, feeling as if someone was choking the breath from her. The bustling of passing pedestrians forced her to gain her composure. Entering the building, Mme Verany rushed to her.

The woman's expression relayed the message before her words did. *"Bernadette est partie."* She held out a note.

Mira took the note, her anger mounting. How in the world could Mme Verany have lost control of Bernadette in so short a time?

Dearest Mirabelle,

Siméon and I could not wait any longer. Meet us at 57 Rue Saint Roche. We shall wait there for you until half past one o'clock. Please do not tell Jaco.

Much love, Bébé

Mira crunched the note in her fist and rushed to the *fiacre* remaining at the curb. "Please, I am in a hurry. Take me to 57 Rue Saint Roche. *Vite.*"

The driver tipped his hat, a bemused look on his face. "*Oui, Mlle.*"

The taxi once again lurched into motion. Mira unwrinkled the note and stared at the address. For her thesis, she had dedicated long hours of research into Léon Gaumont, pioneer of the film industry, and into Alice Guy. She knew this address as the shop of L. Gaumont and Company, where Alice worked in 1900.

She'd convinced herself Jacques was her mission, but Le Veille had enticed her into this mess through the Alice Guy souvenir coin purse with its cryptic message inside.

Does Bernadette's connection to Alice mean the filmmaker needs my help?

She dismissed the idea. Jacques must be her mission. However, did Alice possess information to help her decipher Jacques' secrets?

Damn you, Le Veille. You know how the puzzle pieces fit together. Why can't you tell me? I'm wasting time, spinning in circles like the Carousel that brought me here.

When the taxi turned onto Avenue de l'Opéra, Mira glimpsed the exquisite Palais Garnier designed by Charles Garnier, the same man who'd designed the Luxembourg Carousel.

My time portal.

Impatience for this adventure to be over bubbled within her.

Soon, Mom. I will be back with you soon, for both our hearts to heal.

The *fiacre* halted at 57 Rue Saint Roche, near the intersection with Avenue de l'Opéra. Departing the taxi, Mira felt as if she had entered a Gaumont film. She recognized this area to be Gaumont filming territory from her mapping of films by Alice Guy.

The energetic voice of Bernadette broke into the surreal moment. The teen stood in front of the building whose signage advertised L. GAUMONT ET CIE.

"You are here, Mirabelle. I told Siméon you would come. Did visiting Paquin bring memories for you?"

"Unfortunately, no." Mira quickly moved away from that topic. "You should have waited for me before leaving the residence, Bernadette. Jacques will be angry."

"Why? You are chaperoning us." Bernadette grabbed her arm and tucked it under hers.

Jacques now has more reason to be angry with me. At least I have an opportunity to plead my case before what Jacques tells her hardens her heart against me.

Bernadette dragged Mira toward the studio.

When Siméon opened the door for them to enter, his mouth pursed in pain.

He was disobeying Susette's orders to take it easy, but Mira knew she could do nothing to force him to rest. Once inside the studio, she detected the pungent odor of the film development chemicals permeating the air. She decided to concentrate on the impossible opportunity to meet Alice Guy.

If I'm stuck in the past and facing all sorts of setbacks and difficulties, then why not enjoy this magical moment?

Mira recognized the names on the framed certificate hung on the wall behind the store counter: Léon Gaumont, burgeoning film pioneer; Gustave Eiffel, engineer of the tower; astronomer Joseph Vallot; and financier Alfred Besitier. Displayed behind the counter hung a poster listed the prices for photography supplies including chemicals, photographic papers, card stock, and silver foil.

Gazing at the shop's displays, Mira wished she could tell everyone of the successful future that would unfold for Gaumont, of how he would build one of the most important film companies in cinema history.

A handsome young man and slightly built young woman emerged from the back room.

Mira immediately recognized her from her photographs: Alice Guy.

The young man clapped on his hat. His words sounded like a warning growl. *"Il ne s'en tirera pas avec ça."*

Mira understood his words: "He won't get away with this."

The man left the shop quickly, without acknowledging anyone else.

Mira noticed neither Siméon nor Bernadette projected any curiosity about him, but she could not deny her own. However, filmmaker Alice Guy stood before her, and Mira adjusted her focus to only her. She took note of Alice's appearance. Dressed in an understated and inexpensive business suit with her hair tucked into the pompadour style of the time, Alice appeared far prettier than in photographs.

At twenty-seven in 1900, the young woman would be another contemporary of hers, like Mme Paquin. Mira wanted to warn Alice about events that would diminish her rightful place in the filmmaking world for so long.

Keep your films preserved for future generations to appreciate your genius. Don't marry Herbert Blaché. He will leave you for one of your actresses, force you into bankruptcy, and put an end to your career. Fight for your name so your incredible accomplishments will not go unnoticed until the twenty-first century finds you again.

Bernadette rushed around the counter and offered air kisses, which Alice amusedly returned, and then proceeded with introductions. "This is Mlle Mirabelle Montgomery, an American friend of mine. You do not mind if she accompanies us to Belleville for the filming today?"

"No." Alice smiled at Mira. "I do not mind."

Mira grasped her hands tightly, fearing she might faint from excitement over observing the filmmaker in action.

If only my time traveling were for such experiences, without the worry over solving a mission to earn my return.

Alice cast a concerned look upon both Bernadette and Siméon. "I read about what happened last night. Are you both well enough to assist me today? We can postpone."

"*Balivernes.*" Siméon and Bernadette spoke simultaneously.

"Bumps and bruises." Siméon shrugged, unsuccessfully hiding the look of pain his movement brought. "We were fortunate to have Mirabelle on the scene of the disaster, for she rescued us."

"Siméon exaggerates." Mira cheeks warmed over his bragging about her. "I only helped."

Alice shook her head. "Such an awful incident. Thank you for your part in bringing these two to safety, Mlle Montgomery."

Mira smiled at the formality. "Please, call me Mirabelle." "I shall be Alice to you. Any friend of these two creative young ones shall be a friend of mine. Accompany us if you wish to the Belleville laboratory. I am preparing to re-film *La Fée aux Choux,* using M. Lumière's cinématographe, a 35mm camera. For my original version a few years ago, I used Demenÿ's Chronophotographe, using unperforated 60 mm film." She placed a hand to her forehead, her eyes widening. "Oh, my. I rattle on. I am sure you do not care about the equipment."

Mira grasped her hands so tightly she gasped aloud at her moonstone ring pinching her ring finger.

The three looked upon her with concern.

She gathered her wits. "I cannot hide my fascination, Alice. I am curious about filmmaking. It's magical."

"Yes, magical," Siméon echoed. Bernadette vigorously nodded agreement.

Alice beamed at them. "Lovers of innovation and film surround me. How delightful. When hired as M. Gaumont's secretary, I never presumed I possessed the makings of a filmmaker. He thought me to be too young, but I assured him I would get over that. The one certainty in life is we all age, *n'est-ce pas?*"

She glanced at the wall clock. "We must leave immediately. I have much work upon my return. Let me gather what I need."

Alice disappeared into the back office and returned with her hat and coat, along with *le sac à malices*, a leather pouch bulging with items.

They filed out of the shop.

While waiting for Alice to lock the shop's door, Mira soaked in the displays in the store windows. The binocular- looking Photo-Jumelle cameras. Stereoscopic viewers. The first camera for shooting amateur home movies, the Chrono de Poche. Posters advertising free lessons in photography and demonstrations of the X-ray machine. Film history came alive, right before her.

"Faut se grouiller." Alice took the lead, calling for them to hurry. "We shall go as usual, to Place de l'Opera for the omnibus to Place de la République, where we embark on the funicular to Belleville."

Mira whispered to Bernadette, "I have no money to pay for tickets."

Bernadette pointed to the decorative gold lapel pin. "Those who wear the exhibitor badges have free transportation, for guests as well. Jacques has given one to me and Siméon, thanks to M. Peugeot."

At Bernadette's mention of Jacques, Mira's grasp tightened on her parasol she carried unopened. Bernadette would feel so betrayed by her once Jacques told her of his distrust. Mira could think of nothing else during their short walk from Gaumont's to the famous square, Place de l'Opera. Arriving there, Mira caught her breath at the sight of the magnificent square where the Grands

Boulevards crossed. The heart of the tourist trade in Paris, it was called the Hub of the Universe.

Without the twenty-first century crush of traffic dwarfing its opulence, the Palace Garnier sparkled as the square's undeniable jewel, with the statue of the god of art and music, Apollo, crowning its top.

Even with Mira's troubles pressing on her heart, she breathed in the rarified air of past Paris before scurrying after the others. They boarded an omnibus drawn by four horses that would take them to the large public square of Place de la République.

Mira gaped at the sights of the square as it appeared in 1900, flouting the Hausmann imprint. The twenty-first century brought the redevelopment of the area into a traffic- free open concept, but the focus remained on the large bronze statue of Marianne. This national icon symbolizing liberty, equality, and fraternity represented opposition to the Monarchy.

You've held your age well through the past one hundred- plus years. You gleam with beauty.

They exited the omnibus at the Square. Bernadette and Siméon clambered onto the small car of the funicular and sat together on the bench, which faced sideways. Mira boarded after Alice and followed her to where two open spaces remained farther to the back. Once seated, Alice reached for a notebook and pen in her bag and began writing.

"There." Alice shut the notebook with a relieved sigh. "I needed to make myself a reminder of tasks to complete upon my return to the store. M. Gaumont allows me the time for making the films, if I manage with my other duties."

"I hope he comprehends what a treasure you are." Mira knew that as the years went on, Gaumont took credit for so much of what Alice accomplished, including claiming her films as his own. If only she could warn this lovely, creative woman of how she would be denied her place in film history for so long.

Stay quiet, though. You cannot meddle with this woman's life by sharing your knowledge of her future. You could ruin something you cannot foresee.

Alice returned the notebook and pen to her bag, her expression thoughtful. "I believe my worth will be more recognized if I win the *Diplôme de Collaboratrice* for my film collection shown at the Exposition Universelle. I may not be awarded the honor, though. My competitors include Georges

Méliès, Ferdinand Zecca, and Edwin S. Porter. What chance will I have, a woman against these influential and successful men?"

"Every chance, Alice." Mira knew Alice would win the medal. She felt like a parent keeping secret what Santa would bring.

Alice adjusted her hat with a quick flutter of her hand. "We can only try to shape our own destiny, but destiny will win in the end."

Unless a time traveler can change it.

How she wished her mission were to reshape Alice's destiny. Her thoughts went to the young man in the shop, and her curiosity overtook her. She had walked into Gaumont's at the exact moment he spoke threateningly of someone. She doubted coincidence to be the reason behind anything happening to her, so why had she overheard what he had said?

Each event she experienced provided insight into Jacques. The bridge collapse led her to meet Susette. Susette provided information about Marius Jourdain. The visit to the House of Paquin led her to meet Mlle Brodeur, who provided information about Bernadette's mother, the Queen of Bohemia, providing more puzzle pieces to put together about Jacques' past.

Now, Alice Guy led her to overhearing this young man's threat. Did he connect with her mission? It all must fit together: Jacques, Marius Jourdain, the Queen of Bohemia, Alice, the young man . . . but how?

If only Le Veille would provide direction, instead of leaving me to flounder.

"How do you know Bernadette and Siméon?" Alice asked.

"I met Bernadette's guardian, Jacques, at the American Girls' Club. I am staying there to take art classes while I visit the Exhibition. Jacques provides chauffeuring service, courtesy of M. Peugeot."

Whoa, where did that lie come from? It flowed out without thought.

". . . that's how I met Bernadette, through Siméon. The boy works for M. Gaumont at the request of M. Eiffel," Alice was explaining. "The two men are close friends with Siméon's *grand-père*. Siméon is quite creative and artistically talented. He has caught the film making fever, most unfortunately for him."

"Unfortunately?"

"M. Aubert, who is close-minded about the opportunities in filmmaking, has Siméon's future planned. He believes his *petit-fils* must be an engineer, as himself and Siméon's *père*."

"How do you know this about Siméon?"

Alice's cheek pinkened. "M. Eiffel confides in me."

"I see." Mira wondered why Gustav Eiffel's name would make Alice blush.

The age difference would be quite vast between the widower and Alice. Could they be in love? If only these two married, instead of Alice's disastrous eventual pairing with Herbert Blaché.

Keep the thought to yourself, Mira. You cannot meddle with Alice's life.

"M. Eiffel supports my opinion a woman can stage a film. He even suggests elements of life for me to observe to inspire my ideas for narratives. For example, he has taken me to visit the Pigalle District and talk with the Can-can dancers of Moulin Rouge and the *vauriens,* or illegalists. I have observed first-hand those in the throes of the opium and of absinthe, *la Fée Verte.* The large elephant statue from the last exhibition stands adjacent to the cabaret and serves as an opium den. Quite a sight."

Mira listened intently. Marius Jourdain said he and Jacques met at Moulin Rouge. Jacques clearly detested the man, so their meetings must be business, not social. She must be at their next one, and she knew the one person who could lead her to it.

Her lie about staying at the American Girls' Club could become truth. Jacques' demand for her to leave his residence meant she had no place to stay. Mme Newton would welcome her, and she could keep Winnie under observation.

It did not stretch imagination that Winnie Flanagan would sneak out to meet her lover in Montmartre, a place of Can-can kicks, flowing opium and absinthe—the place where Jacques and Marius meet.

As if Alice read her mind, the filmmaker turned the conversation to her film, *Wonderful Absinthe.*

"It is my comédie in which the man mistakenly thinks he has diluted his drink of absinthe. Have you seen it?"

"Yes, I have." Mira had studied the theme of this film for her thesis.

Alice's animated face relayed her excitement over the film. "I hope the message shines through about the horrible impact of the drink."

"I think your message comes through," Mira replied. The funicular rolled to a stop at the two-spired Église Saint-Jean-Baptiste. Mira breathed in quickly, for the ghost of the great Edith Piaf hovered upon the church's steps.

The scene from *A Star is Born* with Lady Gaga singing the French sparrow's famous **"La Vie en Rose"** replayed in Mira's mind, the haunting love song about a woman allowing a man's love to enter her heart after trying times.

I will not allow you to enter my heart, Jacques Thibaut. You think the worst of me now, anyway. I will accomplish my mission and return to where I belong. I do not belong in your time nor you in mine.

I will leave you to reconcile with your true love Susette. If she'll have you.

TWENTY-FOUR

"We have arrived." Alice disembarked the funicular. Mira followed, with Bernadette and Siméon behind her. The funicular's track dissected the cobblestone street.

Pedestrians and horse-drawn carriages moved about on either side of it. The signage advertised butcher, tobacco, and liquor shops, along with a *théatres populaire,* catering to the area's working-class audiences.

Mira thought about how the Belleville of her own time owed its funky roots to the Belleville of the La Commune uprising and the resulting anarchist and illegalist movement. Did Marius Jourdain call Belleville home? Could this be where Winnie would lead her, instead of Montmartre?

"It's a short walk from here to M. Gaumont's laboratory, where I am filming." Alice quickened her pace. "We will meet my cameraman, Anatole Thiberville, at my little thingy, as I not-so-fondly refer to my place here. Without M. Gaumont equipping it with a bath, I would never have relocated from Quai Malaquais to live here with *Maman.*"

"It must mean M. Gaumont expects you to create more short narrative films?" Mira posed the statement as a question, even though she knew what accomplishments lay in Alice's future.

"Hopefully. He also expects me to be at Rue Saint- Roch as well. He need not worry because I will accomplish all required at the office and film my narratives, also." Approaching the Gaumont laboratory, Alice nodded. "Here we are."

A tall, lanky man leaned against the frame of the inset entryway at 14 Rue des Alouettes. He wore a long white duster and a light-colored derby hat. At his feet sat a large brown wooden box-like camera, a hand cranked 35mm Lumière *Cinematographe.* Mira could not divert her attention from this film history relic. To Alice and this man, it existed as the newest camera technology.

"Mirabelle, allow me to introduce my cameraman, Anatole Thiberville."

"*Bonjour.*" Mira tried to keep the awe from her voice.

She'd studied his films he shot for Alice, and now, here he stood before her in the flesh.

"Anatole, Mirabelle is from America, so let us speak English." Alice waved at Bernadette and Siméon. "Come, you two. We shall begin."

Mira pushed away her worries, comforting herself with the belief her mother would want her to do so. A moment of film history unfolded in front of her, and her mother would advise her, if she could, to fully live in its moment.

Never would Mira have imagined she'd be back in time, standing on a glass-roofed terrace which served as the stage, present at the filming of the 1900 remake of *La Fée aux Choux.*

At Alice's direction, Mira helped the young actress, Yvonne Mugnier-Serand, change into a fairy costume, the white diaphanous dress trimmed at the neckline with silk roses. As Yvonne rehearsed her choreographed moves, Mira worked with Siméon to secure the painted backdrop on the large wall behind the terrace so it would not flutter during filming.

Bernadette arranged on the stage the cabbage props cut from sturdy cardstock painted a light shade of green. Next, the three of them threaded greenery through the white fence in front of the terrace wall.

Alice hid a baby doll behind one of the cabbages and picked up a wand, which she waved to Bernadette. "Please let Yvonne know we are ready. Can you two bring both babies here? Only the babies, no mothers."

"Oh, yes." Bernadette rushed off.

Alice waved the wand toward Mirabelle. "Bernadette will hide behind the cabbages on stage left to keep the baby quiet until its cue. If you could be so kind, I need someone to hide behind the cabbages on stage right to do the same?" "Of course." Mira's adrenalin rushed. She took slow, deep breaths, determined not to faint from her excited disbelief.

When I return to my own time and watch this film again, I'll know the part I played in its making. At least, I hope I will know, if my memory of this time travel remains with me.

Yvonne and Bernadette approached the set with the babies wrapped in blankets.

"Place one behind the cabbage scenery, stage left, and the other stage right," Alice directed. With another wave of the wand, Alice pointed toward Siméon. "Please monitor the area so no one wanders through unexpectedly."

"*Oui.*" Siméon walked to the door leading into the home and stood guard.

Alice handed the wand to Yvonne before calling Mirabelle and Bernadette. "Take your places. Keep those darling babies as motionless as possible."

Mira lay on the terrace behind the large cabbages, hoping the scenery hid her completely from view. If she was wearing less cumbersome clothing, her prostrate position would be less uncomfortable.

"We shall begin. Yvonne, prepare to wave the wand, and keep your eyes on me to follow my direction. And, my dear, *soit naturelle.* Anatole, *commencez.*"

Mira unwrapped the wriggling baby from the blanket and placed her hand on his stomach to encourage him to be still and quiet. She grinned to herself, thinking of how he followed Alice's famous words of direction to "be natural." His cries started low, but by the time Yvonne as the Cabbage Fairy placed him on the ground next to the other already "born" baby, he was letting out full-fledged wails.

Yvonne completed her motions for the scene by picking up the doll and returning it to the cabbage, deeming it not yet ready for birth. Both babies were waving their arms, kicking their legs, and screaming.

"*Nous avons fini,*" Alice called out in a pleased tone, as if unaware of the babies' discomfort. "*Rendre les bébés à leurs mères.*"

Yvonne and Bernadette scooped the babies into their arms. They wrapped them in their blankets and scurried away with them.

"Ah, peace and quiet once more," Alice sighed.

Mira wished she could share with Alice about the Cabbage Patch kids fad of her girlhood. She owned a Cabbage Patch baby she'd named Ashley, born in Babyland General's secret cabbage patch.

The cabbage patch myth was no stranger than other baby-making myths.

She preferred it over the beliefs about the wild women of the forest, owls, foxes, a male water sprite, a raven or a crow or, of course, the stork bringing babies.

One of her mother's top-selling antiques was a porcelain figure from Germany of *Der Kindlbringer,* who dressed like a harlequin and carried a bundle of newborns in a basket to deliver to expecting families. Mira shuddered over the memory of his menacing features.

She joined Bernadette and Siméon in the clean-up. The terrace returned to its normal appearance. The magic dissipated.

Except for my magical, and unexplainable, time travel.

Anatole and Alice were engaged in fervent conversation, the pitch of their voices rising and falling. Mira could not help but eavesdrop.

Alice shrugged as she spoke. "Adolphe came to the shop today and left angry. He cannot dismiss the unfairness to his father. He desires the Le Prince name to be known as Father of Cinematography, even though his testimony in the court case against M. Edison did not allow him to present the evidence. I fear what he may do if he does confront M. Edison in person."

Mira had come across Louis Le Prince's work in her studies and learned about the controversy between him and Edison over who invented the first motion picture camera. There had been court cases, fights over patents, and family tragedies, but the exact details wouldn't come to her.

They bid farewell to Anatole and embarked on their return trip.

Bernadette engaged in flirting with Siméon.

Mira once again sat next to Alice on the funicular. The filmmaker's attention remained on recording notes on the filming, allowing Mira to ruminate on the conversation between Anatole and Alice.

Adolphe Le Prince threatened *he* would not get away with something. Did he mean Edison?

Mira's stomach tightened. Could she have transported to the 1900 Paris Exhibition to stop Le Prince from killing Thomas Edison?

If Le Prince is my mission, then why have I become involved in Jacques Thibaut's life?

TWENTY-FIVE

The visit to House of Paquin.

The argument with Jacques.

The amazing time spent with Alice.

And now, finding out about Adolphe Le Prince's vendetta against Edison.

The exhausting day left Mira with a pounding headache. If Jacques were her mission, which she believed him to be, then why had she become privy to Adolphe's threats? Her imagination raced.

Again, no coincidences. One thing interrelates to another, n'est-ce pas?

Learning about Adolphe's threats provided an excuse to contact Jacques. She could ask for his assistance in intercepting possible danger toward Edison.

When the funicular rolled to its stop at the Place de la République, Mira realized she must soon inform Bernadette about no longer staying with her. Her heart numb, Mira followed the others onto the omnibus, which deposited them back at the Place de l'Opera square.

They quickly made their way to Gaumont et Cie.

Alice unlocked the shop's door. "Much work awaits me."

"I do hope M. Gaumont appreciates how valuable you are." Mira's tone showed her indignance.

Alice smiled. "Do men ever appreciate how valuable we women are in their lives?"

Mira's mouth curved in a half-smile. "You have a point."

"Oh, not true." Bernadette tugged Siméon's arm. "You recognize how valuable I am to you, do you not?"

"*Absolument.*" Siméon drew Bernadette closer.

When they entered the shop, Siméon and Bernadette looked at the camera equipment while Mira followed Alice into the back office to inquire more about Adolphe.

"Forgive me, Alice, but I overheard your conversation with Anatole, about Adolphe Le Prince being so angry toward M. Edison. I vaguely recall a family tragedy in the Le Prince family."

"*Oui.* Adolphe will never accept M. Edison instead of his father being honored as the Father of Cinematography." Alice hung her coat and hat on the hook by the shelf. "Adolphe's father disappeared from a train en route to Paris, on his way to publicly demonstrate his one-lens cinematograph camera in New York City. The police have never found his body nor his luggage. He never demonstrated his camera in New York City, which allowed M. Edison's success."

Something about Adolphe's fate niggled in the back of Mira's mind.

Another tragedy. But what?

"How awful." Mira pushed to learn more about the young man's threat. "Why is Adolphe here in Paris? Is he trying to make his father's name known here at the Exhibition?"

"Adolphe has no exhibit by which to do so." Alice shrugged. "He may be helping the American dancer Loïe Fuller in the lighting of her performances at her Exhibit. Have you seen her dance? I cannot decide which I adore most, her Fire Dance or her Serpentine Dance. You must go to her theater while you are visiting."

"Yes, I must." Mira remembered during her brief time taking dance lessons as a girl learning about how Loïe Fuller pioneered modern dance.

In film studies, a professor showed a silent film of a dancer performing Loïe Fuller's famous serpentine dance.

The graceful movement of swirling fabric and the lighting technique made it appear as if she took flight through flames. It made sense for Adolphe to help with the dancer's special theatrical lighting, but Mira sensed other motives for him being in Paris.

"Adolphe's angry outburst could suggest he is in Paris for reasons other than work?"

Alice returned her shop key to her bag, hesitating before she answered. "I probably should not say, but he hoped to confront M. Edison once again." Alice placed a hand to her mouth. "I should not spread rumors. Please, forget I have said anything."

"Of course."

But I will not forget. If Edison comes to Paris, then his life could be in danger.

She would inform Jacques of what she'd learned, and together they would visit Loïe Fuller's theater to confront Adolphe Le Prince. If Jacques stopped an attempt on Edison's life, his reputation could be restored. At the least, the rumor opened an opportunity to be with Jacques once more and try to set things right between them.

What irony. I am working to restore Jacques' damaged reputation while he believes my own to be sullied. An assassination attempt derailed Jacques' life, while a different assassination attempt might restore him to his rightful destiny.

Alice ushered Mira from the office. "I must get back to my work."

"*Bien sûr.*" Mira followed her into the shop. "*Merci*, for a wonderful day, and for our conversation."

"*Merci*, for your help." Alice clapped her hands. "*Un instant s'il vous plaît.*"

She returned to her office and reappeared with two small items in hand.

At her beckoning, Siméon and Bernadette joined Mira and Alice at the shop's counter.

"Something for you." Alice handed Bernadette and Mira each a coin purse, smiling shyly. "A little souvenir for you two ladies, to advertise Gaumont and my film."

The *La Fée aux Choux* coin purse.

Mira turned it over in her hands, checking the dots above the I's. They were smudged. It was the same purse Le Veille had given her.

She felt as if she were again whirling out of control on the carousel. Everything in her sight slid topsy-turvy. She tensed her body, fighting to regain balance.

"Oh, Alice." Bernadette clasped her purse against her heart. "I love. Mirabelle, you love also?"

Mira nodded, managing a weak reply. "*Oui,* I love." Bernadette opened hers and gasped. She held it out to Siméon. "Look." She jangled the coins the purse held. "Payment for you both, for your hard work today." Alice turned her attention to Mira. "And for you also."

Mira opened her coin purse, half-expecting to find the folded message: *Retrouvez-moi au Carrousel du Luxembourg, à midi.* Instead, her purse held coins as well. "*Merci.* How generous."

Alice smiled brightly. "When you see our little film, enjoy knowing your part in its production."

While Bernadette and Siméon chattered their excited replies, wonderment once again filled Mira. The "little film" would be over one hundred years old once she returned to her world. When she viewed it again, how strange it would feel to know she helped film it.

After a round of À *bientôt,* Mira followed Bernadette and Siméon from the shop.

Siméon grinned. "I will engage a *fiacre* to return us to your place, Bernadette."

"Agree. No walking for us wage-earners." Bernadette's face relayed pride.

Boarding the taxi for their short ride, Mira sat opposite the young couple, watching them exude joy over their day's adventure and their earnings. The parting from Alice left Mira melancholy.

I wish I had told the filmmaker what lay ahead for her, warned her, inspired her. I hate this part of time traveling, being powerless to help others avoid future tragedy, disappointments, failures.

When they disembarked, Mira steeled herself. She must explain her departure to Bernadette without incriminating Jacques, whom the girl adored, and without casting herself in the wrong light.

A tricky maneuver.

"Mlle Montgomery." M. Verany emerged from the pharmacy, addressing Mira. "*Vos colis sont arrivés de la Maison Paquin.*"

Bernadette clasped her hands in delight. "Packages from *Maison de Paquin?* How thrilling. You must model for us." She playfully pushed Mira into the building's entrance. "I have so few outfits. Let me live, how you say, vigorously through you?"

"Vicariously," Mira corrected her absentmindedly. "Live vicariously through me."

"Yes." Bernadette giggled. "Bernadette."

The sharpness in Mira's voice captured the girl's attention.

"What is it?" Bernadette let go of Siméon's hands and stepped closer to Mira, her face awash with surprise. "Are you angry with me?"

"Not at all." Mira beamed a smile to reassure her.

Bernadette frowned. "Then it must be Jaco who has upset you."

Mira could not speak against Bernadette's beloved Jaco. "No, not Jaco. Mme Newton has invited me to stay at the American Girls' Club."

Well, the woman did say she would welcome me anytime. "I have decided to accept. I felt so at home there yesterday, and I believe being around the other American girls will help restore my memory."

How easily lies slip from me.

"I don't want you to leave." Disappointment clouded Bernadette's face.

Siméon flashed Mira a sympathetic smile. "Mirabelle has a point, Bernadette. Being around other American woman could be best for her, *n'est-ce pas?*"

"*Je suppose.*" Bernadette's face set in sadness. "We shall call a *fiacre* for you, Mirabelle."

Mira nodded, grateful for the coins in the purse Alice gifted her. Would it be enough for the taxi? If not, she hoped Mme Newton would take pity and help pay the fare.

Siméon headed toward the street. "I'll help load your packages from Mme Paquin."

"*Merci*, Siméon, but no." Mira rested a hand on the boy's shoulder. "Please, rest now. As Bernadette has said, Susette would be much displeased at how active you have been today."

"I am somewhat tired." An exhausted breath escaped him. "*À bientôt*, Mirabelle."

Mira's heart ached. Likely, she would never see this boy again. She whispered à *bientôt*, though her heart knew she bid him *adieu,* as she must Bernadette.

What will happen to you both? Will you marry? Live happily ever after?

When she returned to the twenty-first century, would an internet search on their names would provide answers to her questions?

The harshness of World War One rushed into her thoughts.

Do I want to know their fates? What if Siméon fights in the war and dies? What if, in the bombings of Paris by the Germans, Bernadette dies?

I should never have allowed myself to become close to them. What happened to the aloof Mira, the one who held everyone at arm's length?

When I travel through the portal back to where I belong, I will leave those I've grown to care about behind forever. A young woman worried about her guardian she adores. A man who believes the worst about me and the worst about himself. A selfless, brokenhearted nurse. I have let all three into my heart.

I must restore Jacques' reputation, and his relationship with Susette before I leave them forever.

She shook her head.

Since when has Mirabelle Montgomery become a martyr for love?

TWENTY-SIX

Mira opened her coin purse to pay for the cab, grateful for the twenty francs from Alice.

The driver assisted in unloading the packages from Paquin before departing.

Mira knocked on the door, remembering that the last time she stood before the American Girls' Club, Jacques was beside her.

Mme Newton did not hesitate to offer her a room, shared with none other than Winifred Flanagan.

Mira did not expect a warm welcome from her roommate, who had glowered at her yesterday during the session with Mary Cassatt. They needn't be friends. She needed information from her about Marius Jourdain's connection with Jacques.

What remained of the evening light filtered through the large bay window of the room. A full-length pedestal-base mirror sat in the bay, along with a table placed between two upholstered chairs, each with a small footstool. A narrow strip of tasseled tapestry hung on the wall, like the one Mme Paquin used as a bell pull to summon others.

Mme Newton moved one to use as a step to reach the gas ceiling light.

Although her mother sold antique gas lighting fixtures, Mira had never witnessed the actual lighting of one. The process mesmerized her.

Mme Newton turned a valve on the chandelier's encased piping that held it to the ceiling to open the gas line. From the large pocket of her apron, she pulled a thin candle and match. After lighting the candle, she carefully lit the mantles of each of the three globes, each of which made a popping sound. While performing the task, she chattered away.

"This is the only unoccupied bed now. The girl rooming with Winifred returned to America because of a death in her family."

The lighting illuminated the room dimly. Mme replaced the footstool and looked around as if searching for evidence against Winnie. "I do hope your roommate will not create issues during your stay."

Mira hoped otherwise. She counted on Winnie sneaking out to meet Marius, so she could follow her.

Don't act innocent on my account, Winifred Flanagan.

While Mme plumped the pillows on the beds, Mira visually examined the contents of the large room. Each side mirrored the other, with a bed and nightstand, bureau, writing desk with chair, and small wardrobe. Mme pointed out in the hallway the water closet with the toilet and a separate room for bathing, shared by all on this floor.

This accommodation may be more comfortable than yours, Jacques, but I miss you and Bernadette already. Have you returned to your home and read the note I left you?

While waiting for the *fiacre* Bernadette arranged, Mira had belabored over each word. She avoided opening with "Dear" and signed it only with her name. She hoped the ending would appeal to his gallantry.

Jacques,

I have relocated to the American Girls' Club. I did not tell Bernadette you demanded my departure. Instead, I explained that associating with American women may help restore my memory.

Bernadette believes the best about me. I beg you, do not tell her you ordered me to leave nor share with her your suspicions about me. They are baseless. I am not a thief, liar, or prostitute.

To prove deserving of Bernadette's trust and to regain yours, I ask your assistance to stop a tragedy that will unfold if we do not prevent it. Please meet me tomorrow morning, and I will explain.

If you accept, send a reply with the place and time. If you refuse, I will face danger, unprotected.

Mirabelle

What if he did not reply? She chased away the negative possibility. *Like good old Scarlet O'Hara, I'll think about it tomorrow.*

"I will leave you to become settled, Mirabelle." Mme Newton paused in the doorway. Concern creased her forehead. "You can summon me by using the bell pull. Please inform me if Winifred's behavior seems alarming."

Mira nodded.

I am counting on it being just that.

Mme Newton's face reddened. "I hope you don't think I am asking you to gossip."

Mira suppressed a smile. "I understand you are concerned about her."

"Yes. Exactly." Mme Newton absentmindedly jangled the keys on the chatelaine hanging from her sashed waist. Her gaze roved over Mira's packages from Maison Paquin. "You have missed dinner. The girls are either out at the Exhibit or in one of the studies, painting or reading. I will send a tray for you."

At the mention of food, Mira's stomach responded with desire. *"Merci."*

Once the woman departed, Mira quickly organized the beautiful clothing and accessories Paquin sent her into the bureau drawers and small wardrobe. She changed into the pale pink dressing gown with horizontal pink satin and lace stripes, ruffled high neck and wrists, and slight ruffled train. She belted it with the wide, matching satin ribbon. With no corset required and the soft flowy material, the gown allowed her more freedom of movement and comfort.

A knock announced her dinner tray, delivered by one of the kitchen servants. The strong aroma of the cassoulet filled the bedroom.

Mira forced herself to eat slowly. Each spoonful of the white beans, sausage, and lamb concoction not only filled her stomach but satiated her taste buds as well. The French pear dessert, *tarte bourdaloue,* balanced out the meal.

With her appetite satisfied, Mira rested on her bed and sipped on another cup of lemon balm tea, wondering if she would find Winifred downstairs, painting or reading. Had she gone to the Exhibition or to see Marius?

Either way, your absence gives me the perfect opportunity to snoop.

Mira took the last swallow from her teacup before searching her roommate's bureau, nightstand, and writing desk. Nothing came of her prying. No love letters from Marius Jourdain. No personal diary or journal. A look in Winnie's wardrobe also revealed nothing untoward.

Closing its door, the flicker of her moonstone ring in the room's lighting reminded her of Winnie's attention upon it. She would keep it on her finger. No doubt the girl would steal it otherwise.

Mira lay on the bed, exhausted. Her instinct told her Winifred and Marius were in an intimate relationship, even if she'd found no evidence among Winnie's belongings.

Her instinct also told her Susette was correct to suspect Marius of derailing Jacques' police career. She hoped whatever she learned from Marius would only help Jacques and not hurt Bernadette. Her breath caught at the thought.

A quiet knock at the door startled Mira, and she bolted upright. *"Entrer."*

The servant returned to retrieve the food tray. "For you, Mlle." He held out an envelope with her name addressed on it in bold, masculine strokes and the initials JT pressed into the wax seal.

Mira accepted it. It seemed like an eternity before the servant left. She opened it and read Jacques' reply.

> Mme Montgomery,
>
> I will meet you at ten o'clock tomorrow morning in Luxembourg Gardens. You will find me seated upon the bench near the Carousel.
>
> Jacques Thibaut

Mira pressed the paper to her lips before folding and returning it to the envelope. Relief and worry washed over her simultaneously. Relief he would meet with her. Worry he said nothing about Bernadette. Had he spoken badly about her to the girl?

Exhaustion settled upon Mira. She looked forward to the close of this long day filled with both devastating and exhilarating moments. Her detective work about Winnie would begin tomorrow.

Right now, she longed for a bath and a good night's sleep. Gathering her sleeping gown, robe, and toiletries Mme Paquin kindly included, she headed for the hallway bath accommodations.

I'll think about everything else tomorrow.

TWENTY-SEVEN

When the morning light awakened Mira, her surroundings confused her for a moment until she remembered her location and why she was there. She expected to see Winifred, but it was as if she were rooming with a ghost.

Rising to face the day, worry nagged at Mira about seeing Jacques again. She must convince him she was not the dishonorable woman he believed her to be.

He'd agreed to accompany her to avert a tragedy, but he would have no idea of her plan to confront Adolphe Le Prince. If Adolphe were planning a confrontation with Edison, Jacques would be credited with keeping the famous man safe from harm, leading to his reinstatement to his job and restoration of his reputation.

Unless Marius Jourdain prevented that, somehow. He is a threat who must be disarmed. If I can't convince Jacques to confide what Marius holds over him, I will uncover it myself. Mira visited the water closet and the bath. She passed other boarders in the hallway who greeted her kindly. The struggle to dress herself unattended gave her more reason to miss Bernadette.

Wearing the pastel blue blouse, skirt, and bolero jacket combination sent by Madame Paquin provided a refreshing change to the dress she had been wearing since the time travel vortex deposited her in 1900 Paris. The skirt's hem, adorned with embroidered purple flowers, matched the facings of the bolero. Erupting from the matching straw hat were bunches of tall purple flowers interspersed with swirls of white tulle.

Mira clipped the small black leather pocketbook Madame Paquin provided to her waist sash. Opening it, she found a lace-trimmed scented handkerchief and cream-colored kid leather gloves with embroidered lavender flowers amidst green vines on the cuffs. She placed her coin purse into the pocketbook, wondering again about how the message came to be in it.

Did Le Veille place it in the coin purse to lure me to the Carousel? Or will I receive the message from someone while here in 1900 Paris? I have questions about everything and no answers to anything yet.

After deftly styling her hair in the ubiquitous pompadour bun, Mira swirled in front of the mirror to check her presentability. Satisfied, she made her walk to the dining hall, looking forward to a strong cup of coffee and a baguette with preserves to start her day.

Mira sat with Eloise, a convivial brown-haired young woman with a propensity to chitchat. Hoping for gossip, she asked about Winifred.

"She is gone more than here, that one." Eloise clucked her tongue. "We try to cover for her, so Mme Newport does not find out about her nightly outings. She has fallen in love with a poor Frenchie. He takes her to Montmartre, where at Moulin Rouge they enjoy the Can-can and partake of absinthe, *La Fée Verte*. So chic. Typically, she returns in the early dawn to make herself presentable before breakfast."

Eloise looked around the dining hall, frowning. "I do hope nothing bad has happened to her."

Her own encounter with this volatile "poor Frenchie" led Mira to imagine something bad could have indeed happened to Winnie. She excused herself. After gathering her cape, hat, and parasol, Mira slipped out to meet Jacques. With gloves on and parasol aloft, she walked toward Luxembourg Gardens, mulling over what she would say to him.

Entering Luxembourg Gardens at the Rue d'Assas pedestrian entrance, Mira paused by *Pavillon Davioud* to gaze upon the statue *Joies de la famille*. The couple with their child and beloved pet at their feet symbolized the joy of a family.

Will I ever experience such? I have held happiness at arm's length. Being drawn into Jacques' life awakened not only physical desire within me but also the craving for something . . . more. Joies de la famille?

With a sigh, Mira continued toward the bench.

As arranged, Jacques awaited her.

Mira breathed in deeply to build her courage. He pledged his assistance to her the last time they sat on this bench together. But the hardness in his eyes, those bluest-of- blue irises ringed with black, had returned.

She gripped her parasol tightly, resolved to win his trust once more. She reached out a hand for greeting.

Instead, he acknowledged her presence with a touch to the brim of his hat.

Mira withdrew her offered hand and hesitated over what to say.

Jacques broke the awkward silence. "I am due later today at Bois de Vincennes to prepare for the Olympic automobile racing event tomorrow. I came only because you wrote of facing danger, unprotected. Even under the circumstances, I cannot allow you to do so. Let me escort you to the police station for assistance. I can request Prefect Lépine himself help you."

"No, please." Mira raised a hand in objection. "Before involving the police, I must confirm my suspicions." "Enough with your obliqueness. What is this tragedy you fear will unfold?"

"I have heard someone plans to confront M. Edison. Perhaps harm him."

"You have heard?" Jacques' mocking grin relayed disdain. "Perhaps you are part of this plan, but now you wish to disentangle yourself?"

"You are vile." Mira turned on her heel, holding her head high.

"Mirabelle. Wait."

Jacques' hand upon her arm stopped her from walking away. Without facing him, she asked, "Why? For more of your insults?"

He stepped in front of her, his hand remaining upon her. "Who is this person plotting against M. Edison? Where did you hear about this plan?"

You will be furious about Bernadette's secret outings with her boyfriend. I must lie, once more.

"I overheard a conversation of a woman and young man passing me yesterday while I stood in front of Maison Paquin, overcome with tears."

"I apologize for leaving you in such a state." Jacques dropped his hold from Mira and stared at the ground.

Mira let his apology linger between them before she continued. "The couple were in deep conversation, neither paying attention to where they walked. The woman was begging the young man not to carry out his plan to harm Mr. Edison. He said he needed to avenge his father's murder, which he believed had been ordered by Mr. Edison. When the man rushed from her, he bumped into me."

"You were not injured?" Jacques swept a startled, concerned look over her, as if examining her for injuries. "I could not forgive myself—" He cut his words short.

His reaction instilled hope within Mira of restoring his belief in her, even though his caring expression evaporated as quickly as it appeared. She continued her story, hating that she must lie to win his confidence in her once more.

"No, I only dropped my handkerchief. He retrieved it and mumbled an apology. He told the woman he was expected at Loïe Fuller's theater for rehearsal and hurried off. The woman made sure I was uninjured before she walked from me. Her demeanor seemed distraught, as if she feared the young man would make good on his threat against M. Edison."

Jacques' brows creased. "I don't understand why this man believes M. Edison would order the murder of his father."

Mira wished she could blurt out what she'd learned from Alice, about how Edison stood accused of stealing Louis Le Prince's place in film history, but she must pretend to be ignorant.

"I think we must confront Adolphe Le Prince. If he is planning a violent confrontation with M. Edison, we must stop him."

Jacques stroked his mustache, silent for a moment before speaking. "I have heard M. Edison will not travel to Paris. Le Prince could be planning to sabotage Edison's company which is here, filming the Exhibition."

Mira had not considered that possibility. Those films provided invaluable archival footage. Adolphe would understand their significance.

"Jacques, we must stop whatever Le Prince may be planning."

"We have no evidence, only what you overheard. The police would not spare valuable police assets to investigate hearsay."

Mira could tell by his tensed jaw that Jacques struggled with what action to take. She held her breath, hoping his decision would be to accompany her to meet with Adolphe. Jacques gave a slight nod. "My automobile is parked nearby. We shall visit Loïe Fuller's theater to see if Le Prince is there."

"Yes." When she accepted his arm, a rush of emotion overtook her.

Where is aloof Mira? The one who never allowed herself to be drawn into others' problems? The one who chose her cocoon of self-preservation over friendships and relationships? The one who did not shed a tear over saying goodbye to Rob? Yet here you are, immersed in the messiness of others' lives. Opening your heart to them. Desiring a man with a boldness of passion I've never felt before.

The faint chiming of the Luxembourg clock reminded Mira of the precious time she was spending away from her ill mother's side.

Please, please, when I return to my present, let me be this wiser and open-hearted Mira. And, let me find time has stood still in my absence. Let me find you alive, Mom.

TWENTY-EIGHT

Mira gazed at the scenery they passed on their drive along the Left Bank toward Loïe Fuller's theater at the Exhibition, trying to ease her trepidations over confronting Adolphe Le Prince. They passed the intersection of Quay d'Orsay and Pont de la Concorde, and she caught a glimpse of the Porte Monumentale.

It struck her once again how it and other buildings constructed for the Exhibition were impressive facades only, razed after the event ended. How fortunate that photographs and films existed to document the fantastic, temporary sights.

Films such as those made by Edison's company.

Before she actually traveled back in time, she did so figuratively through her studies of these *Actualités*. They served as documentaries of the time. Protecting Edison and his filmmakers from whatever Le Prince may be planning would mean protecting the time capsules the filmmakers were creating.

Motoring through the crowded intersection of Quay d'Orsay and Pont Alexandre III, Mira admired the Petite Palais and the glass vaulted ceiling of the Grand Palais before Jacques turned onto Rue Fabert, adjacent to the Esplanade des Invalides.

He entered a large bicycle and automobile shelter located by *le trottoir roulant,* which provided transportation to Champs des Mars, where the Eiffel Tower loomed.

The remembrance of meeting Bernadette on the moving sidewalk caused a pang in her heart.

I have grown to love her.

Once the business with Adolphe Le Prince ended, however it played out, Mira knew her next action. She must disempower Marius Jourdain's hold over Jacques, meaning she must learn the truth about the Queen of Bohemia.

What if restoring Jacques' destiny means breaking Bernadette's heart over learning about her guardian's lies? About her mother's ill-reputed past? I could destroy their relationship. I'll do whatever I can to avoid that, but what if it can't be avoided?

With the automobile at a stop, Jacques leapt out and offered her assistance from the passenger seat. His guarded expression remained in place.

Straightening her hat, Mira asked, "How far is it to the theater?"

He motioned toward the left side of the Seine. "We shall walk along Quay d'Orsay, past the Rue des Nations pavilions, and cross at Pont de l'Alma. Loïe Fuller's theater is small but opulent."

They walked in silence.

Mira soaked in the flurrying excitement around her of tourists visiting the pavilions of different countries. Again, it amazed her that these impressive buildings were temporary facades. Her favorite was the pavilion for Italy built as a replica of the Venetian Palace of the Doges. Its gold rounded domes reflected the sun.

When they reached Loïe Fuller's theater, Mira admired its art nouveau design. She'd learned about the dancer's experimentation with staging and lighting effects in her film studies. The pictures of this theater designed by the famous art deco architect Henri Sauvage did not do it justice.

A statue of the dancer by the famous French sculptor Pierre Roche topped the arched entryway. The exterior walls resembled pleated, billowing skirts evoking the dancer's movements. The inanimate theater seemed to flow with movement.

What a shame such a gorgeous building did not remain past the Exhibition.

She and Jacques passed the placard inside the entryway announcing the times of the performances. They found the doors unlocked and went through. A hubbub of activity surrounded a round-faced, plumpish, short woman whom Mira recognized as Loïe Fuller.

The dancer stood in the center of a transparent glass stage floor with a black velvet backdrop. Reams of white silk fabrics swathed her body, the rigid hems stiffened by unseen rods sewn into the edges.

In front of the stage, musicians sat in the orchestra pit, a cacophony blaring from their tuning of instruments. In corners of the theaters stood light fixtures with men each holding colored glass plates in front of the projectors to beam different shades onto the dancer. Among them, Mira recognized Adolphe Le Prince.

Before she could point him out to Jacques, a woman dressed in men's clothing leapt to her feet from the front row. From having studied about Loïe Fuller, Mira recognized her as Gab Sorère.

Gab raised her arms and shouted, "Silence."

The theater lights went down. Disoriented by the sudden darkness, Mira instinctively held on to Jacques' arm, and he did not shrink from her touch.

Could it be that your anger toward me is diminishing?

The violins began strumming the beginning strands of Wagner's "Ride of the Valkyries."

Mira gripped Jacques' arm more tightly, realizing with awe that they were about to witness *La Danse du Feu,* Loïe Fuller's famous Fire Dance in which flames consumed her.

When the lights hit the darkened stage, the dancer appeared completely covered in shimmering diaphanous white fabric. She held her fabric-draped arms aloft to create a squared fabric top, projecting an illusion of a moving boxed figure. In rhythm with the powerful crescendo of the music, she glided about while the lighting upon her morphed to green. In a dramatic manner, she dropped her arms downward to show her face. Floating her arms sideways, she rotated into multiple balletic spins, so her body appeared swallowed into a cloud of mist created by the undulating fabric.

She finished spinning and stood still, wrapped tightly in fabric to appear like a human core of white light. A reddish glow of light shone upward from under the glass floor, and it inched upward upon her, until she became a column of flame.

When the fabric loosened from her, she glowed white, as if extinguishing the fire. At the closing notes of the orchestral music, she swept the fabric dramatically about her, fading into the darkness, with only a flick of red seen at her feet before it disappeared.

"Amazing." Jacques breathed the word reverently. "She is the phenomenon they say she is."

The intense grace and power of the performance awed Mira, and she whispered, "Yes."

Realizing her grasp remained on Jacques' arm, she disengaged from him and tipped her chin toward Adolphe. "There is the man."

Jacques strode toward him. "Young man, I hear you have threatened M. Edison."

Panic spread across the man's face. He attempted to run past Jacques but collided with Mira. "*Pardon*, Mlle, *pardon*." Mira straightened her hat, closely observing the nervous young man who squinted at her as if trying to place where he'd seen her before.

If you are dangerous, you wouldn't be so conciliatory. I think you are all bravado. Talk, but no action.

"What is happening?" Gab Sorère rushed toward them. "Adolphe, who are these people?"

Jacques hurried to Mira's side. "Are you hurt?"

"No. I am not." Mira enjoyed Jacques' concern.

Loïe Fuller descended the stage and joined them. She wore a robe loosely tied at the waist, allowing a glimpse of her ballet tights and tunic worn underneath. Off stage she seemed shorter and of flesh-and-blood, the opposite of the graceful apparition floating upon the stage.

She tilted her head to address Jacques. "As Gab has asked, who are you? What business do you have at my rehearsal with Adolphe?"

Mira spoke before Jacques could. "This is Jacques Thibaut, and I am Mirabelle Montgomery." She motioned to Adolphe. "I overheard him yesterday speaking with a woman. He threatened M. Edison. I fear he is plotting harm to the man."

The knowing look exchanged between Gab and Loïe worried Mira. Were these women part of Adolphe's plan?

Jacques addressed them sharply. "What do you two know?"

"Are you here upon authority or curiosity?" Gab answered, with a hint of provocation.

"Both," Jacques answered, allowing them to assume he was with the police. He stepped toward Adolphe. "Who are you and what is your intent toward M. Edison?"

"I am Adolphe le Prince. M. Edison robbed my father Louis Le Prince of his rightful place in history. It was my father who produced the first moving picture. Yet before he could be so acclaimed, he disappeared. Convenient for M. Edison who is renowned for my father's invention." Adolphe straightened his posture to stand tall. "The only harm I wish toward M. Edison is to discredit his reputation built on the blood of my father."

Loïe pulled her spectacles from the pocket of her robe and put them on. "I communicate with M. Edison about my patents and experimentation in lighting. I would never work with anyone harboring felonious ideas against M. Edison. Besides, he is not in Paris for any harm to come to him from Adolphe. Leave my theater and take your ridiculous accusations with you."

She motioned to Adolphe. "Come, we need to discuss a slight adjustment to the lighting."

Mira spoke up. "What about M. Edison's employees sent to film the exhibition? Are you plotting to sabotage their efforts?"

"I would not do such a thing." Adolphe walked away with Loïe, her arm around his shoulder.

Gab shoved her hands into her trouser pants and tossed her head. "Despite his bluster of hatred against M. Edison, physically harming someone is not in Adolphe's nature. Nor would he sabotage M. Edison's filming. He would know in his heart his father would not approve. Adolphe will continue fighting against M. Edison legally. He plans to return to New York City, once more to testify against him."

At the mention of his trip to New York, butterflies pummeled within Mira's stomach. She remembered Adolphe's fate. He would die under suspicious circumstances, shot to death by an unidentified perpetrator while hunting on Fire Island in New York.

Adolphe's death would prove beneficial to Edison, as had the disappearance of Louis Le Prince, casting more murderous suspicions upon the famous man.

If only I could warn you, Adolphe, of your fate.

Mira rushed from the theater.

Jacques joined her. "Why did you leave so abruptly? Did Loïe Fuller change your mind so easily about Adolphe Le Prince? Or did you use him as a ploy to see me?"

Mira placed a hand to her heart which was beating wildly. "I have done nothing to deceive you."

Yet, she knew the opposite to be true.

I have done everything to deceive you . . . because I must.

"You lied to Bernadette." Jacques' eyes narrowed with accusation. "Bernadette told me you moved to the American Girls' Club to help you recover your memory. I did not tell her I asked you to leave. Be aware, I will if you come near her again."

"Jacques, you have set your mind against me without allowing me to defend myself. Please, sit with me for a moment."

She crossed the sidewalk and took a seat at one of the tables lining the patio area across from the theater, hoping he would join her.

The time spent chasing Adolphe Le Prince, only to find it to be a wild goose chase, irritated her. Why had this red herring appeared to derail her?

Perhaps to bring Jacques and me to this moment, where I confront him over his destiny? I can't continue to run around in circles, or I will never see Mom again.

Jacques sat facing her with his arms crossed.

His stiff body language told Mira he remained distrustful of her. As much as she wanted to confide her truth about being a time traveler, she decided on a mix of truth and falsehoods. "What I have told you is the truth. I am lost in Paris. I do not know Marius Jourdain. I do not remember anything except my name."

Lying again so easily. Think of it as acting, your Oscar- winning performance, remember?

Her voice quavered. "I do know my mother is close to dying." Heartfelt tears over that truth wet her cheeks. She retrieved her handkerchief from her pocketbook and patted at them before continuing.

"I did mean what I said to Bernadette. I do hope being around other American ladies will help restore my memory."

Jacques' posture relaxed.

Mira pressed her point. "If I were a person of low morals, an unethical person, then wouldn't my ill nature show, even if I suffer amnesia? And, with all you've been through, wouldn't yours? But you are a decent person, even after accusations of being an anarchist sympathizer caused you to lose your position as a police detective. You broke off your relationship with Susette because you felt she deserved someone better."

Jacques flinched.

Mira continued, hoping to prod him into sharing his confidences. "We are both trapped in false situations. Me by the amnesia, you by vicious rumors. Our true destinies have been waylaid. You are more fortunate than I. You know your truth, which can set your life back on track. Tell me, and let me help you."

"I do not need your help." Jacques stood so quickly his chair toppled backward. "I admit your heroism the night of the bridge collapse and your kindness to Bernadette are not actions of one who is immoral or unethical. The strangeness of your circumstances misled me to think the worst of you, and I apologize."

Thank heaven I have reversed his negative opinion about me. At least, for the time being.

He righted the chair before offering his hand. "I must go to the racetrack to prepare for tomorrow's event. Let me return you to the Club." He hesitated, before adding, "M. Peugeot is sending a car to bring Bernadette to the competition. I can arrange for you to join her."

"*Merci.* I do have a special Paquin gown to wear." Mira smiled, remembering the saleswoman's disappointment over not wearing it to the automobile fête.

Jacques' grin told her he remembered the saleswoman's reaction. "Mme Paquin expects you to let everyone know it is her design." His amusement faded to seriousness. "It will be a well-attended Olympic event, so there is a possibility someone could recognize you."

"I can hope so." Mira inwardly winced. She hated lying to him.

She walked with him to the car, sorting through her mixed emotions. She had worked her way back into his good graces but failed to learn about his secretive past.

Winifred Flanagan, I hope you plan to sneak out to see Marius Jourdain tonight. The sooner I confront him, the better. I must learn what he holds over Jacques, or, I will fail in my mission. Then what? Remain in 1900 Paris, until...?

TWENTY-NINE

The 1900 street noises and smells of Paris to which Mira had grown accustomed punctuated the ride to the American Girls' Club. Lost in thought, she did not pursue conversation with Jacques. The silence between them was not rife with his animosity, as before. He assisted her from the Peugeot, and his touch set her insides tingling.

"Good luck tomorrow at the race." She gripped his hand tightly. Worry chased through her. "Please be careful. Think of Bernadette and do not take any risks."

"I always think of Bernadette. As well as others." With a leap into the driver's seat, he sped away.

Mira wondered who he meant by others. Her? Susette? The tango of desire between Jacques and her would lead nowhere for she would not allow it. Her emotions tightened inside her like a tangled mess.

When she signed in at the lobby desk as required, Mira flipped through the pages, finding signatures in various handwriting falsifying Winnie's ins or outs. The most recent indicated she was at the Club.

You are quite a sly one, aren't you, Winifred Flanagan? Hopefully, tonight I will learn your secrets of slipping out to be with your lover, Marius Jourdain.

When Mira entered her room, she discovered Winnie asleep on her bed, dressed in a long-sleeved nightgown more suited to a cold evening than the warmish spring weather. Her hair resembled a bird's nest. The pile of her clothing on the floor reeked of cigar smoke and alcohol.

I hope your exhaustion will not prevent you from partying again tonight.

Mira changed into the comfortable dressing gown. She would enjoy relaxing in it until having to change into an evening dress to follow Winnie, if she did sneak out.

Unable to resist the allure of her own bed, Mira plumped the pillows before reclining. Her moonstone ring flashed in the slant of the afternoon sunlight through the window. Drifting in and out of a light sleep, Mira kept watch on her roommate.

Finally, Winnie stirred from her exhausted, alcohol-and- drug-addled sleep. She perched on the side of the bed. After a prolonged stretch, she stumbled to her feet and pulled on a robe.

From the rear view of her, Mira noticed Winnie's broad- hipped and heavyset figure and felt sympathy for her. In this era of wasp waists, it must be difficult to be overweight.

Winnie stepped over her mess on the floor to gather her toiletries from her bureau top. She studied the belongings set out on Mira's bureau before walking toward the armoires and boldly opening Mira's to examine the clothing hung in it.

"Paquin. *Oh là là.*" Winnie cut an envious look toward Mira. "Someone is keeping you in high cotton, as they say in Mississippi where I come from." Her Southern accent had a touch of Irish lilt. "I would possess such a wardrobe, if my family's plantation and wealth survived the War."

Mira decided to remain quiet. She realized Winnie referred to the War Between the States, which ended in 1865. Winnie's grandfather and maybe even father probably fought in it. If not for the American Civil War, she would be living the life of a Southern Belle and probably be mistress of her own plantation.

I bet you'd have no issue with being a slaveowner.

The nasty thought provoked a tad of remorse within Mira. She assumed Winnie's family's circumstances jaded her life outlook. Traveling from

Mississippi to Paris as a young woman whose family no longer possessed wealth or means must have been difficult.

You must have quite a story to tell about how you manage to be residing at the American Girls' Club and associating with a Parisian criminal. Love and poverty do make strange bedfellows.

Watching Winnie collect her clothing from her armoire, Mira noted she chose an evening dress.

Good. You must be planning another night out.

Mira rose from her bed and straightened the covers. "I haven't seen you since I arrived last evening." She poked with a pointed toe at the clothing pile. "You must have enjoyed yourself last night."

"What business is that of yours?" Winnie fastened a taunting look upon her.

"I saw you with Marius Jourdain the other day. After you walked away from him, he argued with the man accompanying me." Mira shrugged. "My curiosity is piqued."

"What is the saying? Oh, yes. Curiosity killed the cat." Toiletries and undergarments in hand, Winnie moved with quick steps to the door. Opening it, she turned toward Mira. "If Jacques Thibaut sent you here to spy on me, he must not value your life." She exited the room.

Her casual threat chilled Mira. She had wondered if Marius Jourdain abused or blackmailed Winnie, but no. They were equals in whatever unlawful activities they undertook. Mira must be certain Winnie would lead her to Marius Jourdain tonight. She held her arm out to study her moonstone ring once more. The day of Mary Cassatt's painting lesson, Winnie's gaze had remained affixed upon the ring, clearly coveting it. Twisting it around and around on her finger, Mira remembered what her mother said. "It's your tell, Mira. The more upset you become, the more you play with the ring."

Twisting it now brought a plan to Mira. She would set a trap Winnie would not be able to resist—a Lalique moonstone ring. If left unguarded, Mira knew Winnie would steal it and take it to Marius.

The exchange of the ring for my return to my mother's side . . . Dad would understand.

Mira chose the evening gown with the shortest train from the two provided by Mme Paquin, needing to be as unencumbered as possible by material in case she must chase quickly after Winnie. The ivory silk taffeta and chiffon dress with three-quarter sleeves, with its modesty lace panel and high neckline, would not encourage men's attention.

Draping the dress across her bed, she admired its chiffon flowers embroidered with silver thread and the vertical rows of silver sequins extending from bodice to the beginning of the ruffled lacey hemline. She required assistance to fasten the pearl buttons running down its back. She would have to take a chance and ask her next-door neighbor Eloise for assistance.

Mira slipped from her room with the dress in hand and knocked on Eloise's door. She answered and did not hesitate to offer help while peppering Mira with questions about her plans. Mira dodged through them, explaining she promised to meet an acquaintance for dinner.

Returning to her room, she fastened into her hair the turban-style hat with crisscrossed folds of light blue crepe and darker blue chiffon fastened with a large rhinestone jewel. An attached blue aigrette rose high from the hat's rear. While securing the chapeau with long, sharp hat pins, Mira thought of dangers she could face alone in Montmartre. She placed a hat pin into one of the double inner compartments of the silver mesh evening bag. It could serve as a weapon if she needed to protect herself.

In the other compartment, she placed the coin purse containing the rest of the money given to her by Alice Guy, hoping it would be enough to support her efforts for the evening.

If not, I will be stranded, vulnerable and alone.

Mira slipped the moonstone ring from her finger and kissed it before placing it on her bureau, where it would stand out noticeably among other items. Before she could change her mind about using it as bait, Mira wrapped the lacy cape around her, gathered her gloves and handbag, and exited the room. She secreted herself where the hallway made a turn to another wing of the floor to wait for Winnie.

Her timing could not have been better. Within moments, Winnie emerged from the bath with her robe lightly closed around her. She entered the bedroom.

Mira hoped no one would come across her in the hallway while she waited and spied. When Mme Newton appeared, approaching Winnie's door in a stealthy manner as if on a secret mission, Mira's mouth opened in surprise.

Mme Newton tapped three times, as if using a code. Winnie opened the door, and the woman scurried in without a word passing between them.

Why would Mme Newton help Winnie dress, especially considering how lowly the woman speaks of her?

Mira's impatience grew as minutes ticked by.

When the door opened once again, Mme Newton peeked from the room before she walked out and hurried away. The door opened once more, and Winnie appeared in a daringly low-cut brown velvet evening dress, the hem of its pleated skirt trimmed in fur to match the trim on her tall hat.

Mira noted that Winnie wore the dress looser around her waist than fashionable and carried her brown cape over one arm. She held her gloves and purse in one hand. Her outfit was unseasonable for April, and from what Mira saw at Paquin's, out of style. All these observations underscored to Mira the reasons Winnie would turn to a life of crime.

Poverty, and greed. It makes sense Winnie would fall in love with Marius Jourdain, who offers her an opportunity for a life better off than what she has, even if one based on illegal means.

When Winnie closed the door, a flash on her ungloved hand announced she wore the moonstone ring.

A wave of sickness hit Mira.

I will not return through the Carousel portal without my ring.

Pacing herself behind Winnie enough to remain undetected, Mira followed her into the lobby. She paused to pull on her gloves before exiting onto the street without signing out on the register. Multiple *fiacres* were lining the road, their horses flicking their tails. A street sweeper stood on standby to clean the manure piles, which accosted Mira's nose.

She assumed Mme Newton must arrange for this service nightly to provide the women from the Club transportation to the Exhibition or other evening activities.

Winnie motioned to the first waiting taxi. "Moulin Rouge."

Mira's galloping heart matched the hoofbeats of the taxi's horse as it clattered away. The Montmartre location of Moulin Rouge could be dangerous, especially for an unescorted woman.

She approached the next waiting horse cab. *"Suivez ce fiacre."*

The driver tipped his hat. He raised his eyebrows over Mira's request to follow Winnie's cab.

Mira pretended to laugh. *"Je la surprends."*

He returned her presumed gaiety with a wink, believing her explanation she planned to surprise the passenger ahead, and requested the payment for the ride.

Mira plucked the coins from her purse with a sinking feeling over her sparse finances becoming sparser. She settled into her seat, her heart beating hard over the eventuality of confronting Marius Jourdain. He would not be forthcoming, but she must force him into explaining his connection with Jacques.

Her moonstone ring on Winnie's finger proved her a thief and could be leveraged to get the criminal talking. Mira could threaten to call a police officer to arrest her. Jacques could be a witness to the ring belonging to her.

Mira shifted in her seat, wishing Jacques were accompanying her to protect her. Her vanity could not deny she wished he could also see her in this dress, which sculpted her figure. The hat set off the blueness of her eyes.

If Jacques knew the dangerous adventure upon which she embarked, he would be furious. She could not help but think once again that if she died in 1900 Paris, her mother would never know what happened to her. Her Jujitsu could be less effective with her movements constrained by the gown she wore. The hat pin could only do so much damage. She doubted it would be enough if Marius and Winnie attacked her.

Mira breathed as deeply as the corset allowed, building courage.

I will survive the night, and I will return to you, Mom.

She looked out the carriage window to get her bearing. They were passing over Pont St. Michel toward Pont Au Change. Ships, their exterior sides lined with lights and decks crowded with people, floated on the Seine.

The shadowy outlines of Sainte-Chapelle to her left and Cathédrale Notre-Dame to her far right inspired her to lift a prayer. The image of Le Veille intruded into it, as if mocking her. She would not let him keep her captive back in time. At whatever cost, she would succeed.

Even if it means destroying Bernadette? Yes.

Please, no.

There must be a way to keep Bernadette from learning about her mother yet help Jacques. Questioning Marius Jourdain is my first step in figuring it out.

THIRTY

The *fiacre* climbed against the rise of the cobblestone road, alerting Mira they neared Butte Montmartre. As she peered from the cab's window, the brilliant electrically lit sails of its red windmill atop the small red building welcomed her to 82 Boulevard de Clichy, the location of the infamous Moulin Rouge. The oversized stucco elephant positioned adjacent to the cabaret loomed over it, casting an eeriness to the location.

As she stepped from her cab onto the sidewalk, the throngs of people milling shoulder-to-shoulder swept Mira up. She trained her eye on Winnie and followed her into the cabaret. If not for the woman's carrot-red hair showing from under her tall hat, she would have lost her.

Inside, Mira confronted a club environment more frenzied than any modern-day techno club she'd frequented but preferred to avoid. She choked on the thickened air saturated with musky body odors, cigar smoke, heavy perfume, and absinthe, the pungent and spicy drink made from wormwood, anise, and fennel known as *la fée verte*— the Green Fairy. Mira hoped when she confronted Marius Jourdain, he would not be under its alcoholic effects.

She slowed her walk through the lobby to admire the fabulous Toulouse Lautrec posters, which complemented the garishness of the place. As she entered the main room, the vibrant music of the horns, strings, and percussion from a live orchestra permeated through her. They were playing the famous Can-can song "Infernal Galop."

Mira remembered it to be from an operetta entitled *Orpheus in the Underworld.* Its title described the surreal atmosphere enveloping her, an underworld of sorts.

The scene before her resembled the set design for the movie she loved, *Moulin Rouge,* come to life. Billowing red and gold canvas fabrics draped the ceiling. The mirrored walls reflected the light from the huge crystal chandeliers. Small electric windmills turned from where they were mounted on gilded columns.

Keeping an eye on Winnie, Mira dodged the waiters rushing in and out of the crowd, serving those seated at small tables ringing the dance floor. She drew no one's attention while making her way amidst the chaos around her.

Winnie sat at one of the tables. She clapped and cheered the high-kicking Can-can dancers performing amongst everyone on the dance floor.

Mira stood partially obscured by one of the columns from where she could keep an eye on Winnie, whose sparkling eyes showed her enjoyment of the cavorting, rouged-cheeked dancers with bright red lips.

They wore their hair piled under large picture hats set coquettishly at a slant and adorned with high plumages. When they lifted their skirts high to kick their black- stockinged legs, they swished their frilly white petticoats lined underneath with black and scarlet. Some of the dancers sidled close to men and kicked off their top hats, sending all into gales of laughter.

One of the hats flew onto Winnie's table. She laughingly returned it to its owner before making her way out a back door.

Mira hurried to follow her and stepped from the claustrophobic cabaret into a crowded garden patio. She had hoped for a breath of fresh air, but a haze of cigarette smoke permeated it. Yet, it was less polluted than inside.

Couples sat at the tables and chairs scattered about the patio area. They were watching the Can-can dancers on the covered stage protruding from the rear of the Moulin Rouge structure. The dancers performed to the orchestral music wafting from within. Mira observed the strange occurrence of young boys leading donkeys upon which women sat sideways, their tipsy laughter ringing out.

She sat at a table for two across from where Winnie stood by the huge stucco elephant looming over the garden area. Its torso sported a red velvet blanket with braided gold trim and sparkling silver sequins. Its trunk and each foot were wrapped in wide bejeweled gold-roped chains. Upon its head sat an ornate gold crown. To Mira, its large eyes projected a sense of solemnity, as if it disapproved of the decadent behavior of the humans surrounding it, and in it.

Mira noted men coming and going through the door in the elephant's right foreleg. They staggered about in various states of drunken or drugged stupor. Opium vapors reeking of ammonia stench drifted toward her. Disgusted, she pressed a handkerchief to her nose, realizing the rumor of opium dens located there must be true. She'd also heard that prostitutes worked in the dens.

When Marius Jourdain emerged from the elephant, a man followed him. Mira swallowed against the lump of disappointment that lodged in her throat.

Jacques! How could you be part of all this?

The men approached Winnie. She stood with her feet planted apart to control her center of gravity. One ungloved hand drew her cape back from her body. Her other ungloved hand, from which Mira's moonstone ring shone, rested on her large baby bump.

Mira's lips parted in surprise.

Winifred Flanagan. You have gotten yourself pregnant. You're near-term, by the looks of you. No wonder you have been lolling about at the America Girls' Club in your nightclothes at all hours, according to Mme Newton. And, no wonder your waist lacks definition. And, your poor baby. You've exposed it to drink and drugs, and what else?

The loud braying of a donkey walking near her at the patio edge snapped Mira from her shock. She focused on the body language of the three, noticing Winnie's grasp on Marius's arm and Jacques' angry gestures toward them both. Without thinking through her actions, she snaked through the convivial, careening-out-of-control crowd to get closer. The cacophonous sounds around her prevented her from overhearing their argument until she arrived at Jacques' side.

"I am through, Marius. You get nothing else from me. Nothing." Jacques pounded a fist into his palm. "Nothing."

Winnie's eyes widened at the sight of Mira. She hastily hid her hand wearing Mira's ring behind her back. "Mirabelle." Jacques' scowl told of his displeasure at her appearance.

Before Mira could speak, a drunken man's stumble through the elephant door knocked Winnie forward.

Marius steadied her. "You need to sit."

He guided her to a chair on the garden patio. His solicitous behavior toward Winnie prompted Mira to consider that he cared about this woman and the baby she carried.

Concern painted Jacques' face. "Mirabelle, why are you here? It is not safe for an unescorted lady."

Mira hesitated over how to answer.

Should I lay my cards on the table? Why not?

"I followed Winnie here hoping to find Marius Jourdain. He is extorting you, and I want to know over what."

The color drained from Jacques' face.

"Susette told me you called Marius Jourdain's name while you lay recovering under her care at the hospital. Neither of us believe you sympathize with anarchists, or you conspired to assassinate President Faure. Marius must have been involved. Did you come face-to-face with him and allow him to escape because of whatever he is holding over you?"

Mira's voice vibrated with emotion. "Is he blackmailing you about Désirée Blanchet, the Queen of Bohemia? Are you Bernadette's father?"

Jacques reeled from her, as if she'd physically wounded him.

His stricken expression cut into Mira's heart. She hastened to add clarification. "What I said comes from me, not Susette. Because you will not confide about your past, I am left to conjecture."

She motioned to the elephant's door, where another man in a stupor emerged. "I find you with Marius at an opium and prostitution den. What am I to think? If I am to help you, I must know your secrets."

The blackness around his blue irises grew darker.

If eyes are the windows to one's soul, his are nailed shut. I must pry them open.

"Everyone holds secrets, do they not?" Jacques regained his composure. "I can assure you, though, I was not intimate with Désirée Blanchet. Nor do

I frequent dens of opium or prostitution. You observed me tonight delivering a message to M. Jourdain."

His answer left so much unknown. Frustrated, Mira pressed her gloved hands together, missing the presence of her moonstone ring biting into her fingers.

Jacques squinted an eye toward her. "Your amnesia makes you the one needing my assistance, not the reverse."

Mira suppressed the urge to confess the truth.

He grasped her arm. "Let's depart from this craziness." Moving through the throng once again, Mira saw Winnie and Marius seated together, deep in conversation with their heads almost touching. Winnie looked physically ill.

Mira worried the woman may deliver the baby in the midst of the Moulin Rouge decadence. She lifted a prayer for Winnie's protection, and that of her unborn babe.

At the curb outside the cabaret, Jacques hailed a *fiacre*. Mira settled inside, assuming he would have the driver return her to the American Girls' Club.

Instead, Jacques entered the cab and sat across from her. He removed his top hat and placed it on the seat by him. "You look too beautiful for the evening to end."

His compliment caught Mira unaware and brought a flush to her cheeks. "Your admiration will not sway me from finding out about your connection with Marius—and Désirée Blanchet."

"I thought we closed that topic." Jacques pressed his gloved hands into the tops of his muscular thighs.

Mira allowed herself a moment to drink in his sexiness before pleading once again. "Jacques, confide in me. Please." "*Comme ci comme* ça." He shrugged. "You do not need to learn more about me, other than I once served as a police detective and now work for M. Peugeot. I once lived alone, and now I provide an orphaned relative with a home. It is about you we should worry."

He leaned toward her. "We have yet to find out your identity. Your trauma must exhaust you. Let's bring a pause, though, and enjoy tonight."

Jacques settled against the back of his seat and smiled. "I have asked the driver to take us to *La Grande Roue de Paris* at the Exhibition. We shall drink in the stupendous sight of Paris from the top of the Grand Wheel."

"I agree, under one condition." Mira tilted her chin toward him, to show her determination. "You tell me your secrets while we ride."

Jacques lifted a corner of his mouth in a crooked grin, but his eyes reflected sadness. "Perhaps. But only if upon reaching the wheel rounding the top, you kiss me."

"Secrets in exchange for kisses?" Mira knew the bargain to be dangerous. His lips against hers would intensify their desire. "*Oui*. I agree."

Only kisses. Nothing more.

THIRTY-ONE

The jolting of the cab ride set Mira's nerves on edge. Jacques fell into an unapproachable silence, and she feared he was re-considering sharing anything with her. He'd promised secrets in exchange for kisses, and she would keep him to his promise. She thought about what she overheard him tell Marius.

You get nothing else from me.

The criminal must be extorting Jacques. Mira agreed with Susette. Everything leading to Jacques' dismissal from the police force pointed to Marius Jourdain, and Désirée Blanchet.

When they turned to cross Pont d'Iéna, Mira glimpsed the fountain of Jardins du Trocadéro. The Eiffel Tower materialized, ablaze in its temporary golden glory. If not for the pressing nature of her mother's health, she could allow herself to become lost in amazement at the sights of 1900 Paris.

"We have arrived." Jacques' announcement broke the silence between them. "The walk from the Eiffel Tower toward the Palais de l'Électrique allows spectacular views of the lighted water fountains. The steam-powered engines and generators inside the Palace produce the light for the Exposition. Nearby stands La Grande Roue, by the Galerie des machines."

He took leave of the cab and held its door open for her. "Shall we stroll, Mlle Montgomery?"

"*Oui.*" Mira accepted his assistance from the *fiacre.*

With her arm linked into his, she walked the Champs de Mars. She again marveled at the huge exhibition buildings, whose sheer magnitude of size made her feel tiny.

She allowed Jacques to guide her through the crowd, thick even at this late hour. Soon they arrived at the lighted fountains of the Palace and Water Tower. Its structure resembled a giant peacock with its tail spread wide. Upon the central tower stood a chariot with a statue in it, holding aloft a bright torch, the lights illuminating the fountain's rushing waters, which continually changed color.

Mira stared, mesmerized. "It reminds me of Loïe Fuller's dancing, which is as fluid as the waters of this fountain."

"Yes." Jacques motioned to the large Ferris wheel. "Shall we board?"

Mira nodded, her heart rapid firing in her chest. Once they settled into a passenger car, she would learn Jacques' past and know what she must do to correct his destiny. She could be home soon. Leaving him and Bernadette tasted bittersweet, but she found comfort in Jacques being with Susette and Bernadette with Siméon. It was she who would be alone once more, without a lover or even close friends.

Will this experience return me as a changed person, one open to sharing my life with friends and lovers? At least I have let go of my anger and grief over Dad. That's a start.

Standing in the long ticket line, Mira stared at the Ferris wheel. The passenger cars seated at least two dozen. How could she have an intimate conversation with so many people surrounding them? She refused to accept that the night could end without her learning from Jacques what she needed to know.

"Remain here." Jacques hurried toward the front of the line.

When the minutes ticked by without his return, his absence triggered Mira's anxiety. She stretched on tiptoe to peer over those in front of her, but she did not see him until he called to her.

"*Viens avec moi.*" He rushed to her side and took her hand.

They bypassed those in line to reach the ticket taker. He waved them through to enter an empty passenger car at the loading level. Its gate shut behind them.

Jacques drew her into a seat next to him.

Mira looked around in amazement. "We ride alone?"

"I bartered tickets to the race car event tomorrow for our privacy." Jacques held his chin high, a gleam of boasting in his eyes. "Tomorrow, you will cheer me to win. Champagne will flow afterward."

Mira smiled. "Tonight, though, we are locked in this car, and you shall answer all my questions."

The wheel began to turn, and the passenger car lurched forward.

Jacques put his arm around her. "Our ride begins." He leaned in for a kiss.

"Not yet." Mira placed a finger against his lips, and his mustache tickled against her touch. "When we reach the top." She let her hand fall to her lap. "You promised to tell me about Désirée Blanchet. The Queen of Bohemia. Bernadette's mother. You insist you two were not lovers."

Jacques' expression projected relief, as if he were relieved to lay bare his secrets. "I arrested Désirée Blanchet because of her lewd performance as Cleopatra at the Moulin Rouge, seven years ago. Each year the Ecole des Beaux-Arts holds Bal des Quat'z'Arts, a raucous revelry."

Mira did not share that Mlle Brodeur had told her about the night.

"Désirée performed nude, or so rumors said. Once proper society heard, pressure mounted to dole out consequences to reign in such immoral behavior. My police unit was sent to arrest Désirée and the men on stage with her. The judge imposed a fine for their release. She had no money, and no one came forward to aid her. She pleaded with me to find Luc Roget and ask him to pay."

Roget. Bernadette's surname.

That revelation—and the Ferris wheel's movement— brought queasiness to Mira. She held her crossed arms against her stomach. "Did you go to him?"

"Yes. I did. He refused." Jacques shrugged. "I have seen so many women like Désirée. Alone and mired in a life of desperation. Pitying her, I paid the fine for her release."

A life of desperation.

Mira remembered Jacques used those words before, when expressing his concern if Bernadette were to marry Siméon. He spoke then of trying to help women with ruined lives.

Girls who married young and became old before their time. Grisettes who were taken advantage of and abused by their Bohemian lovers. Courtesans who were cast off by their lovers and sank into lives of obscure poverty.

Désirée Blanchet was one of these women.

When Jacques spoke again, anguish dripped from his words. "The Ecole des Beaux-Arts students began protesting. It turned into a drunken, frenzied riot, throughout the Latin Quarter, and we tried to contain it. We used our batons to confront them, but I lost mine in a scuffle. In the chaos, I hurled a heavy match holder off a café table."

Jacques' body tensed.

Mira prayed he would not say what she feared.

He breathed out his confession in a low whisper. "The holder hit someone. I made my way to where the person lay, and I recognized him as Luc Roget."

His voice dropped lower. "I found out later Luc sent a message to the precinct saying he would pay Désirée's fine, not knowing I had done so and she had been released. He became ensnarled in the crowd on his way to the station."

"Oh, Jacques. You can't blame yourself for what happened." Mira placed her arm around his shoulder.

He recoiled from her touch. "I haven't told you the rest. Marius Jourdain knew Luc Roget. He saw him at Moulin Rouge begging for Désirée to return to their marriage. She abandoned both Luc and their daughter after giving birth to her."

Jacques looked at Mira, his eyes glistening with unshed tears. "You know her."

Mira nodded. "Bernadette."

"In the confusion of the night, only Marius witnessed Luc Roget's death. So much blood covered them both. Marius said he would keep quiet if I made it worth his while. "The next day Marius contacted me to meet him. He brought Désirée. They presented the extortion terms I must meet, or they would turn me in for Luc's murder. Marius demanded I help him escape the law when he asked for it. Désirée demanded I provide a home for Bernadette. What choice but to accept the terms? If I turned myself in, the girl would have no home. Désirée would not take her. I became Bernadette's only hope for a decent life."

Jacques ran a hand through his hair. "Désirée became ill and died soon after the night of the riot. I could have abandoned Bernadette then, but the thought never crossed my mind. I took her in to save myself, but I grew to love her as if she were my own."

He hunched forward, his broad shoulders sagging. "When I brought ten-year-old Bernadette to live with me, she believed her mother died soon after her birth from illness and her father died in a carriage accident. If she learns the truth I've hidden from her, she will hate me forever."

"Oh, Jacques." Mira touched his shoulder, wishing she could take away his pain and guilt. "You are not a murderer. Bernadette would understand."

"She would understand her father died because of my actions? She would understand I have perpetuated the lie about her mother? I think not." He straightened his posture, shrugging Mira's hand from him.

"Tell me more about Marius Jourdain. What has he demanded of you?"

Jacques turned his head sharply toward her. "You and Susette already know. I did not see Marius Jourdain again until four years later, at Président Faure's assassination attempt. He came from out of the crowd with a knife, intent on killing Faure. When I tackled him, I took the strike from the knife. He recognized me and uttered only one word: Roget."

Mira nodded. "If you arrested him, Marius would tell the police about the night of the riots. Bernadette would find out."

"Yes." Jacques looked out across the Paris landscape below them. "Not only Bernadette. While in hospital recuperating from the knife strike, Susette cared for me. We fell in love. I hoped to marry her. We would become a family, Susette and Bernadette, and me. But Marius ruined that."

"You mean by framing you as the would-be assassin." "That provided him another layer of protection from arrest. How could I pursue Susette after being fired from the force? When everyone believes me to be conspiring with anarchists, as well as attempting an assassination? Susette deserves better."

"She deserves the truth. You have hurt her deeply by turning away from her and living recklessly. Your womanizing hasn't helped, either."

Jacques sighed. "No woman has come close to replacing Susette in my heart." He placed a hand on Mira's. "Except for you."

"You are confusing our lust for love." Mira slid her hand from his. "I won't deny it. I have dreamed about us making love. What stops me is knowing you and Susette belong together. She loves you, Jacques, in spite of everything."

"She needs to move on, find someone more deserving of her." Jacques' voice cracked with emotion. "There can be no future for Susette and me. I am under Marius Jourdain's control forever, Mirabelle."

"Jacques, we cannot let that continue." Mira beat a defiant fist against his shoulder. "You told him tonight you were through. What is he demanding of you?"

"For me to lose the race tomorrow." Defeat resonated in Jacques' voice. "Renault and Peugeot are the only two of the twelve automobiles racing tomorrow capable of reaching the top speed of 50 kilometers, so either I or the driver of the Renault will win. The champion manufacturer receives international kudos and investment money to fund the next prototype. Marius approached someone on the Renault team. He told them he would ensure Peugeot loses, for the payoff of one thousand francs and a Renault automobile."

"And if you win?" Mira knew the answer but needed Jacques to confirm it.

"He will go public about Luc Roget. Bernadette will learn all I have hidden from her. If Susette thinks she still loves me, once she hears I am a murderer, her love will turn to disgust."

Jacques balled a fist and twisted it into his other hand. "I hoped if I confronted him, offered him the money as one last payout and told him I no longer will be extorted, he would retreat. But . . ."

Mira understood without Jacques finishing his thought.

The Ferris wheel ceased moving. They dangled at the highest point in its rotation. The passenger car pitched to and fro.

Mira met Jacques' gaze once more.

His eyes relayed his torment.

She cupped his face with her hands and kissed him gently. "We will find a way to right everything. Marius Jourdain must be stopped."

The wheel began moving on its downward journey.

Mira leaned into Jacques' embrace and looked into the star-strewn sky, feeling shredded by his secret. How had he lived with it all this time? No wonder he distanced himself from Susette with his womanizing and reckless, amoral persona.

Breaking Marius Jourdain's hold over you is the key to restoring your reputation—and my return through the portal. Even if Bernadette must learn the truth in the process. She and Susette both love you too much not to forgive you. At least, I hope so.

THIRTY-TWO

The horror of what Jacques had shared weighed heavily upon Mira's spirit. When they reached the American Girls' Club, Mira bid Jacques a tearful good night.

Her encouragement for him to tell M. Peugeot about Marius Jourdain's threats had fallen on deaf ears. He appeared resigned to losing the race and remaining under the criminal's hold. She could not let that happen.

Upon entering her room, Mira gaped at Winnie's strewn bedclothes, open bureau drawers, and armoire door. All of her belongings were gone.

Mira feared Winnie had robbed her. She let out a whoosh of relief when she found all her belongings intact.

My moonstone ring must have satisfied you, huh, Winnie? Or, did you not have enough time to make a clean sweep of everything?

Sleep did not come to Mira easily. What she'd learned from Jacques replayed in her subconscious, and bad dreams awakened her again and again. At the first hint of daybreak, she rose and bathed before ringing for Mme Newton to help her dress.

I need to find out why you helped Winnie dress for a night out when you claim to be shocked by that very behavior of hers.

A tap came at her door, and Mira opened it to Mme Newton's arrival. *"Bonjour. Merci* for coming. I am dressing for the Olympic events at Bois de Vincennes. M. Thibaut has a car coming for me."

"How exciting, Mirabelle." Mme Newton entered the room. "Any memory returning?"

The woman's expression and tone expressed maternal concern, but Mira doubted her sincerity. She decided to answer the question with one of her own.

"Why were you helping Winnie dress last night? Did you know she went to Moulin Rouge to consort with a known criminal?"

Mme Newton's face flushed.

"I followed her there." Mira flung her arms around the room. "You know she is gone?"

"Yes." Mme Newton wrung her hands together. "I beg you will keep my confidence?"

"Perhaps."

"Oh, my. I am embarrassed." Mme Newton perched upon Winnie's bed, her face drained of color. "The truth is that the girl is my niece."

"Your niece?" Mira's mouth fell agape.

"Yes. My sister Alice's daughter. I warned Alice not to marry the horrible Flanagan man. A Catholic."

Mira winced.

What prejudice for a minister's wife.

"When Winnie began pursuing undesirable young men, Alice asked for Winnie to come here, in hopes she would find a proper young man."

Mira gave a cynical grin. "Find a wealthy non-Catholic Frenchman, you mean. Winnie told me of her family's post-War dire financial circumstances. Marrying a wealthy European, preferably one with a title, would be a solution for them all."

"Yes. You have interpreted the situation correctly." Mme Newton let out a deep sigh. "I did arrange for her to meet suitable young men, but she could not bridle the streak of wildness in her. The fruit doesn't fall far, you know. She is so like her mother."

She lowered her voice. "Except she has the coloring of an Irish girl."

Mira winced once again.

How much more despicable can this woman become?

Mme Newton wrung her hands more energetically. The pitch of her voice rose. "However, the true reason why my husband did not evict Winifred Flanagan is not because she is my niece. It is because she caught him in the kitchen, late one night after all had retired. He had been partaking of too much of the cooking sherry."

She brushed a hand over her forehead. "No need to parse words. She found my husband drunk. Winnie threatened to awaken the entire house so all could see him in disrepair. I had to protect him, so I agreed to look the other way regarding her behavior, no matter how I disapproved."

Mira gestured to her empty ring finger. "The night you assisted her in dressing you must have seen my moonstone ring on her hand. Yet, you allowed her to steal it?"

"She would not take it off." Mme Newton's tears flowed. "I feared she would strike me again. She slapped me once before."

The last bit of information moved Mira to a tad of pity, but it faded quickly. "Do you know where she has gone?"

"No. She said she no longer needed to remain with me. I warned her she needed to remain close for medical care." Mme Newton's face now flushed scarlet.

"Her delivery time is approaching, isn't it?"

"You know?" Mme placed her hands upon her cheeks. "How stupid of her, unmarried and in a family way. I dread letting Alice know how wayward she has become. However, as harsh as it sounds, I am glad she's gone."

"Don't concern yourself with the infant's welfare. We wouldn't want scandal." Mira smiled cloyingly. "I hope your husband has sought assistance for his drinking problem?" She wanted her words to sting.

Mme Newton stood and held herself haughtily. "You rang me to assist you in dressing?"

"*Oui.*" Mira retrieved the dress Mlle Brodeur hoped to model at the car race.

"Lovely," Mme Newton exclaimed. "You will look beautiful."

Upon completion of dressing, Mira dismissed Mme Newton without agreeing to the woman's begging to keep secret what she'd divulged. Studying herself in the mirror, Mira admired the gorgeous Paquin design.

The pale green silk taffeta accented her reddish-auburn hair and the bodice's neckline showed cleavage, helped along by the corset. The thin sash accented the corseted wasp waist.

While pinning in place the large picture hat adorned with tulle, flowers, and plumes, Mira remembered the hat pin she'd carried in case to defend herself. Learning Jacques' secret confirmed the danger Marius Jourdain posed. The hat pin hardly seemed enough if she engaged in a confrontation with the criminal, but it would have to suffice.

What will you do, Jacques, about the automobile race? If only I could intervene and stop Marius's blackmailing of you. Will he be at the car races today, to intimidate you further? Will Winnie be with him? She is so close to giving birth.

Mira knew the harrowing statistics of maternal mortality in this era. Many women died in childbirth, of puerperal fever or sepsis, hemorrhaging, eclampsia, or other emergencies not diagnosed and treated properly in 1900. Many babies did not survive. Despite Winnie's choice of a criminal life, her baby should be born safely, and she should live to mother it.

What help can I provide her, though? She has chosen the life of a criminal.

After tugging on her gloves, Mira collected her parasol and handbag, with the coin purse and hat pin secured inside, and headed to the lobby. A Peugeot awaited her at curbside. Bernadette and Siméon sat in its back seat, a small basket between them. Bernadette waved energetically, a broad smile upon her face.

Mira returned the wave. "*Bonjour.*"

"Mirabelle, you are gorgeous. Isn't it a grand day for an Olympic motoring race?" Bernadette patted the top of the basket. "We have brought refreshments to keep our energy high to cheer Jaco, though the entire event frightens me to my bones."

"I am sure Jacques will drive safely. He knows how you worry," Mira answered.

After the chauffeur assisted her into the passenger seat, she shifted sideways to smile at the young couple. A surge of protective love toward the girl overcame Mira.

Bernadette would be devastated if she ever learned the truth about her parents and her beloved Jaco's part in it. Mira understood why Jacques went to extremes to protect Bernadette's family myth of a loving mother and father who died explainable deaths.

What would he do today? Would he succumb to Marius's extortion and purposefully lose the race to continue protecting his ward? She could see him doing so. He loved Bernadette as if she were his own.

Mira clapped a hand onto her large picture hat and braced her feet into the floorboard to balance herself during the bumpy ride. If her worry over Jacques was not preoccupying her, she could enjoy the sights they passed on this sunny spring day. The picturesque journey to Bois de Vincennes took them by the Luxembourg Gardens, Notre Dame, and across Pont de Sully bridge, where they drove for a while along the Seine River.

The chauffeur pulled to the roadside by the Porte Reuilly exhibition entrance into the large Bois de Vincennes Park. Remaining silent, he rushed to assist Mira from her seat.

Bernadette and Siméon scrambled from the back of the automobile. In one hand, Siméon carried the basket. He grasped Bernadette's hand in his other.

With a tip of his hat, the driver left them.

"Do either of you know where we are to go?" Mira asked, holding her parasol aloft. She felt like a speck amongst what she estimated to be hundreds of people streaming into the park.

"*Oui.*" Siméon swung the basket straight ahead. "The race is around Lac Daumesnil. There is a grandstand where we may sit instead of having to stand with the other spectators in the roped-off area to the side of the track. We follow along to de la Croix Rouge, and we should see the stands from there."

Bernadette grasped Mira's hand.

The three passed signs pointing to the large warehouse- type structures where motor cars were on exhibit before entering the racing venue. Mira noted both the spectator stand and the large, high platform built for the racing officials seemed hastily constructed. The raw wood was unpainted.

A large wooden placard erected behind the officials' platform would show competitors results. The black flag to signal the start and finish of the races flew from the stand.

Top dust swirled from the unpaved track, tickling Mira's nose. She could almost taste the dirt and the contagious excitement vibrating in the air.

To the left from where they entered the lake area stood twelve tents pitched in a clearing of manicured grass. The automobiles to be raced were parked under each.

"Look!" Bernadette waved to a group of nurses setting up a first aid area by the racetrack. "It's Susette."

Mira joined in waving to the nurse, wondering if Jacques knew of her presence. "The medical team is an extra precaution, I'm sure."

"Don't worry." Simeon leaned toward her and kissed her cheek. "Let's find Jacques to wish him luck, not that he'll need it."

Everywhere Mira looked she saw clusters of men wearing either straw hats or flat caps and long duster coats of white or black. Other men wore formal day suits, and silk top hats adorned their heads. Elaborately dressed women holding parasols strolled about, their large hats providing flashes of color. She wondered which of the ladies might be modeling for a fashion house, as Mme Paquin requested of her.

"There he is." Bernadette rushed ahead to the tent marked by a shield-shaped logo with the profile of a snarling lion and the word Peugeot above it.

At the tap of Bernadette's hand upon his shoulder, Jacques turned and caught her in a hug. Mira thought he seemed pleased to see Siméon. His gaze landed upon her, and she tossed him a wave.

Mira made her way to the tent and Siméon followed. They stood amidst the men who were working through the checklist for the car.

"Look at you, Jaco." Bernadette made open circles with her hands and brought them to her eyes, pantomiming wearing goggles. "How dashing you are, in your white overalls, cap, and goggles."

"Amusing." Jacques smiled.

Mira read the anxiety in his manner.

"You and Siméon can help the crew with the checklist." "*Oui.*" Bernadette almost skipped toward the man holding a clipboard.

Siméon placed the basket on the ground and picked up an air pump to test the air in the back tires.

Jacques took Mira's hands. "Thank you for coming. You look beautiful."

"*Merci.* Bernadette is correct. You do look quite dashing." She pulled him toward her and dropped her voice low. "Have you seen Marius?"

Jacques shook his head. "I have not, but does it matter? What choice do I have but to do as he demands? Bernadette is more important than winning a race."

"Marius will continue imposing threats upon you and keep forcing you into unethical actions." Mira's breath came shakily. "We must find a way for this to end."

I need it to end more than you know. I do want to right the wrongs that have ruined your life, but I have to so the portal will re-open.

Jacques rolled his hands into fists and shook them at her. "How? I see no way out of the handcuffs Marius has placed upon me except for his death. I admit it. I have considered murdering him. I've killed one man."

"Jacques, you must not condemn yourself for an accident."

"Who else is there to condemn?"

"No one else witnessed what happened, except for Marius. How do you know he is telling you the truth?" "Why would he lie? And if so, why choose me? There were many police officers at the scene. He could have accused any of them."

"Did any other policeman approach M. Roget?"

"Only I checked on him. When I reached where he lay, Marius knelt on the ground by him."

"Was Marius harmed?"

"I saw blood on his face, his hands, and his clothing from trying to assist M. Roget."

"Had you ever met Marius before?"

"No. I wish to God that I had not met him then."

"I do wonder. How in all the confusion could Marius clearly see that what you threw struck Luc Roget?"

"He held the heavy match holder covered in blood. Why would I doubt his claim he saw me throw it?"

Mira shook her head, unconvinced. "I don't trust him or what he says."

The revving of the Peugeot caught Jacques' attention. "I must prepare for the race. I will have someone walk you to the stands."

"Do nothing reckless, Jacques. Concentrate on your driving. Follow your conscience. Be safe."

He squeezed her hands. "I will be safe. For those I love."

Mira's insides swirled. He included her among those he loved.

Love of close friends, not paramours. But love, nonetheless.

"Jacques." Mira pulled her hands from his grasp. "Susette is here, with a medical team. Be careful, for her sake as well."

"Mirabelle, come," Bernadette called. "We must go to our seats."

Jacques smiled. "Thank you for caring about me and Bernadette. I'll look for you in the stand."

Mira walked from him, unsure if Jacques would stand up to Marius. Her doubt distracted her from responding to those complimenting her Paquin outfit. Luckily, Bernadette enjoyed chatting with them.

Seated in the grandstand, Mira closed her parasol. Her bird's-eye view took in the medical tent. She counted at least five nurses, with Susette in charge.

Susette should know how Marius Jourdain was manipulating Jacques and why Jacques felt unworthy of her love. This criminal had ruined Susette's life, as well as Jacques'.

What if I cannot return to my real life? If I were to remain in 1900 Paris? Would I be so altruistic about reuniting Susette and Jacques? The physical connection between us is real, but he doesn't look at me the way he looks at Susette. The way a man looks at a woman who owns his heart.

Mira dismissed her what-ifs. Jacques and Susette belonged together. She would ensure that outcome before she traveled back through the Carousel's portal.

She craned her neck around to study the other onlookers. The covered seating at the top of the grandstand was divided into sections by car manufacturers, with the middle section set aside for French government officials. A man wearing a police commander's uniform seemed keen on observing the proceedings through binoculars.

"Do you see someone familiar, Mirabelle?" Bernadette looked toward the man, and her face whitened. "Do you know M. Lépine? The Prefect of Police?"

"No, I do not know him. Why are you upset at the sight of him?"

"He is the one who dismissed Jaco from the force." Bernadette almost spit the words. "Because of him, Jaco is endangering his life by racing these contraptions for M. Peugeot. Jaco faced danger as a police detective but for the greater good, not for entertainment."

Siméon put his arm around Bernadette. "Try not to worry. Jacques knows what he is doing."

Mira hoped Siméon was right. She glanced quickly at the Prefect Lépine once more, and their gaze met. His overt interest in her could not be mis-interpreted. She wondered if she could parlay it into an introduction. If he leaned toward believing Jacques to be innocent, she needed to convince him to declare his stance publicly.

Perhaps if he became besotted with me, I could lead him into making such a declaration?

Her skin crawled over considering seduction in exchange for Lépine's assistance. If she must stoop to enticement, she would. But only enticement. She would draw the line there. A parade of vehicles began to promenade on the track, being driven slowly by the grandstand for inspection. The styles and sizes ranged from petite voiturettes to huge steam- powered omnibuses. According to Bernadette and Siméon's running narrative, those in the parade were celebrities of the day, including Renault, Peugeot, Michelin, and M. Picard, the Commissioner of the Exhibition.

Once the important attendees were situated in their place in the grand-stand box, the race car drivers of the twelve automobiles drove onto the track, accelerating to a fast speed and then braking fast into an assigned position.

"Do you see Jacques?" Bernadette pointed. "He's there."

Mira sought him. The tree growth on the two islands in the middle of the lake would partially block the view of the track opposite where they sat, but the start and finish line were in front of the grandstand.

Bernadette nudged Siméon. "Do you know the length of the track?"

He nodded. "I asked one of the men preparing the automobile. It is fifty kilometers, and they lap it three times. The braking we saw is required to demonstrate control of the automobile. Once the race commences, the allowed speed is between thirty to fifty kilometers, although it has been said none have accelerated to the top speed before."

Bernadette clasped her hands. "I pray Jaco will not do so."

Mira hoped not as well, but she could tell Siméon's expression reflected her own opinion. Jacques would not hesitate to push to the top speed.

Unless he decides to pull back to lose, as Marius demands.

Siméon continued his explanation. "After each lap, the automobiles return to their tent for refueling, tire, and brake checking. We are fortunate to have seats and to have brought refreshments. The day will be long."

At the sight of an official on the high observation deck raising the flag, Mira said a prayer for Jacques' safety.

Upon the flag's dramatic drop, the cars accelerated, and the engines roared over the noise of the spectators. Jacques edged to the lead, sending dust flying behind him when he swerved into the first curve. Once he reached the opposite side, Mira lost sight of him.

Bernadette hid her face against Siméon, her words coming in anxious pants. "I shall never watch Jacques race an automobile again."

Siméon sent a crooked grin to Mira. "I have another shoulder, if you need it."

Mira answered with a slight shake of her head. Her fear would be at the closing minutes.

What will you do, Jacques? Win? Or, let Marius?

THIRTY-THREE

Awe descended over Mira while witnessing this Olympic event. Her attention remained riveted on Jacques' race car. The drivers careened into the home stretch of race one, sending dust spiraling behind them. Jacques remained in the lead, crossing the finish line well ahead of the Renault and others. According to Siméon's explanation, the cars left the track for inspection.

"*Rafraîchissements.*" Siméon opened the basket filled with mini loaves of bread, cheeses, fruits, and stoppered glass bottles of lemonade.

Mira accepted a lemonade, but her thirst longed for a cold beer. While partaking of the picnic, she felt eyes upon her. She looked around but could detect no one watching her. Mira tried to dismiss the foreboding feeling, but it lingered, keeping her on edge. When the automobiles emerged onto the course for the next race, her impatience for the end of the entire event kept her even more on edge.

Jacques held the lead again, until the Renault pulled slightly ahead at the finish line.

Mira wondered if Jacques held back to ensure the Renault would be in position of winning in the third lap, to give Marius what he demanded. That possibility and being miserably overheated under the afternoon's intense sun sickened her.

Her body screamed for release from the weight of the gown and all the undergarments binding her tightly. Her picture hat, though providing shade, weighed heavily upon her head. Her palms sweated inside the gloves, which she wished she could strip from her hands.

When the third and last race commenced, dread prickled her skin. What would happen if Jacques refused Marius's demand? Would the criminal tell Bernadette everything, devastating her? Or was he blustering?

Once more, Mira felt eyes upon her. She looked around, as inconspicuously as possible, but could not detect who observed her. When the cars swerved into the turn heading to the finish line, Mira caught a flash of carrot red hair among the spectators.

So, it's been you watching me, Winifred Flanagan. Where is your comrade-in-crime, Marius Jourdain? I know he must be nearby, waiting for Jacques to do his bidding and lose.

The cars neared the finish. Unlike races one and two, Jacques slowed behind the Renault, making the competitor's first place win certain. The spectators in the stands stood to cheer their driver onward.

"*Aller plus vite,*" Siméon yelled, urging Jacques to drive faster.

Bernadette clasped her hands over her face to avoid the scene.

Mira's pulse thrummed erratically.

Please, do not give in to Marius, Jacques. Whatever happens, we can get through it. Bernadette will understand and forgive you.

Another car came from behind and passed Jacques, pulling alongside the Renault to leave a gap between the two cars, both within striking distance of the finish line. Jacques accelerated.

Mira wrung her hands.

Did my plea to win reach you?

His Peugeot threaded between the two cars, and Jacques streaked at top speed past them over the finish line. The wave of the flag declared him the winner of this lap and the overall race.

"He must have reached 50 kilometers." Siméon gasped. "He is losing control!"

Bernadette fell into Siméon's arms, sobbing.

Terror gripped Mira. Her gaze went to Susette, who stood frozen. Mira assumed they were both saying prayers for Jacques to control his fast-speeding automobile.

Instead of slowing, the Peugeot accelerated at a faster speed toward the first curve of the track. Jacques steered it into the turn. The churning dust from the tires created a thick cloud, obscuring him from view.

A hush fell across the spectators. Those who stood behind the roped-off track scattered in fear of collision.

The Peugeot emerged from the dust cloud swerving once again. It tipped sideways onto the two wheels of the driver side and slid to a skidding stop.

Thrown from the automobile, Jacques lay on his side motionless.

"Siméon, take care of Bernadette." Mira said and scrambled from the stand. She ran toward Jacques, a prayer tumbling from her lips. "Please, be alive. Be alive. Be alive."

Susette reached Jacques before Mira and rolled him onto his back.

Mira sank onto the ground next to him.

Susette looked up, her face drawn. "Mirabelle. Thank God you are here for him. Use your lap as a pillow for his head."

Mira did as Susette instructed. Removing Jacques' goggles and hat, Mira brushed the dirt from his face while trying not to gag at the bloody scrape across his forehead.

"Use this to cleanse the wound." Susette provided a dampened washcloth smelling of antiseptic. "I will tend to his arm. He has dislocated his shoulder."

Mira again did as Susette instructed.

Jacques' eyes fluttered open. "Mirabelle."

"Shh." Mira stroked his cheek. "You will be fine. Susette is here."

"I am a fool. Why couldn't I lose?" Jacques struggled against Mira, attempting to stand. "I must find Marius before he confronts Bernadette." With a moan, he fell against Mira.

She cradled him, shushing him.

Susette glared at Mira. "Keep him calm."

"Jacques, let Susette treat you," Mira whispered. "We will deal with Marius."

"Marius?" Susette looked at Mira, her expression filled with questions. "You will tell me later, but now, we concentrate on Jacques."

The horse-drawn ambulance arrived where Jacques lay. Two nurses exited from it and hurried to Susette.

"Jacques, we must brace you into a seated position." Susette directed Mira to allow the nurses to take her place.

Mira remained kneeling at his side.

Susette leaned over Jacques and spoke quietly. "I must reset your shoulder. It will not be pleasant, but you will feel relief once I do so."

She held his arm and placed a hand firmly upon his shoulder. "Are you prepared?"

Jacques spoke through gritted teeth. "Go a—"

Susette performed the procedure before he could complete his sentence.

He yowled in pain.

A nurse offered Jacques a sip of water, but he waved her off.

Mira took it from the nurse's hand and held the cup to Jacques' lips. "Please. A swallow."

Once Jacques took a sip, he drank the entire cup. "*Merci*, Mirabelle."

He smiled weakly toward Susette, love shining in his eyes. "Once again, Susette, I am your patient. *Merci*."

Susette placed a palm on his cheek, tears trickling down her face.

Mira pressed a hand against her pounding heart. What would happen now that Jacques stood up against Marius's extortion demand?

A man's voice reached them. "You are a fortunate man, Jacques."

Mira rose to her feet to the arrival of M. Lépine with M. Peugeot. The two men did not address her but focused their attention on Jacques, who remained attended upon by Susette and the two nurses.

M. Peugeot tipped his hat to the spectators in the stands, who were hushed at the spectacle of Jacques' crash. "Thibaut, raise your hand to let the crowd know you have survived."

Jacques waved with his uninjured arm.

The spectators clapped and yelled their hurrahs.

"You pushed the speed to the maximum." M. Peugeot frowned. "Did you lose control?"

"I did not." Jacques gritted his teeth against his pain. "The brake failed to engage. I managed to force the car onto its side to bring it to a stop."

M. Peugeot gave an authoritative nod. "Then we have more testing at higher speeds needed to ensure safety. Heal quickly, M. Thibaut. You must continue as our test driver."

"M. Peugeot is correct. You demonstrate excellent driver control, Jacques." Prefect Lépine shrugged. "It's unfortunate you have not shown such control in other aspects of your life."

Lépine and Peugeot turned without a farewell and walked toward the mechanics gathered around the wrecked automobile.

Mira started after the men.

"Mirabelle." Susette scrambled to her feet and grabbed Mira's arm. "Where are you going?"

"I must set the record straight." Mira wriggled from Susette's hold. "Prefect Lépine has to know about Marius Jourdain."

"What about that criminal? What have you learned, Mirabelle?"

"Your suspicions about Marius ruining Jacques' life are correct, Susette."

Mira left Susette calling after her and rushed to where the inspector stood. "Prefect Lépine. May we speak?"

The man faced Mira, glancing over her from head to toe. "I am flattered such a beautiful woman pursues me."

"We have not been introduced." Ignoring his flirtatious comment, Mira held her hand out. "My name is Mirabelle Montgomery."

He took her hand and bowed slightly over it. "You are American? And, an *acquaintance* of M. Thibaut?"

Mira's face reddened from his inference. "M. Thibaut is a *friend*, Prefect Lépine. A good man whom you released from the police force on the word of a criminal."

"A criminal?" The police prefect narrowed his eyes. "What do you mean?"

"M. Thibaut is guilty of nothing except defending your city the night of the student riot. An innocent bystander, Luc Roget, lost his life, leaving his young daughter, Bernadette, orphaned. Having known the girl's mother, Jacques took in Bernadette, becoming her guardian."

"I am aware about the girl." Lépine tapped his walking cane impatiently.

"You are not aware of the entire situation that robbed Jacques Thibaut of his true destiny."

As Mirabelle explained Marius Jourdain's extortion of Jacques, Lépine's unwavering attention emboldened her to leave out no detail.

"Well, well. We have a saying. *Quelqu'un qui met son grain de sel.* It describes one who shares an opinion even when not asked." Lépine ran his hand over his gray beard. "I once held your M. Thibaut in high regard, as M. Peugeot does now. I shall consider your suggestion to review his situation."

"Please." Mira held clasped hands toward Lépine. "Question Jacques today at the hospital. I fear Marius will try to harm Jacques and Bernadette because Jacques drove the Peugeot to victory."

"I see." Lépine struck his walking cane once more against the ground. "I will be returning to my office located by Hôpital Hôtel-Dieu. When Jacques is ready to receive my visit, have word sent to me."

He gave a slight bow. "M. Thibaut is most fortunate to have a beautiful and forceful American woman such as yourself advocating for him." He swiveled on his heels, dismissing her.

Mira exhaled a relieved sigh. Her straightforward and indignant manner appealed to the Police Prefect.

I bet no woman has spoken to you as bluntly as I.

She returned to Jacques, who had been moved onto a stretcher and placed inside the ambulance.

Susette and the other nurses were gathering the first aid materials, preparing for departure. One sat in the vehicle with him.

Mira signaled to her. "May I have a moment with him?" "A moment, only." The nurse climbed from the ambulance and assisted Mira into it.

Mira sat by Jacques and placed his hand to her cheek. "You frightened all of us." She fought tears. "Bernadette will never let you drive an automobile again. It will be back to horses for you."

Jacques gave a small laugh. "Please take care of her for me. Do not take her to the hospital today. She need not see me so battered." His words slurred. "I think Susette gave me something to calm me."

He brought her hand toward his mouth and kissed her palm. Mira could feel the heat from his lips through the glove. "Mirabelle, I am glad I did not die. I would have expelled my last breath without thanking you. I am drawn to you, in spite of my love for Susette."

"I cannot deny I have felt the same. We've fallen into infatuation with each other." Mira stroked his hair from his bandaged forehead, her tears escaping. "We both know you and Susette are meant to be."

"Now possibly we can be. Thanks to you instilling courage within me, courage to rebuke Marius."

"Only because Susette made me aware of your true inner goodness."

"I must explain everything to her." Jacques struggled to sit. "And to Bernadette, also. I cannot lose either."

Mira gently pressed his shoulders to keep him reclined. "There is time for that. You must remain still." She leaned close to whisper. "I believe Marius Jourdain has been lying about how M. Roget died."

"Does it matter? I cannot prove he did not witness what he says." Jacques' eyes shut, but he battled them open again. "Keep Marius from Bernadette, until I can gain my strength to face her."

"I shall." Mira gave him a gentle shake to ensure he remained awake for a moment longer. "Jacques. You must listen. This is important. I have spoken to Prefect Lépine about the riots, the assassination attempt, and Marius blackmailing you. Lépine will visit you at the hospital later to hear your side of the story. He appears sympathetic to you. M. Peugeot's belief in you carries weight. This is your chance to clear your name. Restore your reputation. You must take it."

"How can I thank you? You are giving me back my life." Jacques drew her face toward his, and she pressed an ear close to his lips to hear his fading voice. "Forgive my selfishness. I talk about my heartache while you suffer your own. When I am healed, we shall continue our search for your identity."

"Do not worry. I have found myself, being with you." Mira kissed his cheek. "Rest now. Susette will accompany you to the hospital. Tell her everything. Tell her you love her. Be with her and find happiness."

Jacques' eyes closed.

Mira felt his body relax from the sedative. She kissed his cheek once more. She would locate Marius Jourdain, keep him from Bernadette, and demand from him the truth.

Please, be lying about Luc Roget's death, Marius. You must be lying, for Bernadette's sake.

She stepped from the ambulance.

Susette was gathering the remaining nursing materials into her bag.

Noticing her trembling hands, Mira took the bag from her and closed it.

"*Merci.*" Susette wrapped her arms around herself. "Tell me what you told the inspector."

Mira handed her the nursing bag. "Send for Prefect Lépine once Jacques can be interviewed. Before Lépine comes, though, ask Jacques to tell you what he shared with me last night. Then tell him you love him."

Susette's eyes filled with tears. "I will. You will meet us at the hospital?"

"I will come tonight. First, I must check on Bernadette. Jacques asked me to keep her from seeing him today. I will need the strength of a lioness to hold her back."

Susette embraced her. "You have such strength, and more, Mirabelle Montgomery."

Hurrying from the accident scene, Mira refused to look back. She left Jacques with the woman who loved him and whom he loved.

The future for Jacques, Susette, and Bernadette depended on controlling Marius Jourdain. She would demand the total truth from him about M. Roget's death. He was hiding something. Or lying about something.

Hopefully, the truth will set Jacques free, and myself, as well.

THIRTY-FOUR

Walking toward Siméon and Bernadette, Mira caught a glimpse of carrot-red hair and her heart seized with dread. Winnie was dragging a struggling Bernadette from the stand. Behind them stood Marius, with an unconscious Siméon slumped against him.

"No, no, no." She quickened her pace, fighting against the heaviness of her long dress.

Marius let Siméon fall into the grandstand and joined Winnie.

Together they started their escape with the abducted Bernadette. The girl's head lolled against them, as if she were drugged. Her limp body slowed their progress.

"Stop, now!" None of the departing spectators reacted to Mira's screams. She continued running, retrieving the hat pin stowed in her small purse. If she used the pin to attack Winnie, surely Marius would release Bernadette to help the mother of his unborn?

She didn't wish to harm the baby. She aimed for Winnie's neck and plunged the hat pin into it.

Screeching like a wild animal in distress, Winnie released Bernadette.

Marius shouted in anger. "*Ferme ta bouche.*" Instead of aiding Winnie, Marius continued to drag Bernadette forward. "Marius. Help me." Winnie screamed. "I have been stabbed." She whimpered.

Marius turned, keeping his grip on Bernadette strong. "Come, now. Help me." His gaze met Mira's. "You. Let her go."

Mira held the hat pin against Winnie's cheek and addressed Marius. "No. You let Bernadette go."

"No, Mlle Montgomery." Marius pressed a knife against Bernadette's side.

"Please." Knowing she had no choice, Mira dropped the hat pin. "Do not hurt her."

"Wise action." Marius nodded. "Now, smile, as if you are among friends helping a poor girl who has become ill from the heat."

Winnie pressed a handkerchief against the back of her neck, cutting an angry glance at Mira. The moonstone ring glistened from her hand. "You have provided us with another ransom, *la chienne.*" With a trill of laughter, she looped her arm with Mira's.

Marius encircled Bernadette's waist with one arm. He kept his other arm bent at the elbow with the knife in hand, pressing against Bernadette's rib cage.

Unable to disentangle from Winnie's hold, Mira walked by her side. She sent pleading glances to those passing, but no one paid attention.

The walk to the exhibition entrance seemed miles long. At the street, a poorly maintained *fiacre* awaited, its horse old and in poor health and the driver in tattered clothing and a battered top hat.

Marius lifted Bernadette into it and flicked the knife toward Mira. "In."

She stepped into the cab and sat by Bernadette, who fell against her. She shook her gently. "Bernadette?"

The girl's eyes fluttered open. "Mirabelle? Where are we?"

Marius assisted Winnie into the cab, and they sat opposite.

Winnie closed her eyes and rested her head against the back of the seat. Her hands lay folded over her pregnant stomach.

Mira assumed the due date must be imminent, judging how low Winnie was carrying. She almost felt sorry for the woman because she had to be in such discomfort. She did feel sorry for the baby, having these two as parents.

When the cab lurched into motion, Bernadette fell into a semi-conscious state once again.

Mira lay the girl's head in her lap and glowered at Marius. "What have you given her?" "Tincture of laudanum. She'll survive." "What about the boy?"

"Same. He has come to his senses by now. I stuffed a note in his hand addressed to the great Jacques Thibaut." "You mean a ransom note."

"Yes. You have only Jacques to blame. He won the race, and I lost my payoff. Now, I must obtain the money I need in another way."

"By kidnapping us."

"You were not part of the plan until you made yourself part of it."

Mira looked out the cab's window. "Where are you taking us?"

"Ahh. Where time and death come to cross their scythes."

Her skin crawled at the imagery evoked by his words. "I don't understand."

"Do not bother yourself with understanding." He drew the shades on the cab's windows. "Lift prayers Jacques can afford to pay for your release in addition to the girl's."

Mira remained silent the rest of the journey, praying Siméon recovered and took the note to the police, not Jacques. Perhaps to Prefect Lépine, himself.

When the cab stopped, Marius awakened Winnie. "We are here. Go and light the candles." He waved his knife at Bernadette. "I need her to be able to walk."

"Bernadette." Mira shook her gently. "Wake up."

The girl stirred and sat up, swaying side-to-side and blinking hard. "Where are we?" She held her forehead in her hands. "Oh, my head is pounding."

Mira placed her arm around Bernadette's shoulder. "Are you feeling strong enough to walk? You can lean on me."

"I'm not sure." Bernadette dropped her hands to her lap. Her face paled. "You are the man who followed me." She nudged closer to Mira, her body shaking. "Do you remember, Mirabelle? I pointed him out the day I met you."

"Yes, I am he." Marius jutted the scarred side of his face toward her.

She cowered against Mira.

Marius sneered with amusement over frightening the girl. "Thanks to Jacques Thibaut, once you see me, you do not forget."

Mira stared at his scar. When had an altercation occurred between them, leaving Marius so injured? A shivery sensation moved through her. Only Marius could confirm what she suspected. She needed leverage over him before he would do so.

Marius kicked the cab's door and pointed the knife at Mira. "You get out and join Winnie at the entry door where she awaits. I'll bring this little one. Remember, I will have this knife pointed at her heart."

"Do not hurt her. Please." Mira stepped from the cab and looked around to gain her bearings. Within a moment she recognized the location, closed on this day. The Catacombs. The place of 6,000 people's bones. Where time and death come to cross their scythes.

Sylvie's jest came to her. "We know how you adore scary places."

The thumping of her blood passed through Mira's ears. Her body flashed cold, then hot. Her breathing came sharp and shallow. Her vision shrank, dark and narrow, and stars burst before her.

I cannot enter this place of death.

Marius's threatening voice tore through her faintness. "What are you doing? Get moving."

"I cannot." She gulped her words out, shuddering. "Mirabelle. I am with you. You can do this." Bernadette walked beside her, whispering, "We shall not be here long. Death did not claim Jaco today, so he could rescue us."

Mira squeezed the girl's hand, hoping he would. She took a step toward the entrance, forcing herself to breathe through the fear.

Winnie awaited them inside the door. In her hands she held squared pieces of cardboard with lighted candles poked through each. "Come through. Take a candle."

Obeying her snapped order, Mira went first, with Bernadette close behind her.

When Marius closed the door, darkness descended except for the illumination of the candles casting their singular glows. He lit a torch whose flame provided them with more light.

"Follow me." Winnie began her descent of the narrow spiral stone staircase with triangular steps.

Mira stepped gingerly. She rued the fashions of the era which encumbered lithe movement. Having to grip the candle in one hand and the banister in the other meant she couldn't hoist the long skirt. She could easily trip.

So could Winnie. One misstep causing a fall could kill her baby, if not them both. Greed must have overcome her good sense.

"Is it terribly steep?" Bernadette's voice relayed her trepidation.

"Go slowly, and you will be fine. Do not hurry." Mira projected more calmness than she felt.

At the first curve of the stairwell, Mira could see Bernadette with Marius behind her, his knife pointed at the girl's back. She called out, with hopes of reassuring her. "See? It's not too awful."

Bernadette tried to put on a brave face, but her lower lip quivered.

Mira's heart went out to the scared girl.

Together, we will survive this.

She noticed the air turning cooler and more humid the farther they descended. Remaining underground for long would prove unpleasant.

When Mira began wondering if the stairs were endless, they finally reached a small hallway leading to a maze of narrow corridors with damp walls and varying ceiling heights. Mira felt lost in a labyrinth of caves.

Winnie led them forward, appearing to know the way.

At last, they came to an archway and stopped.

Marius raised the torch to light the words etched into the keystone: *"Arrete! C'est ici l'Empire de la Mort.* Shall I translate for our American beauty? *Stop! This is the Empire of the Dead."*

Bernadette cringed. Mira pulled her close.

"Beyond here are the bones and skulls of the dead." Marius leered at them. "You will be among them, if Jacques Thibaut does not pay for your release."

His threat galvanized Bernadette into standing tall. "You both shall be the ones to pay, once Jacques rescues us."

"Oh. Oh, my." Winnie looked down. "Marius. The baby is coming."

"What do you mean?" Marius held the torch over her. Mira saw a pool of wetness at Winnie's feet.

Her waters have broken. The fool. How could she be stupid enough to descend into this underground place of death in her state?

"Did you not hear me?" Winnie sank to the floor, dropping her candle. "The baby is coming."

"You." Marius waved the torch at Mira. "Assist her."

When Mira knelt by her, Winnie pushed her away. "I do not want your help."

Mira stood and crossed her arms. "Suit yourself."

"Don't be a fool." Marius held the flaming torch over Winnie, making the woman's red hair appear on fire. "You need her help." He looked at Mira. "What should we do?"

Mira knelt once again by Winnie. "She will begin to feel contractions soon. If we get help quickly, we might be able to take her to a hospital for the birth. Send Bernadette. She knows a nurse."

Marius pushed Bernadette toward Winnie. "The girl will remain. You, go. Return with only the nurse. No one else." He brandished the knife against Bernadette. "If you return with police, I will kill her."

"Do not be stupid, Marius. I should remain with Winnie." Mira spoke angrily. "I assume you planned for Winnie to watch us while you met Jacques for the ransom. Your plan has fallen apart. Let Bernadette go for help."

"You know nothing about my plan. Bernadette goes nowhere, but you will. I repeat. If you return with police, she will die."

"Go, Mirabelle." Bernadette nodded toward her. "You are brave enough to find your way out and back."

"I will return as quickly as possible." She studied Winnie for a moment before addressing her. "You cannot give birth in all those clothes. While I am gone, Bernadette will help you undress to your chemise. Use your cape to lie on and your dress as a blanket."

Bernadette knelt by them. "What if the baby starts to come before you return?"

Mira tapped the watch pinned to Bernadette's blouse. "Once her contractions begin, time them."

"How will I know her contractions have begun?"

"Winnie will know." Mira stood. "Hopefully, her labor will progress slowly. But keep track. The nurse will want to know how close the contractions have become."

"Oh, Mirabelle." Bernadette held a palm to her forehead. "I am frightened."

"I know, but you must be calm for Winnie." Mira unpenned Bernadette's watch and handed it to her. "When you remove her hat, use one of her hat pins to scratch the timing into the wall."

Marius poked the torch toward them. "What are you two whispering about?"

"I am instructing Bernadette what to do while I am gone." Mira stepped close to him. "If the girl is harmed, you will pay with your infant's life." Her threat against the baby sickened her, but a man such as Marius would understand only viciousness.

Marius let out a disdainful laugh. "You have no power over this situation." He threw handcuffs at her. "Cuff the girl to Winnie."

"No." Mira swept her hand toward Winnie. "How can Bernadette help her if they are chained together?"

Marcus lunged toward her. "Do as you are told, or both you and Bernadette will pay with your lives, as will your dear Jaco."

Mira stooped to pick up the handcuffs. She fastened Bernadette and Winnie wrists, whispering, "Don't worry, Bernadette. I will be back quickly with help."

Bernadette raised her clasped hand and gave a slight grin. "I will be here."

"That's my girl." Mira shot her an encouraging glance. She hoisted her skirt and hurried from them.

Gripping the candle, she held it high to light the path through the labyrinth of hallways. Her layers of clothing hung heavily upon her sweaty, clammy body. Reaching the stairwell, she peered upward with dread. The climb would be arduous.

One step at a time Mira. Each step brings you one step closer to those who will help.

With determination, she began the ascent. Her legs ached with each step she took, but she continued climbing. She fought gagging over the musky odor of the catacomb's dankness.

Halfway, she lost her footing and stumbled forward, tearing her skirt, and grazing her shins against the step's edge. Her cry of pain echoed through the steep, narrow stairwell. Choking back tears, she rubbed the injury.

You cannot let the pain stop you, Mira. Keep going. Cry later.

She pressed onward, thinking of how she must rescue Bernadette and of the poor baby about to be born. By the time she reached the door leading outside, her muscles throbbed as if on fire.

Mira stumbled into the warmth of the sun, squinting against the light until her vision adjusted. The cab remained parked at the curb. She needed to be careful in approaching its driver, assuming he was conspiring with the kidnappers. He must be convinced that Marius allowed her freedom to fetch help from the hospital.

"*Bonjour,*" she called. "*La fille est malade. Marius dit de m'emmener* à *l'Hôtel-Dieu.*"

With a grunt, he nodded.

Mira entered the *fiacre* and crumpled against the seat. She prayed Winnie's labor would be slow and the baby would not go into distress until she returned with Susette and the police.

Did Marius love Winnie enough to barter his confession of his crimes for her and their baby's medical care? Mira intended to find out. She needed Marius to be arrested for *all* his crimes to clear Jacques' name of the assassination attempt and of what happened to Luc Roget the night of the riots.

Then, Le Veille, you will reopen the Carousel portal, and I will return home, after I tell Jacques the truth about me. I cannot disappear from his life with no explanation. Can I?

THIRTY-FIVE

When Mira arrived at Hôtel-Dieu, she asked the driver to wait. He tugged the edge of his tattered top hat to acknowledge her request.

You don't know you're on the verge of arrest. Surprise.

Mira rushed into the high-ceilinged lobby, she blundered face-to-face into Prefect Lépine standing at the lobby desk, flanked by two police officers.

"Mlle Montgomery?"

She caught sight of herself in the mirror behind the lobby desk and understood his shock. Grime streaked her face, and her hat sat comically askew upon her head. Strands of hair were dislodged from her upsweep. Her tattered outfit carried smears of dirt and dust. Her once-white gloves were blackened.

"Prefect Lépine. I have escaped from being kidnapped by Marius Jourdain and Winifred Flanagan." Mira blurted out the situation while pressing a hand to her chest, trying to control her irregular breathing. "Jacque's ward, Bernadette, is still captive."

Lépine rapped his knuckles on the desk.

The startled nurse who had been staring at Mira from behind the desk jumped.

Rapping his knuckles on the desk again, this time in sync with his words, Lépine spoke brusquely to the woman. "Call for Nurse Godard, immediately."

Mira rested upon the lobby's bench where Jacques had sat the night of the bridge collapse. "The driver of the *fiacre* waiting at the curbside is an accomplice in the kidnapping." Lépine ordered an officer to arrest him before joining Mira on the bench. He maintained a posture stiff and regal befitting his rank. "It is fortuitous you found me here. I have come to visit M. Thibaut. You say these two kidnappers sent a ransom note?"

"Marius Jourdain sent Siméon Aubert to Jacques with it." Mira twisted her hands in her lap nervously. "You know nothing of it?"

"I have just arrived to visit Jacques. Nurse Godard is preparing him to receive me." He studied Mira, frowning. "I shall order you a sedative to calm you after such an ordeal." "Absolutely not. I will return with Susette and the police to rescue Bernadette. I suggest you come, as well."

"The presence of the prefect should be unnecessary." Lépine's tone projected self-importance. "I believe my officers can oversee the situation."

"If you want to learn the truth about the assassination attempt on Faure straight from the would-be assassin's mouth, you need to be present." Mira lifted an eyebrow, in a conniving manner. "You should invite journalists and photographers. Think of the headlines."

Lépine's expression turned calculatingly thoughtful. "You are certain a confession will be made?"

"Yes. To the assassination attempt and other crimes, as well." Mira let mystery cloud her tone to further engage Lépine's curiosity.

"Mirabelle." Susette's urgent call echoed through the corridor.

Siméon rushed from behind her and ran full tilt at Mira. "Where is Bernadette? Is she alive?"

"She is alive. She has been brave." Mira clasped Siméon in a hug. "How are you?"

Siméon thumped a fist against his chest. "I am furious with myself for not protecting Bernadette."

"You were drugged. You could do nothing." Susette worriedly wiped a hand against her forehead. "It's Marius Jourdain who is responsible, not you."

Siméon groaned. "It is my fault. I delivered the ransom note."

His gaze darted back and forth from Susette to Mira. "When he read it, Jacques bolted from his bed and removed his arm sling, cursing Marius Jourdain. He bound and gagged me with his bedsheet before leaving. Until Susette checked on him, no one knew about his departure."

"Calm down, son." Lépine put his hand on Siméon's shoulder. "What demands has Marius Jourdain made?"

"One thousand francs and a Peugeot," Siméon cried out. "Jacques is to meet him at the windmill tower in Montparnasse Cemetery at six tonight."

Susette pointed to the clock in the lobby. "It is five-thirty now."

"We have little time." Lépine motioned to the police officer remaining at his side. "Get precinct headquarters on the telephone. Mlle Montgomery, where were you being held?"

"The Catacombs." Mira shivered, remembering the horror of the place. "At the entrance to the ossuary."

"Poor Bernadette." Siméon balled his fists in anguish. "The darkness frightens her."

Siméon's statement surprised Mira. Bernadette must have confronted her fears to comfort her.

Dear, dear girl.

"Siméon, she has candles for illumination, so she has not been in total darkness."

Yet, the candles were burning quickly. Remain brave, Bernadette.

"You need to take lanterns with you to shine brighter light." Mira hesitated, knowing her next words would further alarm Siméon. "Marius allowed me to come for help, but he did make me handcuff Bernadette to Winnie. I am certain he plans to leave them to collect the ransom."

Siméon balled his fists more tightly. "If he has injured Bernadette, I will murder him."

"You will do no such thing," Prefect Lépine admonished. "Remain here in case Thibaut returns. I will lead a unit to the cemetery. An officer will take you, Mlle Montgomery, to the Catacombs. You'll meet the rescue unit and the medical team. Nurse Godard, you will attend to Winifred Flanagan." Lépine marched to the lobby desk, where the officer had precinct headquarters waiting on the telephone.

Susette's expression conveyed confusion. "Mirabelle, who is Winnie?"

"Of course, you did not hear me tell Prefect Lépine." Mira forced a calmness belying her mounting anxiety. "Winnie is Marius Jourdain's accomplice and the mother of his baby. He released me to bring help because she has gone into labor. She is feverish, and I saw quite a bit of blood flowing from her."

Susette breathed in quickly. "Let's go, right away. Every moment counts."

"You go." Mira lowered her voice to prevent Siméon from hearing. "I am going to the cemetery. I am positive Marius will be there to collect his ransom. He will have left Bernadette alone with Winnie. She will be frightened out of her wits attending to a birth alone."

"I will bring Philomene with me and leave immediately." Susette hugged Mirabelle tightly. "Please, be careful. Come back safely, with Jacques."

Mira returned her hug. "I will." She watched Susette scurry off, confident in the nurse's unflappable ability while under crisis to help Winnie deliver a baby under such dire circumstances.

"I have dispatched the units." Lépine pointed his walking cane toward his officer. "Take Mlle Montgomery to the Catacombs and await reinforcements before descending with her and the medical team."

"No." Mira waved the officer away. "I am going with you, Prefect Lépine. We must force Marius Jourdain into confessing his crimes, which will clear Jacques Thibaut of all suspicion."

"I cannot allow you to place yourself in danger, Mlle." Lépine gave a curt nod to the officer. "You have your orders."

Before Mira could debate further, Lépine exited the hospital and entered a police vehicle.

"Mirabelle," Siméon called from where he stood behind the officer. "May we have a moment before you leave?"

Joining him, Mira tried to placate him. "Siméon, you must believe Bernadette will be fine."

"I am not waiting here. I am going to the cemetery. Marius Jourdain drugged me and kidnapped Bernadette." Siméon spoke through gritted teeth. "I shall extract my revenge."

"You cannot," Mira pleaded. "Bernadette will need you once she is freed."

"I did not protect her from being kidnapped." He walked from Mira. "I must prove myself a man and avenge her." "No." Mira clasped his arm.

"You cannot stop me." He stalked through the lobby. Mira rushed to Siméon. "We go together." Passengers emerged from a *fiacre* at curbside.

Siméon commandeered it, offering a fare to the driver. "Montparnasse Cemetery. *Vite.*"

Mira settled into the coach across from Siméon. Worry over what he plotted to do once they arrived made her stomach ache. She did not need him to interfere with her gaining a confession from Marius within earshot of Lépine. All the better if any journalist captured it for publication.

They came to a halt at the cemetery entrance where a horse-drawn police patrol wagon and the automobile carrying Lépine were parked. Siméon leapt from the cab and did not stop to assist Mira.

She emerged to see Siméon running into the walled cemetery through its gate, to which either side stood columns adorned with a winged hourglass motif. Not knowing the way to the remains of the ancient bladeless windmill in the huge cemetery, Mira hefted her skirt and ran after the boy, fearful of losing him.

The cobblestone walkway threatened her footing. Rushing past the funereal statuary and tombs disoriented her. Some graves she had visited during walking tours with her godmother did not yet exist, for those people died after 1900. The time warp felt surreal.

Once she saw the winged bronze sculpture *Le Génie du Sommeil* éternel, Angel of Eternal Sleep, in the roundabout, Mira recovered her bearings. The short windmill tower stood nearby.

Siméon was stooped behind statuary with two men, one with a notepad and pencil and the other with a camera.

Mira saw Jacques standing in a small open green patch of land at the windmill base, facing Marius. Lépine and a circle of officers stood behind Jacques. At the sight of a gun in Marius's hand, her already aching stomach twisted into a knot.

"Marius Jourdain! You are outnumbered!" Lépine's voice echoed in the mournful quiet of the cemetery. "Surrender yourself!"

"I did not bring the police, Marius," Jacques called out. "I have done what you asked. I have brought the money. The car is parked outside the gate."

Mira crept next to Siméon.

He jerked her behind him. "He is not telling the truth. There is no car. I doubt Jacques brought money. He is bluffing."

Her mouth went dry. Unarmed and injured, Jacques faced poor odds of success against a desperate man pointing a gun at him.

Marius laughed. "I must assume Mlle Montgomery went to them. You will have her to blame for your precious ward's death. If I do not return with the money and the car—if I die here—my accomplice will kill Bernadette."

"She will be unable to do so." Mira scrambled past Siméon into the open. "Winnie will not have the strength, Marius. Do you forget she is about to deliver your baby?"

Lépine waved his officers toward her. "Restrain that woman."

Mira rushed to Jacques' side before they could obey. "Marius, unless you confess to your blackmail of Jacques, no assistance will be sent to Winnie. She will be alone, except for a scared girl, to give birth in the dank horror of the Catacombs. Winnie could die. Your baby could die."

"Mirabelle, please." Jacques grabbed her wrist and flung her toward the police. "Do not try to bargain with this soulless man."

Regaining her balance, Mira shouted, "Think about Winnie! She must be in such pain by now."

Jacques again pulled her to him. His anger hissed from him. "You can't reason with this madman."

"Let me try." Mira wrested free and inched a step closer to Marius, keeping eye contact with him. "I have seen you and Winnie together. I know how much you love her. Do not let her die. We have medical help on standby. Once you confess to the assassination attempt of Faure and framing Jacques for it, Prefect Lépine will dispatch the ambulance to her."

The gun wavered in Marius's hand.

Mira decided to push on his emotions further. "You also owe Jacques the truth, about the night of the riots. You have blackmailed him all these years, threatening to tell Bernadette that Jacques killed her father, Luc Roget, the night of the riots. But, that is not true. Tell us how you got the scar on your cheek."

"Mira?" Jacques cast a shocked look at her. "What are you saying?"

Marius steadied the gun in his grip. "*Tu vas fermer ta gueule.*"

"No, I will not shut my mouth. It's time you opened yours, Marius. You have been lying to Jacques all these years. The heavy silver match holder Jacques threw that night of the riot did not hit Luc Roget."

"You speak lies." Marius cocked the gun's trigger. "Lies for which you shall die."

"I speak the truth. Your truth, which you shared with Bernadette and me earlier today. Remember? You said *thanks to Jacques Thibaut, once you see me, you do not forget.* Why thanks to Jacques?"

"You are the clever one." Marius pointed the cocked gun at her. "You tell me."

"Put down the gun, Jourdain!" Lépine's voice roared through the quiet cemetery, startling the surrounding birds into taking flight. "Or I will order my men to shoot."

"I will kill the girl before your men fire a shot. Tell them to stand down."

Lépine waved his hand, and the officers lowered their guns.

"Mlle Montgomery is correct, Jacques. Luc Roget lay dead before you pitched the match holder into the crowd. It struck against my cheek. Even with the pain of my injury, I could think quickly enough to set you up. How easy it was to convince you that you killed Luc Roget."

Jacques sprang toward him.

Marius fired a warning shot into the air. "Stop, or my next bullet will be for Mirabelle." "Please, Jacques!"

At Mira's scream, Jacques stopped moving forward.

Mira cajoled Marius to confess more. "How you have Jacques at your mercy is worthy of admiration."

Arrogance infused Marius's smile. "When the anarchists paid me to assassinate Faure, to my great fortune, Jacques Thibaut stepped into my knife. I only had to speak the name of Roget to convince you to let me escape, Thibaut." He lifted his shoulders in a slight shrug. "If you had lost the race today, as I asked of you, we would not be here now."

Marius motioned the gun at Mira. "I shall now depart, with the lovely Mirabelle for my safe keeping until I receive word Winnie has delivered my baby and both are well. Oh, yes. You must provide the money and car, as well."

Mira held her hands up, acquiescing to Marius's demand. She whispered under her breath, "Jacques, remember. The hairbrush. I know how to fight. Be ready."

"Now, Mirabelle!" Marius shouted. "I lose patience."

When Mira came close enough to him, Marius jerked her around and jabbed the gun into her right rib cage. "Do not follow me, or she will die."

Mira and Jacques locked their gaze.

His slight nod told her he knew her plan. A jiu-jitsu move.

With lightning motion, she simultaneously rotated her body to bump into Marius and trapped the gun with her left hand, swerving it away from her. She pulled her right arm through their bodies, and using her right hand, she chopped against his wrist to free the pistol from his hold.

Pivoting on her left foot, she swirled backward away from him, freeing herself. Turning sidewise, she faced Marius with the gun pointed at him in the precise moment Jacques reached her. Adrenalin coursed through her, and her nerves tingled raw over the violent combat.

"It's over for you, Marius." Pride laced Mira's breathless words.

As well as it being over for me, here in 1900 Paris. I have done what you sent me to do, Le Veille. Prove Jacques' innocence. Reset his destiny. Now return me to the time where I belong, over a century apart from those I have grown to care about so much.

THIRTY-SIX

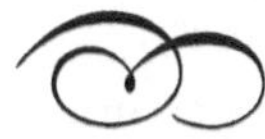

Jacques removed the pistol from Mira's grip and aimed it at Marius. "Why shouldn't I kill you?"

"No, Jacques. Don't throw your life away on him. You've been cleared of any wrongdoing. You can have your life back now." Mira cast an imploring look toward Lépine. "Listen to her, Thibaut." Lépine swiveled his head to address the officers on either side of him. "Take Marius Jourdain into custody."

The police approached with guns drawn.

Marius crouched, as if preparing to take off.

Siméon stepped from hiding. "You cannot escape." He raced toward the criminal. "If there is any justice, you will die here."

"Siméon!" Jacques yelled. "Stay back!" Marius sprang into a run.

"Halt, or you will be shot." Lépine's matter-of-fact tone left no doubt he would fire.

Jacques grabbed Mira's hand with his free one and pulled her out of the line of fire.

Marius did not heed the warning.

Lépine did not hesitate. He drew his pistol and fired, hitting Marius in the back.

Marius fell face-first onto the ground.

The gunshot reverberated through the mournful atmosphere of the cemetery.

The faint scent of acetone and the thin plume of smoke trailing from the gun's barrel mesmerized Mira. She adjusted her gaze to the blood oozing from Marius, unable to conjure regret over his death. Not even when she thought about his baby, now fatherless.

What kind of father would this murderous criminal make, anyway? He'd probably lead the child into his own criminal footsteps.

Lépine strode to where Marius lay. "Fool." He bowed slightly toward Mira. "My compliments, Mlle Montgomery. You managed the situation admirably. I have never seen anyone so competent in self-defense especially a woman. Who taught you such maneuvers?"

Mira turned her head from his admiring stare. What explanation could she offer for her jiu-jitsu training?

Lépine offered a handshake to Jacques. "Thibaut, I expect you in my office first thing tomorrow. We shall straighten out this mess. Full reinstatement to the force will be yours if you desire."

"*Merci.*" Jacques shook Lépine's hand.

With a nod toward the reporter and photographer, Lépine added, "They will be sure the full story reaches the public. Your name will be cleared."

The photographer held the camera up. "A photograph with the body, Prefect Lépine?"

Mira half-smiled.

Vanity, thy name is Lépine.

Jacques turned over Marius's gun to one of the police officers before taking Mira's arm. "We must find Bernadette." "We know where she is." Siméon's voice radiated urgency. "At the Catacombs."

"Don't worry." Relief swept over Mira. "Prefect Lépine ordered a unit there to rescue her and Winifred Flanagan."

During the ride to the Catacombs provided by Prefect Lépine's driver, Mira sketched out for Jacques the story about Marius and Winnie.

The driver stopped in front of the entrance to the Catacombs where Bernadette and Susette stood.

"Bébé." Siméon scrambled from the automobile and drew her into his arms.

"Come." Jacques assisted Mira from the car.

Mira approached Susette, who stood by the ambulance. Exhaustion was written on the nurse's grime-streaked face. "Jacques has been cleared?" Susette's voice quavered.

Mira nodded, watching the joyous reunion before her. "Jaco." Bernadette turned from Siméon's hug and threw herself at Jacques, sobbing. "Thank heaven you have come. Are you unharmed?"

"I am fine." He circled his unhurt arm around her. "Except, I confess to a sore shoulder from the automobile racing."

Bernadette stepped from his embrace. Her tears left tracks on her dirty cheeks. "When I saw you thrown from the automobile, I feared you dead."

"We are both alive." Jacques' voice choked. "We are all alive and well."

Mira bowed her head, tears pooling. Her mission had been accomplished. Jacques' destiny had been righted. Even though Bernadette would learn about her father's death and her mother's identity, Mira knew the girl would survive the revelations. The love of Jacques, Siméon, and Susette would ensure it.

A baby's wail from the ambulance pierced the air. Mira peered in to see an unconscious Winnie. Philomene sat by her, holding the infant.

Who will tell Winifred about Marius's death? Who will raise the child while she serves time in prison for kidnapping? Susette placed a hand on Mira's shoulder. "Without you sending medical attention, they both would have died. The delivery was by C-section, without sterility of the surgical theater. Winnie will be admitted to the hospital, and I will keep watch for puerperal fever. I pray she will fully recover."

Mira shook her head. "The baby will have a difficult life. If Winnie does survive, she will face prison time." "What happened to Marius?"

"Shot dead, by Prefect Lépine. After he confessed, though." Mira grasped Susette's hand. "Jacques' name is cleared, and Lépine offered to reinstate him as police detective. As you suspected, Marius was responsible for upturning Jacques' life for the worse."

"Jacques told me when in the hospital after the race, including how he believed he killed Luc Roget." Susette leaned on Mira, her knees buckling. "You are saying he did not?"

"He did not. The object Jacques threw into the crowd struck Marius, not Luc. Injured and angry, Marius let Jacques believe otherwise, knowing he could hold the incident over Jacques. When Marius's cheek was left badly scarred, he desired vengeance against Jacques and began blackmailing him."

"If not for you, Mirabelle . . ." Susette regained her composure. "You and Jacques are free to be together now. With my blessing."

"Oh, Susette. Jacques and I do not belong together. He loves only you." A tumult of mixed emotions filled Mira's heart. "Go to him. You two are meant to be. He needs you. Bernadette needs you. Love them enough for both of us. I can only hope each of you will remember me, after I am gone."

Susette cocked her head. "Have you regained your memory?"

"Jacques told you about me?"

"Only because he believed you placed his crises over yours."

"I must leave." Mira gazed at Jacques and Bernadette, longing to tell them the truth about herself.

I will not. Cannot. They love the Mirabelle without a memory, not Mira, a time traveler.

The air chilled. Silence descended. Fog swirled around her, blurring everyone from Mira's sight. She knew why.

Le Veille materialized. "*Retrouvez-moi au Carrousel du Luxembourg, à midi.*"

The words were familiar ones. "You?" Mira exclaimed. "You wrote the note I found in the coin purse?"

Le Veille disappeared. The fog lifted, and the activity around Mira resumed as if no interruption occurred. She studied the scene playing out around her and knew she must leave.

I am not here, really. I am not part of any of your lives. It is over, now.

Mira walked quickly to Lépine's car, demanding her heart to close itself off. She requested the driver to return her to the American Girls' Club.

A meal delivered to her room, followed by a night's sleep, is what she needed after the day's travails. If the return through the Carousel portal impacted her body as significantly as her trip to 1900, she would need rest before attempting it.

She had been in this time wrinkle for three days. When she arrived back through the portal, would she find only a moment had passed? Would she find her mobile phone in her hand, with the rest of the text on it about her mother?

Will I remember any of being in 1900 Paris? Will I remember Jacques? Will my mother be alive?

THIRTY-SEVEN

Within an hour of her arrival at the American Girls' Club, Mirabelle answered a knock on her door to find Mme Newton.

"M. Thibaut is in the lobby. He is requesting to see you." Mme Newton brushed tears from her cheeks. "He has told me about Winnie. I am in shock."

Mira tugged her sleeping robe around her. Exhaustion claimed every inch of her. She could not trust herself to see Jacques for fear of what she'd say, how she'd react. "Send M. Thibaut away, with my . . ." She hesitated. "With my regrets."

Mme Newton bowed her head and left.

Mira slipped into bed and closed her eyes. However, rest came in fits. As dawn's light crept through the window, she surrendered the night to the new day, one in which she would finally return where she belonged.

Standing and stretching her sore body, Mira noticed a note slipped under her door. Her breath caught at the sight of Jacques' bold cursive. She removed the waxed seal and unfolded it.

With a trembling finger, she traced the words as she read them.

The note had found her again.

Retrouvez-moi au Carrousel du Luxembourg, à midi.

Her breath caught.

How had she not recognized in Jacques' other note that the handwriting matched the note in the coin purse Le Veille had given her? Its bold cursive had faded into spidery strokes. Time had drained the energy of his bold handwriting. But it was this note in the coin purse Le Veille gave her.

Mira refolded the note and kissed it before inserting it into the *La Fée aux Choux* purse. There it would remain for over a century. Until the mysterious antique dealer said those words. "My heart tells me you are she: the one for whom this coin purse has awaited."

If only she had not been chosen by Le Veille for this mission. Yet, she knew she did not mean that.

These past few days have brought me much for which to be grateful. Acceptance of my father's heroic choice. Willingness to open myself to others. Discovery of my inner strength. Above all, I've learned to love fully, completely, and unselfishly.

Remember Le Veille's paradox? The past holds my future, and I'm ready to embrace whatever and whomever it brings.

Mira called for Mme Newton to help her dress in the same Paquin outfit she wore upon her arrival in 1900. Mme Paquin had asked that she return it, but Mira worried if she did not wear it, her return through the portal could be jeopardized. Her suspicion could be unfounded, but why take a chance?

A rap on the door announced Mme Newton's arrival. Mira turned her back for the woman to button the bodice. She directed their conversation toward Winnie. "Have you checked on your niece and her baby?"

Mme Newton hands fumbled over the buttons. "Both the baby and Winnie are showing improvement. The boy will be called Timothy, after our poor brother who died young of a fever."

Her tone lilted upward with hope. "If the court will show leniency to Winnie, maybe she can return with him to America. If not, I shall take him there myself. He belongs with the Flanagan's at their home in Mississippi. My sister wants her grandson with her, and Winnie, also, if possible one day."

Mira took comfort in Timothy Flanagan being given a chance in life. "Please, arrange for my wardrobe to be returned to Jacques Thibaut's residence."

"You are moving in with M. Thibaut?" Mme Newton did not attempt to hide her judgment.

Without responding, Mira walked her to the door for her departure. The woman did not need to know the wardrobe would be for Bernadette.

A strange mix of relief, joy, and worry crowded Mira's heart over her departure from 1900 Paris.

Will I find Mom alive? I did what you asked, Le Veille. You cannot be so cruel to have sent me into the past only to return me to grieve my mother's death.

That thought stole Mira's breath, and she sat for a moment to recover before departing the American Girls' Club. She walked toward the Luxembourg Gardens, wrapping around her the cloak her mother gifted her. It provided comfort as well as warmth to ward off the spring day's chill.

Mira crossed the street where she first saw Marius with Winnie, and her heart tightened. So much happened in her few days back in time. Ahead of her remained her farewell with Jacques. She felt so connected with him, Bernadette, Susette, and Siméon. The thought of never seeing them again settled hard within her bones.

Arriving at the Carousel, she stood apart from the families with young children who were enjoying their outing. Her father's recitation of the Rilke poem "Das Karussell" revisited her thoughts, especially its line about a land lingering before it vanished.

Will my memory of what I've experienced in 1900 Paris linger or vanish?

Mira remembered the line of the poem describing the white elephant and how she declared it her own after her father placed her upon it that day so long ago, a little girl innocent of loss and tragedy. She sought it and saw a young boy upon it.

The white elephant will take me home, as it brought me to 1900 Paris. It led me to uncover painful memories and release them. It led me not to fear love.

"Mirabelle."

At the murmur of her name, Mira turned to find Jacques standing behind her. She recalled how handsome she found him the first time she laid eyes upon him, wearing his homburg and tapping his walking cane.

Jacques removed his hat.

Mira's face flushed under his intent gaze.

"You left so suddenly yesterday." He stepped near her. "I knew if I invited you here, you'd come."

She instinctively drew back, fearing the explosion of her emotions if she were to allow his touch upon her. Though she knew what they had was not the type of love he shared with Susette, she could not deny how her body desired his.

Hurt ricocheted in Jacques' eyes. "Can I not draw you into my arms? After everything we have been through?" "Oh, Jacques. I am so sorry." She allowed him to take her hand. His touch permeated through her glove. Once again, the lines from *Romeo and Juliet* came to her: "'Palm to palm is holy palmers' kiss . . . let lips do what hands do.'" "I came to see you last night, but Mme Newton turned me away." Jacques reached into his inside coat pocket and withdrew Mira's moonstone ring. "I confiscated it from Winnie to return to you."

Mira closed her hand around the precious gift from her father. Her constricting throat rendered her unable to utter her thanks.

Jacques drew her near, his tone vibrating with passion. "Do you remember how being here before so strongly affected you, as if you expected something to occur but it did not? I pledged my assistance to you."

"Yes. I remember." Mira's voice came out hushed.

Will I remember anything, once I leave you, Jacques? Or will all memories of my time with you vanish? Will I feel again with someone else the passion your nearness awakened in me?

Jacques led her to the nearby bench. Their bench.

After my return, will my mind's eye see us sitting here together?

Shifting his body to face her, Jacques' gaze traveled to her lips. He bent his head toward her, his eyes closing.

"No, Jacques." Mira placed two fingers upon his lips. "Your kisses belong to Susette."

His eyes fluttered open, and his brows drew together. "You're right. I do love her, but yet I cannot deny our closeness. How my body craves yours. I suppose that makes me a cad, unworthy of Susette."

"No." Mira took his hand, shaking her head. "That makes us both human. But acting upon our physical yearning would make us both cads. We will not, out of love and respect, not only for Susette but Bernadette as well."

She drew a ragged breath, preparing to share her truth. "Jacques. I have kept a secret from you. From everyone. I am not sure I should tell you. You will believe me insane."

"I once asked you questions. Who are you and from where do you come? What is your life's story? However, I don't care now." Jacques stroked her cheek.

Mira pressed her lips into a straight line, reconsidering if she should confess.

Yet, how can I leave you without doing so? I must tell you and pray you believe me.

"I must tell you. I have not been suffering from amnesia. I have been lying because the truth is too bizarre. I doubt you or anyone will accept it. I barely can." She placed her hand over his on her cheek. "Promise me you will hear me out?"

Jacques pressed her palm against his lips. "Of course."

Mira withdrew her hand and placed it against her stomach, struggling for a deep breath against the tight corset. With a heavy exhale, she stared ahead at the couples strolling on the sidewalk in front of them, their faces set in contentment she longed to feel.

"I met a man in an antiques shop. M. Le Veille. He sent me to Paris, with a mission." She bowed her head and repeated Le Veille's words in a monotone. "Vanish into the past which holds your future. Return only if you right the wrong destiny that has befallen him."

She lifted her head and latched her gaze onto Jacques'. "Le Veille sent me from the twenty-first century to 1900 Paris to correct a man's fate. Your fate, Jacques. Your reputation is now restored, and you will live the life you were meant to live. Love and marry Susette. And I must return where I am meant to be."

Her words hung between them, thick as fog upon the Seine. Mira read Jacques' skepticism in the rigidity of his body. When he leapt to his feet, she crouched from him, fearing he might grasp her wrist and drag her to a hospital for a psychiatric examination, or to the police station.

"I am not a fool to be lied to, Mirabelle." Jacques loomed over her, almost growling out his words. "If I mean nothing to you, there is no need for a fantastical explanation."

The day's sunshine darkened, and thunder rolled in the distance. A blast of frigid air blew against Mira, and she drew her cape around her to ward off the cold. She knew everything and everyone around her would fade away into a state of limbo, and Le Veille would materialize. Her surroundings blurred, and Mirabelle looked for the time shifter.

Jacques grabbed her in his arms.

Mira fell into his crushing embrace. "Jacques, do you feel the cold? Do you see how this moment in time stands still? How no one moves except the two of us? It's Le Veille. You must believe me. He has come to transport me to my real life."

She felt Jacques' heart pummeling his chest.

"I don't know what to believe, Mirabelle. Your explanation sounds like ranting of a lunatic. But what is happening around us defies reality. I refuse to lose you to another time and place. Your absence will break all of our hearts. You must remain here, in 1900 Paris, with the man who owes you his life."

The wind whipped between them. Before it dragged them apart, she slid the moonstone ring into his inside coat pocket. She would leave this gift of love from her father with the man who had awakened her heart to true love.

The gale force pushed them farther apart.

Mira could see Jacques' lips moving, calling her name, although she heard only Le Veille's powerful voice piercing through the wind.

"Mirabelle." Le Veille beckoned her toward the Carousel and its white elephant. "It awaits you. Your mother awaits you."

A burst of thousands of butterflies descended upon her, and Mira floated upon their wings farther and farther from Jacques. She craned her neck to keep him in her sight until she could no longer view him.

Le Veille promised the past holds my future. We'll be together again, somehow, won't we? I will see you all again, somewhere, somehow?

The swarm of butterflies lifted Mira upon the white elephant before dissipating into thin air. The Carousel's spinning accelerated. The whooshing wind pressed hard against her body, and the unbridled acceleration catapulted Mira from the white elephant into a spiraling black tunnel.

Once more, its centrifugal force flattened her into an almost one-dimensional body before dropping her back into her own time where she had stood, the coin purse in one hand and her phone in the other with Carolyn's text displayed. Mira heard the chimes of the Luxembourg clock striking before collapsing into darkness.

THIRTY-EIGHT

Mirabelle's eyes fluttered open. A concerned older man wearing a Stetson knelt by her.

"Little lady, take it easy. Remember me? Bill Cody? We met at the bookstore yesterday?"

Her mind wandered to place him, for she did know him. At least, she believed she did. She struggled to sit, fighting against nausea and a blinding headache aggravated by the glare of the bright sun beating down.

"What's happened?" Mira held on to the man's arm, recognizing she lay on the ground at the Luxembourg Carousel. The park's clock struck the hour, and she counted until the sound ended.

Twelve.

Noon.

Mira stared at the coin purse gripped in one hand. *Retrouvez-moi au Carrousel du Luxembourg, à midi.* Meet me at the Luxembourg Carousel at noon.

She remembered coming to the Carousel on a lark, to follow the directions in the message tucked into the coin purse. She'd stood before the Carousel then as the clock struck the noonday hour. Yet it struck the noon hour again.

"Let me help you." Bill assisted her to her feet.

She willingly leaned against him, disoriented. When strength ebbed from her body, her knees buckled.

"Pardon, pardon." Bill held her upright and waved an arm to cut through the crowd gathered around them.

The onlookers dropped back to give them room to walk. Mira assumed the buzz of voices was expressing curious concern about her, but she could not understand the French they spoke. She allowed Bill to help her to a bench outside the Carousel area.

When she sat upon it, it conjured memories. She'd sat in this exact place before, but in a different era, dressed in a different way.

Mirabelle . . .

A handsome man with bluest-of-blue eyes marked with unusual dark rings circling the irises shimmered ghostlike in front of her, clothed in a style from the turn of the last century.

Your absence will break all of our hearts.

Mira remembered it all in a tumbled rush of images. 1900 Paris, the Paquin clothing, The Exhibition, Bernadette on *le trottoir roulant,* Mme Newton and The American Girls' Club, Mary Cassatt, Marius and Winnie, Mme Paquin, Alice Guy, Loïe Fuller and Adolphe Le Prince, Prefect Lépine, the Catacombs, a baby boy being born, Montparnasse Cemetery . . .

"There, there." Bill removed his Stetson and fanned her. "You suffered a bad fainting spell."

"I did not faint." Mira clamped her lips together. Why attempt to explain? Had her time travel to 1900 Paris even happened?

A teen girl approached. *"J'ai pensé qu'elle pourrait avoir besoin d'un verre d'eau?"*

"A cup of water?" Bill accepted the small cup the girl offered. *"Oui, merci."*

The girl smiled at Mira with sympathy. "I am sorry you are beside the weather."

Mira absently corrected her. "Under the weather." "Under the weather." The girl walked away, pausing for a moment to look back with a grin.

Mira met her gaze.

Bernadette? Could it be?

Bill held the cup to Mira's lips.

She drank sips until she emptied it. Taking a deep breath, she enjoyed the lightness of her twenty-first century clothing. The encumberments of the

1900 lady's wardrobe would not be missed, though she did wonder about the disappearance of the lovely Paquin outfit in which she traveled back in time. Hopefully, Mme Paquin received it, somehow.

Tugging her cloak around her, she felt the weight of her phone in its interior pocket. Removing it, she read the text from Carolyn—the text displayed partially before she had been catapulted to 1900 Paris, the text that had left her uncertain if her mother had died, the text that left no doubt she must return to her own time.

Mira read the complete message over and over, each time with more joy.

Mira, catch the next plane. Your mother's heart transplant is happening!

Mira scrolled to the next text and gasped. "I must return to New York, immediately." She pushed from the bench to stand but collapsed onto it.

Bill placed his arm around her shoulder. "You need to be examined at the hospital before you board a flight."

"You don't understand." Mira's words rattled out in short sobs. "My mother needs me. A heart has become available. She has been near to dying, and now a heart has been found." "Your mother is going to have a heart transplant?" Bill Cody looked dumbfounded.

"Yes." Mira took the handkerchief Bill provided to blot tears from her cheeks.

"Her best friend Carolyn texted me the details. Mom will be having transplant surgery late tonight, once the heart arrives at her hospital in New York City. It's a dangerous surgery because of her eroding physical condition. She might not even survive." She waved the phone in the air. "I need to get on the first flight I can."

"No need to call airlines." Bill pulled his phone from his pocket. "I fly out tonight, and you will come with me. I'll add you to my manifest."

Mira let her phone fall to her lap. "With you?"

"Yes, my private jet has submitted its flight plan, and it departs at five-thirty this evening. We can get you to the hospital in New York City by dawn. Hopefully, by the time you mom comes out of surgery, you'll be at her side."

"Thank you." Mira knew those two words were inadequate.

William Cody's Stetson suddenly looked like an angel's halo.

THIRTY-NINE

While in flight on Bill Cody's private jet, Mira notified Carolyn of her arrival and called her godmother with the news.

Sylvie promised she would be on the first possible flight to New York City, teasing that Bill Cody could send his private jet for her if he'd like.

The next morning not long after dawn, Mira arrived at the hospital as timely as Bill Cody promised. She found Carolyn waiting for her.

"Mira." Carolyn grabbed her in a tight hug.

When Mira stepped from Carolyn's embrace, she recognized the woman's guarded expression. "Okay, what is it? Is Mom okay?"

"She's doing well. It's not that at all. It's her surgeon. I didn't want to tell you while you were traveling here, but Dr. West could not perform the transplant. He is actually a patient here himself. Emergency appendectomy."

"Poor guy." Disappointment and worry tinged Mira's sympathy. "What timing. Dr. West is the best, so who stepped in for him?"

"He called in his protégé, and his reputation is exceeding Dr. West's."

"Have you met him?"

"No, everything happened so quickly. I'm not even sure of his name."

"Oh my gosh. Dr. West is practically a member of our family, and we end up with a stranger performing this surgery whose name you can't remember. I need to meet him. Or her?"

"Him. Go sit with your mom, and I'll ask the nurse to arrange a meeting."

"Thanks." Mira drew Carolyn into another hug. "I don't know what we'd done without you. Thanks for being there for us, always."

Carolyn beamed a smile. "No thanks needed. I'll send the nurse to you, and I'll head off until tomorrow."

Mira watched her hurry toward the nurse's station and thought how fortunate she and her mother were to have Carolyn and Sylvie in their lives.

When Mira entered her mother's ICU, she froze at the sight of her mom who lay helpless in the hospital bed hooked up to so many monitors and tubes. Although she had come through the surgery without complications, she remained unconscious and intubated.

The reality of her mom's long recuperative period tempered Mira's joyous relief over her survival. She prayed for no complications, such as organ rejection.

Within minutes, a nurse entered to tell her an after- surgery consultation with the surgeon was scheduled for early evening, for he would be in surgery for the day.

Mira couldn't wait to say thank you to this miracle- maker whose name she realized she still had not learned. She remained at her mom's side, encouraged by her moments of consciousness and the nurse's positive reports.

At the end of the long day, a nurse entered the care unit. "Miss Montgomery, visiting time is over. We'll take excellent care of her overnight and will contact you if need be."

Mira stood, hesitating to leave the room. "May I kiss her on her forehead?"

The nurse smiled. "Yes, of course."

Bending over her, Mira whispered in her mom's ear, "I can't wait until you are well enough for me to tell you what has been happening in my life."

Holding the door for Mira's exit, the nurse pointed. "You can wait for the surgeon in the waiting area. Or, there's a small chapel."

Praying appealed to Mira. "Please, let him know I will be in the chapel."

Reaching its entrance, Mira realized once more she'd forgotten to ask the surgeon's name. The jet lag and all her emotions impeded her from thinking straight. Quiet time in the chapel would do her good.

The dim chapel lighting and soft music encouraged the restful meditation Mira needed. She settled onto the front cushioned pew before seeing the sign about extinguishing lit candles before leaving, for safety reasons. After lighting one, she returned to sit.

She felt the room's temperature cool. Shifting her body to look back at the chapel entrance, a foggy mist materialized. "M. Le Veille?"

"No, my girl."

The temperature dropped even colder. The fog thickened and then cleared. Mira's blood pounded in her ears. She grasped the back of the pew to steady herself from shock.

The man she'd known as Le Veille had morphed into the man she'd mourned for so long. The man she'd once resented for his heroism. The man she had finally come to forgive. "Dad?"

FORTY

"It's me, but I can't say it's me in the flesh." He laughed. "Bad joke, huh? I always did tell bad ones, didn't I?"

Mira blinked hard. Her mouth felt sandpaper dry. She managed to speak, but in a tremulous whisper. "Am I hallucinating? Or, have I lost my mind?"

"Neither." Her father smiled. "You are my strong, brave, and sane daughter of whom I am so proud."

"I don't understand any of this." Mira's voice rose. "Why did you pretend to be M. Le Veille? Why did you send me to 1900 Paris? Or, did my time travel happen only in my mind?"

"It happened. Let me explain."

When her father floated closer to her, Mira's breath caught in a sob. He remained dressed as she last saw him, prone on the sidewalk with soot covering his face and burns showing on his legs and arms from where flames left his pants and shirt sleeves in jagged tatters.

"Mira, my actions the terrible night of the fire ended my time with you and your mother too soon. When the power of the afterlife realized the flap of a butterfly's wings had derailed the fate of your mother's heart donor, I was allowed to send you to 1900 Paris to correct that action."

Icy fingers clutched Mira's heart. "Why couldn't you tell me exactly what to do instead of making me wander around without any help?"

"There are rules to this spirit world, my darling daughter. I could not share with you why, nor control your movements or protect you once there. I could not appear to you or your mother as my true self, so I became M. Le Veille, antiques dealer."

He morphed into Le Veille and waved his hands dramatically. "Vanish into the past which holds your future. Return only if you right the wrong destiny that has befallen him."

Mira clenched her fists. "You sent me to 1900 Paris on this mission to save my mother's life, armed only with a stupid paradox. You know how I hate paradoxes."

With another dramatic wave of arms, her father's spirit reappeared. "I provided the clue that you were to help a male. I used your interest in Alice Guy to provoke your visit to the Carousel. I used our white elephant, hoping you would think of me and our discussions of time travel and the butterfly effect."

"Our poem." Mira brushed away her welling tears. "I did remember the butterfly effect. I tried to help Mme Paquin, but she didn't believe me."

"Ahh, but what you left behind did cause a wrinkle in time that may cause your return to the past."

"What I've left behind?" Mira held out her hand with its finger devoid of jewelry. "Because I gave my ring to Jacques?"

"Yes. Involvement with Jacques led you to save the life of the donor's ancestor. Leaving your moonstone with Jacques connects your fate and that of your mother's forever to his actions."

"I don't understand. Who is the donor's ancestor I saved? Is it Jacques? Bernadette? Siméon? You make it sound as if the ring has some magical power. It's just a ring."

"Ahh. But so much more. Meet the heart surgeon. All will become clear." The glow of her father's spirit shone brighter. With a wave of his arm, the chapel filled with red- winged butterflies, their undersides black.

Mira remembered seeing one in the lobby of Hôpital Hôtel-Dieu. She'd recalled the legend that these black butterflies were the souls of deceased people who were unable to move on to the afterlife.

Fog encircled father until Mira could not see him any longer. "What does the surgeon know?"

"The donor's name and more." Her father's disembodied voice floated toward her. "Your forgiveness allows me peace in my afterlife. My time as your time shifter is over. Only the moonstone can call you back through the Carousel portal if the fate you corrected shifts once more."

The fog cleared, and the room grew warmer. The candles on the altar flickered.

Mira sank into a pew by the chapel entrance. Her confused thoughts scattered over all she'd seen and heard.

I must be hallucinating everything. Seeing my father's spirit. Learning he was my time shifter. Saving someone— Jacques? Bernadette? Siméon?—whose descendant becomes my mother's heart donor.

Yet, if I am not hallucinating, by giving Jacques my moonstone ring have I endangered everything I accomplished while in the past?

The chapel door opened, and a man uttered her name. "Miss Montgomery?" He stood by the pew where she sat.

Mira looked up into a man's bluest-of-blue eyes, marked with unusual dark rings circling the irises, like Jacques' eyes. A familiar scent wafted toward her, of talcum, sandalwood, and earthy incense. Jacques' scent.

The man wore sharply creased black trousers, a starched white long-sleeved pinpoint Oxford shirt, and expensive vintage sneakers. His long and lean physique boasted a fit shape. He looked as if he stepped from the cover of GQ.

When I first saw Jacques, I thought the same.

He spoke softly. "The nurse told me I would find you here."

The door shut behind him, and the room dimmed.

Mira remembered the burning candle. To cover her uneasiness, she turned toward the altar. "I need to blow out the candle."

"Let me." He walked past her.

Mira observed his sexy, swaggering stride and inhaled once again the manly scent of his cologne. She admired his long and tapered fingers holding the candle snuffer.

The stone in the ring he wore on his pinky glinted in the candlelight. Her heart knocked against her chest.

It can't be mine. Mine is with Jacques.

The surgeon extinguished the flame and placed the snuffer on the altar before returning to Mira.

"The surgery went spectacularly well." A confident smile creased his handsome face.

Mira opened her mouth to say thanks, but she could not speak. The man's uncanny resemblance to Jacques had robbed her voice. She continued to stare at him, trying to process what he was telling her.

"You mother will have a long recovery before we can say she's out of the woods, but at this point, there are no signs of organ rejection, and her vitals are stable. She received a strong heart from the donor. The nurse wanted me to let you know his family has signed the paperwork to inform you of the donor's identity."

Ask the donor's name . . .

"We absolutely want to say thank you. What is the donor's name?"

"Timothy Flanagan, the third, I think, or some number or another after his name. Resident of . . ."

"Mississippi." The word rushed from Mira's lips.

His eyebrows arched. "You know the family?"

"Not really." Mira shivered, remembering the damp horror of the Catacombs where Winnie bore Timothy Flanagan's ancestor.

So, my involvement with Jacques, clearing his reputation and reconciling him with Susette, had been a side accomplishment to my true time travel mission. I'd been sent back in time to save the baby.

The handsome surgeon approached her and rested his hand sporting the ring onto the back of the pew Mira faced. *It's the same setting as mine. One of a kind. It must be mine. How did he get it? I placed it into the inner pocket of Jacques' coat.*

She motioned toward it. "Your moonstone ring. Is it a Lalique?"

"Yes." Pride emanated from his face. "It's my great- great-grandfather's ring."

Mira swallowed hard. "Do you know how he came to own it?"

He smiled, staring at it. "The story goes that someone he once loved gave it to him."

Mira's eyes brimmed with tears.

My dear, dear Jacques.

"When I announced I was going to be a doctor, my father decided to pass the ring to me." His tone projected pride, but not in a boastful way. "Among its many powers, a moonstone is said to —"

Mira interrupted in a whispery voice. "Have magical powers of healing."

"So, you know your moonstones." He ran his hand through his black, wavy hair.

Mira remembered that Jacques used the same mannerism.

"I haven't introduced myself." He stuck his hand out. "My name's Jack Thibaut."

Goosebumps traveled over Mira's skin.

"My mother and I owe you our gratitude, Dr. Thibaut." She shook his outstretched hand, and her breath caught at the electricity of his touch.

Jacques, our destinies cross through your great-great- grandson. He has given my mother a future. Perhaps me as well. After all, a moonstone is also a love stone.

Jack knitted his brow. "Have we met before? You seem familiar."

"I thought the same about you." Mira stood. "If you're free, I'd like to buy you dinner. As a thank you for saving my mom."

"On one condition." The corner of his mouth lifted in a crooked grin.

Mira raised an eyebrow. "Go on."

"We consider the dinner invitation not as a thank you to your mom's surgeon. Let's think of it as a first date."

Mira's laughed. "Agreed."

Jack held the chapel door for her and crooked his elbow. "Shall we?"

Mira slipped her arm through his. "We shall."

Butterflies fluttered within her. She realized she didn't hate paradoxes as much as she once thought.

Author's Notes

Inspiration strikes at odd moments. When I came across the historical image of a woman losing her balance while using the moving walkway at the 1900 Paris Exhibition (image from *Histoire de la locomotion terrestre*, by Charles Dollfus and Edgar de Geoffroy, France, 1935), a story premise began taking shape in my imagination. What if a time traveler landed on this walkway and became involved in the life of the person she stumbles against? From that idea, Mirabelle Montgomery found her way onto the pages of *A Tryst in Paris*.

These Author's Notes provide information about the locations Mirabelle visits, the people she meets, and historical events in which she becomes involved in *A Tryst in Paris*, along with some of the most significant references that helped me create my story. I have taken care to present with respect the deceased historical figures with whom Mirabelle interacts. Their interactions and dialogue are all derived from my imagination.

The Butterfly Effect

While traveling in the past, Mirabelle remembers past conversation she had with her father about time travel, prompted by their shared love of the H. G. Wells' classic *The Time Machine*. She especially takes care not to impose her presence except where she must in order to avoid setting off "the butterfly effect," which in chaos theory hypothesizes that a small change can be the cause of larger consequences (i.e., the flap of a butterfly's wings in one location sets off a tornado in another location). In time travel, this butterfly effect idea manifests in the idea that whatever the time traveler changes in the past results in changes going forward.

M. Le Veille sends Mirabelle into the past to accomplish a mission, her only instructions being his paradoxical statement: "Vanish into the past which holds your future… return only if you right the wrong destiny that has befallen him." Mirabelle doesn't understand what about her presence in the past will impact her own future, and she takes care to limit her impact on others around her except to help the one she believes Le Veille sent her to help. This "butterfly effect" theory weighs on Mirabelle's heart and mind as she tries to complete what she has been sent to accomplish in order to return to her mother's side.

Locations and Events:
American Girls' Club

Located at 4, Rue de Chevreuse @ Rue Montparnasse, the American Girls' Club was founded in the 1890s by American philanthropist and social activist Elizabeth Mills Reid, who created it as place where American girls studying in Paris would be chaperoned in an attempt to derail their wild reputations as carefree and bohemian. The Club welcomed visiting artists to provide lectures and classes and judge its yearly art exhibition supported by the American Women's Art Association in Paris of which Mary Cassatt was a member. The young women paid for room and boarding, which included the afternoon tea known as *le goûter.* During World War One, the location became an American Red Cross Hospital. In 1964, it was bequeathed to Columbia University. Now known as Reid Hall, it is home to Columbia Global Centers.

The American Girls' Club is an important setting in the story. It is where Mirabelle meets the famous artist Mary Cassatt and the mysterious boarder Winifred Flanagan, a woman involved with the menacing Marius Jourdain. Both Winifred and Marius play an increasingly important role in Mirabelle's time travel mission.

Globe Céleste and the bridge collapse
An icon of the 1900 Exhibition, the Globe Céleste was a large blue and gold sphere painted with the constellations and zodiac signs and was located near to the Eiffel Tower. People sat in recliner chairs on the globe's top and viewed rolling panoramas of the solar system, as if traveling through space. The

pedestrian bridge to the Globe collapsed on April 29, 1900, killing nine and injuring many others.

In the story, Mirabelle and Jacques are following Bernadette and Siméon to the Globe attraction when the bridge collapses and traps the young couple. Mirabelle and Jacques work with other rescuers to save them.

Jardin du Luxembourg Carousel

The Carousel in Jardin du Luxembourg, designed by Charles Garnier (architect of the Paris Opera House) is the oldest in Paris, dating from 1879. Under the green circus- tent top and suspended on wooden poles are the animal rides of giraffes, camels, elephants, two carriages, and horses. The old-fashioned Carousel has no lights or music. The riders on the outer circle play jeu de bagues, a game in which the children attempt to spear rings held out by the operator.

This carousel holds sentimental significance for Mirabelle, for it is where her father took her when they visited Paris. He would recite the poem "Das Carrousel" by Rainer Maria Rilke, and Mirabelle would always ride the white elephant, reference in this poem. In the story, the Carousel serves as the portal by which Mirabelle is catapulted back to 1900 Paris when she sits upon the white elephant. Read the poem and an English translation at Ulrich Flemming's blog entry: https://www.andrew.cmu.edu/user/ujf/blog/carousel. html

Shakespeare and Company

Sylvia Beach, an American, founded the original bookstore Shakespeare and Company in 1919 at the location

12 rue de l'Odéon. The expat writers including Ernest Hemingway and F. Scott Fitzgerald and leading French writers gathered there. She offered her bookstore as a place for writers to stay and loaned them money when needed. Her bookshop closed in 1941 when the Germans occupied Paris. In 1951, after George Whitman's "hobo adventures" of his early twenties during which many generous strangers helped him, Whitman opened his English-language bookstore in Paris called Le Mistral. In 1964 he renamed it Shakespeare and Company to carry on the spirit of Sylvia Beach's bookstore. His hand painted sign on the bookshop wall explains his philosophy: "Be not inhospitable to strangers lest they be angels in disguise." Whitman allowed writers, artists,

and intellectuals, known as "Tumbleweeds," to sleep in the store in exchange for reading a book a day, helping at the shop, and leaving behind a one-page autobiography. After Whitman's death, his daughter Sylvia took charge of the bookstore.

In the story, Mirabelle visits the bookstore where she meets Bill Cody, a Texan whom she invites to her mother's antique shop in New York City. While at the bookstore, Mirabelle thumbs through a copy of H. G. Wells' *The Time Machine*, remembering how her father read it to her and how he arranged for her to receive a moonstone ring for her eighteenth birthday, years after his death. Catching sight of William Faulkner's book *As I Lay Dying*, Mirabelle remembers how Faulkner famously referred to the past as never truly being past.

Notable Persons
(Note: Mirabelle's interactions with these deceased persons are completely fictional.)

Mary Cassatt (May 22, 1844 – June 14, 1926)
Mary Cassatt was an American painter and printmaker born in Allegheny City, Pennsylvania, who spent most of her adult life in France. She is most famous for her paintings and prints on the theme of mother and child. Mirabelle's godmother, Sylvia, claims Mirabelle resembles the woman in Cassatt's painting entitled "Woman's Head in Large Hat." Mirabelle meets and sits for Cassatt at the American Girls Club while Cassatt sketches her as the woman in the large hat.

Alice Guy Blaché (July 1873 – March 24, 1968)
Alice Guy Blaché, a French pioneer filmmaker, is known to be the first woman to direct a film and during 1896-1906 was the only female filmmaker. Alice is credited for making the first film to tell a story as opposed to non- fiction actuality films. She worked at *L. Gaumont et Cie*, a camera manufacturing and photography supply company owned by Gustave Eiffel, Joseph Vallot, Alfred Besnier, and Léon Gaumont. *L. Gaumont et Cie* becomes a prominent force in the history of French motion-picture industry. Alice's first film is thought to have been made in 1896, *La Fée aux Choux* (The Fairy of the Cabbages), remade in 1900 with different camera technology and settings. Mirabelle is studying Alice's impact on the fledgling film industry. When

M. Le Veille gives her the coin purse with the message enclosed within it, Mirabelle excitedly recognizes Alice's film title imprinted upon it.

Félix François Faure (January 30, 1841 –February 16, 1899)

Félix François Faure was President of France from 1895 until his death in 1899. An assassination attempt was made on his life on June 13, 1897, while he was traveling to Longchamps to view the Grand Prix horse race. A police detective was erroneously thought to be the would- be assassin. The crowd attacked him, beating and kicking him until other police rescued him. This event has been fictionalized in the story, where Jacques Thibaut is the policeman accused of the assassination attempt. Mirabelle believes she has time traveled to 1900 Paris in order to clear his name.

Gibson Girl

In the late 1890s to early 1900s, the "Gibson Girl" represented the independent and well-educated "New Woman." The name is attributed to Charles Dana Gibson, an American illustrator who created the illustration of the Gibson Girl look: the hourglass figure sculpted by tight corset and long hair pulled into an updo bouffant (pompadour) style.

Jeanne Paquin (1869–1936)

Jeanne Paquin was a leading French fashion designer, the first major female couturier, and a pioneer of modern fashion retailing. She married Isidore René Jacob, also known as Paquin, who owned a couture house that the couple renamed as *La Maison Paquin* located in Paris at 3 rue de la Paix, next to the House of Worth. Unlike other fashion houses where men were in charge of fashion design, Jeanne Paquin was in charge of design and her husband in charge of the business matters. She was the first couturier to market her designs by sending models to public events as well as collaborating with the theater, architecture, and illustrators. She was president of the Fashion Section of the 1900 Exhibition, which featured her designs prominently and where a mannequin of herself was created for display. Mirabelle arrives in 1900 wearing the beautiful Paquin design she admired in the window of M. Le Veille's antique shop.

Some References

Eastman, Barrett and Frederic Mayer. *Paris, 1900: The American Guide to the City and Exposition (1899)*. Kessinger Legacy Reprints.

Harper's Guide to Paris and the Exposition of 1900. New York: Harper & Brothers Publishers, 1900.

Julian, Philippe. *The Triumph of Art Nouveau Paris Exhibition 1900*. New York: Larousse & Co., Inc., 1974.

Library of Congress Film and Video Collection. Thomas A. Edison, Inc - Niver (Kemp) Collection (Library of Congress) - Paper Print Collection (Library of Congress) - White, James H. (James Henry).

Westinghouse Electric & Manufacturing Company. Westinghouse map of the Paris exposition 1900. [TIFF]. [Paris?] : Westinghouse, [1900]. Retrieved from https:// maps.princeton.edu/catalog/princeton-h415pc989

About the Author

 Anne Armistead earned her English literature degree from the University of Georgia and her MFA in Creative Writing from Spalding University and is a member of the Georgia Writers of Romance (GRW), Atlanta Writers Club (AWC), and Historical Novel Society (HNS).

The damaged hero wins her heart and the hearts of the heroines in Anne's stories. Her novels include the historical paranormal *Dangerous Conjurings* and historical romance *With Kisses from Cecile*. Her sweet contemporary romance is A Christmas Cannoli Kiss. Her time travel romance A TRYST IN PARIS, Book One of The Carousel Time Traveler series, introduces Mirabelle Montgomery as a time traveler in 1900 Paris and Jacques Thibaut, a dangerously sexy French rogue who steals her heart.

Learn more about Anne at her website www.annearmisteadauthor.com

DANGEROUS CONJURINGS
. . . a darkly magical tale ~ Historical Novel Society

WITH KISSES FROM CÉCILE
Awarded 2020 Georgia Independent Author Award, Historical Fiction
…captured my heart…I absolutely loved it. ~ Writer, editor, blogger Jessica Belmont

A CHRISTMAS CANNOLI KISS
I highly recommend this romance for a romantic escape. ~ Amazon Review

A TRYST IN PARIS
*. . . an entrancing portrait of 1900 Paris . . . fascinating read with rich descriptions, a delightful mystery, and realistic, well-rounded characters . . . the mystery and the brewing romance between Jacques and Mira are wonderfully interwoven. ~ 5 Stars from **Readers' Favorites***